WOLFSBANE

DISCARDED HEROES #3

RONIE KENDIG

WOLFSBANE

DISCARDED HEROES #3

BARBOUR
PUBLISHING

OTHER BOOKS BY
RONIE KENDIG

Nightshade (Discarded Heroes #1)
Digitalis (Discarded Heroes #2)

© 2011 by Ronie Kendig

ISBN 978-1-62090-527-2

All rights reserved. No part of this publication may be reproduced or transmitted in any form or by any means without written permission of the publisher.

Scripture quotations are taken from the HOLY BIBLE, NEW IINTERNATIONAL VERSION®. NIV®. Copyright © 1973, 1978, 1984, 2011 by Biblica, Inc.™ Used by permission. All rights reserved worldwide.

This book is a work of fiction. Names, characters, places, and incidents are either products of the author's imagination or used fictitiously. Any similarity to actual people, organizations, and/or events is purely coincidental.

For more information about Ronie Kendig, please access the author's website at the following Internet address: www.roniekendig.com

Cover design: Müllerhaus Publishing Arts, Inc.

Published by Barbour Publishing, Inc., P.O. Box 719, Uhrichsville, OH 44683

Printed in the United States of America.

DEDICATION

To my children,
Ciara, Keighley, Ryan, and Reagan

Thank you for your patience,
Your cheers,
Your quiet (so Mommy could write),
Your laughter,
But most important. . .
For being YOU!

I love you soooooo *much!*

ACKNOWLEDGMENT

Special thanks to:

The Barbour Fiction Team—Becky Germany, Mary Burns, Shalyn Sattler, Elizabeth Shrider, Laura Young. . .a hundred-thousand thank-yous!!

Andrew Kendall—For the amazing Nightshade insignia! You rock!

Agent-Man Steve Laube—You RAWK!! No more ledge-pushing for me, k?

Julee Schwarzburg—A million thanks is not enough. Thank you for believing in me and this series and working so tirelessly. You. Are. Amazing!

Michael Lawrence—for surfing help. Thanks, Dude!

Knees-On-Ground Prayer Team—Your prayers have sustained, encouraged, and uplifted me. I pray God will bless you one hundred-fold in return!

My Arsenal of Friends and Crit Partners—Lynn Dean, Lynne Gentry, Kellie Gilbert, Dineen Miller, Robin Miller, Sara Mills, Rel Mollet, John Olson, Jim Rubart, Camy Tang, Lori Twichell, Lara Van Hulzen, Kimberley Woodhouse, and Rebecca Yauger.

First Reader: Shannon McNear—Girl, you are such a Godsend. I praise Him for your friendship!

Chuck Holton—Thanks for being part of my "arsenal" for military advice and direction. (All mistakes in *Wolfsbane* are purely mine.)

Don Brown—Thank you, sir, for your service to our country, and thank you also for your help regarding military law.

Jeanette Windle—For being gracious and helping me with Spanish.

NIGHTSHADE TEAM

Max "Frogman" Jacobs—former U.S. Navy SEAL, team leader

Canyon "Midas" Metcalfe—former Army Special Forces Group

Colton "Cowboy" Neeley—former U.S. Marine Corps Special
    Operations Command, sniper

Griffin "Legend" Riddell—former U.S. Marine Corps Special
    Operations Command

Marshall "the Kid" Vaughn—former U.S. Army Ranger

John "Squirt" Dighton—former U.S. Navy SEAL

Azzan "Aladdin" Yasir—former Mossad

General Olin Lambert, aka "The Old Man"—Chief of the Army,
    member of Joint Chiefs of Staff

GLOSSARY OF TERMS/ACRONYMS

CID—United States Army Criminal Investigation Command

HUMINT—Human Intelligence

IED—Improvised Explosive Device

JAG—Judge Advocate General

Klicks—kilometers

MP—Military Police

NVGs—Night-Vision Goggles

PTSD—Post-Traumatic Stress Disorder

RPG—Rocket-Propelled Grenade

SF—Special Forces

SOG—a combat knife

Tango—military slang for *target* or *enemy*

USACE—United States Army Corps of Engineers

USCG—United States Coast Guard

VFA—fictitious Venezuelan rebel army: *El Valor de Fuerzas Armadas de Bolivarian*

U.S. ARMY SPECIAL FORCES CREED

I am an American Special Forces soldier. A professional!

I will do all that my nation requires of me.

I am a volunteer, knowing well the hazards of my profession.

I serve with the memory of those who have gone before me: Roger's Rangers, Francis Marion, Mosby's Rangers, the first Special Service Forces and Ranger Battalions of World War II, the Airborne Ranger Companies of Korea. I pledge to uphold the honor and integrity of all I am—in all I do.

I am a professional soldier. I will teach and fight wherever my nation requires. I will strive always, to excel in every art and artifice of war.

I know that I will be called upon to perform tasks in isolation, far from familiar faces and voices, with the help and guidance of my God.

I will keep my mind and body clean, alert, and strong, for this is my debt to those who depend upon me.

I will not fail those with whom I serve. I will not bring shame upon myself or the forces.

I will maintain myself, my arms, and my equipment in an immaculate state as befits a Special Forces soldier.

I will never surrender though I be the last. If I am taken, I pray that I may have the strength to spit upon my enemy.

My goal is to succeed in any mission—and live to succeed again.

I am a member of my nation's chosen soldiery. God grant that I may not be found wanting, that I will not fail this sacred trust.

THE INVITATION

Judicial Building, Virginia Beach

Blood dripped into his left eye.

No. Not blood. Sweat. Hands tight against his hips and fists balled, Captain Canyon Metcalfe blinked away the sting. Another salty drop slid down his temple. Eyes ahead, he focused on his reflection in the massive mirror. Between it and him sat an eight-foot table harboring a panel of three Army investigators from Criminal Investigation Command sent for his one-year evaluation. More like interrogation. And he knew they weren't legit. Nobody got a review once they were out. This wasn't about legitimacy. This was about them insuring he'd kept his mouth shut.

Canyon watched his reflection as a bead skidded over his forehead and nose. Felt warm and moderately sticky. So much like...

It's not blood. Not blood.

"Captain, do you have anything to add?" Major Hartwicke lifted the inches-thick file in her manicured hands and stared at him.

"You understand, Captain, if you reveal anything about what has happened here, you will face a full court-martial and dishonorable discharge."

The voice from twenty-one months ago forged his response. "No, sir."

Behind the one-way mirror a ghost of a shape shifted. Or was that a shadow? No, he was pretty sure he'd seen the human outline. So there were more eyes monitoring this so-called review. *They're testing me.* No surprise. As a matter of fact, he'd expected them to drag him out of bed in the middle of the night, haul him into the woods, and try to beat a confession out of him.

Innocence didn't matter. Justice didn't matter.

Only one thing mattered: silence.

Hartwicke pushed her chair back from the table and stood. "Captain, I don't understand." She motioned to the two investigators with her. "We've told you the CID believes there is enough. . .ambiguity in the charges and proceedings from thirteen March of last year to question the guilty verdict." She tilted her head. "In fact, this panel believes you may be innocent."

"You are not innocent in this brutal crime, Captain Metcalfe. No matter your role, you are guilty. As the officer in charge, you bear that responsibility. Do you understand?"

The eyes of the government held no boundaries. They saw everything. Knew everything. One way or another. Always waiting to throw him away for good. Just as they'd done with the villagers.

Her shoes scritched against the cement floor as she stepped nearer. "Why are you doing this?" she whispered. "Why would you throw away your career?"

Throw away his career? Was she kidding? It'd been *ripped* from his bloodied hands in a colossal mistake twenty-four months ago. Canyon ground his teeth together. *Do not look at her; do not respond.* She didn't deserve a response if she thought this was *his* choice.

A chair squawked, snapping his gaze to the second investigator who moved from behind the table, his gaze locked on Canyon. What did they want from him? He'd kept the dirty little secret. Lived with it. Relived it night after painful night. Living when she died.

Brown eyes cut off his visual escape. "Captain Metcalfe," Major Rubart said in a low, controlled voice. "I don't know what they"—he rolled his eyes to the side to indicate the one-way mirror—"told you or what they used against you as a threat in retaliation for talking, but I think you know something."

Despite his every effort not to, Canyon looked at the mirror.

"You know the truth about that fateful night, don't you?"

The words yanked his eyes to Rubart's. Did this officer really want the truth? Or was this another test? What Canyon wouldn't do to tell, to right the wrong, to relieve the burden. . . But that's just what they wanted him to do—relieve his mind and prove they were right, that he could be coerced into talking. That he was weak.

He flicked his attention back to the glass and the shadow moving behind it.

"You disappoint me, Captain." Air swirled cold and unfeeling as

Rubart eased away. "Your sister says you've not been the same since you returned from that mission."

"My sister puts her mouth before her brain." And for that, Canyon would have a long talk with Willow.

"Do you understand what your silence means?" A bitter edge dug into Rubart's words as he glared at Canyon, who stared through the man.

"What I understand is that you've abused a relationship with my impressionable sister to extract information for the military."

Rubart's lips tightened. "Your silence means the people of Tres Kruces receive no justice."

The thick-bladed words sliced through Canyon's heart.

Quiet tension tightened the air.

"Willow says you've wanted to be a Green Beret since you were twelve."

"Ten." Canyon bit his tongue on the automatic correction. He wouldn't do this. Wouldn't cave under the pressure. He'd endured far worse.

"How can you let them rip it from you? Everything you love and worked for with blood, sweat, and tears?" After several slow, calming breaths, Rubart gave a single nod. "Enough evidence exists to open a full investigation that could reinstate you with full honors, full rank. Just give us one word, one inclination that you'll work with us, and it'll be as if you never left."

Everything in Canyon wanted that back. Wanted the career he'd felt called to, the adrenaline rush of battle, the humanitarian work of helping villages after a tragedy or an insurgency. . .

Screams howled through the fires. He glanced back. Where was she? How had they gotten separated? He spun, searching the debris and crackling embers.

A scream behind him.

He pivoted. Two feminine forms raced into a hut. "No," *he shouted.* "Not in—"

BOOM!

His body lifted, flipped as he sailed through the taunting flames and grieving ashes.

"Captain?"

Canyon blinked back to Major Rubart.

"Just give us some indication you'll help. We'll mete out the details later. Just don't let it go at this. You know this is wrong. Don't let them win."

Irritation clawed its way up Canyon's spine, burrowing into his resolve. He saw through the tactic. "Are we done, sir?"

Rubart's cheek twitched. "You're going to walk away?"

"*In a three-to-one decision, you are hereby discharged. Your actions will be mentioned in limited detail in our final report to the congressional oversight committee. Should you speak openly about this again, you will find yourself in a federal prison for the rest of your life. Do you understand the ruling, Captain Metcalfe?*"

"*Yes, sir.*"

"*I cannot express this enough—this favor we are extending you will be revoked completely if you ever again speak of Tres Kruces.*"

"Captain?"

He met Rubart's gaze evenly. "Decision's been made."

"You can't mean that." Hartwicke's voice pitched. "Think—"

"Dismissed, Captain," the third investigator barked from his chair at the table.

Canyon saluted, then pivoted and strode out. He punched open the door. As he stomped across the parking lot, he wrangled himself free of the dress jacket. He jerked open the door of his red Camaro and snatched off his beret. Flung it into the car. Slammed the door shut. Shuffled and kicked the wheel.

Voices behind pushed him into the car. Letting the roar of the engine echo the one in his head, he peeled away from the curb. Screaming tires fueled his fury. He accelerated. First gear. Second. He sped down the streets. Third. Raced out of Fort Story as fast as he could. He shifted into fourth.

They'd stolen everything from him. What did he have now? The last twelve months had been a futile attempt to plaster meaning to the disaster of a thing called life. Can't serve. What was the point? They had him on an invisible leash. Shame trailed him like the dust on the roads.

As he rounded a corner, a light glinted—yellow. Speed up or slow down?

Slow down? *I don't think so.*

Canyon slammed into fifth and pressed the accelerator. The Camaro lunged toward the intersection. A blur of red swept over his sunroof as he sailed through and cleared it.

Ahead, a sign beckoned him to First Landing State Park. The beach. Something inside him leapt.

Sirens wailed.

He glanced in the rearview mirror and growled. Banged the steering wheel. One more violation and he'd lose his license. Two seconds of fantasy had him tearing off into the sunset.

Yeah. Right. A high-speed chase. Wouldn't his mother love that? She'd give him that disappointed look, and in it he'd read the hidden message—"what would your father have said?"

Dad.

His foot hit the brake. He eased the gears down and brought the car to a stop along the pylons that led to the beach. Less than a mile out, blue waters twinkled at him.

He eyed the mirror as a state trooper pulled in behind him. Lights awhirl, the car sat like a sand spider ready to strike.

Canyon roughed a hand over his face. This was it. Career gone. License gone. He gave his all for his country, and all of it had been systematically disassembled in the last two years.

Hands on the steering wheel, he let the call of the Gulf tease his senses. He should've taken a swim instead of unleashing his anger on the road. He was a medic. He knew better than to endanger lives. How stupid could he get?

What was taking so long?

He glanced back to the mirror, only. . .nothing.

Huh? Canyon looked over his shoulder. Where. . . ?

An engine roared to the left. A Black Chrysler 300M slid past him with a white-haired old man inside.

But where was the cop? Again, he double-checked his six.

Don't look a gift horse in the mouth.

With more care and attention this time, he pulled back onto the road and drove to the ocean. He parked and stared at the caress of the waters against the sand that lured him out of the Camaro and to the warm sand. Rolling up his sleeves, he made his way down the beach.

On a stone retaining wall, he stood and watched a couple of surfers ride a wave. Canyon squatted. Hands fisted against his forehead he struggled through Rubart's promise—they'd give him his career back *if* he ratted out the very people who'd made the nightmare go away.

He wanted to. Wanted to set the record straight. Knew they'd done wrong, but blowing this thing open meant they'd pin every drop of blood and blame on his shoulders. He'd go down in a blaze of disgrace. It was bad enough he'd had to tell his mom he was put out of the military for "medical" reasons. She didn't buy it. She was smarter. But she didn't press him.

Maybe. . .maybe he should let the panel dig into the tsunami-sized disaster and find the truth.

But he couldn't. They'd promised to make his life a living hell.

That happened anyway. Everything that felt right and just died. Just like *her*.

Canyon closed his eyes against the pull of memories and allowed his mind to drift. To everything he felt for her. To all the things he'd done wrong, could've done better.

I'm sorry.

Lot of good that did. She had died.

He hopped off the wall and strolled to where the waters stroked the sand. He let out a long breath and ran a hand over the back of his longer-than-normal hair. He'd tried to leave the tragedy behind. Move on. But who could move on after something like that? Even the government was scared of Tres Kruces. Nice PR disaster with the whole world as witnesses.

Canyon drew out the small vial. *Shouldn't do this.* The back pain was gone. The heart pain permanent. He popped two pills into his mouth and swallowed.

His hand closed around the Emerson in his pocket. Canyon drew it out and eyed the gleaming metal. He'd used it to cut her tethers the first night his team had come up on the backwater village. Flipping the blade to the ground, he tamped down the fireball in his gut. He saved her that night only to end up killing her thirteen months later.

She was gone. His career was gone. The government had a shackle around his neck. What was there to live for?

He retrieved it and swiped the sand from the blade on his rolled cuffs. The silver glinted against his forearm. He pressed the metal against his flesh. Wouldn't be the first attempt. Maybe he'd succeed this time. Drew it along his arm—

"Never did understand how they stand up on a piece of wood."

Canyon jerked at the deep voice. He returned his Emerson to his pocket and eyed the old man a few feet away. Looked like the same man from the 300 earlier. What was he saying? Something about wood?

Canyon followed the man's gaze to the water, the surfers. Ah. Surfboards. "They're not wood."

"Really?"

"Polyurethane and fiberglass or cloth. Depends on the board." He might be off-kilter, but he wasn't stupid. The man had a military cut and bearing. "What's your game?"

A slow smile quirked the face lined with age. White hair rustled under the tease of a salty breeze. "Recycling soldiers."

Why wouldn't they leave him alone? Believe he'd keep his trap shut when he said he'd keep his trap shut? "Sorry, I don't have anything to say."

"Yes, that was quite apparent."

Hesitation stopped Canyon from trudging back to his car. This man had been at his evaluation? Where. . . ? "You were behind the mirror."

"While you said little, your actions said much more, Captain Metcalfe."

A knot formed in his gut. "In case you missed the point, I'm no longer a captain. Go back to your leeches and tell them I'm done."

"Is your career worth cutting your wrists, Captain?"

The knot tightened. "My career was everything," he ground out. "It's who I am." He swallowed. "Was."

"Yes." The man smiled. "You wanted to finish what your father started."

A blaze scorched his chest. "Who are you? What do you know about my father?" Who did this guy think he was?

"Major Owen Metcalfe lost his life trying to free his spec-ops team from a POW camp during Vietnam."

Canyon jerked his attention back to the water. Focused on the undulating waves. The way they rolled in, rolled out. Just like breathing. In. . .out. . . "How—how do you know about my father?" The only reason Canyon knew was because the government tried to use it against him in his trial.

Slowly the man turned toward him, his smile growing.

Only then did Canyon recognize him. "General Lambert." He took a step back. "I didn't. . . You're out of uniform."

"Yes, thank goodness. I've put on a few pounds since they issued the last uniform." Lambert laughed and pointed. "Walk with me, Captain."

What possessed Canyon to indulge him, he didn't know. But he found himself walking the quiet beach, curious that the general would seek him out. Was it yet another trap?

"So that you will understand me, I have read the full file on Tres Kruces."

Of course. He'd fallen right into the general's trap, hadn't he? "This conversation is over." He pivoted and started back to his car.

"If my memory serves me correctly, the vote was three to *one*."

Canyon hesitated. Cursed himself for hesitating. *Just walk away.* That's what they'd done to him.

"What would you say the value of that single dissenter is worth?"

"Nothing. I still lost my career, everything."

"What if that dissenter held the power to *change* everything? What would you say it was worth then?"

Eyeballing the man, Canyon tried to think past his drumming pulse. "My life."

Lambert nodded. "Good. . .good."

Good? How could he say that? What use was a dissenter now anyway? But that unflappable grin and knowing eyes—this man knew something.

"You." Canyon stumbled back as if hit by a squall. "It was you. You were the dissenter." He slid a hand over his head and neck. "General, I— It has to stay buried. Or I go down hard and fast. I'm not playing with this fire."

Hands in his pockets, Lambert smiled up at him. "I am not here in any official capacity related to the U.S. government."

Dare he hope that this nightmare was over?

"How do you like working as a physical therapist?"

Canyon shrugged. "Not bad. It's work. I help people." He hated it.

"That's what's important to you, helping people, is it not?" When Canyon shrugged again, Lambert continued. "Thought so. I have a proposition for you, Captain. One that will get you back in your game."

Wariness crowded out hope. "What game is that?"

"The one you do best. The one that allows you to serve your country, use the medic skills crucial to saving lives, and be part of a winning team."

"They benched me, said I was done, no more or they'd—"

"What do *you* say?"

A wild, irregular cadence pounded in his chest. "I'm ready to get off the bench."

CHAPTER 1

Love is whatever you can still betray.
Betrayal can only happen if you love.
JOHN LeCARRE

Bolivarian Republic of Venezuela
Two Years Later

If she had a heart, she might be capable of tears. If she had feelings, she might hurt.

But she had neither. Not anymore. Hard mortar sat in her chest forcefully pumping the blood through her veins. Curled on her side, Danielle Roark closed her mind to her naked body, to the bruises, the blood. Moving had dire consequences—namely waking the snoring slob behind her. When she made the last escape attempt, he'd beaten her unconscious.

She shoved her thoughts toward the plan. Weeks of preparation. Weeks of rape and torture. Were it not for the discovery she'd made, she would lie down and die. But they'd taken enough of her soul to stir the embers of revenge. Now, she'd make sure there was nothing left to identify of these barbaric apes. Back home in the States, her father and stepmother were celebrating Thanksgiving. Today, she'd celebrate with them, by gaining her freedom.

A loud snort and the subsequent long sigh that always signaled when the drunk general entered a deep sleep echoed in the dank room. *Now!*

Using her tongue, she pushed the plastic from her mouth and moved with the grace of the demolitions expert she was. She slipped from the bed, slowed her breathing, and stretched one foot forward. Her toe touched the chilled cement. Shivers danced through her. Darting a glance to the disgusting form on the thin mattress, she glided across the room to his bag. Though she itched to put her clothes on, she knew if he awoke and found her dressing, it'd start all over again.

Eyes on him, she stealthily allowed her hands to search his bag for the thumb drive he used last night. If she could find that, if she could get the proof. . .then she could end this. And in days, he'd be dead.

Her fingers closed around a thin, plastic object. Exultant, she drew it out. Jaw clamped, she watched for any sign of him waking as she encased the stick drive in the cellophane. Shivering in the chilly November night, she unwound the long thread from her back tooth that she'd secured yesterday, tied it around the device, leaving just enough to anchor it to her molar, then forced herself to swallow. She might as well have tried to gulp a grenade, it felt so large.

The savage was still snoring. Temptation pushed her to the chair where his weapon lay on the cushion. All she had to do was lift it, aim, and pull the trigger. It'd be over. Right now. She could kill him. He deserved that. *She* deserved that. Deserved to see his blood pouring over the cement for what he'd done, what he'd ripped from her time and again.

Imbecile thought he was smart. Yeah, right. So smart he hadn't noticed the odd flavor in his liquor. But if she killed him here, another would rise to continue his work. That, she couldn't allow.

Dani drifted to the end of the bed. Lifted the army jacket he'd shed in his haste to have his perverted pleasure. Though she worked for quiet, the sound of her fingers against the stiff fabric seemed to scream through the cement room. Her hand trembled as she fastened the two middle buttons. When she reached for the pants, his foot dragged over the bed.

A grunt.

Her heart pinged off her ribs. Her life was more important than modesty. She snatched his gun and spun.

"Wha. . . ?" General Bruzon staggered upward, his thick salt-and-pepper hair askew. He looked around, his movements sluggish and uncoordinated. "Guards!"

She aimed and fired—at the window. Running, she eased the trigger back again. Glass shattered. With the gun hitting the pane first, Dani dove through the portal to freedom. As the glass sliced her flesh, prickly fire chewed her arms and sides. Pain had no voice tonight. She had to make it.

Blaring and grating, a siren screamed through the night.

Seconds later the lawn lit up brighter than Times Square on New

Year's Eve. Despite pain and fear, she sprinted around the building. Rocks and burrs pricked the soles of her bare feet. She plunged onward, unheeding.

A door flung open from the side of the building, diverting Dani to a nearby truck where she pressed her back against the hull. Even this late at night in late November, the temperatures in Venezuela hit a balmy midsixties.

Can't stop. Not now.

Panting, she glanced toward the ocean that waited beyond the cliff. Even under the glare of the searchlights, the dark water twinkled. Beckoning her. Calling. Luring. If only the wood was where Hugo had promised to leave it.

Betting your life on a man's word—what an idiot!

A commotion rent the bright night. Dani frowned as she tried to make out the noise. It sounded hollow. Pounding, like a bad bass beat. But amid the unfolding chaos, it was indecipherable. She scooted along the truck, inching closer. From beneath the chassis, she drew out a small wooden pallet. A nervous smile skidded into her lips. Hugo had done it. Like he promised.

She peered around the truck—and froze. Dark shadows rippled toward her like a heat wave. Only it wasn't water. Dogs! A dozen of them.

If she ran, the guards would gun her down.

If she didn't, the dogs would rip her apart.

Bullets or teeth.

Either way she was fated to die.

Dani clamped her jaw tight. Faced the water.

God. . .if You're there. . .

He wasn't. Hadn't been for the last six months. She was on her own.

With renewed determination to do everything she could to protect herself, Dani propelled herself the thirty meters toward the churning ocean that waited below the lip of the cliff.

Barking grew louder. Closer.

Snapping jaws pursued her as the killer canines lunged for her. Panic ricocheted off her ribs. Push. Harder. Had to make it. . .

Within a half dozen feet, she flung the three-foot square raft over the edge. As she leapt, red-hot fire tore through her calf—seconds later the needling registered in her mind. A dog had caught her leg! Sailing through the air, she kicked with both feet. The beast finally reacted to the free fall and released her.

RONIE KENDIG

She plummeted—feeling free! In the split second her foot stabbed the water, she spotted the wood bobbing northeast of her position. Icy liquid devoured her. Dani let the ocean take her down. Down. It'd be easy to just keep sinking. Never return to anyone or anything. Ultimate freedom.

But she couldn't. Not if she wanted Bruzon six feet under.

She launched upward, using her arms to gain the surface faster. Gasping, she searched the dark water for the wood. As she did, she saw the dog limping onto the shore, head down. He looked back at her and snarled, as if to blame her for the leg injury. *Guess we're even.* With the salt water, the searing wound he'd given her was enough to make anyone cry.

Anyone but her.

Knowing Bruzon and his men would hop in their boats and choppers to find her and teach her yet another vicious lesson, Dani swam a mean breaststroke toward the raft. The waves struggled against her, but she pushed herself. Had to. Finally, her fingers grazed the sodden wood.

Even once she folded herself onto it, she wouldn't be safe. Bruzon would search hard and long to find her, especially if he figured out what she'd stolen. For her, it was a guarantee the man would never rape another girl. To him, it was the loss of his entire pathetic empire. One he'd seized through brute force over her mother's beloved country.

Gripping the slick wood, she hauled herself onto it, ignoring the chill skittering over her pebbled flesh. The handmade raft buoyed her as the waves tossed and turned on this sleepless night as if ready to belch her back onto the beach. She squinted up at the dark sky, at the thick clouds barricading the stars beyond. Much like Bruzon keeping her from home. A dull moon seemed a homing beacon against her bare legs.

Getting revenge required getting back to the States. Twenty-two kilometers stretched between Dani and hope. Twelve nautical miles that would put her in international waters.

Light stabbed the night.

She whipped around, the army jacket heavy with ocean water as she paddled.

Bruzon's speedboat roared over the waves.

They were headed straight toward her. A metallic flavor glanced off her tongue. Watching the boat, she quickened her strokes, the wood chaffed her arm. No good. The boat gained too quickly. She'd have to go under.

Inhaling deeply, she slid off the raft and swam through the lukewarm

20

ocean. Believing herself a safe distance away, she drifted toward the surface. With great control and tilting her head back, she eased her ears and nose above the surface.

A VFA soldier leaned over the edge of the boat and lifted the raft. *"No es nada. Ella no está aquí,"* he shouted toward the front and dropped the board. *Plunk!*

That's right. Keep thinking it's nothing, that I'm not here.

The spotlight swung in a lazy circle over the water. As it fractured her space, Dani stopped treading water and sank.

Even with her eyes closed against the saltiness, she could detect the brightness probing the waters, disappear, then probe again. Flutter kicking as gently as possible, she remained in place. Her head throbbed. She couldn't hold her breath much longer. A burn emanated through her chest and threatened to drown her. She tensed, knowing she'd have to break for air. Maybe it was okay. . .

The light seemed magnetically drawn to her. It pierced the dark waters again. It glanced over her, pausing. Dani let herself sink again, but her pulse ramped up until it pounded in sync with the drumming motor.

Is this how she would die? Would she never get to see her sister, niece, and nephews again? While she didn't have the greatest family, she did love her father and sister. Abigail, the wicked stepmother, could take a flying leap. It wasn't every day your ex-boyfriend's sister married your father.

But still, Dani wanted to see them again. *Please.*

Finally, water churned under the frantic thrashing of the engine. The boat tore off.

She shoved herself upward—and burst out of the water. Sucking in air, she also caught a mouthful of water. Coughing and gagging, she swatted the hair from her eyes. She spit as she searched for the raft, then swam to it. She dragged herself aboard. Water sloshed her face as the waves tossed her over one crest after another. Although exhaustion tugged at her limbs, she paddled. Had to. . .get. . .to—

Dani yawned.

International waters.

Over the next hour, she heard the grumble of more boats and the thunder of a chopper, but she'd exceeded their search radius. As one chopper loomed close, she mentally drew out an RPG and launched it. Then plotted the plastique she could rig to the rotors so the craft and crew wouldn't have a prayer. Her eyes drifted closed, thinking of the thing raining down fire on the ocean, the craft in a million pieces. Sick how the mind of a demolitions expert worked after six months' captivity. To think, she'd once been the sweet, compliant daughter of a senator.

Well, maybe not compliant.

A loud bang cracked the night. Brilliance shattered the darkness.

Dani jerked, terrified they'd found her. Only to spot a storm surging and racing toward her. The negative image of the lightning lingered in her eyes. Another bolt flashed through the sky. Within seconds rain unleashed and blanketed the area. The waters grew angry and threatening. Had she angered Poseidon? The thought would've seemed comical were she not facing an endless body of night-darkened liquid. A giant wave rose like the god himself.

It'd toss her into the deep and thrash her like whipped cream. Pulse crashing, Dani wiggled her fingers into the bindings that held the boards together.

The mountainous wall of black rose over her. Waaay over her.

Stricken, she inhaled deeply as the water towered over her, seemingly holding its own breath—then lunged at her. It slammed her into its depths. Swirling, spinning, she clung to the raft, praying it would hold. That it would keep her afloat. Finding the surface after being plunged downward often proved impossible—and deadly.

Miraculously, the raft plopped upward and crested another wave.

Dani sucked in a huge breath before clamping her mouth shut and squeezing her eyes shut as the water plunged her deep again. Then. . .up. . . up. . . It hurled her farther—

Crack! Thud!

Everything went black.

Hands pawed at her.

"Careful!"

"Pull her up," a man's voice skated down her neck.

They'd found her! Disoriented, Dani writhed and screamed. Bruzon would beat her, rip out her soul this time. No, she couldn't go back. She kicked. Raked fingers over flesh.

"Argh! Dad, get her," the nearby voice growled.

"I radioed the Coast Guard, Grant." A woman's worried tone spiraled through Dani, easing her fears.

This wasn't Bruzon. These people were speaking English. American

English. Not the butchered form she'd heard for months. She pushed her eyes open as she was lowered onto something hard...and dry. Blurry images danced over her.

"What's your name?" The dark image in front of her swayed and faded.

Pentagon, Arlington County, Virginia

A light rap on the glass door jerked Olin Lambert's attention to the chairman of the Joint Chiefs lingering outside. He punched to his feet, spine stiff, and pointed to the leather seats on the opposite side of his massive mahogany desk. "Admiral, come in, sir. Have a seat."

"Actually," Admiral Langston said, "I'd like you to take a ride with me."

Halfway between returning to his seat and standing, Olin paused, looking over his silver-rimmed glasses. A ride? He knew better than to question the admiral. He straightened and lifted his hat from the desk. He strode out the door, pulling it shut behind him.

"I have something I think you'll want to see," Langston said.

"Very good, sir." Olin nodded to his assistant sitting at her desk and relayed a silent signal to hold his calls until he returned. He eyed the salt-and-pepper hair of the decade-younger chief as he followed him down the hall and into the elevator.

Since assuming his role as chairman of the Joint Chiefs three months earlier, Langston had kept to himself. There was much to learn and even more to unlearn about his new boss. Would Olin be able to woo him into his court with Nightshade the way he had the man's predecessor?

Once the door shut, Langston pressed the elevator button. "Coast Guard picked up a woman in the Gulf."

Olin shook his head. "Illegals just won't learn." But Langston wouldn't call him out for an illegal—that happened nearly every day. So something bigger was happening here.

The doors slid back with a soft whoosh, and Langston stepped into the large atrium of the building. He donned his white hat as the early morning sun embraced them. Inside the Suburban and on their way, Langston leaned on the console that saddled the space between them. "She wasn't an illegal."

Olin arched his eyebrows. He studied the brown eyes that held his, as if a hidden meaning should exist. He shouldn't have waited so long to figure out the madness to Admiral Langston's methods. Should've taken the admiral to lunch to familiarize himself with the man who now advised the president and the secretary of defense.

Regardless if the woman in the Gulf wasn't an illegal, if it hadn't made CougarNews yet, then things were about to get interesting. "Who is she?"

"For security concerns, her identity is being withheld until we can debrief her fully." He huffed. "Not that it's done any good. She's not talking." Langston peeked up at an orange light as they slid through the intersection without slowing. "We think she's Senator Roark's daughter."

"Roark?" Heat prickled the back of Olin's neck. *Jacqueline.*

He'd never forget the night the report came in that a Corps of Engineers team had been taken captive in the Venezuelan jungle. Then his heart sank when he saw the name of Jacqueline's daughter on the list of missing. Although he tried to discreetly search back channels to find out what happened and locate her, he'd been stifled at every attempt. And doing that made it risky to send out his black-ops team to find her; besides, the team had been shelved when Connelly, the former Joint Chiefs chairman, tried to salvage his career. And failed. Thus the new chairman sitting next to him.

"We've had her twenty-three hours. Not an iota of information." Langston dragged his gaze from the road. "She said she'll only talk to one person."

Olin waited.

"You."

Surprise sparked through him. "Me?" Why would Danielle ask for him? The last time he'd seen her, she was thirteen years old and standing beside an oak coffin, begging her mother not to leave her.

Olin held the dash as they rounded the corner to Walter Reed, then parked outside the emergency entrance.

Keeping pace as the admiral worked his way to the third floor, Olin ached for the young woman. If she'd been captured by Venezuelan rebels, held for six months, and managed an escape, no telling what condition she'd be in—mentally or physically.

"Take care of her, Olin." The decade-old admonishment raked over his conscience.

Langston marched to the end of the hall where two Marines jerked to attention, eyes forward. Another man sat across from them in a metal chair, looking haggard in his unzipped navy jacket. He rose as they approached and offered a salute.

"At ease," Admiral Langston said as he scowled at the loner. "You family?" The growl in Langston's voice could not be missed. No doubt he was ready to throttle whoever had violated the security order and contacted family.

The man's pale eyes widened. "No, sir. Chief Petty Officer Range Metcalfe, U.S. Coast Guard, sir." He nodded toward the secured room. "I lifted her from the sloop that found her. I was ordered to remain here until debriefed."

Ah, that explained the messy hair and exhaustion ringing his eyes. Olin eyed the name over the man's chest pocket. Metcalfe. Was it possible...? His gaze flipped to the eyes. Same blue eyes. But black hair, and a bit less suave looking. Could this young officer be the brother to Nightshade's team member, secretly designated "Wolfsbane" in Olin's reports?

"Let's talk." Langston pointed toward a corner as he motioned to Olin to join them. "Tell us what you know."

Back against the wall, CPO Metcalfe stifled a yawn. "The distress call came in at 0217. Vacationers found a woman drifting on a makeshift raft eight klicks from St. Thomas." He shifted his gaze between the two of them. "When I arrived on deck, she was clothed only in an army jacket." His nervous gaze bobbed on that info. "Nothing else."

"Army?" Langston again scowled.

"Venezuelan—VFA, sir."

Olin narrowed his eyes. "Are you certain?"

Determination glinted in the rugged face. "The name on the jacket was Bruzon."

Mind awhirl with that beauty of a piece of information, Olin schooled his response. He met his superior's gaze. Langston went silent, his face like a stone.

Metcalfe leaned forward. "You know who that is, right?"

Olin ignored the question. "Did she say how she came by the jacket?"

"No, sir. Wouldn't talk. And I can't blame her. In the condition she was in, I'm floored she's alive."

It felt like grease chugged through Olin's veins. "What condition is that?"

"Sir, she'd been beaten. Visible signs of rape, torture, too. She wouldn't let anyone touch her. Well, except me when I lifted her out." His throat processed a swallow. "I'd kill whoever did this, given the chance."

Admiral Langston patted Metcalfe's shoulder and thanked him. He shifted to Olin. "Get what you can from her. We're running out of time."

With a large exhale, Olin started for the room. Palm on the door, he looked back to the chief petty officer. "Metcalfe." He toyed with what he was about to do. He already knew the answer, but he wanted the man to trust him. Trust bought loyalty better than any greenback. "Happen to know Captain Canyon Metcalfe?"

Shoulders up, the Coastie looked between Olin and Langston, then slowly nodded. "Yes, sir. My brother—older by a year, and I never let him forget it."

Sibling rivalry. He wasn't surprised. "I don't doubt that." With a knowing grin, he pushed through the room. And froze.

A frail slip of a woman sat curled on her side, legs drawn close under the pale blue blanket she'd pulled over her shoulders. Her gaze rested on the bank of windows overlooking the city, but the vacant expression told him her mind wrestled somewhere else. Dark brown hair hung down her back, stringy and tangled as if she'd showered but never combed it.

She hadn't flinched at his entrance. Or turned to see who entered. Did she even hear him?

He took a few tentative steps to bring himself into her direct view. No response.

"Danielle?"

She blinked. Her eyes darted to the floor, where they skidded and leapt from one object to another.

Noting her nervous reaction, Olin lowered himself into the vinyl chair nestled under the window. His heart sagged at her gaunt face, her right eye swollen shut. Her lower lip ballooned and cut. Butterfly stitches winged over her eyebrow and another on her chin.

If Jacqueline saw her once-vibrant daughter haunted and distant like this, she would roll over in her grave. *I've failed you, Jacqueline.*

Tucking aside his shock, he scooted to the edge of the seat. "Danielle, it's me, Olin Lambert." He set his hat on the table next to her bed.

She followed his movement, her gaze staying on the hat.

He rested his forearms on his knees. "You're home, Danielle. Back in America."

His chest thumped, remembering CPO Metcalfe's description: *"clothed only in an army jacket."* Everything paternal and primal rose up. He fought the urge to go to her, wrap this young woman in his

26

arms, and promise to avenge whatever had happened. But the Coastie's comment about her not allowing anyone to touch her kept him seated.

The clock over the door ticked down the minutes in the haunting quiet. Olin thanked God there wasn't a window in the door because Langston would no doubt have his face glued to it.

"I'll wait, Danielle," he said, keeping his tone soft, fatherly. "You asked for me; I'm here." Sitting back, he crossed his legs. "Whenever you're ready."

Silently, he prayed. Prayed hard. That God would reach into this woman, stop her from disappearing from reality and delving into madness and delirium that sometimes happened to those who endured captivity.

After nearly thirty minutes of silence and one interruption when Langston peeked in and Olin gave a grave, glowering shake of his head, Danielle let the blanket fall from her shoulder. She pushed out of the bed and plodded to the small bathroom in flannel pajamas and bare feet. Bent over the sink, she cupped her hand under the stream and sipped.

Olin stood. Did she need a drink? He looked at the pitcher by her bed. Should he offer water from it? When he glanced back to her, she stood over the toilet, hunched. A minute later, a gagging noise clenched his stomach.

"Danielle!" He rushed to her side. "Are you ill?" Only then did he notice she had a hand in her mouth. "What're you doing?"

A demonic-like sound erupted. *Splat!* Vomit launched from her mouth and hit the commode, wall, and floor. A long string of orangeish spittle dangled from her mouth—wait, no! Not spittle. A string, tethered to something.

His own stomach roiled as he watched her unhook it from her teeth. Spitting in the sink, she held the thing in her hand. An acidic stench devoured the air. The smell proved sickening, but he couldn't take his eyes off the object.

Stunned, he waited as she peeled back what looked like film from... some gray thing. His pulse ratcheted. A thumb drive! His gaze shot to hers.

Danielle cupped water, slurped, swished, then spit. Delicately patting the edges of her injured mouth with the back of her hand, she turned to him. And stretched out her hand, palm open with the device.

Cold, dark, unfeeling eyes came to his. "Everything you need to kill him."

CHAPTER 2

Undisclosed Location, Virginia

Stacked on either side of the point of entry Nightshade waited. The seven members of the team were split into two groups—Alpha Team, led by Max, and Bravo Team, led by Colton "Cowboy" Neeley. They'd been a team for less than two years and when Reyes died, that left them one man down. Instead of merely replacing body count, the Old Man added two former spec ops men to Nightshade. Duty demanded the team work efficiently and with stealth. They'd trained for weeks.

Today would decide if they were ready to face an enemy with cohesion.

After a firm nod, Max trained his gaze on the point of entry. Griffin "Legend" Riddell, who had helped put the team together, stood behind him and patted his shoulder, signaling readiness. Max took a step back, raised his foot, and rammed the heel of his boot into the door. Vibrations rattled through his leg as the door flung open, hinges groaning. Dust filled the air. He snapped up his weapon and supplied cover as Legend moved forward and tossed in a flash-bang.

"Flash out!" Legend returned to the stacked position.

As the *tink-tink-tink* of the canister seemed to count down the seconds to its detonation, Max focused on the dimly lit corridor beckoning them. Itching to take them down.

He glanced aside for a second, waiting for the white-hot flash of the detonation.

Boom!

A gust of warm wind and dust rushed from the building, as if fleeing the chaos descending upon it.

Familiar with the precision and maneuvering required to clear a building and not shoot or kill one of his own, Max hustled across the threshold. He went right, crisscrossing the point of entry with Legend, and buttonhooked.

A tango leapt from the corner. *Tat-tat-tat!*

The target fell.

"Tango down," Max called as he swept his gaze until it intersected with Legend's line of fire.

"Copy." Legend didn't hesitate. "Clear."

The rustle of tactical pants and the soft squeak of boots on the dirty vinyl floor helped Max keep tabs on the team as they filed into the boxed corridor.

He rushed past a kneeling Legend who held a corner, his weapon aimed across the L-shaped juncture that fed them into the rest of the building. The hostages were believed to be in Red Three on the upper level. First order of business: clear Blue Two, Three, Four and find the stairs.

Back to the plaster, Max sidled up to the corner where yet another hall presented itself. T intersection. Not good. They'd have two routes to address in tandem and not get killed.

First things first. The hall that banked to the right. It could hold numerous tangos. Or none.

Canyon "Midas" Metcalfe pied out, starting at the left and sweeping in an arc to the right. He pied out as far as possible, moving forward to increase his angle of fire farther into the dead space, Marshall "the Kid" Vaughn right behind him. The former Army Ranger had grown up a lot since the team's first days together.

Keeping tabs on Cowboy allowed Max to slip into position at the corner, trusting the man would alert them to trouble before anyone ended up exposed. He signaled back to Legend to cover the far corner where they were blind to make sure more tangos didn't pop up.

Finally, Midas stopped pieing. He paused, squeezed his eyes, then shook his head and continued.

What was that? With the muzzle of his weapon almost flush with the corner, Max knelt. More rustling brought up the rear as Alpha and Bravo fell into place. He felt the presence of Legend and Aladdin at his six. He nodded his readiness.

"Move!" Midas hissed.

Simultaneously they entered the dead space. A sniper, Cowboy's movements were stealthy and silent as he hurried forward. Max stayed on his knee, pivoting around the corner, sighting shadows, dust, smoke, searching for—

Tat-tat-tat!

Cowboy fired before the dust cleared enough for Max to spot the tango flipping around the corner at the other end of the corridor. "Tango down."

Using hand signals, Max sent Bravo Team snaking down the hall in a bound-and-cover approach. They'd already met with resistance, so caution should be exercised more than ever.

With the others executing their plan, Max prompted his team to proceed. On his feet, he hustled forward. At the T intersection he waited, knowing Legend had swept to the opposite side. Max and Legend cleared their immediate areas along their respective walls, starting from the corner and continuing to the farthest. For Max, that meant staring down a door marked STAIRS. The hostages should be up there.

Poised to the left of the door, Max nodded to Aladdin, who provided cover for their six.

Like before, they teamed up and provided protective cover as Max busted open the door. His heart rammed into his lungs as he sighted figures at the opposite end of the hall. He got a bead on the closest.

"Friendly, friendly!" Cowboy's whispered call stayed Max's trigger finger.

He blew out a breath. Stairs now. It'd been an easy insertion so far. No doubt they'd meet heavy opposition up that stairwell. Max stalked onward. Up the stairs he went, sweeping his weapon side to side, checking for ledges where bad guys could take out the team. He knew from instinct, from training with these men, that Legend was one step behind him, covering.

Despite their efforts to remain stealthy, the iron stairs rattled as the guys followed. Reaching the point just before he could be engaged from above, Max turned around and covered overhead, searching for an opening, an opportunity for someone to take his head off or add another hole. Sure enough, a clear angle.

Tension mounted. Quick and quiet, he blew out another breath. Another step. He ascended stepping backward. Ever so carefully. . . backward. . .covering the side and above. Legend still covered him and a sea of tactical gear snaked upward. Fluid. Smooth. Man, he loved this team. At the top, Max shifted to cover overhead as Legend remained front oriented.

Groan!

Max snapped his weapon to the right as something flew up. He fired. The tango collapsed. "Tango down."

Like an undammed river, the team flooded onto the second level. Left and right engagements ensued with multiple "tango down" calls. Partitions and cubicle walls created a nightmare of a logistical challenge. As chaos fell quiet, he heard it.

Whimpering and grunts carried through the air.

The sounds drew him onward. Adrenaline sped through his veins. Bravo Team swept wide left, coming around the back side of the stairwell.

Alpha team cleared right. Then left. *The place is like a maze.* With each advance, the rooms brightened. A window? Light? Hopes rose. Had to be close now. Another L intersection. He stepped around—

Snapped back, his pulse drumming. Held up a closed fist, eyed the team. Nightshade had grouped into strategic positions, all within a dozen feet of each other. Working in teams they protected the hostages but also themselves—no friendly fire.

His split-second recon revealed the scene that faced them. A brightly lit open space. Though the floodlights worked to blind him, he used hand signals to relay the layout, as he could decipher it: Two tangos guarding three hostages. In the corner. Guns to the hostages' heads.

Legend nodded.

Max whipped into the open.

Flashes of movement. Max nailed a tango to the right of a hostage. He buttonhooked as more gunfire rattled off and cordite filled the air. Smoke and dust spiraled through the blinding setup.

A shadow flickered to the extreme left. Max turned.

So did Legend.

In the second it took Legend to turn, panic spiked through Max.

As if in a slow-frame action shot like a cheap movie, he saw the scene unfold. Saw Legend's finger coiled in the trigger well. Saw the shadow take shape. And saw *who* it was.

"No!"

Tat-tat-tat! Tat-tat-tat-tat!

Max lunged, slammed Legend's weapon down. "Hold your fire!"

The reel skipped into real time.

Aladdin stepped from the far side.

"Hold your fire. Hold fire!" Max made sure the entire team saw his raised fist. "It's over." Well, at least the drill. The fury roiling off Legend was a totally different thing. When Lambert intro'd the new guys, Legend had been more than clear about his feelings regarding

John "Squirt" Dighton and Azzan "Aladdin" Yasir, especially the latter.

"Fool!" Puffed up and tensed, Legend cursed. "What're you doing over there?"

Shrugging, Aladdin pointed to the walled space from which he'd appeared. "Half dozen tangos waiting in ambush for the team."

It seemed Legend's chest and biceps swelled. "You should be with the team!" He stormed forward. "*With* them, *protecting* them."

When Legend clenched his fists, Max leapt in front of him. "Hold up, stop."

"I just saved every man on this team." Aladdin raised his arms. "What's your problem?"

Brows slamming down and whites of his eyes practically glowing, Legend took another step forward. "You want to know my problem?"

"No, no, he doesn't." Midas rushed into the fray as he pulled Aladdin back.

"Legend," Max snapped. Waited for the big guy to acknowledge him. Finally, brown eyes came to his. Though tamed the storm still raged. "I told you." Lips tight, nostrils flared, Legend scowled. "He's trouble. He don't know how to work with a team. Bravo Team is dead because he wasn't there to back them up."

"They're not dead." Aladdin wasn't backing down. He'd worked solo for too long and didn't know when to yield. "They're alive because I detected an ambush and intercepted."

It sure sounded like Aladdin had moved closer. The man had brains, right? He wouldn't be that stupid, stepping into the cauldron of Legend's fury.

"This team works *together*." Legend came forward as if Max didn't exist. "If you can't work *with* the team, following protocol, maybe you don't belong. Know what I'm saying?"

Angling to the side, Max realized he had essentially been sandwiched between the two, who were ready to throw down. "Hey!" He sent a fierce warning through his expression to Aladdin. "Stand down."

Aladdin's green eyes flickered to Max. The tension in the man's face reduced, though not much.

"Look at this, ladies and gents. The assassin knows how to take orders after all."

Aladdin went rigid. "I just executed four tangos who would've split your heart in two. That is, if you have one."

Air behind him swirled. Images of his friend killing the newest team member flashed through his mind. Max flipped around to Legend.

"No. Don't. I'll handle it."

Hands out to the side, Griffin all but snorted. "I'm good. I'm good."

Max glanced to Aladdin. From his periphery he saw—but could do nothing to stop—the hammer of a fist sailing into Aladdin's jaw. *Thud!* Aladdin stumbled back.

Max shoved Legend away. "Stand down!"

Legend took a step back. "I'm good—*better.*" He grinned, then flicked a narrowed gaze to Aladdin. "I nearly killed you, fool. Why Lambert accepted you, why you agreed, I don't know. What I do know is that the men on this team"—Legend shifted, indicating the other four hanging back—"they'll put it on the line for you." With a swagger, he moved backward. "Tell me, Lone Wolf, will you do the same for them?"

"I did—I saved their lives!"

"No." Max tried to harness his own anger. "You abandoned your team. Who had Midas's six while you were playing hero?" He sighed and pinched the bridge of his nose. "We're a team. Nightshade. Looking out for each other is number one because without that commitment, we cease to exist."

"So you don't care about the six tangos."

Max walked over to the plastic dummy dangling from a spring-loaded axle. He stuffed a finger through a hole in the head of one, where clearly Aladdin had killed the tango. "This guy?" He patted the dummy's head. "No, because I knew he'd be there."

Aladdin grunted his disapproval.

"This exercise was to find out—would you be where we expect and need you to be?" Max let the smirk slip from his face. "Don't fail the team again. Or you'll be gone."

Roark Residence, Virginia
New Year's Eve

Pain turned her inside out.

Darkness held her captive. Pushing her down, farther. . .farther. . .

Fire shot through her pelvis. She screamed—but no sound came out. Instead, gushes of water poured into her throat. She coughed. Gagged.

A sickening, sweaty body pressed on her.

"No!"

Dani bolted upright in bed. Shuddering, she searched the darkened room for the predator, for the man bent on stealing her virtue. But. . .it was too late. That was gone. She had nothing left for him, or anyone else.

The massive room closed in on her. Billowing curtains around the four-poster bed danced like ghosts. A ceiling fan circled lazily over the sitting area. Marble shone brightly against the light she'd left on in the bathroom. All taunting her. This had been the room of a spoiled, naive rich girl. A girl now gone. Dead.

Everything in her trembled. She drew her legs to her chest and hugged herself tightly. Would the shame ever go away? Tears stung her eyes. Slipped past her tight hold and scalded her cheeks. A sob erupted.

Outside her door, light scampered and grew brighter as footsteps thudded to the threshold. Was it Alexandra or her father? She thought about the soft, quick steps. Her sister.

She cupped a hand over her mouth to stifle the cries, ignoring the chill seeping into her bones. If Alexandra heard her crying, if she heard her moving around, she'd come in. Try to act like she knew what to say. Comfort her with empty words.

As quietly as possible, Dani lay back against the pillows and drew the covers over her chest. When had it gotten so cold?

Facing away from the door and peering out through the slit in the heavy baroque curtains, Dani spied the moon. Full and brilliant. After two weeks in the hospital, she'd come home. Life blurred past, Christmas a vague memory—what gifts had she given or received?—and here she lay, still wishing she hadn't survived that tormented water. Back in the States a month, but even now she still didn't want to be home. Where things were normal. She didn't want to go on as if nothing happened. Didn't want to face her friends. Her family. Her niece and nephews. Her father. Anybody.

She watched light invade darkness until it eventually overtook her. Out there, beyond the curtains and small balcony, the world continued as if no tragedy had ever taken place. As if she didn't matter. She was insignificant. The emptiness of the word mirrored the emptiness within her.

A knock at the door made her blink.

"Danielle, I'm coming in," Alexandra called, softly but firmly.

Soon came the creak of the heavy oak door, a click of the lock, then soft padding over the wood floor. . .then stifled steps as Alexandra walked on the handcrafted Persian rug. The lower portion of the bed near Dani's feet sunk down under the weight of her sister. Warm pressure rested on her ankle.

What? Was her sister going to once again tell Dani that she knew she was hurting? That while Alexandra had never been. . .*violated*—her sister was apparently unable to even say the word *rape*—she understood the depression, yet she didn't want to watch her waste away?

"You might want to get dressed," Alexandra said, a surprising strength in her words. "Because in five minutes, I'm sending someone up. He dropped by, brought flowers."

He? Dani whipped around, disbelief and shock overtaking her empty mood.

Alexandra pushed off the bed, a triumphant expression on her face. "Five minutes. If you don't want Chief Petty Officer Metcalfe to see you with hair tangled, clothes wrinkled, and bad breath, I'd suggest you clean up."

Panic beat a wild rhythm in her chest. "No."

Already at the door, Alexandra didn't hesitate.

"Alexandra Norah! Don't—"

The door closed.

Dani darted to it, her head spinning. She braced against the wall, waiting until the hazy darkness faded. She caught her breath—just in time to hear Alexandra speaking in a singsong voice and telling the guest it'd be just a few minutes.

Slapping her hand against the elaborate paper lining the wall, she groaned. Anger morphed into rage. She spun, staring at the bed. If he came up here. . .he could. . .

No. She squeezed her eyes shut. She couldn't stay here with him. If she hurried, she could head this off. Get rid of him before he ever made it to her door.

Fury pushed her to the closet. She stared at the twenty-by-twenty space with its tufted, round bench and chandelier. Row upon row of color-organized clothes hung in obscene order. Cedar drawers. Shoes lined one wall. Gowns another.

Had she really been this spoiled? Why was it just now hitting her? Shirking the annoyance, she tugged a pair of jeans from a drawer. She then stuffed her legs into them, surprised at how they hung off her hips. Six months in captivity did a lot for a girl wanting to lose a few pounds. Nothing a belt wouldn't fix. She strapped one on and flung on a sweater. In the bathroom, she snatched the brush from the marble vanity, raised it—and froze.

There in the full-length mirror hovered a phantom. A girl she no longer knew. A girl with shattered dreams and faded bruises who looked like a bad makeup job. A girl who once believed in happily ever after. Who was a bit naive but every bit as stubborn and determined.

Oh, God...

Laughter from somewhere in the house broke into her awareness.

Dani jerked the bristles through her hair and tied back her long brown strands. She hurried to the door, whipped it open—and stood before a man.

Her heart hitched. She gulped the fear, her gaze diving to the floor. *Friend not foe. Friend not foe.* She pushed her gaze back to his.

A slow smile spread over his face, lighting his bluish eyes. He gave a curt nod. "I don't know if you remember—"

Dani eased past him, then closed the door to her room. "Coast Guard, right?" She tucked a rogue strand of hair behind her ear, trying to forget that he had carried her almost completely naked body to safety.

"Yes, ma'am." He raked a hand through his short black hair. "I... uh...just wanted to check on you. See how you were improving."

If she was right, he'd checked on her twice a week, every week. Eight times. "I'm fine." A sure, tight answer that kept her from having to go into the truth. Or go into anything all. Could she get rid of him? "Look..." She saw the hope in his gaze and lost the gumption. How could she be cruel? He'd rescued her. Kept watch over her.

Didn't matter. The last thing she wanted in her life was a man. "You can go back to your superiors, tell them I'm fine. You did your job." She feigned a smile. "You should get a gold star or something."

His expression fell. She could've sworn she heard it thunk against the floor. "I'm sorry." He glanced down. "I'm not here because of my job."

Was he blushing? Dani's nerves jitterbugged over the realization. Being in the narrow hall closed off her throat and brain. She stumbled toward the light at the end of the tunnel...er, hall. The balcony. Chief Petty Officer Metcalfe remained with her, his steps even and steady.

"Some place your dad has."

Her gaze darted to the paintings that had captured his attention. "Yeah. I guess." It was called overkill. And she hated it.

Stepping into the brilliance of the sun, Dani was startled at how good it felt. A shudder rippled through her.

"Are you cold? Should we go back inside?"

"No," she snapped, glancing toward the dark hall—and her mind plunged into the prison she'd spent so many months being dragged through. Screams. Banging. Sizzling sounds of electrical torture.

Her feet felt like bricks. Her heart careened into her stomach. Hearing hollowed.

A face burst into her vision.

With a yelp, she shoved the man back. *Fight!*

He grabbed her arms.

Dani yelled and writhed.

"Miss Roark, please! It's okay."

Shock rippled through her at the urgency in the voice and her own name. She stilled and stared back at pleading blue eyes. She wasn't in the prison. She was at home. He wasn't here to hurt her. Humiliation crowded out her panic. "I'm sorry," she whispered.

Leave. Get away. You're an idiot.

"If. . .excuse me." She stepped around him and skipped a step back into the house.

"Miss Roark, wait."

His words sent her running. She dashed into her room and slammed the door shut. Knowing Alexandra would come after her, Dani locked the door, leapt into the bed, and yanked the covers over her head.

Buried, she stemmed her tears. Focused on just being. . .safe. Alone. Quiet. He must think her an imbecile, going nuts at the sight of a lonely, dark hallway. She just wanted to be normal again. Wanted to get back to work, wanted to have a life. Not feel the stinging sensation of being raped with every step she took.

Minutes later, Alexandra's frantic voice called from the other side of the door. The handle jiggled. Her sister's quiet crying eventually faded into the oblivion of sleep that claimed Dani. By the time her eyes fluttered open, the soothing blues of dusk had plowed into the sky. She nudged back the comforter—and stopped short.

"Good evening, Danielle." Soft lines creased the eyes under white, short-cropped hair.

Instant panic bottomed out, embraced by relief. She pushed herself upright. "General Lambert." She looked to the door. It sat open. She could run. Evade. Her eyes drifted back to his. Kind. Compassionate. Fatherly. "What're you doing here?"

A sad smile tweaked the sides of his mouth. "Keeping a promise to an old friend."

Mom. The thought pushed her back against the bed.

"But I'm afraid I have bad news, Danielle. Out of respect to your mother and to you, I chose to deliver the news personally." His expression faltered in a very subtle way. What was that look? Sadness? Anger?

Braced against the edge of the bed, she waited. What could be so horrible? It wasn't like he would send her back there. It wasn't like Bruzon could come and get her. So she waited, believing she could brave whatever he told her.

He stood and walked to the windows where he peered up at the sky. Finally, he turned to her. "I'm afraid the government has. . .*concerns* about the validity of the information you delivered."

The veiled accusation drew her from the mattress. "Concerns?" Chest heaving, she tried to calm herself. "Validity? I gave them Bruzon's blueprints!"

He held up a hand as his gaze lowered. "I know. I know." A sigh. "But they question that he would leave that out for you to steal, that he would be walking around with that information. They think it's too tidy, too clean a scenario. In fact, they discovered a significant amount of evidence on your computer." He nodded to the Dell she hadn't touched since returning. "There are pieces of this so-called evidence that anyone with a brain would question the validity of, but the 'proof'"—he hooked his fingers for air quotes—"was too strong for them to deny. There were images of you with Bruzon—"

"Hello? He held me for six months. Of course I was with him!"

"Two years ago. At his vacation home."

"That's impossible!"

"And they've found an offshore account in your name. With a significant amount of money deposited recently."

Dani gulped.

"They believe you've helped Bruzon in some way to obtain either the technology or the contacts to secure the technology you say is in that underground bunker."

"Are they out of their minds? How would I gain the technology for nuclear weapons or WMDs—and that's exactly what's he's building down there!"

Lambert nodded. "I'm just trying to help you understand." He huffed. "Never mind. There is no way to understand it. But that's their position."

She sucked in a breath. That meant— "No. . ."

Sorrow clung to his handsome, weathered features. "I'm sorry, Danielle, but the FBI has been reviewing your debriefing transcripts as well, and they've requested an interview. The Senate Subcommittee on Select Intelligence is launching an investigation, which could lead to criminal charges." He drew himself straight.

"They are investigating you regarding espionage or treason."

CHAPTER 3

Capitol Hill, Washington, D.C.

February should be warm. Okay, for the average Joe, that would seem ludicrous, but Canyon preferred warm*er*. Like San Diego. Or the Caribbean. Not brittle with stinging slush numbing his toes as he climbed the steps of the Capitol building.

Canyon shrugged as he tugged open the door and stepped onto the gleaming vinyl floor on the Hill. A security checkpoint cleared him, and he strode toward courtroom A10 in response to the AHOD sent by General Lambert. Curious. Most all-hands-on-deck relays ordered deployment. This one sent him to a senate subcommittee hearing.

On the second floor, he spotted a small group huddling outside the courtroom. His mind leapfrogged over the heads—straight to one semiwavy patch of black hair. No way. What was *he* doing here?

Movement to the side snagged his attention. Max "Frogman" Jacobs. Their eyes met before the team leader passed through the double doors. Right behind him Legend strolled by, sipped from the water fountain, then disappeared into the same courtroom.

Canyon would go in eventually, but first he wanted answers. He marched up to the small crowd.

"What're you doing here?" Range glanced to the side, eyes wide.

"I could ask the same, little brother."

"I told you last night I had a trial."

Canyon blinked. "When?"

"When you came by the house to drop off Mom's prescription."

Canyon didn't remember that, but whatever. After a quick shoulder-patting hug, he grinned and glanced around those gathered, trying to understand why his brother was here instead of out baiting illegals on the Gulf.

A quasi-attractive woman with short, dark hair clung to a slick-suited guy. A politician, if the condescension oozing from the man spoke loud enough. An older suit joined them, vague recognition flickering through Canyon's mind. Where had he met him before? The man moved toward a fourth person.

A woman. Long hair hung in cascades of dark brown. Thick and silky like the chocolate fountain at the big bash Lambert threw for the team last Christmas. With her back to him, Canyon couldn't decipher age, but the thin frame was too skinny for his liking. Why women these days stayed on the gross side of skinny, he'd never get.

As soon as the older man touched her elbow, she jerked free and took a step back. Defensive posturing. Interesting.

Tension zapped the already chilled foyer. Range sucked in a quick breath.

Curiosity piqued, Canyon gauged the responses. What was going on?

"Danielle," the man spoke to her. "I'm sorry. It's time to go in. Are you ready?"

She glanced over her shoulder—straight at Canyon. The purest honeyed eyes he'd ever seen pierced him. Something deep inside him burned. Attractive? No. Beautiful. Stunning. But the vacancy in her expression pulled at him. He'd seen hollowed-out gazes like that before. Soldiers, dead on the bed of a helo.

Then his mind switched gears. Why were they leading her into the courtroom? The flood of information—and her locked gaze—left his mind jumbled. "Why. . . ?" He tried to get his brain back in gear. "Why are you here?" he mumbled as he angled his head toward his brother.

"I'm here to testify," Range said. "Remember why I missed Thanksgiving?"

Barely hearing his brother, Canyon kept his gaze on the woman. Two fresh scars pinked her forehead and chin. Maybe it wasn't anorexia that had her thin. Starvation? His brain finally engaged with the story his brother had lamented over. At the time, Canyon felt his little brother was letting his Coastie work get to him. But now, maybe he understood his brother's attention to the case. A woman escaping a Venezuelan rebel camp? Surely this wasn't that woman.

A sudden slap to his gut snapped his narrowed gaze to his brother. "I'm talking to you."

He felt the scowl and washed it free. "Sorry." Again he looked at the girl, but the older man herded her into the courtroom, sans touching. "Who is she?"

"Aren't you listening? I just told you—the woman I pulled from the Caribbean over two months ago." Range took a few steps, then pivoted toward him. "And back off."

Canyon couldn't help the grin. So, his little brother had his sights on the hottie, huh? "Isn't she a bit out of your league, rich and what, twenty-five?"

"She's only two years younger than me, and don't do that—she's not like the girls you date. She's nice."

Twenty-six, huh? A bit young but. . . Canyon grinned. "Isn't Valentine's Day soon?"

Range shook his head and closed the gap between them. "Canyon. I'm not kidding. It's not like that."

Chuckling, he enjoyed the torment on his brother's face. "Really?"

"She's been through more than enough." Range stuffed his fingers against Canyon's chest and nudged him back. "This isn't a game. Leave her alone." A warning hung in the stale, air-conditioned air. "I mean it."

Surprise wove through him. Range hadn't gone serious over a girl since the high school fallout. There was something his little brother wasn't telling.

Range sighed, then furrowed his brow. "Why are *you* here?"

Unfortunately Nightshade-related activities were eyes only. "Consultation." He patted his brother's shoulder and stalked into the courtroom, showing his ID to the guard.

Canyon planted himself in a chair in the far corner of the balcony, lower level. From this angle he had a perfect line of sight on her profile. Surprisingly, Lambert eased into the seat on her left and whispered something to her before moving into the gallery of seats fenced off behind the floor of the committee room. Sitting over her. Like a godfather. The older man—her father?—leaned down and planted a kiss on her head.

She twitched and swallowed hard.

What was that about?

As her father sat next to Lambert, the Old Man's gaze tracked the courtroom, probably searching out the team. Canyon winked at Nightshade's sponsor, then glanced back to her—and froze when his gaze collided with those caramel eyes. Something wormed through his gut, unable to break the electrified connection. The ambivalence and cool facade seemed out of place on her sultry face. As if it hid a dark secret.

"I will defend her."

At the words not his own, warmth shook Canyon. What was this feeling? Where had it come from? He'd only renewed his life to Christ a year ago, but even he had heard stories of God using people to help others. Maybe. . .maybe God could use him somehow.

Yeah, right. A mess like you?

Still. . . He gave her a slow, acknowledging nod. A popping cracked through the hum of conversation in the room as a senator called the hearing to order. Unwilling to break the connection, Canyon held her gaze. But a shoulder surfed into the way, severing the link. His brother squinted at him as he sat next to her at the witness table.

Senator Miller spoke, opening the hearing, then proceeded through formalities. From the corner of his eye, Canyon noticed the way the girl remained ramrod straight and unaffected by the words of the next twenty minutes.

Blah, blah, blah. *Get on with it, lady.* The seats weren't exactly padded to perfection.

"Our first witness will be Lieutenant Danielle Roark."

The rank pulled Canyon forward. Lieutenant? He hadn't pegged her as military.

"Lieutenant Roark, would you please state your profession?"

She eased toward the mic and cleared her throat. "I'm a demolitions expert with the Corps of Engineers."

"Would you please relate to us the events of seven May of last year?"

Hands clasped on the table, Roark drew in a breath that hissed through the speakers, tightening Canyon's gut with anticipation. "My team was sent into a backwater village to blow a bridge believed to be the primary route used by local rebels to transport drugs and kidnap the citizens, selling them as sex slaves." Her soft voice pitched on the last two words. She took a sip of the water sitting on the table, and water sloshed over the side because of her trembling hand.

Range quickly wiped the spot as she continued.

"We'd almost finished the rigging, when they descended on us, en masse. Of the thirteen on my team, five were killed as we engaged the VFA—"

"Excuse me," a gruff, wiry-haired senator cut in. "Please define VFA."

Roark wet her lips and nodded. "It stands for *El Valor de Fuerzas Armadas de Bolivarian.* 'The Courage of Bolivarian Army.' It's the army mustered by Humberto Bruzon, which has recently been legitimatized by the country's president."

The man grunted.

"Our team fought hard against the VFA."

And Canyon bet she gave a solid fight. Which begged the question about why she seemed so broken now.

"What happened then?" Miller queried, jotting notes on a yellow pad.

"We were losing too many too fast, but we were willing to fight to the death. However, an order came from Command to stand down. The rebels rounded us up. Survivors were stuffed on a truck and transported to a facility a few klicks from the coast."

"Who gave the order to stand down, Lieutenant?"

"Sergeant Dean, ma'am."

"Go on. Where were you taken?"

"I—I. . ." Brushing dainty fingers through her hair, Roark lifted her head and composure. Chin out, she continued. "Being the only female, I was separated from the rest of the team. I didn't know at the time, but the others were taken deeper into the jungle and held for ransom."

"And where were you taken, Lieutenant?"

Lips pursed, she hesitated, and Canyon found himself silently encouraging her. "I. . .to a location less than a kilometer from the ocean. A fifteen-story building that looked like any other corporate tower."

"Was it?" Senator Miller prompted, her voice not completely void of compassion.

"No, ma'am. There was a secret military bunker below it. That's where I was held."

Senator Miller, with her perfectly coiffed curls, sent a sympathetic expression to the young woman. "Miss Roark, I realize you've been through a lot, but I need you to tell the panel what happened to you in the custody of the VFA."

Roark's gaze darted to Olin, who gave her a supportive, encouraging nod. She took another sip of water, then drew in a breath. "When I first arrived, I was stripped, hosed down, searched, and beaten." The words came out in a rush, almost tumbling on top of one another. "That was the first night."

"Continue."

"For the next few days, I was left alone. . .naked. . .in a cell." Her gaze fluttered to the floor in front of the long table. "A group of high-ranking officers arrived after four or five days. They. . .they, uh. . .they knew I was the one rigging the explosives to blow their bridge, so they. . .um, they wanted to punish me." Her eyes blinked rapidly. She cleared her throat again. "They took turns raping me."

Merciful God. Canyon recoiled.

The questioning continued, each minute adding to the acid boiling in his intestines. Nausea had nothing on what he felt listening to the horrific testimony. That the woman could sit here and relate the story without falling apart made him marvel. Finally the panel took a short recess. Canyon didn't move. Couldn't. If he did, he might hurt someone. Fury roiled through his chest. But why did he care? He didn't know this girl. And he'd certainly seen worse done to female captives. He wrestled with the thoughts as the hearing reconvened.

"Our second witness is Chief Petty Officer Range Metcalfe," a male voice announced forcefully—Senator Billings. "Chief, can you please tell us about the rescue operation to retrieve Lieutenant Roark?"

"Yes, sir." Range sat forward, crisp and at attention, making Canyon proud. "We received the call at 0217 to rescue a floater. A couple found her adrift. I used the basket to retrieve her from the deck. She was hypothermic and despondent. Once in the bird, we wrapped her in thermal blankets and delivered her to Walter Reed."

"Your report," Billings began, his cold, unfeeling tone grating along Canyon's spine, "says that she was wearing nothing but an army jacket." Billings peered over his reading glasses. "Is that correct, Chief Petty Officer?"

Range stole a nervous glance to Roark. "Yes, sir, that's correct."

"What about her condition?"

"Besides skin discoloration from the hypothermia, she had lacerations to her right temple and lower left jaw. Her lip was swollen, as was her right eye. Multiple lacerations and burns on her legs and arms proved she'd been through a lot."

So, Canyon had eyed the scars right. Two months old. Still a bit pink.

A shift happened when Billings petitioned the panel to return to Roark for more questions that arose from Range's answers. Though Senator Miller challenged Billings, the others felt further inquiry could be beneficial. Canyon wanted to throttle the fat, overbearing Billings.

"Lieutenant Roark," Billings barked, eliciting a jerk from her. "When you were picked up by the Coast Guard, you were wearing a jacket from the Venezuelan army. It is reported the patch bore the name Bruzon. Can you explain how you came into possession of that jacket?"

Bruzon? Canyon's hackles rose. He'd seen the handiwork of that guerilla firsthand. Heard numerous reports of much worse. And yet, no evidence had been lifted that could put him behind bars. In fact, he'd all but seized power in the country through his not-so-subtle and entirely brutal tactics. Admiration toward Roark grew. She'd survived that animal and sat here telling the story.

"As I said," she said, then stopped and drew in a breath she blew out harshly. "I was transferred to the military installation where I was raped." She cleared her throat again. "General Bruzon. . ."

Bent forward Canyon balled one fist and rubbed his knuckles with other.

"Are you saying General Bruzon is one of the men who raped you, Lieutenant?" Senator Miller asked gently.

"Yes, ma'am."

Billings ripped off his reading glasses. "That still doesn't explain how you got his jacket."

Let me explain it with my fist, jerk. Was the guy toting Jell-O in that thick skull? It didn't take a genius to figure out how she'd gotten the jacket. And honestly, Canyon wasn't sure he wanted to hear her tell the tale. It looked painful enough for her as it was.

"Lieutenant?"

Fire danced through her eyes.

Canyon tensed. She'd borne up under the questions like a champ. Clearly, the pukes had made ground meat of her. He pressed his balled hand against his mouth as she seemed to steel herself. *Come on. You can do it.* Shove Billings and his arrogance back to the Stone Age!

"Bruzon held me captive in his quarters. When he had meetings, he'd have me locked up in the underground prison. Then, I was dragged back up to the light of day where he'd—" The fire fizzled out under choked-back tears. She shook her head.

"Lieutenant?" Billings growled.

Range whispered to her.

Canyon wanted to bail. Wanted to storm out, unable to listen to the story of a woman being violated repeatedly. But if he left, he'd draw attention. Couldn't do that. Lambert would have his hide.

Jarring metal scraped against metal. "I can't do this." Lieutenant Roark shoved her way past the guards, past the doors, out of the courtroom. Her father and Lambert went after her.

On his feet as soon as the break was announced, Canyon wove though the crowds. Rushing out a side door, he punched it open, relieved at the outlet for his anger. He jogged down the stairs to the main level. As he hit the door, again feeling the release, he sighted Roark and her family standing in a huddle.

Lambert looked up as Roark's father tried to cajole her into finishing the testimony.

Agitation wormed through Canyon as he held Lambert's gaze, a silent signal drawing the general from the small crowd.

"Why are we here?" Canyon asked.

"I guess you could say it's personal." Lambert sighed. "What do you think?"

Pain radiated through his jaw and into his neck as Canyon ground his teeth. He pushed his gaze to her, where she stood defiant and hard faced. Whatever purpose Lambert had in asking the Nightshade team to attend, whatever services they would need to render, it would never be enough to remove the pain from her life.

But at least she'd have some justice.

"Whatever you want to do, I'm in."

Near Mindanao, Philippines
13:54:15

Nice and easy. Take it slow," Bayani instructed Tem-Tem. "Look at the tree, then to the sights on your weapon." When the warrior complied, Bayani said, "Fire."

The shot echoed across the village, thumping against my chest as I watched him train the men, both old and young, of my village. Hope lingered in my breast that my people would survive. Messages from Hootup and Markoi told of brutal attacks from the other tribes and villages.

Gleeful shouts erupted from where Tem-Tem stood with Bayani, receiving a pat on the back. In all, twelve of our young men had been chosen for training with the big guns and twice that for hand combat.

Were the changes necessary? I was not so sure. Yes, I longed for my people to live, to thrive, to be as our people had been before them. But. . .fighting. . . with training from outside—was it truly good?

My daughter sauntered toward me with a bowl of food and handed it to me. "Mama."

When Chesa did not greet me as was our custom, I glanced up at her. The warriors had distracted her. Well, not our warriors. But the outsiders. One outsider—Bayani. Strong, handsome Bayani with hair the color of wheat. She had been but eighteen years old when the outsiders had come, promising to help our people. It was Bayani who saved her from warriors who held evil in their hearts.

Laughter shot out from the warriors. Even I could not help but stare again. You see, Bayani and Tem-Tem wrestled, the others watching as the two played as boys often do. They were a good match. Where Bayani was keen and patient, Tem-Tem was quick and fierce.

From somewhere in the trees, a long, mournful scream severed the day. I looked around, aware as Chesa raced into the hut to her sisters. Even as I rose to my feet, I saw Bayani and the outsiders grab their weapons and run fast as the leopard to the trees. Our warriors went with them.

Rat-tat-tat! Bang! Screams. All together in a big pot of noise that scared the little ones and made the not-so-little hide their fear behind brave masks.

As the wife of the chief, I gathered the other women, and we all prayed that the men would return safely. Impishly, I even prayed to the Christian God. Any god who would listen and bring back my Awa.

As the torches flickered, the men returned. Bayani and the outsiders were tired but unharmed. Twelve of our men died in the fight. Awa tells it was not the Higanti as we feared but a group who demanded our people embrace their god or die.

It angered me greatly—until I saw Chesa and Bayani standing just out of the torchlight. Alone. She held his hands. Understand, that this was not done in our village. Awa saw as well. And he ordered that Bayani must take Chesa or they must both be killed.

CHAPTER 4

Metcalfe Residence, Virginia
Mid-March

"**W**e shouldn't be here." Dani hesitated on the sidewalk, her gaze traipsing over the green shamrock lights strung along the front porch. *Who decorates for St. Patrick's Day?*

Her father nearly tripped as he moved around her. "Nonsense." He guided Dani and Abigail, her stepmother, up the winding path to the Metcalfes' ranch-style home. "They invited us, and we're glad to be here."

At his not-so-subtle prompting, Dani swallowed hard as they reached the porch. The light came on seconds before the door swung open.

Dressed in a shirt and tie, Range smiled and welcomed them. "Glad you could make it." Shadows flitted over his face as he stepped back to allow them entrance. "Please, come in. The family's in the den. Mom will be down soon. And as you can see, Paddy's Day is important to her."

Hesitantly, Dani moved into the home, her eyes straining to adjust to the dimmed environment. The tiny foyer boasted a large rug that added a coziness to the home. Pictures of children, weddings, babies, and family groups consumed the wall, quickly establishing the focus of the home—family. A light glowed brightly at the far end, bringing with its illumination laughter and merriment.

"Let me get your coats." His cologne tingled her nostrils as Range received their coats, hurried them to a closet, then returned.

Abigail stepped forward. "Have the caterers arrived?"

"Well, yes, ma'am. They set up tents in the backyard and are still working, but we have our own fare Mom insists on."

"Of course," her father said.

Range turned to Dani, his gaze instantly softening as he held a hand toward the living room. "Come on. I'll introduce you to everyone."

Stomach aflutter with nerves, Dani followed him past the stairs and another hall, where he pointed and mumbled something about the bathroom.

They stepped into a tiled area and the change gave her pause. Although the home had probably been built in the seventies, it'd been updated. The entire area gleamed with brand-new appliances, tiled floors, dark cabinets, granite, and luxurious seating. Jutting off to the left, a massive fireplace cradled the den with two sofas, recliners, and a large round ottoman that boasted two giggling children. Several adults sat around, laughing.

"Hey, everyone, listen up." Range's hand came toward Dani.

She forced herself not to flinch or pull away as he touched her shoulder.

"This is Danielle Roark, her father, Senator Roark, and his wife, Mrs. Roark."

A tall, lithe blond shifted, then came toward her. "I'm Willow." She offered her hand to each of them, then paused next to Dani. "We're all named after elements of nature, so just guess if you can't remember."

"Yeah," a guy called from the sofa. "There are too many of them anyway."

Willow rolled her eyes. "That's Mark, Brooke's husband." She angled herself closer and pointed toward the stone fireplace where an older teen slumped on the edge of the sofa. "That's the littlest Metcalfe. You can just call him Runt."

"Whoa. Huh-uh." The guy shoved to his feet, and his large build and broad chest belied the "runt" moniker. Longish, sandy-blond hair accented his brilliant smile. Girls probably swooned at his feet. "Leif Metcalfe." He pumped her father's hand as the other members of his family joined the introductions. "Nice to meet you, Senator." Something about him seemed familiar. He nodded at her in an almost bashful manner. "Miss Roark."

A crowd formed. The air thickened. Too many people. Too much attention. Although Dani forced a smile into her face, she mentally plotted the quickest exit.

"Would you like something to drink?" Range asked, his touch gentle against her back. "We have St. Patrick's Punch, Eight-Inch Leprechauns, and of course sodas. Or I'm sure there's other things out there." He arched his brows and glanced through the windows to the chaos.

There Dani spotted a large white tent, Chinese lanterns, gleaming stainless steel servers, white-coated wait staff. . . In other words, overkill. Her father and stepmother were notorious for lavish overkill and tonight, in their attempt to help Mrs. Metcalfe with the meal, they'd succeeded again.

"Oh." Abigail perked up. "I did some research on Irish stuff and had them make the Blarney Stone cocktails, shamrock cocktail—"

"Hold up!" Leif chuckled. "Metcalfes don't do liquor."

"Shut up, Leif." Willow glared at her little brother. "Sorry. Canyon's not here to keep him in line, so his mouth is running away with him."

"Hey, Canyon isn't my keeper."

A hoot sounded from the guy with the baby—Mark. "Hey, Brooke, make sure we remember to tell Canyon that when he gets here. What about Stone? Is he—?"

"Right here." A broad-shouldered man, slightly gray at the temples, stepped into the living room with a woman and two children. He offered his hand to her father. "Senator, Stone Metcalfe, and this is my wife, Marie. Nice to meet you. I've followed your career closely."

Dani's stomach tumbled at the way Stone Metcalfe said that. As if a face-off was coming. But instead, he and her father launched into a discussion about the recent vote and the direction of the economy.

"Would you like something to drink?" The question whispered against her ear snaked up her neck and made Dani jump. "I'm sorry." Range's face reddened. "I didn't mean to startle you. Can I get you anything?"

Grateful for the diversion from the people and introductions, she nodded. "Please. Some. . .uh. . .water. Do you have water?"

He grinned. "Right this way." As they moved from the den to the kitchen, Range motioned to a stool at the granite counter. "Have a seat. I'll get you taken care of."

A floral perfume swept around them just seconds before Willow eased onto the stool next to her. "This is going to get overwhelming, I promise. Range, get me an Eight Inch, please."

"Sure." He lifted two mugs from the cupboard and began filling them.

"There are six of us," Willow explained, "and even I get stressed when we're all under the same roof."

Whoa. Six. Dani essentially grew up an only child since Alexandra was so much older than her. "So, you don't all live here?"

Willow's strong cheekbones glowed under the warm lighting, highlighting her pale blue eyes. "Heavens no. Well, Range, Leif, and I do, but the whole family comes together for Sunday dinner and anything remotely close to a holiday. It's a Metcalfe family thing. Oh, and wait till you meet Mom. Everything comes together when she's around."

"My father said she had surgery. Is she okay?" Dani asked, grateful for the natural, easy way Willow acted. And for not bringing up who Dani was or why she was here. She tugged the lightweight sweater over her shoulders and clutched the top of it closed.

Wrinkling her nose, Willow sighed. "Healing, but it'll take a while. They completely reconstructed her back after a bad car accident. She'll be in a brace for the next six months as her spine and back heal."

"Bet she doesn't wear it tonight." Range set a glass of ice water in front of Dani, along with a mug. "Give this a try, it might chase that chill away."

"No way would she let anyone see her in it." Willow giggled. "If there's one thing Metcalfes do right, it's pride."

"Pride and parties."

"Well, tonight we have the help of caterers."

Dani didn't miss the way Range's sister rolled her eyes. "I'm sorry about that. My stepmother has this twisted sense of helping—she thinks sending all this stuff, the caterers, is helping. Most of the time, it doesn't. It just makes people feel. . .weird."

Willow sipped her drink. "No worries. Brooke can keep her busy. And I see Stone has already captured your father's attention."

The sprigs of mint on her drink wafted up with a light menthol scent.

"Hey, boy scout," Willow taunted her brother. "Why don't you tell Mom everyone's here."

"But Canyon—"

"Hates parties. He'll be late." She grinned. "Mom will put you *out* on the range if you leave her back there too long."

"Ha, ha. Fine." He glanced at Dani. "I'll be right back."

A gust of wind blew in from the back door. "Sir, we are ready." A man in a white serving coat, black slacks, and bow tie waited with his white-gloved hands folded.

"Shall we?" Her father motioned to the tents. "Fine food, great people, and a perfect evening!"

Dani sipped her drink, wishing her father would take a backseat. Let this family run their own home and party. But no, he had to be the center of attention, the one with the power.

"So, you are a demolitions expert?" Willow asked as she directed

Dani out onto the back porch, then down a pebble path to the massive tents.

Dani nodded, nerves churning.

Willow smiled. "I'm in the Peace Corps." The beautiful blond eased into a chair toward the back of the tent. "I joined right after I graduated from college, all idealistic and everything. Thought I could reform the world."

Dani tugged back a seat next to her and settled in with her warm mug. "I joined the Corps of Engineers because I thought it'd make my father mad."

Willow laughed. "Did it?"

"Mad didn't come close." Dani smiled, remembering how her father all but threatened to disinherit her. "I think my sister saved me." Indeed Alexandra convinced their father to overlook her rebellious streak.

Amazed at the easy conversation between her and Willow, Dani told herself it was okay to relax—at least a little. She honestly felt okay here, didn't feel the need to erect barriers or hide behind rehearsed answers and platitudes.

A while later, Range's lanky form escorted a graceful woman garbed in a burgundy pantsuit. "Senator Roark, I'd like to introduce my mother, Moira Mulroney Metcalfe."

Her father stood and bowed. "Mrs. Metcalfe, it's an honor to meet you."

"Thank you, but the honor is mine. We are so glad you could join us." She waved him down. The woman was elegant and absolutely beautiful—Willow's mirror image. And Range had been right—she stood straight and tall, sans the back brace. Proud. Just like they'd predicted. The Metcalfes definitely did pride well. Instantly, Dani loved Mrs. Metcalfe.

Her father waited as Mrs. Metcalfe took her seat across from him, then pointed to a chair and spoke to Range. "Son, have a seat. Tonight, we honor your bravery in saving my daughter."

Heat slapped into Dani's cheeks.

"Oh, you're the lady Uncle Range rescued?" A blue-eyed angel of a girl peered up at Dani from across the table, mashed potatoes poised on her fork.

Silence dropped on the gathering like a wet blanket.

The attention it elicited unsettled Dani more than the question itself. She let a smile slip into her lips and opened her mouth to answer.

"Kaleigh!" Brooke admonished from down the table.

"No, it's okay," Dani said, remembering how many times Alexandra or her father had reprimanded her as a child for simple, innocent curiosities. She smiled at the little girl. "Yes, he saved me that day."

"I didn't save her." Range's terse voice broke in. "I lifted her to the Coast Guard chopper. The Middletons pulled her from the ocean. That's who deserves the honor."

Appreciating his humility, Dani offered him a small smile. And tensed at the sudden light in his eyes.

"Nonsense, son." Her father leapt into the conversation. "What you did—saving Danielle—means a lot to me."

Movement behind Range snagged Dani's attention. A shadow shifted, then solidified as a man ducked through the opening. Her heart hitched. The man from the courtroom! The one whose mesmerizing eyes had infused her with strength she didn't have during the trial.

"Canyon, 'bout time you showed up," Mark shouted. "You should've heard Leif earlier."

"Traitor!" Leif thumped his brother-in-law on the back of the head.

Again, her father introduced himself and Abigail before Canyon started around the table.

Laughter warmed the party, but Dani couldn't shake the heat flaring up her neck as she watched the man they called Canyon. Sharp in a blue shirt and black slacks, he gave his brother-in-law a cockeyed grin and gripped his shoulder in a friendly greeting. "What's with the tent? You remodeling again, Mom?" He inched down the row of seats, touching his mother's shoulder as he bent toward her and planted a kiss on her face.

"That's right; you'd better greet your mother." Moira Metcalfe patted her son's cheek. "Find a seat. Enjoy the evening."

The warmth in this family seared her heart. If her mother had lived, would this be what she had instead of a stepmother only a few years older than herself, celebrations replete with all-too-expensive gifts, loneliness to tuck her in at night?

Willow set a biscuit on an empty plate. "Canyon, have a sit. I already started your plate."

He wove through the chairs and tables and greeted his sister in the same way he had his mother. "What'd you put on there? Sprouts and alfalfa?"

"If you don't behave, I'll make sure that's all you get."

His deep laugh rumbled through the night—and straight into Dani's soul. As he scooted in and looked around, his gaze stumbled into hers. He stilled, his smile slipping.

Dani's pulse hiccuped. She wanted to look away. Even told herself to. But if she did, she might never find a moment like this again.

Weird knots rolled through his stomach as he stared into the caramel eyes that had haunted him since that day in court. Now three weeks later, she sat in his family's backyard, beneath this absurd tent, with an ethereal glow—compliments of the candelabra and its soft light. Her gaze darted away but came back just as quick, as if some supernatural connection existed between them.

Yeah, she felt it, too.

"Have you two met?" Elbows propped on the table and fingers threaded, Willow glanced between them, her curiosity screaming.

"I—" Canyon ripped his gaze from Roark's. "No." Not technically.

Embarrassed at the way he'd lost focus, he scoured the table for his mother's sweet potato casserole but saw nothing but porcelain containers with things too fancy to recognize. The expense alone could feed an entire Third World country. He reached for a bowl of something green. Hoped it was edible.

"Really?" Disbelief thickened Willow's words. "Well, why don't I introduce you two? Canyon, this is Senator Roark's beautiful daughter, Danielle. The woman our dear, waterlogged brother rescued from the Gulf. Danielle, this is my ruggedly handsome brother, Canyon, who can't seem to keep his eyes off you."

Willow had a mouth bigger than a C-130—and he was about to drive a nuke straight into it. He glanced at Roark, noticing the way she hung her head. Her cheeks pinked.

"We...uh, met." Roark tried to be brave against his sister's directness. "At my hearing."

"Her hearing?" Willow arched an eyebrow. "What were *you* doing there?"

"Consulting." They certainly didn't need to rehash what had happened. "You'd think you would've cultivated some manners at that prep school of yours."

Besides, hadn't Range laid some claim to Roark, warned Canyon to back off? Curiosity made him check his little brother—and sure enough, Range glowered. Temptation to egg his brother on vied for Canyon's submission. And won. He flashed his most charming smile. "Nice to meet you officially, Miss Roark."

She smiled—a tentative, awkward one that wavered.

Whoa, that'd gotten way more reaction than he expected. Wasn't she smitten with his brother? Dark hair curled over her shoulders and swung into her long, graceful neck. Nice, prominent cheekbones had filled out since he'd seen her last. The bruise was gone as far as he could tell in the low lighting.

Willow nudged him. "See? Can't keep your eyes off her."

"Pass the potatoes," he said, giving her his fiercest warning look. "What is all this stuff? Where's the ham and beans?"

"Catered by Mrs. Roark."

Canyon's gaze shot to Roark's.

"Not me—my stepmother." Regret streaked through her tawny features. "I—I'm sorry. She didn't want your mom to have to worry about cooking. And well, Abigail tends to go overboard." She chewed the inside of her lip, her gaze again drawn down.

Everything in her demeanor screamed victim. He'd seen it on others, but on her—he hated it. She didn't wear it well. He'd seen more fire and brimstone in her gaze at the hearing. Where was that woman?

"So, Danielle," Willow said, clearly exercising every ounce of social skill she contained to draw the woman out of her shell. "How did you ever get into demolitions?"

Her fork played hopscotch with her food but never quite made it home. "I love science." What was she hiding behind that tight, controlled answer?

"That is so cool." Willow folded her arms and leaned on the table. "So, you really blow things up?"

Canyon stabbed a red potato and slid it into his mouth.

This time, a real smile spread through the woman's pink, full lips, even tugging out a laugh. The sound eased at least one of the knots in Canyon's shoulders.

"No way." Leif's teenage voice cracked. "Blow up, as in C4 and detonators?"

"No kidding, Sherlock." Willow tossed a roll at him. "What'd you think? Bubble gum and balloons?"

Canyon eyed Roark, whose laugh drifted through the cool night and encircled his mind. This was better. Maybe another hour or two with the insane Metcalfe zoo would have her loosened up and relaxed. What would she be like then?

Suddenly her gaze hit his—and bounced off, taking with it her smile. She set her napkin on her lap and excused herself. He watched her walk up the steps onto the deck and disappear into the house.

He felt the urge to go after her, to. . .to what, he didn't know, but he was on his feet before he knew it.

A hand caught his, snapping his gaze to his sister.

"Be careful, Canyon. She's wounded and Range. . .he's never shown interest like this."

In other words, don't. Leave her to Range. The right thing to do. He remembered the pact he had with his brothers since high school.

"No Metcalfe steps in on another." His response silenced her and gave him the out he needed. But his own words clung to his conscience as he headed into the house. As the families mingled tonight, he'd have to remain distanced, aloof. Nonchalant.

A few hours into the shindig, her father left on an urgent call, and that's when Canyon really noticed Roark's countenance shift for the better. *Not exactly a cozy father-daughter relationship, huh?*

Filling a glass with water, he heard a noise in the hall. He shut off the tap and went to check it out. As he rounded the corner, he heard grunting.

"Stupid thing!" Roark jiggled the door handle, bending down and peering at it closer.

Canyon grinned, admiring the view. "It sticks."

She jerked straight and spun toward him, her long, dark hair whipping across her face. "What?"

"It sticks." He eased down the hall, closing the gap between them. "Here." He reached around her, noticing the way she kept her smooth brown eyes locked on him. Noticing how she didn't pull away. . .not completely. Enough to be nervous and demure, but not enough to say she wasn't interested. Within inches of her, he held her gaze, his eyes tracing the soft curves of her jaw and cheek. Those full lips.

Step off, Metcalfe, or you'll crash and burn.

CHAPTER 5

Capitol Hill, Washington, D.C.

General Lambert?"

Amid shadows cast by the fluorescent lights in the Capitol Hill employee parking garage, Olin paused before stuffing the key in his car. Several shiny black cars separated him from Senator Sarah Miller, one of those on the panel investigating Danielle. Though his pulse hiccuped, he forced himself to remain calm.

"Evening, Senator Miller. Shouldn't you be at home with your family for a Paddy's Day celebration?"

"Shouldn't we all?" After a furtive glance around the garage, she navigated around an SUV, her heels clicking on the cement. "You're not usually on this side of the Potomac, General." Attractive, the middle-aged woman smiled up at him. Her gray wool business suit accented the gray eyes peeking up at him from a wisp of brown feathered bangs.

"Late meeting with the Armed Services Committee."

"Ah." Again she looked around, chewing her bottom lip. She seemed like she wanted to talk to him or tell him something.

"Can I help you, Senator Miller?"

She ducked her head. "I—I, uh, shouldn't be talking to you about this, but. . ."

This time, Olin scanned their surroundings. "Go on."

She wet her lips. "I'll be honest, General, since my voice isn't being heard anyway—things don't look good for Danielle."

"Why?"

The male voice, strong and perturbed, jerked them both around. There, Senator Michael Roark stood with his briefcase. "Why doesn't it look good for Danielle?"

Senator Miller darted a glance to Olin, as if saying she'd hoped to talk to him privately, but they were both caught in the act here. "Despite my efforts to persuade the panel that she isn't acting, that her injuries were real, and the information she delivered could be credible, they won't listen. They're intent on their course of action." She blew out a breath through puffed cheeks. "I'm sorry. I've done everything I can. I just thought I'd let you know."

"Wait—they don't believe her injuries were real?" Olin heard his voice pitch and didn't care. "They were catalogued by two different doctors in two different locations, not to mention the Coasties' reports. You can't fake that."

Her shoulders lifted a little. "I'm sorry. That's what I tried to tell them. But Billings didn't agree." She shoved her fingers into her hair and groaned. "They'll kill me for telling you all this before the findings are released, but you need to prepare Danielle."

"Prepare her for what?" Michael's face darkened.

"Billings and his minions—I still can't believe the power that man exerts when *I'm* the lead on this. Anyway, they're determined that she was and/or is spying for Bruzon. That the injuries were inflicted to help her return without suspicion. They think Bruzon is just dangling this WMD technology in our face, trying to make a spectacle of us similar to Iraq—and Lord knows nobody is willing to go through that again—or force us to respond, thus stirring up an international incident."

"Those sons of—" Olin bit down on the curse. "This is asinine!"

"Are they out of their minds?" Michael shouted.

"Listen." Miller leaned in and lowered her voice. "The schematics of that underground facility do not match the footprint of any known building where she says they held her captive. We've questioned experts and they agree." She let out another hefty breath. "They sent a team to your home, Michael. They found information on Danielle's computer, logs and e-mails dating back fifteen months. E-mails between her and Bruzon. Images of her with him at his island estate."

"Pictures can be doctored, and everyone knows it's possible to remotely access and control a computer." Olin grunted. "That means nothing."

"It means a lot to the CID and JAG. They're back there tossing around one charge after another, General."

"Anyone with a brain can see she's haunted, she's skittish—"

"And they say all that is an act."

When both he and Roark spoke at the same time, Miller held up her hand. "Gentlemen, you don't have to convince me. I know she's not faking. I believe her. And I believe someone has set her up. But I'm the minority and I'm being overruled. They—" She swallowed and looked away.

Olin felt a cold finger trace his spine at the expression on the senator's face. "What? Tell us, Sarah. Help us save Danielle."

Brushing wispy bangs from her face, she sighed. "*Unofficially*, they want to charge her with one count of treason, one count espionage, and three counts rendering aide to the enemy." Her eyes seemed like pools of ebony, shadowed by grief. "If they do that, then they can pursue the death penalty."

"*Death—!*"

"It only shows the reckless desperation of the lawyers," Senator Miller said. "But they *can* do it. And apparently, they're going to try—with Billings's blessing."

Olin clamped his mouth shut, breathing hard through his nose. "What can we do? This is a massive train wreck. Can we stop it?"

"Unless the proof of that underground facility can be obtained"—her gray eyes bounced between them—"then, no. I'm sorry."

"What if we got that proof?" Michael said.

"How?" Miller tossed up her hands. "I personally recruited every expert I could to locate that WMD facility, the entrance—they spent two months trying, and they found *nothing*! How are you going to find it?"

"Danielle."

Stunned, Olin glanced at Michael Roark. Heat rose through his belly, seeping into his chest, then his throat. "*What* are you suggesting?"

"Send her back down there—"

"No!" Though he tried to tame the explosive fury roiling through his body, Olin couldn't. "Michael—stop. You've seen her, seen what this did to her. How can you even think of sending her back down there? She's your daughter, for pity's sake."

"That's right." Michael's eyes sparked with challenge. "She's *my* daughter, and I know her. Know what she's made of." He glowered at Olin. "Was she affected by what happened? Of course. Can she assist a black-ops team to point out the entrance, get the proof needed to clear her name—especially in light of the death penalty? Yes. *Would* she be willing to? I believe so." He jabbed a finger at Olin. "You said it yourself, she'll never survive in a federal pen—or if she faces the death penalty!"

Realization dawned over Olin and smelled like a walk through the dumps. "Yes, you really don't want her found guilty—"

"Of course, I don't!"

"Because then your run for the White House would be shattered."

"How dare you!"

Olin skewered the man with his gaze. *"Don't* pretend your concern is for Danielle. This is about your career!"

"Yes," Michael said in a low growl. "My career will be impacted if she's found guilty. But I believe Danielle is strong enough and that she would *want* to clear her name."

"You can't do this to her. Stop thinking about yourself and think about her for once." Olin shook his head as he looked at Miller. "This will devastate her. I won't allow it." There had to be another way.

"Ignore him. He doesn't have any say in this." Michael turned to the senator. "I'll talk to her. If she agrees, will you stay the ruling?"

Senator Miller hesitated. "I—I don't know. We'd have to present it to Billings. I—"

"Let's do it." Michael hooked her arm and dragged her back toward door that led into the building.

Something thick and rank sliced through the air—the smell of this deal with Michael Roark. *"He doesn't have any say in this."*

Very well. If he wanted to cut Olin out of it, he'd preempt this selfish, insane plan. Olin lifted his phone and dialed.

Metcalfe Residence
No Metcalfe steps in on another.

With a flick of his wrist, Canyon opened the door for Roark. Took a step back. "There."

A furtive smile chased her into the bathroom.

As the door clicked shut, then locked, Canyon blew out a breath and roughed a hand over the back of his neck. Range would kill him if he'd seen that moment he'd just shared with Roark. But Canyon couldn't deny the magnetic field that surrounded that woman and drew him in like scrap metal.

Over the next few hours, he kept to himself. Stuffed himself in a recliner and watched the silenced game. But being the Special Forces soldier that he was, he also kept tabs on Roark. Especially how she seemed to tolerate Range's attention but didn't encourage it. Or was that his imagination?

Range had gotten there first, so as far as Canyon was concerned, Danielle Roark was off the map.

A boom of laughter severed his thoughts. Canyon glanced over his shoulder and found his mother and Abigail Roark laughing as they stood by the spread of desserts. But then, just as fast, his mother's face paled. Her face went slack.

Canyon launched out of the seat and darted to her side. "Mom?"

She smiled bravely as she tried to maintain her composure. "Such a nice evening."

Only one other time in his life had he seen her try to save face like this. She needed out, and fast! "Can I talk to you?" he asked, shifting so that he shielded her from Mrs. Roark's gaze.

"Well," she said, her voice weak, "if you think it's important—"

"I do." And with that, he led her from the kitchen and down the hall. She pressed into him more with each step. By the time they reached the hall to her room, she crumbled.

He lifted her into his arms and rushed into the bedroom where he laid her over the thick blue comforter. He stuffed two pillows under her legs. "How're you doing, Mom?"

"Better now," she mumbled, her words thick. "Water. . ."

From her nightstand he grabbed the glass and aimed the straw toward her lips. "You overdid it."

With a soft snort she set down the glass. "I gave birth—"

"To five screaming babies." He finished her infamous rant as he pressed two fingers against her carotid artery to monitor her pulse.

A weak smile trembled over her lips. "And one silent tormentor."

Him. She'd always said he'd never cried until he was two.

Her pulse thumped steadily, enabling him to take a decent breath. With the back of his hand, he checked her temperature. Warm. "You shouldn't have invited them. It was too soon after the surgery—and why weren't you wearing the brace?"

"Oh, stop worrying. Range wanted to have them over. I thought it was nice." She sighed. "I think he likes Danielle." Her head rolled toward him. "Such a pretty name for a beautiful girl. I like her."

You and me both.

Encouraging her would only churn what little food was in his stomach. Everyone in their family had already assigned Danielle the spot next to Range. The spot beside Canyon remained empty. And he'd better not mess with that, or he'd be dubbed a cad. *Wouldn't be the first time.* They almost hadn't let him live that down.

Eyes closed, she drifted to sleep.

Canyon laid a blanket over his mom. He stood beside her for several minutes, debating whether or not to call her doctor. Had she just pushed too hard too fast as always? Or was something really wrong? He lifted the advanced thermometer and swiped it over her forehead: 99.9—not stress worthy.

Scratching the back of his neck, he stepped into the hall.

Range met him. "How is she?"

"Resting." He pulled the door closed. "What were you thinking inviting the senator and his family over so soon after Mom's surgery?"

A scowl dug into his brother's dark brows. "She said she'd love it."

"Grow a brain. Mom would welcome anyone even if she were dying!"

"Give her more credit—"

"I'm giving my medical advice. She shouldn't have been up and around. If you'd cared more about her than entertaining your girlfriend—"

"Excuse me." A timid, feminine voice dashed into the hall.

Canyon turned—and his stomach cinched when he saw Roark a few feet away.

Range strode toward her.

Suddenly not in the mood for company, Canyon slipped back into his mother's room and stuffed himself in the wingback chair. Hands tucked under his arms, he closed his eyes and let himself relax. Maybe if he fell asleep, he'd wake up and they'd all be gone.

But he'd miss *her*.

He cleared his throat and shifted. Didn't matter. She belonged to Range. Which was odd because the feisty ones had normally repelled his kid brother. Then again, maybe her withdrawn actions from the captivity had snuffed out her fight. Come to think of it, what little of that strong nature he'd seen at the hearing had disappeared tonight. What was up with that?

Laughter outside drew his eyes open and his mind out of the fog of sleep. At the telltale thunk of car doors, he pushed to his feet and checked the window. The lone streetlamp lit only his Camaro and Willow's car parked in the drive. The other vehicles were gone. Good. He could unwind and maybe go for a jog. His stomach gurgled, reminding him of how little he'd eaten. When he stepped into the hall, he heard Willow, Range, and Leif talking in the den.

Light peeked out from under the bathroom door. His siblings were in the den. Everyone else had left. Who. . . ? He knocked. When no sound came, he pushed open the door—movement flashed to the side. He jerked back as he saw Roark. She stood stiffly, hands at her sides, one slowly moving behind her.

"Sorry, I thought everyone was gone," he mumbled and back-stepped, his gaze swinging down.

Instincts blazed.

In rapid-fire succession the pieces hit him—her wide eyes, heaving chest, tear-streaked face, stiff composure. The way the semi-new scars had brightened. The red spot on the tile. Everything in him went cold and silent at the drop of blood. He dragged his gaze back to her, noticing the way she shielded her left arm.

He studied her face. Ashen. Chin trembling.

Splot! A second droplet hit the tile.

Canyon craned his neck to the side—and he sucked air at what he saw. Blood dribbling down her arm. With the pull of gravity, blood flowed faster.

Adrenaline spiked. In a fluid motion, he stepped in, kicked the door shut, and grabbed her arm. He pivoted and slammed his back against her chest, pinning her to the wall.

She yelped and whimpered. "Please, please..." She hissed. "It hurts. Oh, it hurts!"

He held her arm up, groping the shelf for a towel. Finally he snatched one, spun, and clamped the towel over her cuts. "What're you doing?" He heard the growl in his voice but didn't care. "Are you out of your mind?"

Tears streaked down her face. "Please...please don't tell them."

Anger lashed out. "Tell them what? That you tried to kill yourself?" He kept a tight grip on her forearm, feeling the wet warmth seeping through the cloth. If he didn't get this stopped, she'd bleed out.

Pinching the pressure point under her arm, he mentally blocked the panic gouged into her beautiful face. He wanted to curse. Shout. Shake some sense into her.

Shoulders sagging, she shook her head. "I'm sorry. I didn't mean to..."

Blood slid over his thumb and splatted against his cuff. The dark stain swam outward in an ever-widening arc against the pale blue cotton. His gaze flipped back to the towel. Soaking fast. "I'm going to have to stitch this to stop the bleeding."

She hauled in a breath.

"That or call the cops."

"No!" she snapped. "You can't. My father..."

"The father you didn't care about two seconds ago when you sliced open your veins? What about my brother? After all he's done for you..." His fury unleashed, mixed with the adrenaline at seeing her life slipping away. About to really let her have it, he faltered when she swayed. "Lie down. On the floor."

Clumsily she complied, her limbs trembling.

"Keep your arm up." He stepped into the tub to give her room to maneuver. "Put your legs on the ledge." He shifted and grabbed another towel, placing it over the first. "What in the name of all that's holy were you thinking?"

"Y–you don't understand."

"You got that right!"

"My dad made a deal. I have to go back—they said I have to." She shook her head frantically. "I can't. I can't go back there."

"Where? What're you talking about?"

A sob leapt from her throat. Her eyes rolled.

Out of time. Time for triage. "Keep your arm up. Don't move." Canyon propped her arm against the throat of the sink. "I'll be right back." Rolling up his sleeve where her blood had stained it, he darted through the house and outside to his car. From the trunk, he pulled his field kit and slunk through the side door, hoping to avoid attracting attention. Back in the bathroom, he knelt beside her.

"How're you feeling?"

"Woozy. Sick."

"Good." He dug through the pack and tugged out the sewing kit. "Serves you right." With care, he peeled back the towels. Dabbed the wound, assessing. Swiping an antiseptic swab around the skin, he wanted to wring her neck. What was so horrible that she couldn't fight and get through it? She had it in her; he knew she did.

Having tried to off himself before, he knew how it felt. But he'd also come out of it realizing *nothing* was worth killing himself over. And she had so much going for her. For some strange reason he couldn't justify, it ate at him that she wanted to end it all. He should be nicer. No, she didn't cut nice. She needed a good jerk on her reality chain, wake up, and see the good things around her.

She tilted her head to look at her arm. "Do. . .do you know what you're doing?"

"Stay quiet and still."

She sniffled. "I'm sorry."

He glanced at her before focusing on numbing the spot and stitching her up. "I should report this."

A ragged intake of breath. "You can't. Please!"

"Yeah? Well, just because a beautiful woman bats her eyes at me and says please isn't enough cause to keep this under wraps. Your family

65

needs to know, so they can take care of you. Help you."

Roark lay still, staring at the ceiling, tears slipping over her rosy cheeks. "You were at the hearing. . ."

Tension bottomed out as he remembered that day.

"My godfather, General Lambert—you know him?"

He wanted to smile but kept it to himself. "Heard his name once or twice." Stitching completed, he slumped against the tub, holding her elbow on his knee and appraising his work. This wasn't something she'd be able to hide. At least not without long sleeves.

"The subcommittee doesn't believe me." Fresh, fat tears oozed from her brown eyes. A sob racked her. "If I don't want to go to prison or face the death penalty, I have to go back."

"What? Back where?" He groaned and slumped back, shaking his head. He knew exactly where. "Never mind." He held her gaze, wishing he could wipe this travesty of justice off the map of her life. She didn't deserve this.

Was the government serious? Yeah. . .they were stupid enough. Mentally and physically traumatized, she didn't have a prayer of staying alive down there.

At least. . .not without help.

Nightshade.

CHAPTER 6

Stark white bandages covered her left arm. Rubbing her fingers over the white tape, Dani released a shuddering breath. Had she really sunk so low she thought the only way out was to kill herself? Exhausted, she set down the toilet lid and sat. Realization of what she'd done finally settled in.

Tears again stung her eyes, but she stuffed them down. She had sobbed like a hysterical fool in front of a man she didn't know. In a few minutes she'd have to face Range, and the last thing she wanted was more of his doting concern. He hovered. Crooned. Suffocated. While she just needed space, not a reminder that the "perfect man" worried over her. Yeah, he was perfect—perfect life, perfect family, perfect temperament. He certainly wouldn't understand.

"You got that right!"

His brother's snarled words as he worked to help—no, *rescue* her—wormed through Dani. Even with his mumbled curses as he worked to save her life, she saw the understanding that held back his anger. Somehow Canyon understood. Understood that the court had found her guilty, that she'd lost hope, that she was terrified of ending up a victim again. And he hadn't babied her the way his brother had. Rather, he looked like he wanted to pound her.

The door creaked open.

Dani jerked up, then stilled as Canyon's familiar build filled the bathroom, every crevice and nook, with pure confidence. Beneath the sandy blond crop and eyebrows, twinkled eyes that said he'd seen much, done much, and took everything in stride. Yet she'd rattled him with her little stunt. He must think her a mental case.

Well, who else would carve her own arm?

67

"Here." He held out a black shirt and blue cardigan, the veins in his arms taut and strong. "Change behind the shower curtain." Without a word, he bent and started packing his kit.

Hesitating for only a minute, her gaze locked on his broad shoulders and his straightforward methods, she hiked over the ledge of the tub. Tugging the navy curtain closed, she glanced at the shirt. Similar in style to the one she'd worn to the party. And with the cardigan, no one would know the difference or see the bandages. How many men would think like that?

"Remove the bandage when you get home." His words sailed through the thin barrier. "Air the wound out and let the healing start. The stitches will dissolve, but you'll need to keep it clean."

Changed, she stepped from behind the curtain.

Canyon stood with his arms folded over his muscular chest, the kit gone from sight. He gave her a nod. "Ready?"

Dani adjusted the sleeve of the sweater as it caught on the bandage. Why did the thought of leaving this little sanctuary scare the wits out of her? She wasn't a scared baby. As a matter of fact, hadn't she hated being in confined settings with men since returning? So, why was his presence in the small room more comforting than disturbing?

"Imagine Range is looking for you by now." He reached for the knob.

She caught his arm, her breath in her throat. "I. . .please. . ."

He paused, blue eyes fastened to hers, then softening as he smirked. "I don't kiss and tell."

Not exactly what she wanted to hear. A strange feeling spiraled through her, warming her belly. Attraction? The thought made her stomach flip. Then flop.

No. That couldn't be. She didn't want anything to do with men.

He slipped into the hall and glanced both ways. "You're clear." He motioned her out.

Moving into the chilled darkness, she hesitated as laughter erupted from the living area. Several voices mingled. Who was still here? Two hours ago, when her father got paged and had to leave, Range offered to take her and her stepmother home if they wanted to stay and hang out with the others, an idea her father instantly agreed to. But then she got the call. . .and rushed from the room. Range followed, but she told him she'd be fine and locked herself in the bathroom.

Or so she thought until Canyon walked in on her. How exactly did he get in if she'd locked the door? Her mind flitted to earlier in the evening when she couldn't get the door open and he'd told her that it stuck. Maybe it hadn't locked. Was it providence he'd come in on her?

How did he figure out what she'd done?

"Here." Canyon's gruff voice snatched her attention back. He passed her a slip of paper. "That's me."

She glanced at the scrap with scrawled numbers.

"I expect two calls: one before you bed down and another first thing in the morning. If I haven't heard from you by 2359 and 0800, I'll bang down your front door and bring the cops with me." Laugh lines pinched the corners of his eyes. "Got it?"

Although a smile dug into her mouth, Dani feigned offense. "I don't recall being put under your command."

The amusement faded from his face.

She lowered her gaze to the paper, feeling the full idiocy of her actions. "I'll call." Drawing up her courage, she tucked a strand of hair behind her ear. "Thank you." A lump formed in her throat. "I owe you my life."

"You owe it to yourself. You're stronger than this."

"I don't know that I am," she whispered, her words thickened by the emotion pulsing through her. "What if I don't make it. . . ?" She couldn't finish the sentence. Didn't want to.

But Canyon must've known. He inched closer, his woodsy scent washing over her. "You survived it once. That means it's in you." He peered over her face, something unfamiliar in his expression. "You're strong, Roark." A cockeyed smile pulled his lips apart. "You might have to dig it out, but don't ever forget it's there." His hand came up—

A throat cleared.

Dani flinched.

Canyon didn't.

She looked down the hall. Willow stood, hands on her hips, watching. Within seconds Range joined them. He grinned—until he noticed Canyon.

Unease slithered through her. Range had gone through so much to make this evening nice for her and her family. And she had tried to kill herself, then stood here with his brother, wanting more time and more attention. How stupid. Canyon only meant to look after her injuries.

She shot Canyon a quick look, then moved to his brother.

Range hovered, his attention bobbing between her and Canyon until he caught her elbow and led her into the hall. "Are you okay?"

"Yeah, just. . .an upsetting phone call. I'm fine." She pushed a smile she didn't feel onto her lips, her mind snagged on the way Canyon had looked at her. The way he'd almost touched her. "Can you take me home?"

Uncertainty flashed through Range's face. "Uh, yeah, okay. Let me grab the keys."

"Where's Abigail?"

"I drove her home a while ago," Willow said.

Waiting by the front door, Dani held her throbbing arm close. Seconds later, Canyon strode down the hall toward her, his head down. Dani's heart hammered.

The light from the lone amber sconce accented his handsome features. His jaw muscle popped. Was he mad? As he rounded the corner and started for the stairs, he glanced at her. Held up two fingers, then flicked them into a phone gesture. Two phone calls. He wasn't letting her off the hook. Dani smiled her agreement—then stiffened as Range hustled down the carpeted steps.

"Doc Henry's coming by in the morning to check on Mom," Canyon mumbled as he passed his brother.

Range slowed but didn't stop. "What time?"

"Eight." Canyon glanced at Dani again. Eight, the time he demanded she call.

"Okay." Range opened the door.

As she was ushered into the dark night, she rubbed the scrap of paper in her hand, remembering the silent signal and the intensity of Canyon's steel gaze that vowed he'd make good on his threat to break down her door.

Oh, she hoped he did.

Soft footsteps climbed the stairs. Canyon clamped his teeth as the floorboards creaked, heralding Willow's arrival. A subtle swirl of the air told him she waited in the bathroom doorway. He wouldn't indulge her. She'd wait. A very long time because what brought her up here was something he'd never give: information.

At the sink he worked the soapy lather over his arms, the images of Roark's blood seeping through his fingers a vivid reminder he tried to scrape away with the suds. He concentrated on scrubbing properly with the brush, something he hadn't had time to do before she left.

"Want to explain what you were doing in a dark hall with Range's girl?"

Range's girl. Huh. Could've fooled him with the way she all but leaned into his touch moments ago. *Scritch. Scritch. Scritch.* Wrists, knuckles, fingernails.

"Okay. I'll take that as a no."

"Always were the bright one in the family."

"Why were you in the bathroom with her?"

How she knew that was beyond him. To his knowledge, she hadn't seen them exit together. She must've seen or heard something. Or maybe she was just fishing.

"What about trying to kiss her?"

"Did no such thing." He dried his arms and hands, finally eyeing his sister in the mirror. Irritation tightened her mouth. She never did like not getting her way. Too bad. After he tossed the towel in the hamper, he turned and pushed out of the bathroom. Headed back downstairs. In the kitchen, he drew out a glass and filled it with water.

"He likes her. How can you step in on him like this?"

"The only thing I'm stepping into is the kitchen."

"Whoa, wait," Leif said as he joined the conversation. "Who's Canyon making moves on? The senator's daughter?"

"Not making any moves on anyone. Willow's looking for a gossip column piece." Canyon pierced her with a warning look. As he lifted the glass, a dark spot on his sleeve caught his attention. He cursed himself for not seeing it sooner.

"I am not looking for gossip. I'm looking to stop an older brother from stealing Range's love interest, from hammering a wedge of resentment into our happy family." Willow folded her arms over her chest. "Again."

"What's Willow being overdramatic about now?" Stone wrapped an arm around her, kissed her temple, and said good night.

"How did Canyon's poor sportsmanship become my drama? I wasn't the one—"

"Night, Stone." Canyon drank the water, set down the glass, and rolled up his sleeves, feigning casual comfort. "Better head out. Got an o-dark-thirty meeting."

"This is not the time to go all mysterious, Canyon Metcalfe. You need to explain yourself."

"That I don't." He started for the hall, where he removed his jacket from the closet.

"Why is there blood on your sleeve?"

Teeth ground, he looked to the side, tempering his aggravation. The frustration pumping through his chest made his breathing uneven.

"Canyon," Willow said as she came closer. "If you don't want to tell me what happened, then. . .just answer me this—is she okay?"

"Good night, Willow." Without another word, he waved good-bye to Leif.

Trailing him into the night, Willow called, "He asked her to the Coast Guard gala. She agreed. Let them have this chance, Canyon."

Waving over his head, he hurried out of the house. The thought of Roark and Range. . . He'd never lost to his little brother. Never. Was that what upset him this time?

No. It was about a woman. A very broken woman.

Which, in his professional judgment, blazed warning enough for both of them to stay off.

In his car, he tugged the small black phone from his pocket. Dialed.

"Wolfsbane, good evening. What can I do for you?"

"I've got an idea."

CHAPTER 7

Roark Residence, Virginia

She might as well die.

Oh right. She'd tried that and Canyon interfered. Okay, so maybe life wasn't as desperate...

No, it definitely was. Dani slid her feet into the sandals and headed downstairs, adjusting the coral sweater where the material snagged on the stitches. As her foot hit the bottom step a reverberating gong carried through the floor and tickled her feet. She stopped as another gong rang out from the antique grandfather clock. And another...another...

Hand on her phone she paused in front of the tall wood pendulum swinging back and forth. Each intonation thudded against her conscience. Eight o'clock. It was time to call him again. Let him know she was okay.

That would be lying. And her mother, a devout Catholic, had raised her better than that. *But Mom's not here.* Besides, nobody cared. Life was pathetic and depressing.

The painful thought felt weighted and louder than the eighth gong of the clock. What she wouldn't have done to have her mother's arms gather her into an embrace of love, understanding, and fierce protection.

"Danielle?"

She flinched at the sound of her sister's voice as Dani turned and found Alexandra standing by the entry to the family room. "Morning." Though she mustered the dregs of her energy for the smile she offered her sister, Dani knew she'd failed miserably.

"Chad is making his specialty for breakfast." Her sister smiled and ambled over the gleaming marble floor. "Would you like to join us?"

Chad. Her father's clone. But on a smaller scale and, unlike her father, Chad had some semblance of family values and good enough

73

sense to spend the morning making breakfast for his wife and children.

"Dani?"

"No. Thank you." She smiled again. "I think. . .I think I'll just sit on the patio for a while. Enjoy the sun."

"I could join you."

With her fingers on the brass lever for the patio door, Dani faced her sister. "This is your family time. Go be with them." She waved Alexandra away.

"Please, consider—"

"I already answered that." Crisis counseling. Her sister had mentioned it almost daily. She didn't want to expose a complete stranger to her nightmare—she wanted to forget it!

Putting on the facade of well-being and happiness drained her. She stepped onto the pebbled cement and strolled toward the table and chairs by the pool. Standing beneath the partial shade of the table umbrella gave her a view of the gardens. Her stepmother had insisted on making it as much like a true English garden as possible. Never understanding the point, Dani avoided the extravagant display. But somehow, for some reason, today she wanted to explore the grounds.

Gravel crunched beneath her feet as she traveled the path between parallel hedgerows that dumped her into a rectangular-shaped space. In the middle, a smaller rectangle boxed in a fountain. Water spewed and dumped from the jug atop the shoulder of a peasant woman, the tumbling waves foaming at her feet. Another stream flowed from a smaller jug propped on her hip. The woman looked as much gypsy as she did princess.

Absurd. Yet it didn't surprise her considering the ideals of her father. He wanted his wife to stay at home, raise the children—do wife things. Make him look good as a senator-cum-vice-presidential candidate. He'd threatened disinheritance when Dani told him she joined the Army Corps of Engineers. But that was nothing compared to his face when she explained her job with the USACE was blowing things up with explosives.

Explosive. Yeah, that's about how she could've described his reaction.

"I'll build you a lab out back. Just don't do this. Think what the constituents will think if my daughter is building bombs!"

Dear old Dad never considered that his daughter wanted to get away from him and his trophy wife. Tugging a leaf from the wall of shrubs, she kept walking, enjoying the soft cushion of grass beneath her feet.

Somewhere in the distance the squeal of tires stalked the quiet morning. Rich kids with expensive cars and no brains. She'd grown up with them. Maybe. . .maybe at one time she was one of them.

General Bruzon changed that—changed her.

She squeezed her eyes tight to block the images that assailed her. His hands. . . "No." Dani pinched the bridge of her nose. Alcoholic breath. . . "No!" Shoulders hunched, she pulled closer to the shrubs and wished they'd drag her into their foliage, help her disappear.

Noise erupted.

Dani paused and listened, blinking back the memories and panicked tears. What? When loud voices intruded, she glanced in the direction the sound came from.

Shouts spilled from the house. Brow furrowed, she started back along the path. As soon as she returned to the fountain, she stopped short.

From between two shrub columns burst Canyon. A deep scowl carved a mean line down his face. His gaze collided with hers. He stalked over the stones, his fists balled.

Her breath backed up into her throat as he stormed toward her. Behind him—blurred since she didn't dare take her eyes off him—Alexandra stopped, hand over her mouth.

"Two phone calls," he said in a terse, low voice. "Midnight, eight o'clock."

"I. . .I—"

"You're late. The cops are here." With a huff, he halted not a foot from her.

Cold rushed through her stomach and chest. "You brought them?" She glanced at her sister, who watched with a curious expression, then turned and hurried back to the house.

He towered over her, eyes ablaze and nostrils flaring. "I told you. Two phone calls or I would come and bring them with me."

"Well yes, but I didn't—"

"Didn't believe me?"

Mouth dry and words gone, she stared up at him, at the challenge so clear on his rugged face. He'd come? For her?

He took another step, his brow wrinkling then smoothing out. Anger replaced by. . .concern? "You were crying."

Dani jerked her gaze away, heart pounding. "You have no right to be here." She started away but he caught her arm.

"Roark."

75

RONIE KENDIG

Her eyes slid shut as she felt him draw closer. His cologne—light and yet thick—swirled around her mind as he stood a head taller.

"Are you okay?" His breath brushed against her cheek with those deep, quiet words.

Swallowing the swell of grief over the memories, yet relief that he'd come, she steadied herself. Curse being a hormonal woman—her chin trembled. Which made her angry. "I'm fine." She tried to pull out of his hold, but his grip tightened. She flashed him a glare.

"This isn't a game." The intensity roared back into his words and expression. "Your *life* isn't a game."

"Yeah, what do you know?"

"I know a strong, beautiful woman who's trying to pretend the pain cutting her heart open doesn't exist. Instead, she cuts open her wrist."

"Dani?"

She gasped, noticing for the first time her sister standing to the side. He communicated so much through those blue eyes, could she do the same? She shot him a look that said she'd kill him if her sister had overheard. "Alexandra, go inside."

"Are you sure?"

"Yes."

They waited, locked in a silent duel, as her sister's steps faded.

"What I did last night was stupid."

"Ya think?"

She huffed. "That's not what I meant."

"Enlighten me."

Dani rotated, grateful when he let go of her arm. She walked along the grass, turning her attention away from the churning in her body to the feathering, glossy leaves against her palm. "When General Lambert called and said I had to go back, everything inside me—all the walls and braces I'd established after what happened. . ." She drew up her courage and shoulders. Took a deep breath. "Well, they vanished when that call came. When you found me, helped me, I knew I had a second chance. I saw how stupid it was." She faced him. Put on the plastic face she'd rehearsed since her father remarried. "I'm fine."

Tension radiated from his eyes. Slowly, that faded and with it, she hoped he'd back off and leave her alone. When he gave her a soft nod, she realized she'd won again. Was it always this easy to make guys think you'd given in?

He smirked. "Sell your sad tale somewhere else."

"What?"

"I'm not buying it."

Glancing away, Dani scrambled. He wasn't buying? Why not? What could she say that would send him on his way? To get rid of him? "Look—"

"I'm not going away. We have a deal. If you break it again, I'm not playing nice."

"Nice! You call this *nice*?" That stupid smirk turned her stomach inside out.

"Do you really want to find out?" He narrowed his eyes. "We have a deal—"

"There is no deal. You said two phone calls."

"And you missed one."

Dani stared at him. Was he serious?

"You owe me a call."

Lips taut, she tugged the cell phone from her pocket. Dialed.

A song—"American Heroes"—blasted out. She glared at him.

Another smirk. He slid the phone from his pocket and answered, his gaze never leaving hers. "Metcalfe."

"I'm a little late," she said into her phone, "but I'm calling. I'm *fine*."

"I'll give you that—you are a fine woman, but you're late."

Heat crawled into her cheeks, unable to look away from the man whose fastidious focus had brought out the worst in her. "So?"

"So, it'll cost you." His eyes twinkled.

She shouldn't smile. She really shouldn't. But she did. "You're as bad as my father or any politician."

Something flashed through his face. He stretched his neck and broke their eye-locked connection. Slowly he lowered the phone and stuffed it in his pocket.

Feeling as if the world had just crashed, she lowered her phone. "Wh—what just happened? What did I say?"

He pursed his lips. "Nothing." The bright sun pinched his eyes into gleaming slits. "I should go."

Her heart tripped and fell over his drastic attitude change.

When he stepped back and turned, she couldn't help what leapt from her tongue. "So you really are like my father."

Canyon rounded on her. The storm returned.

No way she could've known how that flaming arrow had pierced the center target of his soul. Pure adrenaline had shot him through the door to her home, searching, demanding to see her. When her sister said Roark was out on the grounds, he hunted her down. Though relieved at seeing her alive, he'd wanted to throttle her for not calling.

And now—*now* she compared him to a politician. To her father. The blow hit below the belt.

"Canyon?"

Gorgeous brown eyes peered up at him. Was that hurt? Or confusion? "Wh–what. . .what did I say?"

He'd been so determined to make sure she was still on this side of paradise, that he hadn't thought through coming or how seeing her would make him feel.

Range will kill me.

Dark wavy strands framed an olive-toned face and pinkish lips. He had to get out of here. Before he did something stupid. "Take a ride with me." Like that.

A smile flitted across her lips. "Yeah, sure."

He started walking, not trusting himself to talk, and dug the keys from his pocket.

As they passed a ridiculous fountain, she broke the silence he'd created. "Did you really bring the cops?"

"Of course. You gave me your word. When you didn't call, I took it to mean the worst." He eyed her.

Her face went slack and a rosiness filled her cheeks, but she said nothing. She'd looked like she was about to say something or like something he said had stunned her. She wasn't fighting or snapping back. What did that mean?

A shadow dropped over him as they stepped from the crushed gravel path onto the pebbled sidewalk. Canyon glanced up, the ornate home looming over them. Lots of taxpayers had spent years paying for this house. He distinctly remembered her sister saying their father was on a conference call. The last thing Canyon wanted was elbow rubbing with a politician.

"Is there a side way to the front of the house?"

"That way." She stepped off the path and turned onto another walkway alongside the home.

He should probably say something. But then he'd gotten himself in trouble that way too many times before. Like two minutes ago when he'd asked her to go for a drive. About to round the corner of the house, he heard a door open behind them.

"Danielle?"

No, don't stop, he silently willed Roark. *Pretend you didn't hear him.*

She stopped. Turned.

Canyon continued a few more paces. Everything in him said to keep going. Don't show this man that he could control *this* Metcalfe. But Roark. . . Canyon slowed and shifted, facing the front of the house now but looking back at the father and daughter.

"Where are you going?"

Don't tell him. Just. . .let's go.

Roark glanced at him, her dark wavy hair glistening in the early sun. "Just out."

"Mr. Metcalfe, is that you?"

Sucking up his disgust, Canyon nodded. "Senator."

"What a nice surprise. Is your brother here as well?"

"No, sir." He would not give this man any information he didn't need. Besides, he was sure Range would end up hearing it anyway. "If you'll excuse us . . ." He started walking.

"Bye, Dad."

Canyon stalked to the circular drive, keyed into Roark's steps hustling behind him.

"That was borderline rude."

He pressed the fob. The Camaro bleeped as the locks disengaged. He held the door open for Roark.

"Nice car. Red—a power statement." She eased around it and tucked herself into the car.

He shut the door and hurried to the other side. As he opened his door, he caught movement in a far corner window. Senator Roark. Looking down from his pedestal.

Inside, Canyon started the engine and peeled out of the drive. The speed, the sharp corners, helped empty the venom that had dumped into his system at the senator's intrusion on their morning. Despite keeping his focus on the road, he could also feel Roark's eyes boring into him.

He didn't want her quizzing him. "Thought we'd go to the beach." She'd have to wait a long time to hear the story behind his reaction. That was, if ever.

"Somewhere there's no stiff-shirted politicians or my father?"

So she understood his basic motives. He'd let her think she had scored a piece of intel on him.

Take her back. You have no business taking her out.

He slowed as they approached an intersection, backpedaling on this outing. Could he find an excuse that wouldn't offend her? No. No way.

She'd called him on his treatment of her father. And he couldn't stand the thought of hurting her.

Scrounging for something to say, something to add legitimacy to his being alone with her, he knew he couldn't mention the conversation he'd had with the Old Man. Too many things were still being meted out. If the team couldn't secure approval, they wouldn't go. He tightened his fingers around the steering wheel at the thought of her going into the jungle, without him.

Fifteen minutes of silence delivered them to the beach. He parked and climbed out of the car. By the time he reached her side, she'd already opened the door and planted her feet on the pavement. He held the door all the same.

She gave him a look he couldn't decipher as they started toward the water. "I didn't even know you could get to this side of the beach."

"Most surfers know the quiet spots."

"You surf then?"

"Every time I can." He slid his hands into his pockets as they walked the shoreline. "You ever tried it?"

She shook her head. "I prefer being *in* the water, not on top of it."

He chuckled. "Synchronized swimming?"

With a light backhanded slap, she bristled. "Competitive. Made it to state once. I've always wanted to learn to surf, but. . ." The cool March wind tousled her hair and flipped it into her face. She tucked the strands back as she wrinkled her nose. "Swimming to save my life kind of ruined the water for me though."

Something strange slid sideways in his gut. "Imagine it would change things for me, too."

"I doubt you could ride a board as far as I swam." She laughed. "I make that swim every night in my dreams."

He heard the opening and debated on pursuing it. Did she want to go there? Could he handle hearing the truth? "Nightmares?"

"Nightmares, daymares. The oddest things trigger them, too. The rattle of keys. A Hispanic person shouting. . ."

"Are you afraid of going back?"

Roark stopped and stared out over the water. "Terrified."

"But what if. . . ?" He picked up a twig and snapped it in half, then in fourths. "What if you get a good spec-ops team to go down there with you?"

Derision filled her voice. "Who do you think was with me and my team in the first place?"

"Maybe this new team will be better." He couldn't tell her about Nightshade. Not yet. Not unless his follow-up with the Old Man tomorrow night went well.

A disbelieving laugh trickled through the salty air. "Okay. You think that, if it makes you feel better." They walked for a while along the beach, dodging occasional sunbathers, boards planted in the sand, and kids building a sand castle.

"So, are you going to tell me?"

"Tell you what?"

"Come on. You aren't that dense."

"I don't know," he said with a chuckle. "Maybe I am."

"The way you treated my dad."

Singular focus. She'd come back to his reaction already. Canyon flung the stick pieces to the side. "It's not something I talk about."

"I see."

The hurt in those two little words felt like a meaty wave knocking him from the board. "Sorry, it's not personal."

"Wow, that was lame. My father can do better than that."

Ka-pow, right in the gut. "Excuse me?"

She stopped and turned to him. The sun sparkled against her eyes, making them appear as pools of melted caramel, like his mom used to make for harvest festivals. "Look, I've poured my heart out to you, you've seen me cut my wrist, and you came to my house convinced you'd have to rescue me again." She planted her hands on her hips. "Turnabout's fair play."

"I never asked you to pour your heart out to me." Wow, that was juvenile, even for him.

"I told you all that because. . ." Her head angled to the side, her gaze dropping to the sand, and she went quiet.

"Because what?"

When she didn't answer, Canyon grew concerned. Had he missed something? He shuffled closer, touched her arm. "Roark?"

"Never mind." She folded her arms over her chest. "Besides, I saw the way you reacted when I accused you of being as bad as a politician. Then the way you behaved toward my father—which was quite rude, considering how courteous he was."

"Politicians always have an ulterior motive for what they say and do. I don't."

"So, you're just out here on a Saturday morning, walking the beach with me because you're a medic and you want to make sure my arm is okay?"

He couldn't help but smirk at her.

"No ulterior motive, huh? Okay, fine." She tugged up her sleeve. "There. It's stitched. And itchy." She pulled the sleeve back down. "I'll be going now."

Busted. "All right." Canyon slumped down on a clump of boulders and propped one foot up. This was a really bad idea. He should probably return her to the house, grab his board, and catch some waves. Work off some of the tension bunching the muscles in his back.

"A congressional oversight committee put pressure on a particular general in the Vietnam War to pull the plug on a top-secret op, right in the middle of the mission when the armchairs thought it was going bad." He shrugged. "The team got captured—save one man. My father. He tried to get backup, but the Brass abandoned him and his team. So he went in alone to find them. Two years later, my father's headless body came home."

She gasped.

"Nobody talked about it. The government even tried to deny my mom benefits."

Eyes wide, she covered her mouth.

"When my mother and Stone tried to get answers, they were essentially told to sit down and shut up. The congressman responsible denied everything. I've seen it happen enough times to know politicians are corrupt. End of story."

"How do you know it was his fault? Maybe he didn't really do anything."

He leapt to his feet, letting all the heat of his loathing erupt in his words. "And maybe you're really guilty of treason."

DAY ONE

Near Mindanao, Philippines
14:45:02

*B*ut the story does continue, yes?

For many days and nights, Bayani and the outsiders trained our warriors—and the people as well. He taught the women how to do many things to save time, to preserve food. Bayani great in our people's eyes. All would give him their daughters, but he would not have them. He had his Chesa and would not look at another girl.

Soon, word come from other villages—the Higanti had attacked. I would never, ever forget what happened in the days after. My husband said to us, "The Higanti are fighting everywhere and everyone. They wish to wipe out all that is not Tagalog, to keep our island pure. Great fights between the Muslim people who would push their religion on us, and the Higanti, who would push their beliefs on us as well."

It is very messy, yes?

"Bayani, Bayani," Awa said and ran toward the warrior training area. "The Higanti are coming to our village. Our elders fear they will attack because outsiders live among us." Then Awa said, "Bayani—you must leave or my people will be killed."

"No," Bayani said, angry. "We will not go. We are here to train your men to fight, to defend your territory. Let us show you."

"You are outsiders! We cannot win against the Higanti. They are fierce warriors—the most fierce of our people."

"Please, Bayani," Chesa said, tears in her eyes. "They will kill you."

Eyes on fire with anger, Bayani said, "If I leave, they will kill you, and I will not let that happen. It is my duty to stay here, to teach you to fight and survive. I will not leave."

One by one, the outsiders circled around Bayani. Fists in the air, they shouted and agreed with their leader.

I lay in my hut that night, still as a panther by my husband's side, listening to the music of the jungle, the laughter of Bayani and Chesa in a hut close by. As I stared into the blackness, something made my heart tremble. A smell so familiar yet so. . .wrong.

Smoke. I rose from my bed and stumbled toward the door, half-weary, half-scared. As I reached the opening—

Chesa banged into me with a yelp. "Mama, back!"

Bayani rushed in behind her. He pointed to Awa, who was stirring. "They're here. The Higanti are here."

CHAPTER 8

Sayan Mountains, Siberia
One Week Later

Who turned off the heat?

Pine branches laden with icicles drooped toward the blanket of snow. Unforgiving brutal beauty. Pristine whiteness glared back at Canyon as he crouched with his back against a rocky edifice. He peeked up at the overhang, praying those foot-long icicles didn't break free. What a way to die.

His breath puffed out through the extreme-weather mask covering his face. No matter how still, how stealthy he remained, seeing his own breath couldn't be helped at forty below. If he weren't frozen like a dummy on a Popsicle stick, he might be impressed with the beauty of the Sayan Mountains. But breathing hurt too much to enjoy anything right now.

A scritch of boots drew Canyon's gaze to the other side of the gorge—the Kid squatted, his attention on their planned route.

Canyon turned toward the rock wall towering over them. Where it smeared down and collided with the path, Frogman huddled. To the left, a gaping hole in the mountain beckoned. Through the cave, into the heart of the mountain, they'd locate the facility. Rescue Sokoleski and catch the next wave back to the States. To sunshine. Warmth.

Bring it!

Even with the swirling wind, the howling within the cave sent chills racing down Canyon's spine. Chills that had nothing to do with the forty-below temperature. His numb toes warned him if they huddled much longer, the team would go home with fewer digits.

Frogman pointed toward Canyon and Aladdin, motioning them into the mouth.

Peering down the stock of his M4, Canyon eased himself around the rocky wall. Stepping deeper into the cave, he let his gaze track over every crevice, shadow, and jutting space, searching for motion sensors, trip wires, anything that would alert the facility five meters below that they were about to be invaded.

Subtle crunching, not detectable by most, came from behind. Aladdin had his back, tight and clean. Darkness bit down on them. Canyon popped down his night-vision goggles that ghosted the room in a spray of green. In the corner, a pair of eyes glowed back. The small animal had probably come in for warmth. Couldn't blame it.

Too quiet. He slid along the wall, anticipating an ambush.

A strange scratching noise drifted to him on the wind searing through the wool mask. He fisted a gloved hand and held it up, giving the all-stop. Adrenaline spiking, he peeked around the bend in the cave. Two more eyes peered toward him. Then looked away, burying its muzzle into something. His stomach clenched as he realized the animal was eating a large creature. Probably found out in the frozen wilderness and dragged in.

Crack.

Slowly the carcass came into view. Pretty big. *Oh man. . .* Not something, *someone.* Canyon rushed forward. The body must still have warmth to draw the hungry fox. He swiped the animal away from the fallen man, but the thing snarled and lunged.

Thump.

The fox fell like a limp rag, snapping Canyon's attention to his partner.

Aladdin nodded over his silenced Glock and continued monitoring.

Kneeling beside the body, Canyon plucked off his gloves. Iciness prickled his warm hand as he pressed two fingers to the throat. Dead. But not frozen solid, which meant the kill had been recent. His gaze swept the body looking for the cause of death. A dark stain gaped from the partially open jacket. The fox had eaten some of the man's fingers. Sick.

White lab coat. Normal shoes. The guy had been in a rush to get out, but why? Who was chasing—and shot him?

"What's the word?" Legend whispered.

Canyon shook his head and stood, coming in line with the others as they continued forward. Tension ratcheted with each crunch. Echoes shouted their approach.

As the tunnel burrowed into the mountain, a strange sick-sweet smell permeated the air. Being a medic, he knew that scent. Teeth clamped, he prepped himself for the worst. That they'd get in here and find everyone dead, including their objective, Viktor Sokoleski, a physicist who'd promised some juicy intel in exchange for safe passage to America. The important parts were to get in, get the objective, and get out—alive.

His NVGs hit another body. Canyon darted to the prostrate form, but even before he reached the person, he knew it was too late. A half dozen spots mottled the jacket. Irritation coiled around his gut and clenched. What was going on? Who had silenced these scientists? And why? Did someone beat them to Sokoleski?

Pop! Pop! Pop!

Ahead, Frogman dropped to a knee, firing his M4 into the darkness. Shouts reverberated through the cave. The team pressed against the wall, each man taking a different position to optimize coverage.

A lone figure rushed toward them, hands up. "No shoot! No shoot." He patted his chest, yellowish green eyes peering back at them. "I Sokoleski. Help! He kill all. Still here." He waved behind him, breathing frantically.

"Get down! Get down! On your knees!" Frogman shouted as he hustled forward, pointing toward the slick ground.

Sokoleski dropped to his knees, arms still raised.

Swiftly Legend patted him down. "Clean." He jerked the guy up and tossed him toward Canyon, who pinned the guy against the frozen cave wall, let his M4 drop against his chest in the sling, then unholstered his Glock.

"Let's get—" Frogman snapped his M4 back toward the tunnel. "Stop!"

Another form appeared. Hands raised.

"Don't shoot me," the man said, in a weakened but adamant voice. "He's not the right man. I am Viktor Sokoleski."

"No, *no*. I Viktor."

Weapon raised and pointed at the newcomer, Frogman sidestepped between the two men. "Legend, check him out."

After a quick look to the first man, Legend patted down the second, then moved to the side where he kept a gun trained on him.

Was Canyon's mind playing tricks on him? In the green hues, the two men looked exactly alike. Twins? With his forearm against the first man's throat, he aimed a Glock at his head.

The Kid groaned. "This is messed up."

"No trust him," the first man rasped from beneath Canyon's hold. "My brother kill all."

"Dmitri, quiet!" The second surged forward but Legend's muzzle urged him back.

Frogman shifted, glancing between the two. "Gimme light."

Canyon flipped up his NVGs as shafts of illumination burst out, pouring brightness on the man under his restraint. Legend's shoulder lamp cast strange shadows over Viktor as Frogman assessed his face. The Kid moved closer, flashing his torch at Dmitri.

A curse sailed through the frigid air. "They're identical."

"No," the first argued as he pushed against Canyon's grip. "He killer. I escape. He know I tell you everything, so he kill me. Pow!"

Canyon would bet his life the good guy was in his grip. Something about the too-perfect English and ultracalm demeanor of the second Siberian unsettled his gut. But there was no way to sort this out here.

"Watch him." Canyon handed off his prisoner to the Kid, who grabbed the man's jacket—

Thwat!

Canyon spun at the sound of the silenced gunfire just in time to see the man's stunned expression frozen in place. Sokoleski One gasped. Gurgled.

"He's shot!"

Canyon pushed the Kid aside.

Blood streamed out of Sokoleski's mouth.

Shouts and fights jerked Canyon's gaze around. Legend and Frogman had the second guy face-planted into the icy terrain. Sokoleski Two peered up, past Canyon, saw something, and smiled.

"Down, fool!" Legend slammed the guy's head into the ground.

Canyon caught Sokoleski One as the guy slid down, his breath wheezing out of him. He eased the man down and pressed a hand to his chest where a red stain blossomed.

The man groaned. His eyes focused. He gripped Canyon's hand. "I good guy."

Canyon nodded. "Just hang in there."

A gasp. Another gurgle. "Mir. . .ann. . .da."

"Just be quiet." He shrugged off his medic pack and dug in it. But even as he did, he knew it was useless. With the way the guy was drowning in his own blood, he had massive internal bleeding.

Canyon stepped back and reached into his medical pouch, riffled through the first layer, and finally curled his fingers around a dart. On his feet, he walked over to the tangling trio of Frogman, Legend, and Sokoleski Two, and fired a dart into the guy's neck.

As the fight leeched out of the man, Frogman and Legend released him. Secured his hands.

"Good work," Frogman said. "He had a hidden weapon."

"He wanted to silence his brother."

"Yeah, but why?" Legend asked.

"Someone named Miranda."

First Street Jetty, Virginia Beach, Virginia
13 April

"Not bad, not bad." Canyon grinned at Azzan as he sloshed out of the water, board tucked under his arm. "Dude, you ready to paddle?"

Azzan smoothed a hand over his short-cropped black hair and smiled. "More than."

"Then let's hit it."

But his friend hesitated, glancing over Canyon's shoulder. "You know her?"

Canyon looked back—and stilled. After the way he stormed off the last time he saw her, he'd bet she wouldn't speak to him again. Apparently she liked defying odds.

"Roark." The sun glistened against her loose hair as she hung back. "I see you got the Rash Guard." He couldn't help but notice the way the black and silver nylon-spandex material hugged her upper torso, streamlined her curves.

"It seemed like a hint that I should come out." She closed the distance.

He shrugged. "You said you wanted to learn." Though he wanted to smile, he wouldn't. Not in front of Azzan. He tossed his head in the former assassin's direction. "He just started an hour ago. Think you can outlearn him?"

"Willow said you just got back in town, so I wasn't. . .if it's a bad time. . . I don't want to interrupt." Roark flicked her gaze to Azzan but quickly brought it back.

When she took a step away, Canyon moved into her path, planting the BZ beginner board in front of her. "Giving up already?"

Her chin drew up and with it a defiant gleam trickled through her brown eyes.

"I got back last night. Ten days spent like an ice cube makes a man enjoy warm water and smiles." He liked the way that made her high cheekbones fill with color. "So, you ready?"

She nodded.

"Good. Let's run through some basics." He smoothed a hand along the board. "This is called a surfboard."

"Gee. Really? I wouldn't have guessed."

Azzan slapped him. "I've got her beat." With a wicked grin, Azzan dragged his board back to the salty water.

What Canyon didn't miss was the streak of indignation that darted through Roark's expression. "Come on. We'll run through it."

He led her to a clear stretch of beach where he laid out the board, careful to bury the fins in the sand. "Okay, first things first. This is the nose." He toed the front portion of the board. "It's a beginner board, so it's not narrow like mine. Then you have the tail and rails." He pointed to the sides. "Of course, on the bottom, fins." He patted the center. "The deck."

Canyon stood and walked around the board, which brought him behind Roark. He gave her a slight shove between her shoulder blades.

She pitched forward but caught herself. "Hey!"

"Relax, I was checking your footing. You're a right footer."

"Excuse me?"

"When I pushed, you stepped with your left foot to regain your balance. Tells me how to instruct you on the board. Now, watch. I'll demonstrate, then it's up to you." Canyon pressed his gut to the fiberboard and gripped the rails. "You'll ride it out like this to get into position. When you're ready, push your shoulders up and arch your back. Make sure your hands are under your chest and then raise up.

"Push upward from your toes and hands." He mimicked as he instructed. "Bring your back foot up, front foot forward, level with your hands. Then stand with your knees bent, arms apart, looking toward the nose."

After tying her hair back, Roark spent the next twenty minutes perfecting her technique. He kept a watch on Azzan still riding the smaller waves. Chicken. Canyon had a feeling Roark's competitive edge would push the two into a silent contest.

"I think you're ready to show Aladdin there a thing or two."

Roark eyed him. "I'm not here to compete."

"Why *are* you here?"

She dipped her head and though the sunburn made it hard to tell, it seemed more color infused her cheeks. The noble thing to do was to tell her to go home, wait for Range to call. Spending so much time with her certainly wouldn't help his sibling rivalry or relationship. But the fact that she'd come, sought him out, when she withdrew from every other male he'd seen around her. . .

"Come on." BZ in hand, he plodded the shoreline to a clear spot. "Okay. Hold the rails and walk it out until you're waist deep. Then hop on and paddle out."

"You want me to go out there already—*alone*?"

"I'm not leaving. You aren't ready." He motioned to the board. "Take 'er out."

With a nervous glance at him, she positioned her board into the water. He monitored the water depth, noting he stood at least a foot taller than Roark. When the ocean encircled the top of her board shorts, he stopped her. "Okay, lay on it so the nose rises out of the water. Not a lot, but enough."

Complying, she moved with expertise.

"Okay, good. Good." Wasn't this her first time? As he waded out, hands still on her board, he noticed the determination gouged into her face. "Roark."

Her gaze darted to his.

"Relax. Enjoy it."

A sharp nod.

"If you tense up, you're going to make yourself sick out here or get wicked cramps." Chest deep, he paused and held her board. His words seemed to have worked because she blew out a short breath. "Now, get your feet on the board like you practiced on the beach."

As she shifted from belly position to feet position, the board wobbled. "Keep it nice and fluid. Try again." Canyon waited as she repeated the maneuver. "Okay, good!" He searched the surfers and found Azzan coming off another small wave. "Hey, Aladdin! You'd better pony up to a big wave or Roark's going to wipe you out!"

"Bring it," Azzan said just seconds before he flipped into the water.

After an hour of more lessons, Roark had grown comfortable enough to attempt a decent wave. Canyon stood at the shoreline monitoring her as she tackled it.

Azzan sloughed through the water, board under his arm. For a minute or two, he watched Roark. "She's good."

"Yeah." Canyon folded his arms over his chest.

"I need to bug out. After this morning's exercise, I'm feeling a bit worse for the wear."

Canyon chuckled. "It'll take time. Don't let Legend get to you."

"His fist sure got to me a couple of weeks ago."

"At least you've haven't made that mistake since."

"I don't want to go through that again." Azzan handed off the board. "Next week?"

Canyon nodded. "Yep."

As his teammate took off, he turned his attention back to Roark. In the water, she'd apparently fallen off but was already climbing back up. *Atta girl.* She lay on the board and started toward shore.

At the moment she waved to him, grinning, he saw the dark, discolored water. Choppy and rippling. "Oh no." He hurried to the water's edge and cupped his hands over his mouth. "Go with it! Don't fight the pull."

Too late.

Her brows knitted. She paddled harder.

Canyon grabbed his board, secured the leash to his ankle, and rushed into the water. Long, determined strides pushed him into the rip. The board struggled beneath him. "Roark, paddle into the pull. Don't fight it."

Brown eyes hit his. Wide. Panicked.

He pointed a couple of yards out. "Aim that way."

She glanced in the direction, then nodded. The water writhed beneath them. Canyon finally made it to her. "Keep going. You're doing fine."

Minutes later, they eased along a diagonal path and made it out of the riptide. Roark slumped against the foam base with a groan. Face partially flattened against the board, she looked at him. A half grin made its way into her face.

"You're not a beginner."

She shrugged.

"But you're not a pro."

"Hardly." She sat up on the board and straddled it. "My dad and Abby got married in Hawaii. I learned the basics while they were honeymooning."

Canyon grinned. "Promise me one thing."

Squinting against the setting sun, she smiled at him. "What?"

"Don't tell Aladdin."

CHAPTER 9

Metcalfe Residence, Virginia
18 April

Danielle, you look absolutely stunning, my dear!" Mrs. Metcalfe took her hands and held them out to the side. "My, my. Look at this dress." She arched an eyebrow at Dani, making her feel self-conscious in the satiny navy dress with sequined bodice. Her gaze shifted to the long sleeve of the lightweight sweater that concealed the marks the stitches—long since dissolved—left. "Never mind the dress, look at *you* in the dress. I think I might need to chaperone you two to this spring ball."

"Mom, you're embarrassing her!" Willow laughed. "Come on, everyone. Out back for pictures."

Range inserted himself, tucking Dani's hand into the crook of his arm as he smiled down at her. "You look beautiful."

Nerves and nausea swirled through her stomach. She appreciated his attention, but her mind kept racing back to Venezuela, to a similar look far too many men had given her. She had to mentally dissect the look, reminding herself that Range had more honor in his little finger than Bruzon's men had in their whole bodies.

A series of photographs took close to a half hour, but Dani was glad for the company of his sister and mother, grateful she wasn't alone with Range. But the padding of their presence wouldn't last forever. She and Range posed this way. That way. Always his hands on her, whether at the small of her back, her shoulders, her waist. Dani fought the urge to squirm away from him. Out of his reach.

"We need to get going." Range led her back into the house and patted down his pockets. "I think I left my house keys upstairs. I'll be right back."

Willow's lighthearted laugh seemed to mingle with the rose-patterned wallpaper and nostalgic photos. "You might want to hold the

93

keys for him tonight. He's notorious for losing them."

The front door jerked open. "What's with the—?"

Dani's breath jammed into her throat as Canyon stopped in the foyer. His gaze fell on her. Though she thought she saw appreciation in his expression at her appearance, a stronger emotion crowded it out: irritation. Or anger. Either way, his mouth clamped shut and he didn't move.

"Just in time, Canyon," their mother said. "Doesn't Danielle look amazing? She'll be the belle of the ball."

Canyon's jaw muscle popped. He gave a curt nod. Stalked down the hall to the kitchen, taking her heart with him.

Why did he have to show up? She didn't want him to see her like this—all dressed up and going out with his brother.

"Okay, we're good to go." Range hustled back down the stairs.

Sultry and blue, evening welcomed them. A cool breeze mingled with the thickness of an impending storm. As she turned toward the drive, gravel crunching beneath her feet, she froze.

A sleek black limousine waited.

Impressed, Dani couldn't help but smile at Range. But as she did, she saw in his eyes the hope of something more. . .of a future. *Oh no.* A limo like that meant Range wanted to express a promise of things to come. Things she wasn't interested in seeing fulfilled. Clearly this was his attempt to woo her.

But maybe that wasn't so bad. Handsome in his own right, Range Metcalfe had a heart of gold. Gentle manners. Almost shy in a charming sort of way. Really, she shouldn't rebuff his attention. A man like him outshone every date her father had pushed on her over the last five years, trying to marry her off. She could get used to the treatment, especially since it was obvious Canyon didn't have an interest.

They arrived at the Marriott Resort amid a flurry of dress whites and glittering gowns. Their limo pulled to the porte cochere and a valet opened the door. Range climbed out first and once again offered his hand.

Dani accepted it, glad to have his protection against the crowds and pomp of the evening. How her mother had ever borne up under it, she didn't know. They'd shared everything—characteristics, appearance, and sentiments. Then her mother died.

A wretched thought rammed into her, shoving a steel rod down her spine. If Range was here and he'd rescued her, wouldn't there be more of the Coasties who'd rescued her as well? She slowed.

"You okay?" Range asked as they entered the resort.

"Yeah." It seemed not only possible but a grim reality. And the last thing she wanted was to have some officer or Coastie staring at her, remembering her naked broken body laid out in that basket.

"Why, Chief Metcalfe," an older officer with more medals and ribbons than most of the Coasties approached them with a perfectly coiffed woman. "Who is this beauty you've brought with you?"

Was it her imagination or did Range's chest just puff out?

"Lieutenant Commander Greene, this is Danielle Roark, my date," Range said. His blue eyes—so much like Canyon's—sparkled against his tanned face. Another thing like Canyon.

Stop comparing them!

"Miss Roark, it's a pleasure. I've always wondered what kind of woman it would take to ensnare this officer." Commander Greene laughed and shook her hand. "May I introduce my wife, Elizabeth?"

Dani shook the woman's hand, surprised at the tight, firm grasp. "Mrs. Greene, it's nice to meet you."

"Thank you, Miss Roark." She rolled her expressive eyes to Range. "Chief, I'd say you've outdone yourself with your date, but we've been waiting so long for this night."

"Well, we won't keep you two. The dance floor's that way," the commander said with a laugh. He patted Range's shoulder with a "well done" and vanished into the crowd forming behind them.

Blushing—was he really blushing?—Range tilted his head toward her as they crossed the patterned floors. "He was one of my dad's good friends." He led her through another set of doors and paused. "Shall we?"

With a mustered smile, she allowed him to guide her onto the dance floor. Dani turned into his arms. She needed to put her mind elsewhere, away from the fact that he had his arm around her waist and was holding her hand.

Get the small talk going. "Why'd you get into the Coast Guard?"

"I wanted something water based but knew I didn't want to go through BUD/S or special ops, like Canyon." His gaze pinged off hers, and he gave a halfhearted smile.

She'd ignore the temptation to ask about his brother. Even she knew better than that. Tonight was Range's night. And he had treated her with respect and courtesy. She could certainly return that favor. "Do you like being a Coastie?"

"Yeah, I do. It's fulfilling and keeps me challenged. I protect the borders of our country, I've saved a few lives, and I get to be out on the water."

"You know." Dani wet her lips and stared at the brass buttons on his navy blazer. If she met his gaze, she probably wouldn't be able to voice this. "I never thanked you. . .for. . ." Why had she even brought it up? She dropped her gaze as a stinging awareness of what she'd looked like, what he'd seen that fateful night, washed over her.

Range squeezed her hand. "You're welcome." He craned his neck to see into her eyes. "Let's make a deal."

Dani braved a glance at him.

"We don't mention it again. Let's leave it where it belongs."

Acute relief cleansed the nausea. "Thanks." She relaxed. "That means a lot."

"So do you." Range straightened almost immediately and peered out over the dance floor, as if afraid to see her reaction to his words. With subtle pressure on her back, he drew her closer. The knots in her stomach tightened.

After two more dances, Dani begged off. "Maybe we could get a drink or something."

"Sure." Range led her to their table and pulled her chair out for her. "What's your flavor?" He sat sideways in the chair, a hand over hers.

"Water."

He nodded, then made his way through the crowd and disappeared.

"Hey," a guy in full dress said as he slipped into the seat beside her. "You look familiar."

Her palms grew slick. "I'm not sure why." *Oh please don't be one of the Coasties who rescued me. Please don't.* "I don't recall meeting you."

"No." He shook a finger at her. "I've seen you. . ."

Hopefully he hadn't seen more of her than he should've. The knots tightened even more.

"Hey, Moore, bug off."

A roar of laughter shot past Dani as the guy stood. "Metcalfe!" He winked at Dani. "Wait." His smile dropped. "Are you—?" He glanced at Range. "You're the girl we picked up out of the Gulf."

"Leave off, Moore." Range's tone bore a sharpness she'd never heard from him before.

"Hah, this is cool." His friend patted his shoulder. "Way to go, Metcalfe. Take advantage of Stockholm. Know what I mean?" The sickening laugh seemed to push Range over the edge.

"To be Stockholm, I'd have to be her captor. You're drunk, Moore. Leave off." The punch sloshed over the cups, and he dropped them on the table and drew up straight.

Dani shoved to her feet. "I'm ready to leave."

Moore gaped at her, then quickly diverted his humor and attention to another couple nearby. He glanced back at her and Range and smirked. The expression on the man's face cracked her resolve to enjoy this evening.

The burst of strength and fortitude slid through that crack. Her courage and willingness went with them. And through that opening came a swift squall of memories. Foul breath. . .near-rabid dogs. . . leaping from the cliff. . .

"Dani?" Range's soft voice came very close, almost against her ear.

She closed her eyes and tried to squeeze away the memories. But even with his comforting tone, she felt herself caving. "I want to leave."

"Sure, no problem. Let's go." Range took her elbow. Helped her to her feet. Directed her out of the building with swiftness. "I'm sorry."

She should be strong. Shove this very far away from her mind. But the humiliation of that nightmare coming back to life. . .

"I'm really sorry that happened. Moore is a loser. Ignore him." Range eased his arm around her shoulder and pulled her against himself. "Please don't cry."

Only at his words did she feel the warmth of the tear slipping down her cheek.

Inside the car, she burrowed into the darkness, wrapped her arms around herself.

"I'm sorry," he said as he hovered next to her. "It was a bad idea to take you there. I had no idea. . ."

She couldn't argue. Though she knew propriety would dictate she exonerate him from guilt, remove the weight he felt for what happened, she couldn't. As if standing on the edge of a dark precipice, she felt ready—no, *willing*—to fall into the dark fathoms of despair. Why did she think she could survive this, beat it? It'd haunt her for the rest of her life.

"We're here."

Dani lifted her head, surprised to find the limo snuggling up to the home. Seconds later, they emerged into the warm, sticky night.

"Hey, you two," Willow's singsong voice rang out. "You're back early."

Unable to look up at the question in Willow's statement, Dani shuffled around, trying to hide her face. Looked toward her car.

"Everything all right?"

Canyon. A piece of her wanted to spin and rush into his arms.

Insane. But that's what she could see herself doing. Yeah, that'd go over well with Range.

"Want to go inside?"

She looked up. . .but stopped at Range's shoulder. "Thanks for the evening. Really, I did have a good time." But she couldn't stay. Not with Canyon. He'd know. "I should get home." Again, she managed that weak smile and started toward the car. Fumbling with her bag as she plodded down the flower-strewn path, she dug for the keys.

Behind her, she heard the siblings mumbling. A terse word here and there. No doubt Range relaying the events. Embarrassment chased her to the car, but not before Willow glided up on her right. "Here, let me help you." She reached for the key.

Numb, Dani let her take it. "Thanks."

"Sure thing." With a smile that held both understanding and pity, Willow looked over her shoulder and tossed the key in that direction.

Dani whirled just in time to see Canyon snag the keys from the air, then pivot and walk back up to the house. Turning back to Willow, she felt the cloud of confusion descend. "Wha—why did you do that?"

With a shrug, Willow smiled. "I guess we're having a sleepover."

Metcalfe Residence
19 April

Am I my brother's keeper?

Cain had killed Abel. For a split second, Canyon understood. The feelings churning through his gut at the sight of Range with Roark last night. . . She'd looked ethereal. Sexy. Sultry. Jealousy was one thing, but seeing them together last night and then this morning, the green-eyed monster had fanned the flames of his anger that Range claimed her first. And she sure didn't seem to mind being Range's date. Maybe she had more politician's blood than he'd thought.

It was stupid. Brothers fighting over the same girl.

But the girl was Roark. The futility of what he felt for her left him feeling whacked. Which is why he kept his distance all day, while she hung out with Willow and Range.

As quiet bathed the house, Canyon ventured from his self-imposed isolation with his golden retriever, Daisy, who plodded beside him as he headed to the backyard to throw the ball for her. His shoes thunked against the wood as he moved onto the back porch.

"Canyon's on my team!" Leif's shout stopped the hustle on the back forty, as it was called.

Stone, Willow, Range, and Roark turned as Canyon froze. *Crap.* He wondered where they'd gone. Sunday with the Metcalfes meant family time. Meant big meals. Meant nobody left till darkness came.

"We're teaming up for football," Stone said. "You game?"

" 'Course." Trudging down the steps, Canyon rolled his agitation over Range and Roark into a tight ball and pitched it into the cesspool of indifference.

"Dani and I will take Willow." Range tugged the girls aside.

"Wait a minute. Two girls and a guy against three hard players?" Willow shook her head. "No way."

Roark leaned toward Willow and whispered something. His sister laughed, then said, "We're good."

"They're ready to be buried." Leif flung the ball at Canyon, who snagged it from the air.

He glanced at the group as they lined up. "Where are Brooke and Mark?"

"He's on a trip; she's prepping for a case." Stone clapped. "All right, let's bring it."

"Marie?" Canyon asked about Stone's wife.

"Just play."

In a squat, Canyon planted the ball on the ground. With three on three, it wouldn't be bad, but it also wouldn't be a fulfilling game, not with these odds.

Range, Willow, and Roark prepared.

"Ready. . .set. . .hike!" Canyon thrust the hide to Leif, then burst down the green. Running, he glanced back and spotted Stone running parallel to him.

Leif palmed the ball, lifted it, and sent it spiraling straight to Canyon. To catch it, he'd have to double back. He skidded and backpedaled.

Range and Willow were coming fast.

Stone cut in and blocked Range.

Willow continued the straight line for him.

Canyon launched into the air and caught the ball. He landed and rolled, came up and kept going. Close by he heard a grunt. Glanced back. Roark was within three feet. Without a thought, Canyon threw himself over the marked line for the goal.

"Touchdown!" Leif shouted.

On his back and staring up the sky, Canyon could only laugh. A hand came into view. He craned his neck and found Roark standing over him. "You're ruthless. You think I'll trust that offered hand?" With her help, he came to his feet. Considered her. "You're good."

"Sweet play." Leif retrieved the ball and started back to the fifty yard line. "Guys one, others zip."

Range jogged toward them. "Nice try, Dani. Nice try."

Canyon stalked away, ready to pummel some more yardage—or his brother. Anything to get away from Range and Roark. If Canyon stood around, the buzzing in his head at seeing his brother take the lead with her would make him mental. In the huddle, he listened as Leif plotted their next play.

"We'll need to keep an eye on Roark," Canyon mumbled. "She doesn't play like Willow."

Stone chuckled. "No kidding. Willow plays for fun. Dani plays to win."

The grin couldn't be helped. She wasn't afraid to try to take him down. They slapped hands and turned to the painted line.

"Come on," Leif taunted. "We ain't got all night."

When the trio turned, Willow had the ball. She stuck her tongue at Leif and bent into position. Roark came up behind her.

Stone gave Canyon a knowing look, and he returned his brother's sentiments. Almost in sync, Canyon and Stone backed up a couple of paces.

In play, the ball passed from Willow to Roark. She spun around and instantly, the other two gathered up. Seconds later, all three burst down the field.

Canyon scrambled to see who had the pigskin.

Easily, Stone took down Range. No ball. Canyon jogged after Willow and Roark. There! Under Roark's arm. She was close to their goal. He pushed himself hard. Willow banked into his path. Leif nailed her. Canyon had to leap over them to keep going. He reached toward Roark. She looked back and jerked left.

"No!" Lips tight, Canyon lunged. Caught her shoulders. Pulled her down. They rolled and slid to a stop.

On her stomach, Roark didn't move.

Canyon touched her arm.

Her shoulders bounced. Was she crying? "You okay?"

She flopped onto her back, laughing. Thrust the ball into the air. "Touchdown!"

"No way," Leif said. "You went down before the line."

Canyon didn't care about the score. What he liked, what made him stare was the massive smile on Roark's face, the exultant glow in her mahogany orbs.

Roark propped herself up on her elbows, looking down at her toes. "Check the smear marks."

The others gathered around as Canyon pulled himself to his feet. Something knocked him sideways.

"What do you think you're doing tackling her?" Red colored Range's face. "It's a *friendly* game."

"Hey, back up, Range." Stone stepped between the two, a hand on each chest as he nudged them apart. But then he looked at Canyon. "Maybe you should take it easy. Tackling—"

"It's fine. I'm fine." Roark's voice stabbed the tension. "I thought this was a football game. Or is it junior high?"

Canyon stepped off. "She's right. The point is good."

"No way!" Leif growled. "That's—you took her down before the line."

"Give it up." Canyon shot Range a frown. "It's fair. Besides, we're tied now. Let's get it going. I plan to win."

"Keep thinking that if it makes you feel better."

He spun, staring down at the spunk that came in a package called Roark. "You don't seem to realize who you're playing against."

"Enlighten me."

Canyon smirked.

Stone tugged him back. "Leave it." He pulled him around and walked him back to the line. "You pegged her. Glad you went after her. I wouldn't have had the guts to tackle her."

"If she wants to play with the big boys. . ." Canyon high-fived his older brother.

"Just remember"—Roark sauntered past them, twirling the ball— "big boys fall hard."

Stone bent, touched the ground, and grinned at her. "Bring it, little girl."

Uh-oh. Roark had no idea the man before her earned his way through his law degree on a football scholarship. This should be interesting.

Amusement sparked in Roark's eyes.

Canyon wasn't sure whether to call a time-out and regroup the guys or let this play out. His younger brother made the choice. Leif stuffed the hide into Stone's hands. Within seconds, the teams flew into motion.

But Canyon held back, watched Stone's challenge get met head-on. Literally. Roark charged him, dove into his gut. Canyon couldn't help but laugh as she tried to knock Stone from his feet.

"All right, Mighty Mouse." Stone patted her back. "I'll give you an A for effort."

Batting hair out of her face, Roark glowered at him. "I don't need charity grades."

Stone guffawed.

Roark lunged. Caught him off guard. His brother went down. Hard. On his backside.

Laughter roared through the late afternoon. Shock riddled Stone's face. Slowly he pulled himself off the ground. He looked to be dusting off the humiliation as much as the dirt from his clothes.

"See?" Roark, arms propped behind her, grinned unabashedly at him. "I was right. Big boys fall hard."

In sickening slow motion, Canyon watched Range pull Roark into a laughing hug, then kiss the top of her head. Ready to vomit, Canyon stalked off the field. He might not have any latitude regarding his feelings for Roark, but he sure didn't have to sit around and watch them get cozy. What if they got serious? Got married?

Abs tight, he ripped open the screen door—right off the hinges.

CHAPTER 10

Crack!

The screen door clattered to the wood porch. Dani brushed the hair from her face as Range released her. Heat slid through her face as she spotted Canyon's hulk disappearing down the hall inside.

"Door's been threatening to fall off for months," Leif said with a laugh.

But Dani knew exactly why he'd left. At least, she thought she did. The reason was touching her shoulder. Well, to be precise, wrapped around her shoulder. Range had suddenly become quite comfortable with her. Too comfortable.

Rigid, she battled her first instinct—to slap Range's hand away. Why was she so conflicted? It was like she couldn't choose because the decision had been made for her. This wonderful family wanted her to be a part of their group, but as Range's girlfriend. Not a horrible thing, but she didn't want this brother. She peeked up at him as he talked with Stone and Willow, mumbling something about Canyon.

Stone went into the house after him.

Range shrugged and turned back to her. "Ready to eat?"

The Metcalfe family had it all—warmth, laughter, games, family, camaraderie. Everything she'd longed for as a little girl.

A buzzing noise seeped into the night. Range snatched a black device from his belt and grunted. "Man, I have to go." He turned to Dani and touched her face. "I don't want to leave you but they've called me up."

Inclining her head conveniently removed his hand from her face. "I understand."

He planted yet another kiss on her head. "Thanks."

"We'll cover for you." Willow led Dani back to the covered porch where tiki torches flickered in the evening breeze and kept the mosquitoes at bay.

"Mighty Mouse," Stone said as he and Leif stood. "We're going to watch a *real* football game—we recorded this year's Super Bowl. You want to see how to really play?"

"I wouldn't want you to be embarrassed," Dani replied, the retort so quick, she felt bad after she said it.

Stone laughed hard. So did Leif, and they managed to con her into coming inside. Seated amid the men, she let her gaze rest on the massive flat-screen TV, but her mind roamed the house. Where had Canyon gone?

Thud.

She glanced at the back door, once again seeing Canyon disappearing outside. On her feet before she could stop herself, Dani knew following him would look bad, so she headed to the bathroom. Washed her hands. Ran her fingers through hair. Then maneuvered her way back into the kitchen. Nobody had noticed her; they were too engrossed in the game. She eased the french doors open and stood on the porch.

At the foot of the stairs, Canyon grabbed a ball from the grass. He threw it, and the dog sprinted into the yard, circled, and returned with it in her mouth. After a half dozen throws, Canyon eased back onto the step. He pitched a few more.

Dani slipped onto the steps and sat. "It's a beautiful evening."

Though he flinched at her voice, Canyon watched the dog as she returned with the now-soggy ball. He shook it out and then tossed it again.

"Canyon?"

He glanced to the side, in her direction, but not at her.

"Why did you take my keys last night?"

"I like your car. Thought I'd give it a spin."

Nice save. He seemed to have as much trouble talking about painful things as she did. "Someone at the ball. . .recognized me." Jitters scampered through her veins. Why did she bring it up?

As the golden retriever reclined on the grassy yard, Canyon pulled his feet up a step and rested his elbows on his knees.

Fidgeting with the trim on her sweater, she pushed on. "All I could think of was diving into the water the night I escaped, wishing I hadn't come up for air."

Canyon nailed her with a fierce expression. "*That's* why I took your keys."

She tilted her head and whispered, "I know."

He frowned. "Then why'd you ask?"

She scrunched her shoulders and leaned forward, arms resting on her knees. "You always seem to know what I'm thinking or feeling. I guess I just wanted to thank you." Why wouldn't he just talk to her instead of blasting his icy attitude? "I didn't mean to intrude. . ." She started to get up.

"My brother's wife is leaving him," he mumbled, drawing her back down. "She had an affair and decided she liked the other guy better."

"*Stone?*" Dani gaped. "Stone's wife is leaving him?"

He nodded. "I can't figure it out. From what I can tell, he did everything right, ya know? Lived by God's Word, did mission trips before college." Canyon ran his hand through his sandy blond hair. "My life was screwed up but it was my fault. I got what I deserved. But Stone? He had it all—bent over backwards for her. Worked his rear end off." He shook his head. "I so wanted to be like him, make our parents proud. When Dad died, Stone stepped up to the plate and became the family spokesman."

"Bet your mom didn't appreciate that."

Canyon snorted. "She put him in his place, but she appreciated his gesture. She's very old school." He looked up at the blanket of stars and let out a long sigh. "I've tried to get my life back on track, do what is good and right—for a change." A soft laugh rattled between them. "I've never been exactly compliant, but after. . . A year ago, I renewed my commitment to God."

"Is it working?"

Canyon shrugged. "I'm learning. Life hasn't been entirely cooperative."

"When is it ever? I'll never forget when my dad announced he was marrying Abby. She was a senior in high school when I was a freshman."

He watched her.

"My mother hadn't been dead two years when Dad married Abby." She pushed her fingers through her hair with a groan, then clasped them together. "Abby wanted the security and the prestige. Dad—I think it stroked his ego that someone as young and attractive as her would want him. But I don't get why anyone would leave Stone. He's intelligent, he's rich, he's handsome."

Canyon's eyebrow winged up.

"I mean—" She diverted her gaze. "That sounded wrong."

"Yeah, it did."

The tone of his words lured her into looking at him again. In the evening light, his profile was strong and stern. "You're jealous."

He gave a half chuckle-half snort.

"So, it *was* anger that drove you out here when Range had his arm around me."

Canyon shook his head and watched the yard again.

"And why you stalked off during the game."

He ran a hand over the back of his thick neck. "You seem to be enjoying this."

"Yes." But then she realized. . . "No."

He tilted his head toward her but didn't meet her gaze again, his straight Greek nose seemed to point to the thin lips permanently parked in that smirk of his.

"I don't like seeing you jealous or angry."

His blue eyes bounced to hers. "Why? Do I scare you?"

She smiled. "Only your anger."

He nudged her shoulder with his. "Well, don't worry. I'm not violent."

"How. . . ? That night you found me cutting, how did you know what I was doing? I mean, I get the medic skills, but it was like. . .you understood."

He drew in a long breath and slowly let it out. Fidgeting with his sleeve, he unbuttoned the left one and turned it back. Then a second time. Was he ignoring her question?

Gradually, a tattoo peeked at her. Fisting his hand, he flexed his muscle and angled his arm toward her. At first, she only saw the wings and sword, but then the light hit his forearm just right. And ridges seemed to rise from his flesh.

"What. . . ?" Dani tucked her hand under the crook of his elbow and touched the ribs of the wings. "What is that?"

"I tried the same thing you did about four years ago."

"You tried to end your life?"

He cocked his head at her. "That surprise you?"

"Yeah." Her gaze collided with his. "I'm glad you didn't succeed."

Only inches apart, arms partially entwined still, their eyes were locked. "Why's that?"

"I never would have met you."

When Canyon's gaze dropped to her mouth, hope took flight. His breath dashed against her cheek. Warmth soaked her muscles as she anticipated the kiss he seemed to be considering. His touch was firm as he used two fingers to angle her chin up. Nervous jellies swarmed her stomach.

His lips swept over hers.

Thrilled—yes, he felt the same way!—and eyes closing, Dani leaned into his kiss that caressed her mouth, warm, hovering, then pressing. Why did everything with this man feel right and beyond wonderful? Something about him, about his gaze, his touch, spoke to her. To all the wounded places in her heart.

His hand trailed along her jaw—

Canyon jerked back. Turned away. Hung his head. Cursed. He shoved to his feet, hustled down the steps, and stalked to the white fence that separated the open yard from the small garden closer to the house.

Following him, Dani tried to gather her wits and roiling emotions against the heat that had blossomed at their intimacy. "Canyon?"

At the fence, he gripped the rail and arched his back.

"What—why—what'd I do wrong?"

He kicked the dirt. Rattled the fence with a growl.

"What's wrong?"

Head down, he rested his mouth against his upper arm. "Range," he ground out. Snapped straight. "I can't do this." He looked at the sky, hands on his belt. "I gotta go." Running a hand through his hair, he stalked toward the front of the house.

Unable to move, feeling jilted, cheated, and used, she struggled against the tears burning her eyes. Range. This was because of Range. Canyon, the man she wanted to be with, the man she was falling for, the perfect gentleman, wouldn't cut in on his brother. And how did Range ever decide she was *his* girl? Because he'd made his moves and Dani didn't oppose him?

"You all right?"

The quiet masculine voice pulled her around.

Leif Metcalfe hesitated a few feet away, hands tucked into the pockets of his jeans. The youngest brother so resembled Canyon the awareness caught her off guard. He'd come from the side of the house, which meant he had a perfect view of them as they kissed. Had he seen the exchange? Somehow, something in his expression said yes, he'd seen everything.

An engine roared to life.

Dani turned in the direction of the sound, the same direction Canyon had gone.

Pealing tires rent the night.

She shuddered against the sound but recovered. Stiffened her spine. "I think I'm ready to leave." Canyon—he'd had her keys! How would she get home now?

107

Seconds later, Stone and Willow burst onto the back porch. "What was that?" Willow asked as she rushed down the steps.

"Canyon," Leif said.

"What happened?" Stone asked his little brother as his gaze skipped to Dani, then to the front of the house.

Leif cast a look to Dani, and she willed him not to say what he'd seen—if he'd seen anything. Guilt and shame mingled, making her muscles ache. Who was she kidding? She'd allowed Range's attention for the sole purpose of being around Canyon. How could she be so callous and cruel? And now, the family she adored would find out she was an awful person. It would happen sooner or later. She never understood why they'd accepted her—they were perfect. Perfect Christians. Perfect family. And she was. . .far from it.

"You know Canyon," Leif finally mumbled.

"Yeah, I do, which is why I came out." Willow frowned at Dani.

"Same here. He's never angry."

Except with me. Ashamed and guilt ridden, Dani stared at the ground.

"Mom needs your help in the kitchen, Leif." Willow tucked a hand through Dani's arm and led her away from the house, Stone on her heels. "Want to tell me what happened?"

"Nothing."

Stopped, Willow checked the house. "Canyon left here ticked off. My brother. . .you might not know him very well, but it takes a *lot* to get him riled. He's been to hell and back, and he can roll with just about any punch."

Dani felt her chin trembling and chewed the inside of her lip to stop the involuntary reaction. "Look, I've just been here too long, okay? I'm tired and should get home—my dad had called my cell phone several times."

It wasn't a whole lie. He'd called. Twice. Because he couldn't find something. He wouldn't worry about her. Never had. Nobody had.

Except Canyon.

"Dani?"

"Look. I know everyone in your family has decided I'm Range's girlfriend. I get it. I do. And I'm very grateful to him. He's handsome, he's sweet, he saved my life—" It felt as if a spark had lit her fuse. "But I've spent time with Canyon. Took a walk with him. He taught me to surf. And last night, he knew I was—"

"Wait." Hand up, Willow's brow knitted. "How many times have you and Canyon been out?"

Wow, why did that sound so bad the way Willow said it? Dani shrugged. "Just a couple of times. Maybe three."

"*Three?*" Stone's face personified his name—a granite expression, hard, unpliable.

Panic ping-ponged through her belly. "I know how it looks, but you don't understand—"

"No," Willow said. "I think you're the one who doesn't understand—"

"Leave it, Willow," Stone ordered.

Wait. What were they hiding or protecting her from? "What?" Dani shifted between the siblings. "What aren't you telling me?"

In the darkening night, Willow seemed to pale. "Never mind." She pushed her hair back, then pointed to the car. "Canyon put your keys in the ignition." She backed away, unwilling to look at Dani. "Excuse me."

"Willow?" Dani whirled to find Stone watching her. His expression inscrutable. His eyes unreadable. "I know you think I'm horrible, but—"

"No, it's. . ." A shaky smile drew across his face. "Don't worry. Everything will be fine."

The last time someone said that, she spent months as a sex slave.

Virginia Beach, Virginia
29 April

"Man, you suck."

Gulping the pill, Canyon whipped around, planting his board in the sand. "Stone." Had his brother seen him down the painkiller? He'd hidden it all this time, buried the pain, the memories, the guilt. . .buried them with a hefty dose of medicine. As a medic, he knew it wasn't the right way to handle his issues. But seeing a psychiatrist would only get him diagnosed with PTSD. A label didn't help. He knew what he was dealing with.

Correction. Running away from.

He smoothed a hand down the back of his neck. Maybe he should talk to them, come clean. For a moment he considered his brother. Yeah, right. With all Stone was dealing with, he didn't need Canyon's trouble. Besides, it would beg questions about the pills. No way would he face questions about taking them.

He glanced to the bank of cars lining the street and swept the salt water from his face. "What're you doing here? Is everything okay? Marie?"

"Marie is. . .Marie. Nothing has changed there. I'm not sure why I ever thought I could tame her." His older brother pushed off the rock and sauntered closer, his hands in the pockets of his slacks. "I've watched you compete at this sport for years." He bobbed his head toward the tumbling waves. "But I've never seen you fall off as much as you did in the last half hour."

Half hour? Had Stone been here that long? Canyon grabbed a towel and dried his face. "Water's choppy, unpredictable." So was his heart. And mind.

"That's never bothered you before."

"Doesn't bother me now but makes the ride different."

Stone nodded to the bottle resting at the top of Canyon's pack. "Back still giving you problems?"

"Yeah." Warmth speared him. He'd never lied to his brother. But Stone had a reason for being here, and it didn't have to do with surfing or back problems.

"Board needs more wax." With that, Canyon started priming his board for another run to work off the tension.

"What happened at the house, Canyon?" Firm, stern, and direct. Stone had never been any other way. It's what made him a good lawyer and city councilman.

"Nothing." Why did he feel like he was seventeen again and coming to painful terms with his idiocy and arrogance, terms that had severed his relationship with his family for two long years? He smoothed the wax over the deck, working the knots out of his shoulders with each circuit. Anything to keep from seeing the disappointment in Stone's face.

"This has a lot of the same earmarks as—"

"Don't!" Canyon spun. Pointed at his brother. "Just. . .just leave it alone. Same as I'm doing. Okay? I've changed. That's a lesson I don't need to learn again."

Stone studied him.

Since when did his brother have the same eyes as their father? Or the same tight, disapproving lips as their mom? When his brother finally turned back toward the water, Canyon realized he'd been ready for a fight. He let his shoulders ease down. Took a calm breath. Used the towel to wipe off his hands.

Stone squinted against the setting sun. "It's been a long time since you were mad enough to snap at me."

Canyon wrung the towel.

"If you don't want to talk, I get it. But I'm worried."

"Well—"

"Don't tell me not to worry. I can see it written all over your face, *Midas*."

Canyon gritted his teeth. The high school moniker carried through during Special Forces training and right to Nightshade. But nobody— save Stone—knew how much he hated that name. Which was why Canyon kept using it. To remind himself of the mistakes, his stupidity.

Stone swiped a finger across his upper lip. "Okay, listen, I can't leave here without saying this."

Defenses up, heart perimeter armed, Canyon stood ready for the lecture.

"I know you like her."

That wasn't a lecture. And stupid lug that he was, Canyon looked at his brother.

"A lot."

Truth pushed Canyon's attention to the sand.

"From what I saw at the house Sunday, the feelings are returned."

Pulse racing, he swallowed. Man, he'd never forget kissing Roark. How everything in life faded away during that moment.

His brother huffed. "You've always had a special touch when it comes to women." Stone held up his hand. "No, even I can admit it. But I don't know if what Danielle feels is because of your charms or if it's real. Either way, it makes me wonder. . ."

"What?"

"If you were out of the picture, would she welcome Range's attention?"

The question hit center mass. Canyon thrust the towel onto his pack. "Not a problem."

"What do you mean?"

"I'm going to make it clear there's only one Metcalfe she can date."

"Is that why you've avoided her and the family for nearly two weeks?"

He shook his head against the warning in his brother's voice. "I've made up my mind. I crossed a line. It won't happen again. I swore thirteen years ago I wouldn't interfere again with Range." He fastened his attention on his brother. "I keep my promises. No Metcalfe cuts in on another."

"You're scared."

He scoffed.

Stone stretched his jaw, peeked out at the water again. "What happens when you realize your plan isn't going to work?"

"Of course it will."

"Why?"

"Because I'm not going to repeat high school."

Stone tilted his head. "You think this is high school all over again?"

Arms wide, Canyon chuckled. "What else? I mean, isn't that what everyone's thinking? There goes Canyon again. Stepping in on Range's girl."

Closing the gap, Stone frowned. "You're dealing with a grown woman who has been severely traumatized."

Was Stone really angry? "Actually," Canyon said as he moved back, still assessing his brother's reaction. "I'm not." When Stone scowled at him, Canyon raised his hands in surrender. "Like I said, I'm not going to repeat my mistake. He wants her. . . ." The words caught at the back of his throat. He couldn't finish the thought audibly.

"Canyon, you're headed for trouble."

He laughed. "Dude, chill. I just told you—I'm out of the picture. Gone. Range can have her." Acid had nothing on the way those words ate at him. "I'm not going anywhere near her." That was the truth. He'd resolved to stay away from her now. He'd gotten close, stolen that kiss—*man, what a kiss!*—and then his brain returned. Range would kill him if he knew.

"You've been out with her three times already."

He scowled. "You're out of your mind."

Stone shoved a fist between them. "One"—he raised a finger—"you went to her house." He raised another finger. "Two, you took a walk with her on the beach." A third. "Then you gave her surf lessons."

"So what?"

"What happened to your self-imposed rule of only one date?"

Canyon shrugged. "Those aren't dates. We just. . .talked." How could he explain without violating Roark's trust, without telling his brother she'd tried to kill herself? "Listen, I was helping her work through the trauma." He gave another shrug. "Seriously. That's it."

"When your feelings for her catch up with your denial, you know where to find me." Stone turned and trudged up the beach.

Denial. Canyon snorted. Whatever. He grabbed his board and started back into the water when his phone rang. He riffled through his pack and found the phone. His adrenaline cranked at the caller ID. He pressed the button. "Go for Metcalfe."

"AHOD now."

The gruff all-hands-on-deck command told him two things. One, the Old Man had gotten things lined up. Two, Nightshade would escort Roark back to Venezuela.

Which meant his vow to Stone was a lie.

Roark Residence, Virginia
29 April

"It's time."

Dani shifted in the early morning sunshine streaming onto the patio. The general, dressed in uniform, had come on official business. The business of the U.S. government determined to dump her in a jungle. She was unable to move as his ominous words slithered around her heart. Choked off the singular hope that this nightmare would meld into the dark void where she'd hidden the memories of captivity. Rape. Bruzon.

Now, she was headed straight back into his territory.

Denial webbed her feet to the floor. "Time?" Why did she act like an imbecile and ask a question she already knew the answer to?

"Yes."

It'd been weeks since the hearing. Enough time to believe this day might not come. "Now?"

"I'm afraid so. And we must hurry."

"Hurry where?" Her father emerged from the house, decked out in one of his slick Italian suits and sporting a glare that bespoke the famous tension between the two men.

Trepidation held her fast. Even though she knew what General Lambert referred to, she could not bring herself to speak it.

"It's time, Michael."

Her father stilled, his hazel eyes flicking between the two of them.

"I. . .I, uh, guess I should get my things." Dani skirted the table and started toward the house.

"Pack light."

"Danielle," her father said. "See me in my office before you leave."

"I don't think that's wise, Michael."

"*Don't* tell me how to manage my own affairs."

Pulled around by the sharp tone, Dani waited at the french doors. Her father looked ready to blow a fuse. One that led to a twelve-kiloton blast.

"I meant no disrespect." The general nodded to her. "We have little time."

"She certainly has time to say good-bye to her *father*." With that, he stalked to his office.

After a furtive glance at the general, she darted up the stairs. She stepped into a pair of black jeans and a burgundy T-shirt. Once she managed to tie her hair up, she grabbed a few unmentionables, a pair of jeans, a couple of T-shirts, and toiletries, then stuffed them into a duffel bag. She'd been on enough military operations to know to pack only the necessities. The Corps of Engineers had taught her a lot about discipline and efficiency. She could only hope those got her through this rerun of a nightmare she'd hoped to blot out of her mind.

Back downstairs, she debated whose patience to tempt. Her father's by not saying good-bye, which was weird anyway. He'd never been an emotional person. Never liked good-bye. Even insisted her mother's casket be closed for the ceremony. Or she could tempt the general's, and what would she lose? Not getting to go—yeah, right. Like Lambert would let her get away with that.

She diverted from the stairs and quickened her pace. At his office door, she raised her hand to knock.

"Leave her out of this!" her father shouted.

Another voice rumbled but the words proved indiscernible.

Dani eased open the door.

Her father's gaze snapped to hers, his hardened expression remained fixed.

The general moved into her view. "Are you ready?"

No. "I have my things."

Olin nodded.

"Danielle." Her father came closer. "Here." He lifted a gold chain with a ruby-embedded rose dangling from the pendant. "It was your mother's. She wanted you to have this."

Dani let her father slip the beautiful piece around her neck. But a weight plunked against her stomach. Why did this gesture feel so much like, "Good-bye, I'll never see you again"?

CHAPTER 11

Nightshade Shack, Virginia
1 May

Dude, I think you need a new call sign." Calling one of the newest members of Nightshade "Squirt" didn't sit right with Canyon.

John Dighton quirked an eyebrow. "Why?" He grinned. "Is it intimidating?"

"No, just makes me think you're some punk kid—worse than the Kid."

"Hey, I heard that." The Kid sauntered into the Shack and dropped his duffel.

Canyon nodded. "See what I mean?"

Grinning, the former Navy SEAL bent over the table, palms pressed against a large map.

"If you would like a new call sign," Azzan said as he joined them, "make sure Midas doesn't give you the name."

"Why?" Dighton considered Canyon warily.

"Because of him, they now call me Aladdin."

"Dude, what can I say?" Arms held out to the side, Canyon chuckled. "On a surfboard, flying over the water, you look like Aladdin."

"That is a discriminatory and derogatory statement. Being half-Palestinian, half-Jewish doesn't make me a medieval character from Arabia."

Canyon eyed him. "You're learning American political correctness fast."

Aladdin shrugged. "I must blend in, right?"

"Gather up," Max said, hands on his belt as he stood at the head of the conference area with Cowboy beside him. "We've got a lot to work out. The Old Man is en route with the girl."

Should've greased up. Maybe then she wouldn't recognize him

115

painted up. Like when they went deep into the Philippines and Max's wife hadn't recognized him. Was it too much to hope for that Roark wouldn't realize he was there?

"Squirt is going to give the rundown on the details."

Squirt faced the team. "First, I appreciate your trust. It's not taken lightly—"

"Whoa." The Kid stood straight. "Is that an accent I'm hearing?"

Scowling, Squirt speared the Kid with a fierce look. "Be careful, Kid. You start getting smart, they might mistake you for someone else."

Laughter trickled through the room but Canyon had noticed it, too. Dighton had an accent. "Down Under?"

With a huff, Squirt planted his hands on hips. "Grew up in the Top End."

"As opposed to the bottom end?"

Though sincerity bled into the Kid's question, Squirt looked ready to kill. "Northern Territory, Australia."

"How'd you end up here?" Legend asked.

The guy might as well spill his history. The team wouldn't let up until they knew.

"Long story. Gist is my mom divorced my dad right after my kid sister was born."

"You have a sister?"

Cowboy patted the Kid's shoulder. "Down boy."

Dighton glared but went on. "My mom moved us back to her homeland—Australia. When I was sixteen, she died and my sister, Rel, and I came back to the States to live with my dad. I went into the Navy after high school." He gave another huff and looked around. "Any more questions, or can we get back to this mission and why I'm helping lead?"

"Wicked," the Kid said.

Max smirked. "Go ahead."

"Since I spent time on special ops in South America and my specialty was logistics, I offered my services in the planning and implementation. I'm familiar with the countries, their people, and their language."

The Kid perked up. "You speak Spanish?"

"Más que un cabrito como usted sabrían nunca."

Running a hand over his mouth, Canyon hid his smile. *More than a kid like you would ever know.* Would the Kid realize he'd just gotten owned?

The Kid stared at Squirt for two blinks. "What'd you say?"

Expression flat, Dighton said, "You're wise beyond your years."

"Awesome." The Kid nodded. "But. . ." Then grinned. *"La próxima vez, asegúrese de que el niño no sabe español."*

Shock gaped across the Shack.

The Kid shifted. "For those who *don't* speak Spanish, I said, 'next time, make sure the Kid doesn't know Spanish.'"

Head thrown back, Dighton guffawed. The laughter reverberated off the metal beams crisscrossing the ceiling. He slapped his hand into the Kid's and pulled him into a man hug, only to end up noogying him.

"Hey, hey, hey!" The Kid extricated himself. "Give me some respect, will ya?"

"Let's focus," Max said. "We're headed into Miranda, Venezuela." He pointed to the maps on the table. "We'll hop a C-130 down south, then chopper in." Handing off the conversation to Dighton, Max nodded at his SEAL buddy.

"Okay, we'll drop in ten klicks inside the Venezuelan-Colombian border." His finger trailed over the map, from one X to another. "This is where we'll pick up vehicles. It's deemed hostile, but it's not."

"Come again?" Wiping the blade of his SOG against his pants leg, Legend looked over at the map, an apple dangling from his other hand. "Hostile but not?"

"There's a military presence, but they should be easy to avoid."

"How can we be sure?" Canyon was all for not encountering bullets and blades, but he wasn't going in blind.

"I've taken a team down there myself. I know the routes, their territory." Dighton shifted his focus back to the penciled-in plans. "Vehicles here, we drive through the night to reach this." He drew an imaginary circle around a spot that bordered what looked like water. "This is the reputed location we're to recon and report."

"What do you think?" Legend asked, eating the apple he'd sliced. "Think this information is legit?"

Palms on the table, Dighton peered up through a tense brow. "If this is right, if what I read in the hearing transcript is accurate. . ." His pale eyes darted over the map. "It's brilliant right there on the coastline. Access to land, air, water. In and out, nobody's the wiser."

"If the facility goes deep enough, there's no sat imaging," Max added.

"Don't get me wrong," Dighton said, his voice deep. "Bruzon is no idiot. If he finds out we're there, it won't be pretty."

"What's our timetable?" Cowboy eased against the couch and folded his arms.

"Ten days," Max said. "Two weeks at the most. But it's rugged, brutal terrain—and we'll probably get hit with rain."

"You worried about the girl?"

Aladdin's question, though targeted at Max, pulled at Canyon's heart. Roark was one of the toughest women he knew. But she'd tanked after returning from the mission that went horribly wrong, and then plummeted off the will to live when told she'd have to go back. What was her frame of mind now that they were gearing up to leave?

"She's former Army Corps of Engineers, ordnance. They discharged her medically after her return," Max said.

"Demolitions is one thing," the Kid said. "Black ops is another. Besides, wasn't she wigged out when they pulled her from the water? I mean, that transcript from the hearing was messed up."

Head down, Canyon glared at him.

The Kid shrugged. "Just sayin'. Why are we doing this, anyway? I mean, wasn't there enough evidence she was brutalized down there? How'd it get whacked and suddenly she's the bad guy?"

Max shifted. "The intel on that stick drive was too precise—too perfect. CIA sources checked it out; government sent black ops down there—all came up with one thing: zip. Nothing like what she reports." Knuckling his lips, he stared at the spread on the table. "And—this goes no further than your ears—Lambert thinks it might be connected to Siberia."

Legend grunted. "You mean something might come out of me freezing my assets off?"

"How's Siberia connected?" Cowboy asked.

With a shrug, Max said, "Don't know. Old Man's not saying."

Roughing a hand over his stubble, Cowboy grunted. "There's a lot that doesn't add up or make sense."

"Like the Bermuda Triangle of bad ops. Never know what will be what till it's too late. Know what I'm sayin'?" Legend mumbled.

Max nodded. "There's also question about the girl's loyalties."

Canyon's chest tightened.

"According to the Old Man, agents checked out her home computer, found all kinds of intel, including vacation photos tethering her to this guy." He leaned forward, shaking his head. "Think about it. Not that I agree with their accusations, but she's held by this perv for six months, then suddenly escapes with the USB drive—the keys to his kingdom, to a facility that holds weapons of mass destruction?"

"Tss," the Kid said. "I can gain remote access of a computer with my eyes closed. Anyone could've planted that information. And everyone has seen CougarNews reports about Russia sending missiles to Venezuela."

"True. But they've also found a bank account with enough money to float her to the moon."

"But she's not complicit," Canyon nearly growled. "She's innocent."

"Midas is right, I think. The question is, who planted that stuff there? Where'd the dough come from?" The Kid frowned, his gaze thoughtful. "Seems mighty coincidental, don't you think, that all this stuff is *suddenly discovered*? I say someone's trying to get rid of her."

"That's not going to happen." Max glared at the Kid.

The men wanted to know what they'd have to deal with, what sort of mental and physical shape Roark was in. The questions were standard. Needed to be asked. But still. . .it rankled him. The question was not whether she could do this—because somehow, he knew Roark had the courage to gut it up and get it done—but whether Nightshade would keep her safe.

But he couldn't say anything. Couldn't let them know how things had *shifted* between him and her. Even though he had shifted it back, would Max or Lambert yank him if they knew?

Nah, better to keep his mouth shut. Ensure he went on the mission. He dare not look up and show what he felt, what ate at him: One misstep, one mistake, and she could end up in the claws of a man who would not hesitate to rip her apart.

"Realize what we could be dealing with if Sokoleski is involved. He killed his brother, and he won't talk, but it's not hard to imagine what Russian physicists would be developing in an underground mountain facility."

"Nuclear weapons."

"Or something to make it possible." Max waved his hand over some gear. "We need to get images of Bruzon's facility, environmental readings. All the supplies are there; we just gotta get it logged. If they are building nuclear capabilities—well, it goes without saying that we need to stop this."

Canyon straightened. He grabbed the imaging and stabbed a finger against the name. "Miranda." He looked at Max. "That's what Sokoleski said to me as he died."

Someone cursed.

Canyon's mind raced. Roark was caught up in a nuclear plot. And more than ever he believed her. Not that he hadn't before, but this added cement to it.

"Midas?" Aladdin speared him with inquisitive eyes.

Canyon started at the attention. "Sorry?" He noticed the others watching him.

"You've spent time with her. Do you think she's up to it?"

Aladdin had no idea the gem he'd just revealed to the team. And Canyon certainly didn't want to explain anything. He kept his secrets in a vault with the combination buried.

As expected, the question caught the attention of their team leader. Max frowned. "You've spent time with her?"

Defensive talons dug into his chest and needled his shoulders. "She's up to it."

Hand on his shoulder, Max forced Canyon to face him. "Do I need to know something?"

Too many variables. Too much involved.

"Attention on deck," Legend's voice boomed as he nodded toward the main bay.

Saved by the arrival of a visitor, Canyon slipped to the rear of the room.

Through the sea of black-clad bodies, he spotted a black Chrysler 300 gliding through the doors. It rolled to a stop at the four-foot bank that boasted stairs with no handrails. The Old Man emerged.

He's my godfather. Roark's words the night she cut her arm roared through his head. What kind of godfather would send his goddaughter into the gaping maw of a communist jungle laden with rebels?

The kind of godfather with an elite team of warriors at his disposal.

Shadows scampered from one corner to another as Dani climbed the concrete steps into the warehouse. Grimy windows. Dilapidated. Broken windows high up. The building had all the earmarks of disuse. Until she passed through the first door. Night and day difference. Back there, dust and abandonment. In here, clean and remodeled. A consecutive series of walled-off areas defined the cavernous space into distinct rooms. To the left, bags and gear piled high in the middle of the room. Immediately to the right, the wall curved around and opened, revealing a brown leather couch—torn and well used—and a three-legged table with a stack of books serving as the missing fourth leg.

In the semidarkened room, shadows wavered. A lone, tinkling light dangled over a table around which several men huddled. Seven, in her quick appraisal.

Dressed head to toe in black tactical gear, the group seemed to tighten as the general guided her into their sanctum. Pockets protruded from the legs, ubiquitous bulges hinted at the weapons they carried, and thick chests bore testament to armored vests—most likely Interceptors. But the vests had nothing on the bulky bodies stretching T-shirts and filling jackets. Grit and determination had been gouged into these men through one method—experience.

Despite the temptation to relax, to believe she'd be safe with these men, Dani held her ground. She'd had no fear with the last team either.

"Gentlemen," the general said. "This is Danielle Roark, your primary objective."

Objective. It sounded so sanitized, and she knew the reason behind the term—to make it easier for the men to do their jobs and not get attached to the objective—*me.*

The general's stoic mask remained in place. "You are charged with Danielle's protection. If anything happens to her, you will answer to me." For a minute, he seemed to falter but then he looked at her. "I trust these men with my life. You can, too."

Dani bounced her attention from man to man. With their proximity to one another, she couldn't see the two at the back. All the same, the men here bespoke a powerful confidence.

"For security reasons," Lambert said, "we'll use call signs only. In the front, there's the team leader, Frogman."

Dark eyes matched the black clothes of the man who gave a curt nod. "In and out. We'll have you back before you know it."

Though she tried to smile, it fell from her lips. Nice sentiments. She'd heard them before.

"Don't let the big guys scare you," the general continued. "The one on the right is Cowboy."

He tipped a black baseball cap. "Ma'am."

"Next to him is Legend."

A nod.

"There you have Squirt and the Kid." Lambert pointed to the side where one from the back eased around the broad shoulders of Legend. "Then there's—"

"Aladdin." A smile made it into her lips this time. "How could I forget?" The playful tone haunted her words with memories of the surf lesson with Canyon.

Soulful eyes twinkled. "I am never going to live that down."

"Maybe it's the magic you work."

Aladdin laughed. "I knew I liked you."

"And of course," Lambert said, "you already know the last team member."

Blue eyes blazed, stuffing her heart into her throat as the last man stepped into view. "Canyon?" In the lighting, his sandy blond hair almost looked brown. Was it really him? Her gaze trailed over his body—the tactical gear only emphasized his muscular yet lean build. The look added an aura of intrigue and intensity to his already mysterious persona. Clearly he was a part of this team, but he'd never spoken of it. *Business trips.* He'd taken one not too long ago. Was it really a mission?

A curt nod. "Roark."

The formality and distance in his greeting shoved her heart back down, past her chest, and into her stomach as she relived the night he'd kissed her, the night he'd murmured his brother's name, then pealed into the night.

Legend took her duffel. "I'll take care of this for you."

She glanced over her shoulder as he headed to the other bay and flung it into the pile before returning. "Thank you."

"...a problem. What am I missing?"

The terse question drew her round. Frogman had Canyon pinned in a corner. Toe to toe the two were the same height, same build. But Frogman exuded a ferocity that made Canyon look like a lamb. Beside her, the general talked with a couple of the other men, and although she feigned interest in that conversation, her ears were trained on the one in the corner.

"I said it's not a problem." Canyon scowled at Frogman.

"What I'm seeing says different."

"What you see and what's real—"

Frogman leaned in. Said something hissed and angry.

Fire lit through Canyon's expression.

More heated words.

Two-handed, Canyon shoved him back. "Step off!"

With speed that frightened her, Frogman grabbed Canyon's shirt and hauled him up against the wall, his forearm pressing into Canyon's throat.

Silence dropped like an anchor on the room.

Dani started forward, but an arm flashed into view and held her back. She frowned at the general. Disconcerted, she could do nothing but watch. Conversations died. Movement ceased as all eyes pinned on the confrontation.

"At the first sign. . ." Frogman's voice carried low and menacing, his face pushed up against Canyon's. What he said next got lost in her whooshing pulse and his guttural words.

Face red and bulging against the air deprivation, Canyon struggled. Planted a hand against Frogman's elbow, trying to dislodge the pressure.

"Got it?" Frogman asked through clenched teeth.

A strained "yes" carried through the deadly quiet.

With a grunt, Frogman released Canyon and stood there, shoulders rising and falling under labored breaths. "*Don't* make me do that again." He turned.

Dani recoiled at the ticked-off expression. His dark eyes tracked over those watching, then he headed through an open doorway. The sound of his boots thudding as he stormed down the hall was soon severed by a slamming door.

Whatever just happened, it'd brought an icy blanket of dread. She dared not move. The others, gazes locked on the floor, said nothing. But she couldn't tear her eyes from the man slumped, holding his knees. Canyon. He looked broken, furious. . .and something else she couldn't figure out.

He stretched and rubbed his reddened neck. When he pushed himself upright, his gaze lingered on the floor. For several seconds he stood there without moving or talking. Then he strode toward them, a scowl gouged into his handsome face.

The men stepped aside, the sea of bodies parting to allow him exit. He stalked down the open corridor toward a steel door with a lone lightbulb flickering overhead.

Pangs shot through Dani. Why did Frogman do that—and Canyon yield? Was the mission already in jeopardy? "Where's he going? What does that mean?"

"Showers." Legend sauntered out of the room.

"It means we're a team and hold each other accountable." Cowboy soon followed.

Accountable? Accountable for what? Did this mean Frogman didn't like her? She glanced to the general.

He cupped her elbow and gave a light squeeze. "They've worked together for more than two years, dozens of missions." The smile he offered didn't fool anyone. "It'll be okay."

She should leave. Right now. Being locked up in a federal pen was better than being captured or killed in Venezuela, and if this team was divided, she wasn't going anywhere with them.

Then again, there was the death penalty. . .

"They are *the* best, Danielle." He touched her arm and a sorrowful smile clouded his normally vibrant eyes.

"How do you know?" she whispered. "After what I just saw—"

"I can't tell you more. Just know that these men will put their lives on the line to carry out this mission." Were there tears in his eyes? "I wouldn't entrust you to anyone else."

The vehemence in his words pushed her back. His comment seemed out of place. . .odd. But then she remembered the promise he'd made to her mother.

A presence loomed over her. Dani glanced to the side and jumped, yelped.

Legend hovered, his milk-chocolate skin practically glowing under the amber light.

Beside him stood Cowboy who pushed his ball cap off his forehead and winked at her. "Don't let them worry you none. Frogman might be hotheaded sometimes, but he knows what he's doing."

"That include roughing up his own men?"

Cowboy grinned, a dimple peeking at her. "Reckon Midas needed it."

"We all do at one point or another." The deep bass voice echoed Legend's large size. "Tell you what," he said as he tugged out a metal chair. "Why don't you sit here and show us on the map what you know."

Tucking a strand behind her ear, Dani nodded, grateful for the shift in focus. "Okay." Seated, she let her gaze skip across the gridded map. "The entry point is here."

"There's no door," Cowboy said.

"I know. But it's there."

Legend spread satellite photos in front of her, along with some images that looked as if they'd been taken by hand. "Show me the door."

And yet, she couldn't. Brick. Uniform. No breaks or cracks. But no door. "I don't understand." Her stomach knotted. "It's there. I know it is." It had to be. "Once I was on the ground level, they blindfolded me and led me through the—" Her gaze hit an empty lot beside the building. She pointed to it. "There—I thought. . .a parking garage. I remember the hollow sounds of the cement walls and ceilings. Cars. . ." She cradled her head. "This doesn't make any sense." Was she losing her mind?

Aladdin scooped up all the images and the map. He tossed aside the pictures but swirled the map to face him. "Close your eyes."

Dani looked around, confused. Concerned.

"Go on. I have an idea." His smooth words calmed her.

With a sigh, she obeyed.

"Tell me what you remember. Try to remember number of steps, stairs, floors, sounds, feelings, smells—anything."

Dani took a breath and blew it out as she honed her focus. "Okay, once on the ground floor, we exited the elevator and went left. Through one set of doors—secured with a side-panel control. I remember the sound of the plastic swiping and the beep before a lock disengaged." What next? She bit her lower lip. "One more secured door, and then we walked down a ramp, it's really damp smelling. I guess it was—"

"No, no guessing. Just keep going."

She nodded. "Down the ramp, then a door—without a secure code box. It smells normal in here. Nothing special, but a bit windy. But then the ground is different, cement, I guess. This is the garage. We walk about twenty yards, then climb a set of stairs. Up, probably a dozen steps, then the landing to the right and up a dozen more steps. Then...two feet or so to a door. No code box. And we walk thirty paces or so and get in a car." Dani opened her eyes, expecting to find the men looking at her. Instead, their gazes were fixed on the paper that Aladdin was drawing on.

Aladdin stood, flipped the pages over, ripe with the stench of a permanent marker, and laid them out.

"Son of a batch of cookies," the Kid muttered.

"The entrance isn't at the building," Aladdin said. "It's right here, two buildings down. There's a parking garage." His green eyes met Dani's. "They took you underground."

Sitting on the bench in the locker room, Canyon stared at the wadded-up socks in his hands. Humiliation clung to him like body odor. Max had seen straight through the tough facade he'd tried to conjure up when Lambert singled him out.

He rubbed his thumb over the ribs of the socks, feeling the pattern that mirrored the dissonance in his own life. He could feel it, feel his entire life slipping right through his fingers. He couldn't let this happen. It'd happened before. All this. A mission. A girl. His feelings. Death.

Punching to his feet, he sought to avoid the squall of memories. Fingers threaded behind his head, he paced the length of the shower well. Had to get it together. Get it together or the past would repeat itself. *Mind in the game.*

He stalked toward the lockers.

She's just a girl.

Back to the showers.

Doesn't mean anything.

He jerked around, rammed his fist into a locker. Grabbed the side of the locker and held it, willing his fingers to dig through the metal.

"Let's go."

Canyon spun, surprised to find brooding Max standing by the side door. If Canyon had expected an explanation, he wouldn't get one. Max stormed back out without another word.

Pulling his wits from the frayed ends of his nerves, Canyon grabbed his pack and followed. Down the hall, lights tinkling overhead. Dressed in the same black duds, Max blended into the shadows at the far end of the dimly lit corridor. Hand on a knob to an office, Max waited.

Canyon slowed. "What?"

With a nod to the room, Max opened the door.

Inside, Canyon looked around.

Bam!

He jerked at the slamming door just as his gaze connected with Roark's. *Crap.* This wasn't supposed to happen. Violated his self-imposed restrictions.

She started toward him but stopped.

Had to get out of here. Now. Before it was too late. He shifted back to the door, but a shadow from the other side danced across the frosted pane. Max. Self-appointed guardian of the team. Dropping the bag on the cement floor, Canyon sighed.

She'd turned to the window, her profile strong against the dull gray walls. "Why didn't you tell me about this?"

"Can't tell you about the team. But me being here doesn't matter."

Her gaze snapped to his. "Do you believe that? Does being here mean so little to you?" The hurt in her question lodged itself against his conscience. She shoved her arm out and yanked up her sleeve. "Does *this* help you remember how I feel about this mission?" Two steps closer. "Do you not remember how this terrifies me, especially knowing it's not just my life on the line but my father's career?" Another step and she flung her arms out to the side. "And you're going to tell me your being here doesn't matter? The only man who knows *everything*—"

"On this mission, I am a member of the team, nothing more."

She blinked those large caramel-colored eyes, awash with unshed tears. Roark drew back and straightened. Did she shake her head? He couldn't quite tell. Moving back, this time she definitely shook her head. "Then forget it." Facing the window again, she wrapped her arms around herself. "I'll take my chances in prison. Or with the lethal injection."

He might've distanced himself, might've walled off his heart and feelings for her, but he wouldn't let her give up like this. "Roark, listen. . ." He checked the door. The shadow shifted. Canyon returned his focus to her. Stepped closer. "I. . .you can trust these guys."

Her chest and shoulders contracted. "No. Sorry. Did that a year ago and it didn't turn out so well."

Within reach, he paused, remembering the first time he'd seen her at the courthouse—wraith-thin, gaunt. . . His gaze traveled over the length of her body. Curves had rounded out. Shape accentuated with a pair of black jeans and a dark red top. She'd filled out. Flourished. Mentally, he hauled his thoughts back into line.

"Then trust me." *What're you doing, Midas?*

Wary, glossy eyes came to his.

"I won't let anything happen to you." Man, he needed an O_2 line. Couldn't breathe. This was stupidity defined—to the nth degree.

She turned. A tear streaked down her pink cheek. Slid over her full lips. Jarring, the memory of kissing her barreled into him. He'd never forget it. The one glimpse of paradise, the one second that pulled back the dark night that had shielded his life from happiness.

Roark swung her head back and forth in denial, painful denial. "You can't promise that. Nobody can."

"I can." Somehow, he'd moved forward another step. Someone had taken control of his body because it sure wasn't listening to him, to his willful determination to put distance between them. See? There went his hands, holding her shoulders. "And I do." His voice thickened.

"Who's doing this to me? Why would anyone want *me* locked away or killed? It's got to be Bruzon." Her gaze darted over his chest, as if connecting dots. "He was so obsessed with me, maybe he wants revenge." She sucked in a breath—hard. "I'm terrified, Canyon." Her forehead dropped against his shoulder. "I trust you, but I know how things can get screwed up. If I get caught again, I'll kill myself rather than be taken."

"Don't." Canyon gripped her shoulders and pulled her straight. "Don't say that again." He crouched to look into her eyes. "I mean it.

Not ever. You hear me?"

She nodded.

"If you only know one thing, know this—whatever happens down there, I'm *not* coming back without you."

DAY TWO

Near Mindanao, Philippines
09:15:32

W*ar had become as breath to our people. Thanks to Bayani and his outsiders we were fighting, no longer fearful the way we once were. Still, the choking smoke and the crackling fire pushed tears down my face. Chesa trembled in my arms as I held her and her sister close.*

Through slits in the hut, I saw the men fight. Higanti warriors killed ruthlessly. Our warriors fought with honor, died with honor.

As we sat alone in the darkness, I wondered at Bayani. We were not his people. We were not bound by blood or oath to defend him. Yet he and his outsiders fought for us, taught us how to live. He had taken my Chesa and honored her, protected her. He had spoken in recent days of more of his outsiders coming, to help and to learn. It scared me—would the Higanti, if they did not kill Bayani tonight, return to kill him later? Would his outsiders draw the breath of evil upon our people?

Only as I pondered these things, did I realize that Chesa had left my side. Now she hung near the door.

"Chesa! Come away from there."

"I don't see him, Mama. Where is Bayani?"

"It matters not." What if he had been killed? "Come—"

She screamed.

A warrior towered over her, his blue-streaked face a mask of terror.

Chesa screamed and thrashed against him.

My heart climbed into my throat. I could not move as he dragged her from our home. It was our way—to cower and hide. Not to fight. Not to invite death to our door. But as he hauled her out into the gathering middle, I saw the fight had stilled.

"Let her go!" Bayani shouted at the warrior.

"She is my daughter," Awa shouted. "If you harm her, it will mean war."

129

*The warrior turned, Chesa wrapped against his chest as he came around.
"Who leads these Christians?"*

*With a shout, Bayani came forward. He dropped his gun and lifted his
hands. "I do. Let the girl go." Why did he not tell the warrior Chesa belonged
to him? In our village that would warrant death, touching or harming
another's woman.*

"Get back, Corazine!"

*The command startled me. When had I left the hut? As I turned to go
back, I saw Bayani approach the warrior and drop to his knees.*

I gasped and clamped a hand over my mouth.

"Release her," Bayani said. "It's me you want."

When the warrior shoved Chesa away, he gloated. Like he'd won.

But this bloodthirsty man did not know Bayani.

*As quick as lightning, Bayani whipped a knife from under his shirt and
plunged it into the warrior's belly.*

CHAPTER 12

Somewhere in Miranda, Venezuela
2 May

Arms crossed over her chest, Danielle dropped the half dozen feet from the skid of the helicopter. Tall grass swayed, as if waving and inviting her into its silky arms. Warm, sticky air enveloped her as she plummeted to the earth. She landed, feet together, knees slightly bent, and rolled to the side then onto her back. Her pack arched her back off the ground. She moved to squat with one knee, squinting through the darkness to the black shapes drifting across her field of vision.

A tree there. Another to her left. Where had the guys gone? The black night shrouded everything in its oppressive cloak.

Something clapped against her shoulder. Dani jerked away and turned. Dark eyes pierced her with a glare. His finger pressed against his lips as Legend bent toward her. At least, she thought it was Legend. The paint scrawled over his face camouflaged his features well. However, it would take a lot more than camo or a ghillie suit to hide the man's gargantuan size. Even kneeling, he towered over her.

The thunderous roar of the helo dissipated with the whipping wind. Slowly her ears cleared and a whistle sailed through the air. Had they been seen already? Her heart skipped a beat as she probed the darkness for guerillas or the VFA.

Where had Canyon landed? She looked over the field, knowing full well she'd probably never spot him. Or any of the guys. They'd been trained for this stuff. Fed off it. Now where was he?

A long, sonorous response sounded from Legend. A countersign. He patted her shoulder—a weight that nearly shoved her face-first into the dirt. Scrambling to stay upright, she saw his shadowy form hustle away. . .fading. . .fading. . .gone.

Panic pushed her in the direction he'd gone. *Don't leave me.* Grass and vines clung to her legs, as if the jungle had come alive and worked to take her captive again. She plunged through the waist-high blades. It all felt familiar. Eerily, hauntingly familiar. She'd been here before. In this very jungle.

Perfect peace. . .the mind. . .the man. . .mind. . . Ugh! How did that verse go? She'd heard it in church when she'd gone with a friend a couple of years ago. She hadn't darkened the door of a church since her mother's death. Though she groped for a tendril of hope, it evaded her.

Blind in the moonless night, she pushed ahead. A vine slapped her cheek. The sting was nothing compared to the wild rhythm thundering in her chest.

When she found Canyon, she would give him a piece of her mind. How could he abandon her so quickly after making the promise that turned him into her knight in shining armor? Everything about him spoke to her. His quiet strength. The unflappable belief in her mettle. The commitment to see this thing through with her to the end. It was probably naive to even go there, but was she in love with him? It couldn't happen that fast, could it?

Ahead, she spotted Legend. They rushed into a small huddle of trees. Nearly colliding into the wall of muscle, she spun around him and stopped. Adrenaline stabbed her. What made him stop? What happened?

Directly in front of her, three shapes solidified out of the hazy night. Two directly in front, another to the right—no, wait. Three more. In a semicircle knelt the Nightshade team. All the men save Canyon. What happened to him? Had he. . .?

A breeze swirled from the side.

She glanced right and found Canyon easing up beside her. Where had he come from? Was he behind her the whole time? He knelt, eyes on his team leader.

"As discussed, we head northeast eight klicks," Frogman said in a controlled whisper. "Tight and fast. At the village, we retrieve vehicles. Take them to the pass. Ten hours into the heart of the beast."

The pass. Her stomach squirmed. The pass had a bridge. A bridge she'd been sent to blow twelve months ago. Where the guerillas had captured her team. A complete mission failure that scarred her physically and emotionally.

One by one, the men lumbered to their feet and hiked off. The trees swallowed them. Dani shook off the foreboding sense. *Get it together.* She'd been trained in basic, but despite that training, all she could think about was captivity. Had to shake that off. If she didn't, she'd get herself killed.

The climb increased, with fronds and foliage, slippery from a recent rain, swatting at them. Frogman and another man walked a parallel course but fifteen, maybe twenty, feet apart. She let her gaze drop to her right and left. Flanked. She glanced back and left. Legend moved with stealth that belied his size.

"You okay?" Canyon's voice skittered along her spine.

Over her left shoulder, she discovered he'd taken up a closer position. She gave a curt nod. Though she'd love to give him a piece of her mind, chatting would endanger them. Besides, what did he care if she was okay? He was so bullheadedly determined to step out of the way for his brother. Clearly the kiss they'd shared hadn't meant what she thought it did. At the very least, it meant more to her. Did he know that she'd never kissed anyone? Of course not. And who would believe her in this day and age? She didn't want to end up like her mother, trapped in a loveless marriage.

Still, it was the truth. She'd never found anyone she wanted to kiss. Until Canyon.

Hands on the straps of her pack, she hiked it into a more comfortable position and continued behind Aladdin. She stretched her neck and something snagged her attention. She stopped. Stared into the trees. What caught her eye? Straining to see through the dark void, she mentally convinced herself it was just shadows. Trees seemed to dance. But then...

Shadows took substance.

"What is it?" Canyon asked.

"I thought I saw something."

"It's Cowboy. Keep moving."

Why would Cowboy be way out there? Her foot hit a slick stone, and she skidded over the small surface. The mishap pitched her forward. Her hand glanced off the moss-covered spot.

Crack!

A weight plowed into her back. She sprawled to the ground. *What...?* Dirt burst into her face.

"Stay down," Canyon growled, pinning her to the warm earth. "Down, down, down!"

Squinting around at the team, Dani spit the dirt out. The others had dropped as well. The sound of gunfire spiked her adrenaline.

Thwat-thwat-thwat!

Whoa. They're close.

"Cowboy, taking fire!" a voice hissed through the com piece in her ear. "Midas, how's the objective?"

She angled around to see Canyon partly on his side, weapon drawn and aimed behind them.

Light twinkled in the night: muzzle flash. Even a hundred meters off, it was weird and discordant with the danger it signaled.

"Alive," Canyon said through gritted teeth as he pushed with his legs and rammed his back into her. He kept pushing backward, and finally Dani rolled onto all fours.

"Keep it that way," Frogman hissed.

Crack! Crack!

Rocks pelted her face.

Way too close. They had to get to cover or they'd be dead.

"Up! Move!" Canyon snapped.

Her pack jerked up. The straps strained and yanked her backward...up the hill. Dani scrambled to her feet and launched herself in the direction Canyon led.

"Cowboy, kill me some rebels, man." The voice—had to be Frogman's—sailed through the coms.

A sudden thrust sent her spiraling toward a cluster of trees. Fingers raking rough bark, Dani swallowed the yelp crawling up her throat. Canyon pressed her back against a tree and covered her with his own body. He peeked out.

A whiff of cordite stung her nostrils.

Canyon's hand came back and grabbed her again. Whipped her to the side. Her legs tangled in the roots of the tree. She stumbled. Tripped over an exposed root, but an invisible force kept her upright.

Canyon spun, pulled her into his arms. They went down, rolled. When she felt gravity clawing at her, she dug her fingers around the drag straps of Canyon's vest.

They tumbled. Down. . .down. She flipped. Her fingers ripped from the nylon. She rolled more. She tucked in her arms, anything to avoid snapping an arm or hand. Momentum slowed until finally she thudded against something solid.

Silence dropped like a vacuous concussion after a detonation. Dani blinked. Tried to gain her bearings. Movement to her left froze her.

"Don't move," Canyon whispered, his mouth suddenly against her ear as he once again pinned her.

Gee, ya think? Only then did she notice he'd drawn his weapon again and aimed it back up the hill. Waiting. Watching.

"Cowboy. . ." came the stiff warning from Frogman. "I don't like swiss cheese. Got it?"

"Target one acquired." Calm, smooth words. "Target down."

Dani let out a small breath.

"Target two acquired...and down." Quiet bathed the night. "Midas, you have a tango coming up on your—"

Rat-a-tat-tat-tat.

In a split second, Dani registered four things: the brilliant flash of the muzzle, the way her hearing felt ripped out, the man looming ten feet away, and the report of yet another assailant.

Their attacker dropped forward, his body somersaulting down the incline. Straight toward them.

Dani rolled away—away from the guerilla and away from Canyon. Her gaze locked on the face of their attacker. Like so many faces she'd seen while Bruzon kept her locked in his facility.

She whipped her weapon around and fired.

"Tango down," Canyon said with a grin.

"Frogman, two meters from your seven."

An almost inaudible *thwat* drifted on the warm, thick wind that rustled the leaves overhead.

"Clear," again the calm voice came.

"Regroup." Terse and stiff. Frogman.

Pack pressing into and arching her back, Dani stared up at the silent dance of the canopy. It afforded brief glimpses of the heavy clouds cluttering the sky. Looked like... "Rain." Oh no. Why hadn't she thought of it before?

Canyon stood over her. "What's wrong?"

"Rainy season."

"Midas, what's your twenty?"

Canyon grabbed Roark's hand, tugging her upright with him. "Bottom of the ravine, twenty yards down and east." He guided her back up the steep hill, using trees, twigs, and roots to pull themselves along. "En route."

"Roger."

At the crest of the hill, he crouched and surveyed the area. The team stood, weapons at the ready, shifting, probing, expectant.

He whistled.

Two shifted toward him, the bore of their weapons vanishing against the black uniforms. An answering whistle gave him the clear to move into the open.

"Anyone hurt?" Cowboy asked.

"Negative," Canyon said as he and Roark rejoined the team.

"Let's move out. Time's short."

As if in response to Frogman's announcement, the sky dumped its bounty. Rain pelted them, chilling and drenching.

A growl emanated from the side. "You *got* to be kidding me," Legend said, irritation skidding across his dark face.

"Dude, you knew it was coming," the Kid said.

Legend scowled. "It could've waited till we left."

"Move, people!"

Back on track, the team trudged through the downpour. Roark had been right—the rainy season had come. Canyon had felt it in his bones since they'd dropped onto the side of the mountain. It'd be too much to ask, of course, that they have clear skies and unfettered success. Easy didn't cut it when dealing with special operations and elite soldiers like Nightshade.

All the same, the rain would aid them—less likely to encounter patrols and less likely to be heard. Besides, on a time-sensitive mission like this one, they couldn't take cover and wait it out. Every second mattered. He couldn't help but think how this terrain reminded him of. . .

Canyon squeezed off the thoughts. Shoved them down into the foxhole where he'd buried them and stole a look at Roark. Tough. Determined, yet vulnerable. She had training and skills, but part of her was still broken. Head down, she trudged onward, shielding herself from the downpour.

He had to hand it to her. She'd gutted it up. Set aside her fears. Okay, maybe setting them aside was going too far, but she buried the hatchet and boarded that C-130. Now, eight hours later, she'd hiked halfway up the mountain she'd vowed never to set foot on again.

It's why he'd tripped up and kissed her. That dogged determination. Resilient. Focused. A bit of pride seeped through the sodden clothes to his heart. *Knew she had it in her.*

Man. He'd spent the last several klicks thinking about the very woman Range had set his sights on.

Canyon huffed. Why? Why'd it have to be Roark that his brother had fallen for? Why'd it have to be Roark that *he* had fallen for?

Legs sloshed through the mud.

Roark was slowing down.

Her foot dropped into a hole, and she wrenched to the side.

Canyon caught her arm. Drew her up out of the sludge. She gripped his forearm and got her footing. "Doing good."

Seemingly unconvinced, she nodded as rain dropped into her eyes and set off again.

Range doesn't deserve her.

Stifling the thought, he pulled up the rear. If Frogman didn't call a short break soon, he'd have to insist on one or Roark would collapse. She might be tough, but she was also still recovering. She'd been emaciated when Range had pulled her from the water. Though she'd filled out, she probably still wasn't the woman who'd entered this jungle nearly twelve months earlier.

Another dozen feet and the team slowed to a stop. So had the rain. Wait. No. Canyon glanced up, surprised to find an overhang protecting them from the drops that battered the rest of the jungle.

"Take ten," Frogman said.

Tucking themselves farther into the cleft, the team took cover from the rain.

"That is some nasty stuff." The Kid plopped down and shook his head hard. Water whipped in every direction.

"Dude, we don't need your backwash." Canyon angled toward Roark and propped himself against the back wall of the pseudocave. He nodded toward her pack. "Grab a bar and take a sip."

Roark obeyed, nibbling on the end of a protein bar. Weariness dug at her grease-painted face. No. . .not weariness. Cracking open a green glow stick, Canyon slumped next to her. Took the bar from her hands. Chomped into it.

Her eyes widened. "Hey!" she said in a tight, controlled whisper and snatched it back.

Grinning, Canyon chewed. He leaned closer and whispered as she bit into the protein bar, "Didn't your mother teach you to share?"

After another bite, she darted him a glance, and it was as if the sun had broken through the storm clouds—she smiled.

Yeah. That's what he wanted. A smile. To know she still had it in her. To know that defeat hadn't latched its wicked talons into her soul. He eased his shoulder against hers in a nudge.

Caramel eyes came to his. Dark brown hair plastered her cheeks. A rogue strand clung to the curve of her neck. Even looking like a drenched cat, she was gorgeous. *Back on task, Midas.* "How you holding up?"

She licked her lips and swallowed. "I'm here."

"About three more klicks to the vehicles. Should help, make things quicker."

"And drier."

He nodded. Head against the rocky face, he closed his eyes. Focused on the mission. Not on the beauty sitting next to him. But even with his visual cues cut off, he could feel her. Hear every breath. The rustle of her wet clothes as she shifted. The light pressure of her shoulder against his.

She had no clue how much that knotted up his mind. Smoothing a hand over his head gave him reason to remove his arm from touching hers. He rested his elbow on his knee and kept his eyes closed. He'd promised himself he'd get this mission done, get her home safely. . .to Range.

Canyon balled his fist.

Weight bumped his right oblique muscle—actually, his Interceptor vest that protected that muscle. He glanced over his bicep at Roark. His gut cinched. She rested her cheek on her arm that wrapped around her knees—all placing her within two inches away of his nose.

Eyes fastened to his, she watched him. Intently. "Are *you* okay?"

"Yeah."

"Liar."

"You first."

A breathless laugh. So, he'd been right—she wasn't okay. Then again, who would be in this dripping jungle, slogging toward peril?

The ominous green hue of the stick played tricks with his mind. Her eyes weren't just brown—or caramel. The caramel color had flecks of a darker brown. Intriguing. High cheekbones. Coral-colored lips. *Soft* lips. That curved into a smile.

Dude, you're staring! Canyon blinked. Adjusted the straps on the pack that didn't need adjusting. Retied his boots.

The order came to move out, and with it came the rain. As if it'd waited for the team to return to its mercy. He'd never seen the intensity of a storm like this. Not with this much rain. Not this constant. Within a mile of the village, an itch started in his boots and shoulders. Blisters. That'd make the journey interesting.

"All stop."

Canyon came up on Squirt, Legend, and Frogman huddled near a stump. The others gathered round, including Roark, who hovered to his right.

Squirt peered through a pair of binoculars aimed toward the congested village. "They're there."

"As planned." Frogman traced a finger along a map pressed over his knee. "Head northwest—stick to the trees. We'll rendezvous here."

On the other side of the village.

Frogman and Squirt jogged south a dozen feet, then burst across the open field toward the village, zigzagging from one point of cover to another. Finally they vanished into the crowd of shacks.

"Let's move," Cowboy said.

Silently the remaining six slunk around the perimeter of the open field that separated trees from the tangle of cement buildings, laundry strung from roof to roof, and kept the team from exposure.

Attuned to Roark's movements, Canyon worked his way to the rendezvous point with precision, ears trained on the swish of the tree limbs, the creak of the Kid's boots. Twenty minutes found them laid out flat on the ground, hidden from view by the natural slope of the land. Darkness draped over them like a wet blanket.

The throaty—and noisy—rumble of a diesel cracked the stormy night. Canyon peered down the scope of his M4. Two metal hulks lumbered out of the small town. A flicker of light from the interior of the first vehicle—an old Jeep Forerunner. The other, a beat-up Hummer.

"That's them," Cowboy said. And with that, they crawled toward the road.

Though the vehicles slowed they did not stop. Canyon grabbed Roark's hand and sidled up next to the Hummer. He ripped open the rear passenger door and swung her toward it. She clambered into the darkness. Canyon dove in after her.

Dry. Warm. Stale. He wrinkled his nose.

"Aw man," the Kid said from the right front passenger seat. "This thing stinks."

"It's dry and it runs." Squirt glanced in the rearview mirror, the light of the instrument panel glowing against his greased-up face. "Might want to buckle up."

Canyon glanced over his shoulder. Lights fractured the night, jouncing in hot pursuit.

CHAPTER 13

Somewhere in Miranda, Venezuela

*P*ing! *Tsing!*

"Down!" Canyon grabbed her head and shoved it forward.

Wind ripped at her—and only then did she realize the window had rolled down. She peeked up and her breath backed up into her throat. Canyon leaned out the window, his M4 aimed at the vehicle behind them. Between the wind and the rain and the speed of the Hummer, she was amazed he could maintain his grip on the weapon.

Shots riddled the night.

The Hummer trounced and pitched. Dani slipped to the floor and braced herself. The din of the elements almost devoured the report of his weapon.

Ping! Ping! Thud-crack!

Glass dribbled down on her with fat drops of rain. Canyon slid back into the Hummer, groping in the dark for something.

"What do you need?" she shouted.

He straightened, something in his hand. *Clink!* He stretched an arm out the window and flung the object. "Frag out!" With that, he dove down—at her.

Brilliance ripped the night in two.

"Hang on!" Squirt shouted.

The Hummer's back end lifted.

"Whoa-whoa-whoa," the Kid yelled.

Gravity yanked them back down. Canyon's head rammed into her cheekbone. The vehicle fishtailed. Straightened. It pitched and bounced. Seconds stretched into long minutes as they huddled on the floorboard, sans flying bullets and panic.

"Nice work," Squirt said. "It's clear."

Canyon eased up, pulling his weapon to the ready as he peered out the back window. He finally slumped onto the console seat, still watching their tail. Dani dragged herself onto the slick seat, brushing glass out from under her. A piece sliced her hand. She hissed.

Canyon frowned but then shoved his attention back to the road. Scowling. The knotted brows, the thinned lips—even with green and black paint covering his face, she could tell he was ticked.

"Squirt," Frogman said through the coms. "Everyone in one piece?"

"Roger that. Thanks to some handy grenade throwing by Midas."

"Hooyah," Frogman said. "Let's make tracks."

They seemed to have accepted their success, moved on from the pursuit. Everyone but Canyon.

Dani reached across the seat and touched his hand.

He flinched but didn't look.

"What's wrong?"

His gaze dropped down and to the left, but not at her. "Nothing. Get some shut-eye."

He was hiding something from her. She'd just have to trust that if Canyon thought she needed to know something, he'd tell her. Though she wanted to do anything but sleep, the lure of the suggestion pulled at her mind. She hadn't gotten much last night, on her soft, thick mattress, worrying over this mission.

You're strong, Roark." How many times had she repeated his words over the last two weeks since he'd admonished her in the bathroom of his mother's home? Nobody had believed in her the way he did. Well, maybe her mother. But she was gone. Her father didn't have the first clue about her or her feelings. He was more in tune with his constituents and polls for his veep bid.

Why was love always messed up? Her mother and father had more of an arrangement than a marriage. Alexandra married prestige and money.

And yet, Dani clung to the hope that she could have a *real* marriage. Where she loved him and he loved her, they had common goals and dreams, willing to work through the good and the bad to come out stronger in the end. And the man who so perfectly fit the template of the type of man she wanted to marry sat right next to her.

Only. . .he wanted to trade her to his brother.

35,000 Feet Above North America

"I did not expect you to call so soon, *mi amigo*." Humberto took a long drag on his cigar and allowed the thick odor and heady revelation to encircle his mind. "What of my package?"

Amazing the way so many had yielded to him since his dramatic takeover. He had one goal left now: dictatorship. With the arsenal sitting under his skyscraper, total power was guaranteed. In time.

"On its way."

"So soon?" Another puff as he stared out the small framed window of the Lear. "I am not in the country."

"That's not my problem."

Humberto chuckled. "Actually, it is. We had a deal."

Silence gaped.

"You want your little problem taken care of, then mine must be taken care of *también*." He smiled. He had this man wrapped so tightly around his fingers he couldn't breathe without permission. "Remember, my friend, what will happen if you do not cooperate."

"And remember," the tone seethed with hatred, "what will happen if you don't stop her."

"You dare to threaten me? Without me, you are dead. Your career is dead. What of that pretty wife of yours?"

A quick intake of breath.

Humberto let his pulse even out. "I see we still understand each other." He'd have to send the colonel to find her. Kill the others. "I will contact you."

Miranda, Venezuela

"It's screwed up." When the others gawked at him, Canyon balled his fists. "Think about it. We got nailed as soon as we hit the ground. They were there waiting for us. Knew exactly where we'd insert. That's not coincidence. No way."

Legend shifted.

"Then first village contact. You're in and out without a glitch. Soon as we're all piled in, we've got demons breathing down our necks, trying to pick us off." Sludge pumped through his veins. "This isn't right.

Someone knows we're here."

"Nobody knows but the Old Man," Max said.

"It's no coincidence, and if we don't sit up and get smart, someone's going to get killed."

"Hold up," Max said. Even in the deluge, the guy's eyes radiated a fierceness that Canyon had come to appreciate. "We've had a boatload of bad luck, but let's hold off on tucking tail and running."

"I won't put her life in danger if I think it's there." Canyon pointed at the Hummer parked across the road, cradling a soundly sleeping Roark.

Max's right eyebrow winged up.

Canyon swallowed. Scrambled for something to say that wouldn't sound so pathetically sappy or stupid. "We're charged with protecting her." Yeah. That worked. "The Old Man said if anything happened to her, we'd answer to him."

"Yeah." The Kid frowned. "What's with that anyway? Why does the Old Man care so much about this chick?"

"She's his goddaughter."

"Want to explain how you know that?" If Max ever looked like he was about to push Canyon's nose through his skull, it was right now.

"Look, it doesn't matter." Cowboy tugged the bill of his ball cap down. "We're less than two klicks from the facility. I say let's check it out. If we get there, find something amiss. . .reckon we can figure something out then."

The others seemed to consider the option.

Max leveled his gaze at Canyon. "We already talked. I'm holding you to your word." To the others, he said, "We stick to the plan and let this play out."

Molars grinding, Canyon blinked through the rain. "This is wrong." He could feel it in his gut, slipping and skidding like the rain down his collar and back. "It's all wrong. We can't—"

"Grab the gear."

Fury lit through him.

Max leaned in, chin down. "Wake her. Move out in ten."

Canyon stood there, fists balled. Wanting—thirsting to pound some sense into someone. But it wouldn't do any good. Six to one. *Walk away.* If he didn't, he'd regret it. Without a word, Canyon slogged through the muck to the Hummer where Roark sat in the back. Not asleep but watching them.

"What's going on?" she asked, her words thickened by a still-groggy weariness. "Where. . .where are we?"

"Less than two klicks out."

As she straightened in the seat, her lips parted and her eyes widened.

Fear. If there were more light and her face weren't streaked with camo paint, he wagered he'd find her skin pale. "We're gearing up to head out." Perched on the edge of the seat, he dangled his leg out, resting his boot on the running board. "It's going to be okay."

She looked at him. "You wouldn't say that unless you were worried."

He looked at the team. Max was determined, believed things were in order. He'd have to trust the leader. Trust the team.

What about the knot in your gut? Relying on that feeling had gotten him in trouble before. Chesa. . . He squeezed off the line of memories.

"They want to go in. . .with the rain. . .the mud?" She leaned forward, peering into the storm-blackened sky. "It's not going to let up. Isn't it too risky?"

"We knew it was risky when we left Virginia. The rain just adds adventure." He quirked a grin at her, hoping it worked.

Pensive eyes held his for several long seconds. Then her head swung slowly from side to side. "No," she said quietly. "You don't believe that."

"What I believe is that I said I wasn't going back without you." He locked gazes with her. "I mean it." Telling her that he thought they were being set up wouldn't help. It was hard enough to focus on the mission with a sense of doom clogging every pore; he didn't want her to bear that burden.

"Good, 'cuz I'd hate to have to kill myself."

Fire roiled through his chest. He grabbed the back of her neck and drew her face closer. "What did—?"

"Canyon." She clapped a hand on his forearm. "It was a joke. I—I didn't mean it."

"Get that thought out of your head. Suicide is *not* an option. Not now. Not ever." Where was that O_2 line? The thought of living without her. . .of her being gone. . .of her ending her life. . . "No matter what happens, I'm there. Got it? I'm not going anywhere without you."

She gave a faint nod, then her gaze dropped to his mouth. And he knew—*knew*—what she was thinking. How did the woman switch tracks faster than him? Lord help him, he wanted another kiss. To touch that piece of paradise again. . .

No. He'd made a vow to his brother, to his family.

The world tilted. Vibrated. Shifted beneath the power of—

"Midas!" The shout wailed through the torrential elements and slammed into him.

144

An evil roar devoured all sound. Sucked them into a vacuum where only the angry howl of the wind reverberated through his body.

Rumbling shook the Hummer. It rocked. Forward. Back. Forward.

What was it? A tornado? He glanced to the other side of the road. The veins in Frogman's neck bulged as he shouted and motioned him back. A muted crack sliced through the chaos. Then, as if in some surreal horror movie in slow motion, the Hummer's right side rose upward.

What the. . . ?

No! Not rise—

"Oh crap!" Pure instinct made him jerk the Hummer door closed.

Rumbling increased. Deafening. Numbing.

Roark screamed. Slid away toward the other side. She grabbed at his arms. Her body dropped down. That's when the dots connected. That's when he realized the Hummer was sliding. . .sideways. . .down. Off the side of the mountain.

Mudslide!

CHAPTER 14

Somewhere in Miranda, Venezuela

Greedy and ravenous, gravity clawed at Dani. The door flapped open.

Her legs took on the weight of anchors as the Hummer slid down the face of the mountain sideways. She strained to reach Canyon and managed a weak grasp. Stricken, she locked her gaze on him—his blue eyes nearly lost amid the paint streaked over his face. But nothing could hide his frantic expression.

"Don't let go!"

She clapped her hands around Canyon's forearms, clinging tight, her body dangling over the ripped seat and half out of the Hummer. With his help, she hauled herself back inside.

Feet planted, one on the seat and one on the floorboard, Canyon braced himself as he pulled. "Wedge your feet!"

Scrambling, Dani hefted her legs upward. They hit the steel brace under the driver's seat, then slipped against the slick surface. "I can't! The mud. . ." She whimpered past the lump in her throat.

Her hands were slipping out of his grasp.

Dani yelped as gravity exerted its power, yanking her downward. Her finger slipped over his wet clothes. . .down his wrists. In one last effort, she dug her fingernails into his hands. But still she slipped. Dropped.

"Roark!"

Air sucked at her. Her body plummeted—then suddenly swung sideways. She pitched into the back of the driver's seat. Though the impact felt like she'd been knocked against a cement wall, relief plucked the breath from her chest.

Hands pawed at her. Finally, Canyon latched on to the drag straps of her vest. His hot breath skated down her neck. "We've swung around," he shouted over the roar of the storm.

Swung around. That was good. It meant she wasn't in danger of being snatched out and buried alive in a mud grave. After a shaky nod, she smiled. Braving a peek over the headrest, she froze. The front end dove downward amid a sea of mud, trees, and shrubs. Would they tip over? Resting her face against the vinyl seat, she caught her breath. Already she felt the tremor in her limbs from the adrenaline dump.

"No." He nodded toward the front windshield as he strained across and pulled the door closed. He pushed himself back up.

The wide front end of the black vehicle surged and dipped. Mud splashed over the hood and splatted the windshield. But that was just it. In the black night, only blackness reigned. "What?" She couldn't see anything. What was he worried about?

"It's a mudslide. The entire shelf is gone." He struggled, fiddling with something behind them. "Wrap this around your arm and hold on." He pulled hard on a strap—a seat belt.

"Why?"

"The Hummer is made for this. We're safest inside. Don't want to lose you."

He didn't answer her questions. And that meant he was hiding something from her. Dani grabbed his arm. "Wh–what aren't you telling me?"

Knees wedging him between the edge of the rear seat and the front passenger seat, he looked to her, then back to the belts he wrapped around his arms.

"Canyon!"

He glared at her. Then out the windshield with a curt nod. "The river. It's probably gorged on the rain and mud."

Her heart dropped with the Hummer...straight down. She strained to see in the distance, but again the void of light prohibited her view. "Are you sure?"

He flashed a cockeyed grin. "No, I just thought I'd make it up so life would be a little more interesting." With that, he leaned toward the driver's console. He flipped a few knobs.

"What're you do—?"

Light stabbed the wicked night.

He scrabbled backward and pressed his shoulder against the seat. "We're moving too fast. I think we're going over."

Dani widened her eyes. "Over what?"

"The cliff. A big drop into the Río Lagunita."

As the Hummer pitched and jerked, Canyon keyed his mic. "Frogman, this is Midas. Come in."

"Mi—*hiss*—see you—*hiss*—miles from position—*hisssss*. . ."

He pressed the piece against his ear again. "Frogman, come in." He craned his neck and peered back up the mountain. The distance between his position and the top grew quickly. "Frogman, can you see us?"

"*hiss*—ative. Lost—"

A shriek rent the line.

"Ack!" Canyon snatched the piece out, his ear ringing. *Merciful God, where are You?* He grabbed his SureFire and aimed the flashlight out the side windows.

Roark straddled the middle space between the seats. "Are they going to rescue us?"

A sea of mud, trees, and debris sped down the mountain with them. He could only thank God they were in the Hummer, or they'd have been buried alive in the first two seconds. Still. . . "First things first."

Irritation skidded along her face. "Like?"

"Surviving this mudslide."

"But. . ." She licked her lips. "We're in the Hummer."

"And we're heading for a drop. If we don't slow. . ." It didn't need to be said. Roark was a smart girl. She could figure it out. His light beam struck more trees. Was that a slab of cement tumbling past them? Another reason to thank God—if that'd hit them, they'd have been knocked around, if not killed. The power of the slide must be stronger than he'd figured. Nothing like sluicing twenty miles an hour down a mountain in a river of mud.

"What are you looking for?"

"Debris that could k—" Canyon bit off the word. "Hit us."

"Kill us. That's what you were going to say, right?"

Neither of them needed that image in their heads. "Just keep watch."

Silence—but not silence with the gurgling and slurping of the mudslide outside and rushing against the hull—gaped inside the cabin. He cursed himself. If he'd been paying attention, if he hadn't been yelling at Roark, he would've seen this coming. Maybe gotten them out before the road dissolved.

"The drop-off!" Roark stabbed a finger toward the front of the SUV.

The panic in her voice jerked his attention toward the foot of the mountain where a mighty body of water carved out a trail that led southeast. Far away...very far away from the team. If they got caught in that, if somehow they were shoved into the river—

No. He couldn't go there. Coated with mud and casting dimmer light, the headlamps illuminated what lay ahead. Like lasers pointing the way toward the drop-off. He checked the side window, his focus on a tree that seemed to keep pace with them. He skirted a glance around.

"I think we're slowing." He struck his flashlight beam over the side. "Yeah. Look. The trees are lodged tight." On the other side, debris still tumbled over each other, racing toward the finish. Yet not as fast. Was it too much to hope for that they'd make it out of this alive?

"Seriously? We're stopping?" Roark whipped her head around and peered through the windows. "Are we?" A bubble of laughter seeped through the tension-wrought moment.

Canyon studied the battered landscape. "Yeah, I think so."

As if someone had applied a magical brake, they drifted down the last few feet, sliding closer...closer...

Canyon leaned back, pressing his legs against the seats as the SUV shuddered and glided toward the drop-off. The Hummer swirled at the basin where the mud spiraled to a stop facing the edge of the world. At least, it felt that way. Canyon checked outside. Would something push them over?

"We stopped!" The hope in her voice tugged on his pessimism.

One wrong hit by a tree...if another piece of the mountain gave way...it'd all be over. Canyon took the next couple of minutes to assess the situation. The elements. The debris mottling the river of mud as it trickled farther down the mountainside. Some dripped into the river. Amazingly, the Hummer held. Rain dribbled in through the cracked rear window.

Canyon eased onto the edge of the seat and unwound his hand from the belt. He swept his flashlight beam along the sides again. "I think..." His voice strained as he scanned the upper slope of the mountain from where they'd made their descent. A long gouge defaced it. Two sides lush and green. The middle marred brown and gaping.

He double-checked the distance from the front bumper to the cliff's lip. Not more than ten feet, *if* that. "That was close." Finally he let his focus drift to Roark. Her eyes were fastened to him, waiting... holding her breath, it seemed.

A smile faltered on her lips. She nodded, as if to say they'd made it. Then glanced through the back of the Hummer. She blew a breath through her lips. "Wow." A shaky smile. "Let's not do that again."

"Agreed."

"Think we can get back to the team?"

"Dunno. Maybe." He slumped against the seat, letting the adrenaline bottom out. "It'll be one heckuva climb. First, we need to make sure things are secure before we attempt it."

"I thought it was over."

He eyed the terrain. Some portions were still rupturing. But it was far to the side, away from them. "We're good." He patted her shoulder. "Let's grab what we can and wade out."

Crack!

The sound jerked his gaze to the rear. Up twenty or thirty feet on the lush green side, a tree had its feet seemingly swept out from under it. It tripped into the muddy river.

Canyon drew back, his pulse pinging. "Oh no." He held his breath, waiting as the tree decided its course.

God. . .

Roark looked out the window and gasped. "Canyon?" She whipped toward him, eyes huge. Her fingers coiled around his arm as she pulled closer to him.

The mammoth tree laid back like a slider in the luge. Roots flung mud in all directions as the thing spiraled on its slick bed. It rocketed down. Straight toward them.

"Brace yourself!"

DAY TWO

Near Mindanao, Philippines
13:04:15

N*o more outsiders!"*

Bayani stood before the chief, his hat and humility in hand. "Chief, please—they will only be here a short while. My people want me to train them, to teach them how to live in the jungle."

"No! Already the Higanti seek to burn our village to the ground, steal our women, and slaughter our men."

"Then I must leave," Bayani said.

"Is that your will?" Awa demanded. "I gave you shelter, taught you our ways, and gave you my daughter. And you will leave because I will not allow more outsiders to threaten my people; because I do not bend to your will."

"It is not my will." Lips tight and eyes downcast, Bayani fisted his hands. "I am ordered to train these men. Will does not matter, unless it is I will train these men."

"No. I have given my answer."

Shoulders pressing down, as if rocks weighted his strong back, Bayani stilled. "Then, I must leave, Chief."

"No!" Chesa leapt from the side and threw herself at Bayani. "You cannot leave me. Please, Father."

"Silence."

Bayani removed Chesa's arms from around his neck. "Chief, I say that not to force your hand but to explain that I have no choice. They own me, sir."

Within two weeks, eight more outsiders camped outside our village. The compromise pleased Bayani, who did not have to leave Chesa or the village—which to my surprise seemed as important to him as his men. The new men were dark-skinned, though not dark like Africans. More like from Spain. And they were trouble.

"What're you doing?" Bayani's shout pulled me from the creek. I rushed

up the bank toward the sound of shouts.

A scream.

Heavy thuds.

Finally I broke through some brush and stopped short.

Bayani punched one of the new men, whom he had pinned to the ground. "I'll kill you if you do that again!"

I saw Tortia cowering to the side, her eyes wide and streaked with tears. Chesa rushed across the space and drew her friend into her arms.

Jabbing a finger at the man with the now-bloodied lip, Bayani said, "Hands off. Am I clear?"

The downed man nodded.

"What has happened here?"

Maut came forward. "He seized Tortia and kissed her."

Awa's rage grew. "You must take her at once. Her honor!"

Bayani jumped up. "No." He stepped between Awa and the dark man. "I won't let this happen."

My husband stared at Bayani. "What do you mean? He must take her. You know—"

Bayani glared at the dark man. "He has no honor. He's leaving at first light."

CHAPTER 15

Wedged between the back and front seat, Canyon waited. Expecting the jolt that would launch him into next week. He anticipated what would happen. How he'd need to act. "Loosen yourself from the belt!"

Roark fumbled to get free.

CRACK!

Whiplash had nothing on this. His head felt as if a sledgehammer had rammed it backward while his body went forward. *Crack!* Fire leapt through his skull at the impact.

Like a missile fired, they shot off the cliff. After the initial jolt— nothing. Absolutely nothing. No movement. No deafening scream from Roark. No roar of the elements. Silence. Freakish silence that snatched courage from his chest one beat at a time.

Until the unmistakable sensation of a twenty-foot free fall.

Exhilarating.

Terrifying.

The Hummer's front end flopped down. An anvil slamming toward the water. Despite it being water, at this speed and distance, it'd feel like they hit concrete.

Feet braced against the front seats, he peered down the length of his body. Over the front seats. Past the dash. Out the windshield. A churning river of brown writhed as if in anticipation of their plunge.

His senses snapped to life. A roar punched him in the chest. No, not a roar. A scream. Short but sharp. Roark! She clamped her mouth shut and grabbed her shoulder. The belt had tangled around her wrist. Probably pulled her arm or shoulder out of socket, maybe tore the cuff or ligaments.

"Roark?" The howl of the elements swallowed her name.

He stole another peek at the river. Despite feeling like minutes, the time it took to penetrate the water was only seconds. Hummers didn't float, but their sealed interior would keep them buoyant. But going straight in? They'd submerge. They'd bob back up, right? Whatever happened, he'd have to act fast.

Water rushed them.

Smack!

The impact threw him into the front seat. He flipped. His face hit the console between the front seats. Pain darted across his cheek. Water gushed around him, swirling and taunting. He strained to keep his chin above the H_2O. In the din, he heard Roark coughing and gagging.

He pushed himself backward, toward the sound, toward Roark, battling the powerful force of gravity and the weight of water. Reorienting himself, he twisted around.

Water, tepid and hurried, seeped through the back window. As long as it held—

Crack!

The windshield gave. A torrent of muddy water shoved him back down, feeling like a sucker punch to the chest. Tempted to gasp, he had to bite down hard, remind himself he'd drown. He launched upward, breath held.

The SUV bobbed upward. He squinted through the now-grimy windows. Trees waved in the distance.

Canyon swished around and locked on to Roark, who shoved dark hair from her face and sputtered. "You okay?"

More coughing. A strained, "yes."

The SUV bobbed downward again. "We need to get out of here." Then lifted and tilted back, leveling out. Their gear. . . Oh man. Gear. They didn't have any gear. He'd unloaded the supplies from the Hummer before the mudslide. What did he have with him? *Think!* Mentally he traced the pockets. Paracord, SOG knife, waterproof matches, rudimentary first-aid kit.

Swollen and enraged at their survival, the river tossed the vehicle around. Canyon pressed himself toward Roark. Slumped against the seat, she clamped a hand over her right shoulder, face screwed tight. Her long fingers tracked down her arm to the belt that still held her in its tangled grasp.

As he sloshed closer, water splashed his face. More tumbled through the back. Still contorted, her face betrayed the agony that stretched her lips taut. He drew out his SOG and sawed through the belt, freeing her arm.

Amid the torrent racing past them and the thrashing inside, he thought he heard her yelp as her arm flopped down. She gripped it tightly and grimaced.

"You okay to swim?" He tucked the knife back in his pocket.

"No. . .no," she said with a whimper.

She wasn't focused on survival. He gripped her face with both hands. "Roark."

Wild, frantic eyes. "He can't find me. . ." she mumbled.

"Look at me!"

She blinked. Focused.

"We have to get out of the Hummer." He wrangled out of his paracord survival bracelet and unthreaded it.

"Why? We're floating."

"Water's coming in. The Hummer will sink."

She looked around, comprehension dawning on her face. "What're you doing?"

"It's twenty feet of paracord." He strung it out, then knotted it around the carabiner before tethering himself to her.

"Together?" Straightening, she winced as her gaze hit the rapids outside. "Is that a good idea?"

"Dangerous but it's better than getting separated." *Or losing you.* With her shoulder injury and the distant expression in her eyes, he wasn't sure she could manage the rapids on her own. At least this way he could drag her to shore if need be. "There." He tugged to test its integrity. "Ready?"

"Okay."

Canyon gripped a portion of the window that swung inward and ripped it free. After flinging it toward the front of the vehicle, he crawled through the gaping maw in the back. The steel frame sandwiched his body, rubbing along his spine, then he dragged his legs out. He wedged a boot along the bumper, the other a few inches away. Braced, he turned and motioned to Roark.

She reached for him with only her left hand. He'd had a dislocated shoulder more than once. He wasn't sure if the thought of her in pain or the thought of having to pop it back into place was worse. Hand coiled around her belt, he maintained the grip as she scooted into place, shifted around.

"Got it?"

Roark nodded as she clung to the vehicle, again favoring the arm. One wrong jolt and she'd pitch into the frenzied waters.

Still holding her, he scanned the tree line. They were closer to the southern portion of the river. A tree limb hung over the water, dipping its branches into the tumbling chaos. *Almost as if waving us to safety.* "There," he shouted over the tumult. "Aim for that."

She nodded and turned, digging her fingers along the drag straps of his pants.

"On three."

Her gaze traced the waves.

"Roark." Between the pain he knew to be blinding and her fear of the river, he understood that she didn't answer. But they didn't have time for this. "Roark."

Resolve slid into a hard edge. A nod.

"One. . .two. . ."

Bam!

Roark flipped backward. Off the car. Broke their hold.

Even as the tether yanked him into the water, Canyon saw that a tree had slammed the Hummer out from under them. He turned the flail into a determined dive, reaching for Roark.

They sunk into gurgling, roiling water.

Canyon kicked back up. Breached the top and hauled in a long breath. The cord pulled taut. He grabbed it, tugging. Soon it slackened.

Waiting for her to surface proved excruciating. "Roark?" Glancing behind didn't help. "Roark!" To the side—nothing. Couldn't be more than fifteen feet away, considering the length it took to tie off. He treaded water, waiting, his heart in his throat.

The cord tightened again.

His chest spasmed—she'd gotten too far away. He'd have to go in and find her. After a deep breath, he dove forward.

Thrashing stopped him. Arms. Hands. Flashes of her face above the water. Then a wave dunked her again. Her yelp clawed at him. Canyon lunged for her, his arm slapping the angry water. He caught an arm. He dragged her up.

Roark popped up. Agony rippled through her face. Gagging and crying, she struggled to keep her head up. Using the paracord, he pulled her closer. To him.

An arm coiled around his neck. She buried her face against it. Coughing. Whimpering.

"It's okay; it's okay. Just hold on. I'll get us out of here." Holding her with one arm, he used his right for long strokes, watching the dangling limb wave them to the bank. Though he'd like to think they were safe, this river had a demonic force behind it. They weren't safe till they got to shore. Then they'd have other things to counteract that notion of "safe."

Halfway across the river, Roark released him.

Canyon hesitated, then saw her swimming on her own. Yeah. She was tough. Killer survival instincts. It's what he loved about her.

Liked. He *liked* that about her. A mental snapshot of her and Range the night of the Coast Guard gala smacked his thoughts straight. No, not mental snapshots—the photos his mom had propped on the mantel already.

Roark would never be his. *Get used to it.*

Battling the water was the easy part. Battling the horrific memories of captivity with Bruzon nearly drowned her. Each swell that drenched her had brought different thoughts—the dogs that chased her off the cliff. Bruzon's foul liquor breath. The choppy sea that nearly sent her to its depths.

Then Canyon was there. Holding her. His strength reassuring and commanding as he guided them to safety. When she'd finally told herself to gut it up and pushed off him to swim on her own, she'd seen pride in his expression. At least, that's what she thought it was.

"Grab it!" Canyon's voice sounded hoarse and distant.

She looked up just in time to see a branch dangling overhead, as if to say "here, catch hold." Without thinking, she reached up—

Fire-hot pain spiked her shoulder. She dropped her hand and gulped the cry. Carefully she used her left hand. The slick foliage made a solid grip nearly impossible. She sloshed. The water swept her under the branch. Past it.

"No!" She groped for the branch, fearful she'd miss it and be pushed farther away.

Something wrapped around her waist. She looked down and found... boots. *What...?*

"Roark!"

She peered over her shoulder.

Canyon, muscles bulging as he held on to the limb, locked his legs around her waist. "Grab hold!" With one hand he pressed a long branch toward her. "Now!"

Grinding her teeth through the pain, she caught the lifeline. Then flipped over. No matter the pain, she *had* to hold on with *both* hands. "I'm good." The pressure around her waist lessened.

Once Canyon released her, she hooked an arm over the big limb and shimmied her way over toward shore. The pelting rain and gnashing teeth of the water nearly made her slip, drop into the river. But no way was she going back down there. She swung her gaze back to the five-foot span to the shore. Toeing the slick grass, she tried to gain solid footing. Her boots kept slipping. She'd have to swing onto shore.

Swallowing the acidic taste on her tongue at the idea of how much that would hurt, she balled up her courage and threw it into the fray. Pain ripped through her, nearly blanking out her mind. She bit through the agony and swung. One. . . *"Augh!"* Two. . . She yelped. Launched herself.

Her boots hit. Slid. Dani pitched herself forward. Dug her fingers into the soggy earth. Once convinced she was not sliding back into the river, she flipped over, holding her arm still, and gasped for a decent breath. Wouldn't worry about the pain till she was sure he'd made it safely.

Halfway across the big limb, he alternated his arms monkey-style. He dropped next to her, legs bent. Finally, he slumped to his knees on the bank, the ground making a squishing noise in response.

Head dropped against the ground, she groaned. She wanted to curse him for making it look so easy. Beside her, she heard his deep breaths. Good. She was beginning to think he was Tarzan with the way he'd manhandled the elements of nature. The mudslide, the river, the branch. As easily as he'd tackled her during the football game with his family. *Wow, that seems like eons ago.*

"How're you?"

She craned her neck to where he lay next to her, about a head higher. "Alive."

He rolled and pushed onto his knees again. Quietly he worked, untethering them. "We need to get out of sight." He wrapped the cord twice around his waist before scooting closer. Taking her hand in his, he gently placed the other palm against her shoulder.

She sucked in a breath, frantic at what she saw in his eyes. "What're you doing?"

"Assessing your injury."

Trust him. . .trust him. . . But the pain level rose with each manipulation. She winced and cringed but tried to keep the intensity from her face.

"Dislocated." Canyon shifted closer, still kneeling as he hovered over her. "Ready?"

Horror strangled her response. All she could offer was a *heck-no-I'm-not-ready-but-I-don't-really-have-a-choice* nod. She'd seen this before. It wasn't pretty. Stomach knotted into a tight coil, she closed her eyes.

Cupping her elbow, he tightened the grip on her hand. He lifted her arm parallel to her body and turned it inward, across her stomach. Then drew it back out—straight across.

Pop!

Daggers shot through her arm. She arched her back and screamed— A hand clamped over her mouth.

The pain faded with her muffled scream. She blinked back tears as she looked up at Canyon. Through the patches of greasepaint still on his face, she saw raw worry.

"Better?"

Nodding seemed the right answer. She stared up through the tree limbs where the first rays of dawn peeked through the leaves. Leftover rain dribbled from the swaying branches and splatted against her face.

"We need to head into the trees. Ready?"

She pulled herself up, the ground suctioning her drenched clothes. "Yeah." Though aching and sore, her shoulder only hassled her with an aching throb as they trudged up the slick incline away from the river.

As they hiked Canyon seemed unfazed, alert and tackling the jungle. As if none of that had just happened. No terrifying plunge down the side of a mountain in a mudslide. No diving into the river and nearly drowning. No swimming through angry waters. Remembering it exhausted her, weighted her courage and limbs. But Canyon. . .he seemed made for this.

"I think I'll call you Tarzan."

He paused, for the two seconds it took his gorgeous blue eyes to track over her. The fading paint made him appear mysterious and fierce. Though he looked like he wanted to say something, he grunted and started walking again.

"Are we heading back to the team?"

"No."

Was he kidding? Dani scurried up beside him. "No?"

Without answering, he wound through the trees. Over brush and roots. His wet pants swished loudly, emphasizing his movements. Just like hers. Matter of fact, if they kept this up for long, she'd have a blister or two in a few unmentionable places.

"Where are we going?"

"Out."

She grabbed his arm and hauled him around. "Stop and tell me what's going on."

Frowning, he considered her for a second, then scanned the trees. Muscle taut beneath her hand, he didn't move or look at her again. "What do you want to know?"

"You're wired so tight you're rigged to blow. Why?"

He huffed. "We have no supplies, no radio communication, no weapons, and—" His mouth clamped shut, eyes darting back and forth.

What was he seeing that she wasn't? "And?"

"We're in guerilla territory."

CHAPTER 16

Lambert Residence, Maryland
3 May

W e're in a boatload of trouble."

"I'm seeing that." Olin glanced at the news footage of the mudslide in Miranda, Venezuela. Awfully close to the team's position.

"We've lost the medic," Max shouted, the din of rain and thunder making it hard to hear him. "And the girl."

Olin's knees weakened. He slumped back against the kitchen wall and gripped his head as he clutched the secure satellite phone to his ear. "What do you mean, 'lost'?"

"Went down with the mud. Lost line of sight in the trees."

Olin grabbed the thin threads of hope. "You. . .then they might still be alive?"

"Yeah. . .maybe. I don't know."

Swallowing hard against the daunting news did little to dislodge the lump in his throat. Danielle dying down there. . . He couldn't let that happen. Jacqueline would never forgive him. Then again, he'd never forgive himself.

And the mission. If they got her and Wolfsbane back alive, without the proof of the facility or WMDs, Danielle would still face federal prison. Or death.

Crack-rumble-crack!

"We've tried to find them but no-go."

"Have you compromised your position?"

"No, sir. It's lonely out here."

"Then proceed with the mission."

"Sir?"

"You heard me, Alpha. Get it done." He hated the cold, callous tone, but it was important.

A long stream of static filled the connection.

"Roger. Out."

Stumbling forward, Olin reached for the cold, marble counter. He leaned against it, phone cradled in his hand, and propped his forehead in his other. He couldn't lose her. Couldn't let this mission fail. The ramifications were too big. Quickly he dialed the number of a Special Forces group down that way.

When the line connected, Olin folded his emotions neatly into the foot locker of familiarity in mission planning. "Colonel Hamer, I need a favor."

Somewhere in Miranda, Venezuela
4 May

Squish!

Dani cringed. Not at the sloshing of the mud around her boots, but the telltale wetness that just erupted in her sock. Burning along her heel was now saturated with a warm, gooiness. Blisters. They were forming around her toes, ankles, and collar. But stopping meant surrender.

I won't go back.

Why hadn't she listened to herself? Federal prison sounded really cozy right now compared to this jungle. With the storms dumping rain on them, in guerilla territory. Unable to make it to the facility so Nightshade could take them into the belly of the beast to prove the nuclear program being developed beneath the noses of every UN country actually existed—it all felt so hopeless. If she and Canyon got out alive. . .well, the *if* was too big to contemplate right now.

But the man with her—

Her gaze lifted to his strong, sturdy frame. Hiking without complaint or conversation. Moving with stealth and skill. Her life was in his hands. She gave a soft snort realizing she wouldn't want to be anywhere else on the planet right now than here with Canyon Metcalfe.

Her boot caught on a tree root and pitched her forward. Hands grazed bark, plunged into the earth. Mud splashed her face. On all fours, Dani ground her teeth.

"Having fun?" Canyon squatted beside her.

She flopped onto her backside, let out a sigh, and shook her hands out, making sure the mud splatted him. Rain washed down her face, probably making her look worse. But she just didn't care. Wiping her hands down the legs of her pants, she nodded to him. "Sure." She was everything—hungry, thirsty, exhausted—but having fun.

He glanced around the area. "We can't stop here. I know you're tired, probably have some blisters. It'll be nightfall in a few hours. We'll stop then." He shifted in his squat. "Think you can make it?"

Agitation and humiliation wove a wicked garment around her mind. How could he be so undaunted, unfazed, un-tired? "Yes, Tarzan, I can make it." She would. Even if she died walking.

He smirked and stood. Again, he looked around but this time also up. What? Was he going to swing on some vines and whisk her to safety? Hand held out to her, he grinned. "Come here."

Mud sucked against her jeans as she stood, slipped, then regained her balance. Using the back of her hand, she pushed hair from her face.

Canyon caught her elbow and tugged her to the side. "Here." He reached up, drew her closer, then angled a large wide leaf down. . .to another. . . "Drink." He cupped the leaf and aimed it at her face.

Water splatted her face at first, then Dani tilted her head back and drank. Relief closed her eyes as water splashed her throat. Not a gush, just enough to moisten the parched desert in her mouth. She smiled and pushed her hair back. A small giggle escaped, amazed at how much better she felt for just that small bit of refreshment.

"I'll get you out of here." Husky but strong, his words made her open her eyes. Beneath the mercy of the weather, she peered up at him. Only as what he meant hit her—*I won't leave you or quit till you're safe*—did Dani realize his arm was around her. He had that same look as the night he'd kissed her.

She allowed herself to lean into him, using his strength as her own. "I know. I trust—"

Crack!

Screeching birds in the distance shattered the moment.

Canyon stiffened, his head snapping to her right. Though the foliage blocked their view, they both listened. "We'd better get moving."

Onward and downward. . .down the mountainside. For hours. Their quiet aside and rehydration bolstered Dani's resolve to maintain course. Only as they hiked and her boots rubbed her flesh raw did she realize she'd follow Canyon to the ends of the earth. And that's exactly what this journey felt like right now.

Night crept through the branches and leaves. Again, the rigorous terrain weighted her with exhaustion. She tripped but caught herself.

"Here." Canyon moved off to the side. "Sit."

Too numb to ask why or argue, Dani dropped against a tree and slid down the bark to the ground. Through half-closed eyelids, she watched him draw out his knife, slice through several tall stalks, saw off a few branches, then hack off leaves. With his repetitive motions and noises her mind lulled to sleep.

"Roark."

A nudge against her shoulder resisted her attempt to sleep.

Arms slid under her thighs and around her shoulders. Weightlessness startled her. She jerked, eyes flashing open.

"Shh," Canyon muttered as he carried her to the place he'd been preparing.

Eyes drooping, she barely noticed the lean-to. Robotically, she crawled into the space and slumped on her side. Canyon wedged in behind her. His breath dashed across the back of her neck as his arm rested over her hip. The lean-to's compact size provided no room for propriety-demanded distance. Right now she didn't care. Having him close, having him holding her—all was right with the world.

Sleep claimed her greedily.

Fire licked the walls of the huts. Smaller ones, devoured by the flames, collapsed with a whoosh *of heat and ash.*

Canyon grabbed her arm. "No, don't go back there!"

"Please, I must get my mother!" She jerked free, stumbled but raced toward the burning hut.

"It's too dangerous!"

Behind him, something snapped.

He turned.

A scream echoed through the night. He looked back. The hut she'd gone into pitched forward, then—

Snap!

Canyon's eyes popped open, his heart racing. He blew out a ragged breath. A dream. It was only a dream.

He let his head drop back against the sodden ground, awakened to the fact he lay pressed against Roark. Exhaling slowly, he closed his eyes. Wondered what Range would say about this. He couldn't help the grin. Range had always been a plan-first, act-later guy. It's why he usually lost out. But Canyon couldn't let his impulsive nature loose again. Not with Roark. She was too valuable. In the cacophony of jungle noise, he honed in on her soft breathing. Man, this felt right. Being with her.

God...

He stopped, uncertain what to pray. The honorable part of him would ask God to help guard against temptation. Canyon knew what he was made of, what he was prone to do. But he didn't want any more pain inflicted because of his bullheaded, steam-forward determination.

Crack-snap.

More of the same filtered into his awareness. Soft, steady steps. Several. It wasn't a dream. Someone—several men—lurked in the trees close by.

With great care, he lifted his head off his arm so he could move it. He brought his other hand toward Roark's mouth, in case she jerked and yelped when he tried to wake her.

To his surprise, her cold fingers coiled around his arm, then released. Grateful for her silent signal that she was awake, he reached for his SOG. "Stay."

Footsteps drew closer.

Canyon eased the knife from his side pocket. At the same time, he angled his body away from Roark, so, if discovered, he could lunge at the intruder. Silently, he cursed himself for giving in so quickly to exhaustion. If they'd kept moving, maybe they'd have put more distance between them and these rebels.

No point looking back now.

He tried to squint past the leaves and branches. How many were there? Could he take them? Probably not without getting shot or killed.

"Raul, *rápido!*"

"*Cállate,*" the man near them muttered.

Glancing down the length of his body, Canyon saw into the sprinkling of dawn light, saw the man approaching.

"*Juan encontró la pista. ¡Rápido! ¡El general ordena que sean encontrados!*" Voices called through the jungle, farther away than whoever was near their hiding place.

Dani craned her neck so her lips were near his ear and whispered, "He said the general wants us found."

"*Espere. He escuchado algo.*"

She gripped Canyon's arm tightly. "He heard me."

The guy stepped closer.

His boot hit Canyon's.

CHAPTER 17

Canyon scissored his legs and swept the guy off his feet. He lunged out of the lean-to. *Boom!* Thunder clapped through the air, deadening the man's grunt that no doubt punched the breath from his lungs as he hit the ground.

When the guy went for a weapon, instinct and training kicked in. Canyon pounced on his chest before the guy could draw that first, painful breath. He jerked the man's head to his left. With his reverse hold he drove the blade into the side of the neck.

The man gasped. Gurgled.

Canyon threw hard left into the man's face. The body went limp.

He whipped around. "Roark." He kept his voice stern but quiet.

She scampered from the shelter.

Pointing her away from the others, he growled, "Move!"

Roark hustled down the slippery terrain.

Behind them, dulled by the rain and thunder, shouts gave pursuit.

Together they darted through a grove of trees, down a hill, moving southwest away from the scouting party. He stuffed the blade away and let the downpour wash the blood from his hands as they sprinted through the sloping mountainside.

With her ahead of him, Canyon retrieved the waterproof container tucked in his pocket. His conscience wrestled with him, but he could feel the throb and strain of the mission taking over. He unscrewed the cap and dumped a couple of its contents into his mouth. He swallowed hard and kept moving.

Survival justified his actions. Neither made it easy to sleep.

Fifty Klicks Northeast
5 May

Zooming in gave Max a halo-green image of the facility approximately 150 yards from their current position. "Two tangos on each corner. Security gate with two more tangos. Building's got heavy activity."

"Just like we expected."

Max lowered the high-powered binoculars and glanced at Legend. "Right down to the number of lights."

"So, we do this thing," Legend said.

"And get out." And not a minute too soon because the team wasn't going home without every man and woman accounted for.

"What about Midas?" Crouched beside them, the Kid looked around. "I mean, we're not just going to leave them, right?"

"Mission priority is the facility," Squirt said.

Anger lit through the Kid's face. "Dude, don't—"

Max patted his shoulder. "First things first, Kid."

"Even if we found Midas," Cowboy added, "if we don't finish the mission, the girl is up against a mountain of trouble."

"Then we find them, right?"

A faint noise echoed through the stormy country drawing Max's attention from the guppy-like kid. Max skated a practiced gaze over the terrain. The trees. Hills. Plains. Miles. Nothing stood out, but he was convinced they were out there. Somewhere. Hearing that gunfire reinforced his belief that Midas and the girl had survived. That's when he saw a chopper hovering over a small peak. "Black Hawk."

"Not good," the Kid said.

Legend drew out his sniper rifle scope. "Dropping five—no, six men."

Seconds later, the chopper veered off and disappeared over the next swell in the mountain. Had the helo deposited more trouble?

Gut twisting at the thought of losing Midas and the girl, Max refocused. "Okay, Squirt and Aladdin, let's go. Legend, Kid, and Cowboy, I'm counting on your sniper skills to keep us intact and alive. Rendezvous on the coast."

"No extra holes in my body, please," Azzan said, looking at Legend, who glowered.

"All right. Let's get it done and get out."

5 May

"I can't. . .I can't keep going." Dani gulped air and bit through every step she took, following Canyon down the steep hillside. Who cared if he thought she was weak? A bug buzzed around her head. She swatted it.

A branch snagged her ankle. Stumbling forward, she grunted. Whimpered. And did Canyon care? No, he just kept hiking, climbing over one hill after another. They topped an incline, then started the descent. Between a gap in the branches, she caught sight of miles and miles of nothing but the same.

She deflated. How big was this godforsaken country? She was so tired. Leaves swayed, smacked her face. Whatever. She'd probably hug the guerillas if they came after her. Okay, that wasn't true, but for heaven's sake—when would they find safe haven? In a pout she stomped her foot—and it slipped out from under her. She plopped onto her bottom. Slid.

Canyon caught her hand and stopped her. Dangling from his hold, Dani tilted her head back and stared up at the green, mocking canopy. At least the rain had stopped.

He scooted next to her. "Giving up already?"

"I'm done." She sounded like a simpering, petulant child, but who cared? "I can't do this. I can't. I'm so tired I can't think to even put one foot in front of the other. Everything hurts. And if I slid down this whole mountain, I wouldn't care."

He chuckled. "Give it a try, and I bet you'll change your mind."

Her anger flared as she snapped her gaze to his. "I'm not made of the jungle like you."

He frowned.

"And you can get mad or be disappointed or hate me or whatever." She slapped the wet ground and shook her head. "I'm through."

He pushed up on his knees, disgust clear in his eyes. "So, what, you're going to lie there and let them find you?"

Her heart tripped.

On his feet, Canyon pointed in the direction they'd just come. "Bruzon's men are right behind us. I'm sure they'd love to find you waiting for them." He turned and started down the hill.

"How dare you!"

He waved and kept walking.

Smacking the mud again only splashed more mud on her face. In disbelief she watched as he trudged down the slope, using the branches and trees to maneuver. She stomped to her throbbing feet and yelled, "You're a jerk, you know that?"

"Yeah," he called over his shoulder. "And probably every guerilla around us knows, too, thanks to you."

Tears misted her eyes. Stupid, stupid tears. She didn't have the energy they required. She started after him, determined to. . .to. . .well, she didn't know what, but she'd figure it out by the time she reached him. Maybe punch him in the nose. Or smear that stupid smirk in the mud. The thought propelled her onward. And onward. How had he gotten so far ahead?

Finally, she could coil her fingers around enough material in his shirt to stop him. She yanked him backward.

Canyon turned.

"I have blisters in places I can't mention, but you keep pushing me, taunting me." She batted her hair from her face. "I don't know who you think you are—"

"I'm the man," he said with a grin and a pant, "who just got you to hike another twenty minutes."

Dani stopped short. Glanced back up the hillside. A bubble of disbelief worked its way through her throat and came out sounding an awful lot like a giggle. She slapped his chest. "You could've asked nicely."

"You were beyond that."

"How do you know?"

"Because I know you."

And they were on their way again. She bit through the temptation to complain and whine. Or to cry. He was trying to get her to safety. She knew that. But it hurt. . .hurts on top of hurts radiated through every pore of her body. Combat training could *not* prepare her for this. Stumbling onward, she barreled into him and yelped.

He grunted and shoved her back. "Quiet."

Dani peeked over his shoulder. And sucked in a breath.

Crouched and peering through a grove of unruly trees, Canyon considered the anemic structure. One side seemed to have collapsed. The roof canted toward the south. The brush around and leading to what should be the front stood knee high. Taller in some spots. But not trampled or shorn. More like. . .abandoned.

No light escaped through the thin slats, but that didn't mean anything. With plenty of daylight, if someone lived there, they'd want to preserve whatever they had as fuel for a lamp. No electricity meant an alternate form of fuel and light.

"Think we can go in?" Roark whispered from behind his left shoulder.

Checking for inhabitants could prove hazardous—deadly if they'd stumbled upon the *wrong* people. Rebels. VFA. But with the drenching rain, getting thrashed in the river, and hiking for twenty-six hours without sight or sign of civilization, they needed shelter and food. This crumbling shed wouldn't provide food—unless there were canned goods. Canyon highly doubted it. But they could at least dry out for a while. Keep the rain off their backs, especially with the clouds gathering in the distance.

"Stay here." Hunched, Canyon scuttled out of the trees. Intentionally, he lightened his movement across the swamp-like field. Another ten feet. . .five. . . As he squatted at the southeast corner, he felt his boots sinking. Silky soft weeds swayed in the muggy breeze and tickled his face as he took in the surroundings. Searched the tree line for Roark. Smart girl. She'd stayed out of sight.

Canyon shifted around to the east wall. Sidled along to where it leaned outward, as if reaching for the trees it'd once stood among. Carefully he peered between the slats. Blinding darkness. Slivers of light peeked through from the other side and provided enough visibility that he could see cobwebs sparkling in the beams. Tipped over furniture. A critter scurried along a horizontal plank that lined the western wall. Animals. Cobwebs. But no humans.

If they were around, they'd kept their shanty in disarray to fend off intruders. Doubtful. But he wouldn't rule it out.

Deftly, he poked his head forward, searching for owners.

No one. Taller grass.

A board creaked.

His pulse slammed through his veins. It wasn't him. He had kept clear of the planks.

Creak!

A resounding thunk was soon followed by a gentle swish. Only then did he see the raccoon racing through the field away from him. Time to pony up and see if he was the only biped home. As he slowly pushed to his feet, he drew the SOG from his side pant pocket and extended the blade. Crisscrossing he made his way to the door. He yanked the door open.

Squawk! Squawk!

A large black bird flew at him.

Heart thrumming as he raised an arm to shield himself, he ducked as the bird flailed past. Feathers dusted his face. Fire sliced through his right forearm. Stuffing aside the surprise he surveyed the shack. Empty. Dry.

He let out a weighted breath. The bird had upended his defenses. Had anyone else been here, they could've taken him without much of a fight. Holding the door, he stretched around the building and waved to Roark.

He started when she stepped from the woods, parallel to his location, not where he'd left her. She'd been moving into position, moving closer. And fast. Nice not to have to act like a drill sergeant. She knew what needed to be done and did it. Roark swept around him into the shanty.

As he let the door close, his gaze surfed the surrounding debris. "Find something to barricade the door."

Together, they carried a broken table and propped it against the door. Canyon rigged a rope around a counterbalance, effectively anchoring the door shut. "It's not much, but with the clouds coming, we should be safe. Soon as it lets up, we need to move out and find a town."

Roark turned toward him—light beams seemed to tease her hair and face as she moved. "Is that smart?"

"It's vital. We have to clear out before we're found."

"Then why stop here?"

The ground shook. A rumble snaked through the air.

He raised his eyebrows. The skies had answered for him.

"More rain." She let out a long sigh.

"It's your fault."

She whirled on him, eyes wide. "What?"

Canyon shrugged. "You said it was rainy season."

Lips parted, she stared but said nothing. No doubt trying to discern whether he was teasing or serious.

He kept the smile and laugh to himself.

"Then the river was your fault."

"How do you figure?"

Hands planted on her hips, she stood firm. "You said we were safe. Then the tree hit the Hummer and knocked us into the river."

Though he tried to stop the smile, it snaked into his lips. When she returned with a smile, it warmed him. Deep, deep inside. And angered him. He shoved it aside and refocused. "Grab some rack time. I'll keep watch."

"Sleep? I can't sleep"—she raised her hands—"in the middle of all this."

Wanna bet? She'd tripped twice and fallen once in the last half hour. He'd wager Roark would sleep within minutes of lying down. "You're dead on your feet." When her mouth opened, he shook his head. "Don't argue. Get some rest while we can." He pointed to the back corner. "It's dry over there."

Roark surveyed the shack. "Considering your track record, I'll try the opposite side."

Again, he grinned. Boards creaked and groaned as she settled into a corner. Curled on her side, she tucked her hand under her head. Canyon jerked a three-legged chair toward the wall where the leaning boards gave him an inch of space to watch for trouble. If he straddled the chair and used the wall for support, he could make it work. Seated, he crossed his arms over his chest and rested his head against the wood.

The dull throb of exhaustion pounded through his legs and arms. He yawned. Falling asleep wasn't a worry. His senses were on high alert. This territory hauled out the demons of his past. The jungle so familiar yet unfamiliar. The smells similar yet strange.

I will keep my mind and body clean, alert, and strong, for this is my debt to those who depend upon me.

The words from the Special Forces creed echoed in his mind. He owed a great debt. . .to her. As the thoughts assailed him, the heavens opened up their bounty again, dumping more rain. Drops sailed through gaps and some streamed down from cracks, slicking the walls. The storm washed away the cobwebs in his mind, that tragic night alive and fresh.

She had mumbled something about her mother, then raced off. He was too busy fighting his own panic as he screamed into the coms to call off the attack. The coordinates were wrong. Had to have been.

Canyon pinched the bridge of his nose. *Shut it out. Shut it out.* Couldn't go there now or he'd lose focus. And he *would* keep his mind and body clean, alert, and strong. For Roark. For Range. To bring Roark home to Range.

Something inside him twisted and knotted. He wanted to curse. Their names even sounded alike. Well, enough. Maybe they belonged together.

As darkness and rain dragged them into the night, he noticed a dull halo hovering over the valley below. He strained to decipher what gave off the glow. Lights?

That much illumination meant considerable light—electricity. The thin golden strand stretching across the blackened and wet landscape meant there was a town at least a day's journey. Hours of walking. Could Roark make it?

She would. Because that's the type of woman she was—rock solid. When he'd assessed her shoulder at the river, he couldn't believe how mangled it was. After he reset it, she hollered—he'd done a lot worse when he had his reset after games with his brothers—but she worked through it. Even now, hours later, she made no complaint. He doubted she ever attempted anything without finishing it. They had that in common. His mom called him obsessed. His dad called it focused.

Maybe that's why it'd been so hard to let go of Roark: obsession. That's what it felt like, her beauty—inside and out—digging into his gray matter with a death grip.

He thrust his head back against the wood. Pain darted down his neck. Good. Maybe he'd remember that the next time he got stupid. Even if Range hadn't set his heart on her, Canyon was too screwed up to deserve a woman like her. SOG in hand, he drew the blade along his pants and allowed the splinter of moonlight to skid off the steel. *Cut her loose.*

Elbows propped on his knees, he hung his head. *God. . .I've tried. . .tried to do right so many times and it backfires. But this. . .Roark. . . Help me. . .*

He couldn't finish the prayer. It was wrong to pray and ask for help. Wrong because he didn't want help. He wanted Roark.

Flipping the blade closed, he let his gaze wander to the side, over the rain-slicked boards, past the crate with a can on it, beyond it to the corner. . .to Roark. Chin on his shoulder, he watched her sleep and slid the knife back into his pocket, hooking the clip on his material. Shadows and darkness shrouded her face, but he could make out the contours of her body. Enough for his vivid imagination to spring to life.

Canyon fisted a hand against his lips. *Curse it all!*

He'd screwed up once. Divided the family. He couldn't—*would not*—do it again. That mistake had pushed him into the Army. Not enough pain of punishment, so he went into the Green Berets. Which led to Tres Kruces. And destroyed everything important in his life, including. . .Chesa.

The massacre walled off his heart.

Even if Roark gave herself to him, it wouldn't be fair. He could never provide what she needed and deserved. Because as much as he wanted her, he could never again commit.

The revelation coiled around his mind, drowning his ill-placed longing for the woman sleeping just a few feet away. Implicitly trusting him to protect her.

Just like Chesa.

Canyon stomped to his feet. The chair clattered against the floor.

He cringed, hoping he hadn't woken her, but he couldn't look. Why was it easier to live with and train a hundred non-English-speaking villagers than to deliver one woman to safety? What if everyone ended up dead again?

Canyon pinched the bridge of his nose. What time was it—could he take more? He shrugged. Two more wouldn't hurt. He dumped two tablets into his mouth and swallowed.

"You okay?" Doused in sleep, her soft sultry voice reached through the night and clenched his heart.

Snap!

Yanking the SOG out, Canyon spun toward the north wall.

DAY TWO

Near Mindanao, Philippines
13:34:30

W hat is wrong with me, Mama?"

Wiping the tears from her face, I tried to calm my daughter. "It is normal—"

She buried her face in my chest. "It is not! Mary already carries Maut's baby, and he took her only two months past. Bayani took me four months ago. Why does his child not grow in me?"

"Be at peace, Chesa. When it is right, it will happen."

"But I heard him talking—orders came for them to prepare to leave." She cried harder and louder. "He is going to leave me and with no child. What will I do? No man will have me after I have been taken by an outsider."

I gripped her face in my hands. "He is leaving? When did you hear this?"

"Last night. He said the order came. Bayani was very angry." Her dark eyes darted over my face, as if searching for me to tell her this was all not true. "If he was angry, it means he has to leave. You know those orders must be obeyed just as everyone does what Father tells us to do."

On my feet, I grabbed her hand. "Come, we must talk to the chief."

175

CHAPTER 18

5 May

Rigid and poised to take on an intruder, Canyon faced the door.

With stealth, Dani pulled herself upright just as the glint of a blade flashed in his hand. Images of him taking down that guerilla in the jungle told her she was in very capable hands. But it didn't ease her mind. Watching him fight. . .it wasn't as comforting as Hollywood might portray. Brutal, sickening. The blood. But the other side of her knew his actions were vital to staying alive.

He'd heard something. His dark form deftly moved to the right side of the door. He turned. Back against the wall, he craned his neck to the side as if pressing his ear to the wood.

Easing onto her feet, prepared to fight the way the Army had taught her, she hoped her fear wouldn't slow her. Training in explosives demanded steeled responses to high stress. She'd mastered that. Until now. Seeing Canyon place himself in harm's way sent waves of nausea crashing through her stomach. He was her only hope. Hands knitted and squeezed, she waited.

Creak! Flop!

A furry thing scampered in through a small broken board in the opposite corner. The board flapped behind the animal.

Canyon huffed out a breath.

Dani laughed.

He ran a hand over the back of his neck. "Ready for breakfast?"

Breakfast? What? Oh. "No!" Dani whispered. "You can't—"

With a chuckle, he shook his head.

Stretching her back plied a yawn from her lungs. "How long was I asleep? Hey." She tilted her head to the side. "It's not raining!"

"You slept nearly four hours. The rain stopped just a few minutes ago."

Dani stilled. "Four? Seriously?" It'd felt like a blink. Well, at least until she awoke and spotted Canyon watching her. It'd warmed her through the damp clothes. Then he'd snapped to his feet. At first, she thought he'd heard something, but the way he stood there as if facing off against some unknown assailant. What had agitated him?

"Ready?"

Trying not to alarm the animal, she quietly crossed the room. "What's the plan?"

Canyon pointed through a broken slat. "See it?"

Straining to see around him yielded only darkness. She shook her head, but then— "The light."

The lure of his grin felt like the tidal pull of a full moon. To say he was handsome was an understatement. The way his brows almost hid those pale blue eyes. . .the way his lips seemed permanently parked in that cocky smirk. . .

She just wanted everything to be okay. "I'm sorry I got mad earlier."

"No worries. You were tired."

Silence held them in its vacuum. Couldn't he see there was *something* between them? Must he always wedge emotional distance between them?

Canyon blinked. Looked away.

Apparently he must.

"It'll take a day or a day and half to reach that town," he said.

A soft, tender moment slammed shut every time. Why did he always do that? Why wouldn't he explore the chemistry between them?

Because nobody wanted a used-up woman.

Range hadn't cared what Bruzon did to her. Was that the *real* reason why Canyon kept his distance? Was his rejection because she'd been raped? Was he that puritanical?

No, that couldn't be true. He'd been a hero in every sense of the word since they'd met. So, what kept him so far out of reach? "Why do—?"

Crack! The sound resonated through the night.

Canyon stilled.

Dani froze, listening.

Tat-tat-tat. Tat-tat-tat.

Canyon grabbed her hand, kicked aside the blockade, and jerked her out of the hut. The seconds between hut and trees felt like minutes of naked exposure. He sprinted into the trees and burrowed deep into the dark, balmy jungle. Her foot slipped as he tugged her along but she quickly caught her balance and continued on. Dodging limbs and trunks. She bit down hard when her shoulder rammed a tree. But she kept moving.

Part of her still hated the way Canyon moved, as if born nocturnal, not affected by the darkness, the vine-entrenched forest, or the snaking roots that acted more like gotcha trunks. It was like he belonged to the jungle.

Strands of hair dangled in her face. Taunting, itching, irritating. She batted them back. Wiggling her hair into submission, she pushed on.

As they plunged through the trees and over the forest litter, her legs grew leaden. Die-hard determination dug into her. Canyon liked her strong, so strong she would be. Besides, Canyon hadn't slept and he continued with agility and skill. She wouldn't whine about aching legs even if they were falling off.

Light shoved away the night, but the overcast day hung gloomy and depressing. After what felt like hours, Canyon slowed and led her up around a cluster of rocks. "Take a break." He pointed to a smooth spot.

Dani dropped on the rock and hung her head, gulping air through a parched throat. Hard to swallow with a dry mouth. Even as they rested up, the staccato heartbeat of weapons' fire poked the thick air.

"They're...closer," she said through pants.

"Don't talk." He shook his head, face dripping. Sweat rings darkened the black shirt around his throat. Jaw muscle dancing, he breathed through flared nostrils. "Save your strength."

Read: no idea how long they'd be out here.

Great. Dani nodded.

"Let's go."

With a huff of frustration and irritation, Dani pushed to her feet.

Heat wound through the jungle and wrapped her in sweat. They roved over one hill after another. After a while, the hills and trees all looked the same. Were they running aimlessly? Of course they wanted to put as much distance between them and the guns. But did Canyon know where he was going? Or was his goal just "far away"?

Only when she dragged her feet over a large root system did she realize they'd slowed. She shook off the haze that gobbled her focus and tried to pay attention to their surroundings. Should've been doing that from the beginning. Yeah, the whole *tat-tat* chasing them kinda messed up that plan.

Splat.

But what if something happened to Canyon? She'd never find her way out of here. Okay, bad thought. But realistic. *Everything* bad was plausible right now. Wild animals. Guerillas. A local farmer who thought they'd steal his crops. Gypsies—did they even have them here?

Splat-splat.

She should—*splat!* The drop nailed her in the eye. Dani looked up. Rain peppered her face. "Oh come on." They'd run for God only knows how long through rain. Then hiked the last several hours in the blistering heat of the jungle. Now...more rain? "Give us a break, okay?"

"Who are you talking to?"

She looked at Canyon. "Anyone who'll listen. Ants. Critters. God."

"I think only one of them can really help." He flashed that cockeyed smirk that always undid her pulse. "Come here." His amusement drew her across the five feet that separated them.

When she stood beside him, Canyon angled her to the side, her back to his chest. His breath skidded along her cheek as he leaned closer and pointed through a cluster of trunks. "See it?"

Am I really supposed to notice anything except Tarzan next to me? She glared at him.

Using two fingers against her chin, he guided her attention out through the darkness. "See?"

She shook her head. "No. . ." A white blip on the canvass of green snagged her attention. She sucked in a breath and peeked at him over her shoulder. "A church?"

He grinned. "Probably another three- or four-hour hike."

She shifted around to face him. "But. . .a town!" Hope ripped open the gray clouds that had gathered over her heart. "They'll have food." Her stomach rumbled loud and unfeminine-like.

Canyon started hiking again. "A phone is more important."

She scampered after him, eyeing a large root that she stepped over. "Then food?"

He chuckled. "Then food."

Had she sprouted wings, they would not have carried them as swiftly as her racing heart over the next several hours as the facade of the church grew larger. White, gloriously white. Which meant someone tended it and kept it as a beacon of hope for the weary of body and soul. For a while, it blinked out of sight and took her hope with it, until they crested a hill.

Tugging her down, Canyon dropped to the grass.

Before them, a lavish landscape spread out. Okay, so maybe not *lavish.* The buildings were old, the fences in disrepair, but they'd made it! A town. A full town. Buildings. Homes. Farms with budding fields. Children playing in the street near the church and what could very well be a school.

The children... What if the guerillas found Dani and Canyon here? Their presence could bring a lot of trouble upon this quiet community. Or would the people here capture them and turn them over? Her stomach squeezed. Maybe they should find another way.

"Wires," Canyon whispered.

Dani traced the length of black running between poles at the far edge of the village where the wires passed the church and dropped out of sight. Electricity. Perhaps phones.

"Let's wait till nightfall." He glanced at the setting sun. It'd be an hour or less before they could scamper across the open. With a motion of his hand, he directed her back down the knoll and into the trees. They hovered a dozen feet back.

"Maybe we should find another way."

"Why?"

"The children could get hurt."

"We don't have a choice. It took us thirty hours to make it here. We have no food or gear." He sighed. "It's a risk we have to take."

Red clouds surrendered to night, draping them in a midnight blue canopy. Canyon stayed quiet. Too quiet. Was he as unnerved as she was? Ironically, the only question that came to her mind and found its way out of her mouth was, "What if it starts raining again?"

Splat! Splat-splat!

A Hotel in Washington, D.C.

"There's been an accident."

Humberto sighed as he closed his eyes and slumped against the leather seat. "What is it this time?"

"A mistake, that's all. Someone smoking too close to the flammables."

Humberto came out of his seat. "The entire facility is flammable!"

"*Sí*, General, but it was contained. Nothing was threatened."

"I hope you took care of whoever was responsible."

"He will never cause problems for anyone again."

"Good, good." Humberto eased back into the seat and accepted the glass of wine from the hostess. "What of the troublemakers?"

"Our men are still searching. No sign. I took the liberty of calling in Navas."

Reassured by the mention of the mercenary, Humberto accepted that the girl was still out there. In his country. Images of her curvaceous form flooded his mind. And though he allowed himself the pleasure of remembering her, he also remembered how she had outwitted him, how she'd escaped with the blueprints. They'd taken precautions to conceal the secret entrance, but it never hurt to be prepared. "Double the guards at the facility."

"Of course, General. It has already been done."

"Good because I will be hosting a meeting at my estate when I return."

"*¿Con los Americanos?*"

"Sí." He swirled the crimson liquid around the crystal. "It is time to extract his promise."

Shouts pervaded the connection. Tugging the phone away from his face, he scowled. "*¿César, qué pasó?*"

"General," came the breathy response. "I can't believe it."

"*¿Qué?*"

"*Esto es Fauzi.*"

He slammed the glass down. Straightened, his back rigid. "What of Fauzi?"

"His team found tracks. When he went to investigate, he never came back. The men found him, bleeding out."

"What?" His voice roared through the luxury suite.

"He is dead, General. Fauzi is dead."

"No!" He pounded a fist on the table where several men and women sat. Grief turned him away from the shocked expressions. Turned him toward the vengeance he'd operated under for so long. "Find them, César. Find them! Hunt them down. They will pay for killing my son."

5 May

"Here, put it on." Canyon shoved a yellow dress toward Roark.

"Are you kidding me? I'm wearing boots!"

He glanced around and yanked another tunic from the line. When she made no complaint, he stuffed his hands in the colorful tunic he'd grabbed for himself, all the while keeping his attention focused on the nearly empty street.

Even though the town was bigger than first appeared, they'd have to keep a low profile. Play it safe. Propping against the wall revealed the tremor in his legs as he unclipped the SOG and worked it around his waist, beneath the tunic. Nothing like walking into a hotel or restaurant with a tactical knife to scare everyone off.

A long night's rest would do them both a lot of good, but could they let down their guard? *Never.* He eyed the two-story structure halfway down the paved road with more holes than cement. A sign hung crooked from the eaves and read: HOTEL. The stenciling on a grimy window revealed it was also a restaurant. Chipped plaster and cement marked the building with years of age and neglect. Not a five star but it'd do. Two birds with one stone.

He glanced back at Roark. She shrugged into the tunic and flipped her hair out from under it. The burgundy T-shirt peeked out beneath the yellow tunic but the jeans and T-shirt might give them away. She looked good—too good. And that worried him. People would notice. People would remember. *No choice.*

The greasepaint still clung to her skin. Probably to his, too. "Hang on. Come here." Out of view, he snagged a small shirt and dipped it in a bucket of rainwater perched precariously on a chair. Holding her chin, he swiped the rag over her face. Cheeks, forehead, eyes—he tapped her nose and made her flinch—and then her chin, around her mouth. . .

Her lips parted and her eyes rose to his.

Shake it off.

"Here." He stuffed the rag in her hand. "Clean me up."

She smiled, her pink lips alluring and beautiful. Granted, she wasn't washed and glowing, but the woman before him could take him to his knees with that smile. The rag smoothed over his face and chin. As she craned her neck and wiped, he spotted the greasepaint along her neck and ears. In the last hour something had shifted between them, but he had to focus. On getting cleaned up so they wouldn't attract more attention than tourists normally drew.

He took the cloth and wiped her neck and ear. As he did, he felt her eyes come to his. Canyon let his gaze soak in her beauty, her courage, her strength. He'd not met anyone like her. As much as he loved Chesa, Roark had captivated his heart and mind.

His pulse pounded when she tilted her head and leaned into him.

He let his lips caress hers. Once. Twice.

Range. Canyon jerked back. Range would kill him.

Growling, Dani drove both hands against his chest. "Why do you keep doing that?"

"What?"

"You know what. Every time you kiss me, you veer off. You go from hot to cold in seconds." Fingers plowing through her thick, dark hair, she blew out a long breath. "Is it me? Do you not like me?"

"It's my brother. You know that—or should. You went out with him, dressed in that slinky dress, and paraded around the Coastie ball with him."

Her eyes flamed, then twinkled with amusement. "You're jealous."

"What was your first clue?"

"Well, it's not your brother who I love, okay? I love you."

A two-by-four upside the head wouldn't have had the impact those words did. He steeled himself and shook his head. "Don't say that."

"Why?"

"Because you don't mean it." He bent to the barrel, scooping water and running it over his face and neck. No way she could love him. From his leg pocket he lifted the small vial, and retrieved two pills. He stuffed them in his mouth and swallowed.

She wedged herself between him and the back of the house. "Why does that scare you? That I love you."

Canyon ground his teeth together. "Because it'll wreck everything."

Hurt marched across her face.

"Think my call sign is an emblem of good luck? It's not—I muck things up. Ask my family. Ask Tres Kruces." Everything in him went cold. Had he really said that out loud?

Roark wrinkled her nose. "Tres. . .what? What is that?"

He used his sleeve to dry his face. "The biggest mistake of my life. It cost me everything—my career, my reputation." He shifted and glared down at her. "You deserve Range—he's a good guy, honest, upright. Got it? Me? I'll just screw it up."

"Do you really believe that?"

"I've *lived* it."

"Well, so have I. And you're the only person I feel safe with, Canyon. Look, I admit I allowed Range's attention so I could be close to you. But enough. I'll tell him I love you and no one else."

"Don't. It'll only make things worse."

Cool hands braced his face gently. "Look at me."

His gaze drifted to hers as if in response to the call of a siren who made his pulse race as he stood almost nose to nose with her. Though he scanned around them quickly, he couldn't distract her. Or himself.

Her soft, pink lips curled upward. "I will never love your brother. I love you, Canyon. You're the only one who's been there for me. Ever."

Intoxicated by their closeness and the intensity of her expression, Canyon lowered his forehead to hers. "Please. . .don't do this." He swallowed and wet his lips, tempted beyond all reason to kiss her soundly.

"Give me room, okay?" He couldn't sort this out. Not in the middle of a mission. "So help me, God. I'm trying to do the right thing, Roark."

"That's part of why I love you, Canyon."

An engine roared to life nearby.

Canyon cleared his throat and threaded his arms into the holes. "We should go. You ready?"

A tight-lipped smile accompanied her nod as she pushed off the house.

Regret dug into his fogged brain. He fished in his pocket for the vial again. Drew out two pills.

"Hey." Roark's hand covered his. "You just took two."

"No, I didn't."

"Yes, you did. I saw you."

I did? He frowned.

Her grip tightened. "What are they?"

"Painkillers."

Gold eyes came to his and her brow knotted. "Are you in pain?"

Canyon hesitated.

Her fingers closed around the vial, and she plucked it from his grasp. "Hey."

"You don't need these, Canyon."

"They're for my shoulder and back." And his heart. His mind. When a kid's shout distracted her, he took the pills back. "Remember." He clasped her hand and tucked the vial in the tactical pocket. "We're hiking through South America. Just a couple of tourists."

They stepped up on the wooden porch, his boots clomping their arrival. He gripped the handle and tugged open the door to the hotel. Heavy grease and tobacco odors assaulted him, nearly knocking him back into the street. But he went with it, pretended to enjoy the smells wafting from the small restaurant.

"*Hola.*" A man stood up from a spindle-backed chair near the door and strode toward a counter that anchored the main entry area. "Need a room?"

"Please." Canyon led Roark to the counter, instantly taking in their surroundings. The bar and restaurant on the right. Cluster of chairs and sofa on the left along with two doors marked laundry room and office.

"How many nights?"

"One."

The clerk pointed up. "Second floor. Room twenty-five."

Did this place even have twenty-five rooms? It felt more like an

old-fashioned boardinghouse. With a metal key in hand, Canyon stepped
back and waited, glad when Roark took the cue and headed for the stairs.
The more they acted like a couple, the less attention they'd draw.

Though he had to jiggle the key to get the door to unlock, he didn't
mind. It meant it'd be harder for someone to break into the room quietly.
SOG in hand, he moved into the room, waited for Roark to join them,
then locked them in. As she fastened the dead bolt and secured the chain,
he cleared the closet and bathroom. The sight of a second door in the
bathroom made him tense. Sharing a bathroom posed risks. But again—no
choice. He locked it and would keep it that way. He checked the bathtub.
Rust had eaten through some of the porcelain. He flipped the knobs. Pipes
groaned and creaked. Water dribbled out, then rushed into the tub. At least
it wasn't brown water.

"Looks good." Back in the room, he drew off the hot, heavy tunic
and dropped it on the bed. He stepped to the window and peered
through the shades, glancing up and down the street. "Let's get cleaned
up, then grab some food. We'll sleep and head out before dawn." When
she didn't respond, Canyon looked back at her.

She waited by the dresser, her hands behind her and propped on
the wood. With the greasepaint gone, her face seemed pale. Definitely
not the rosy-flushed cheeks from when she'd kissed him on the street.

"You okay?" He turned, hesitating. Had he ticked her off by trying
to stave off his spiraling attraction? Surely she understood...

She wrapped her arms around herself and took in the room.
Something had drastically shifted in her personality since they entered
the hotel.

"Roark, you okay?"

"Yeah. Sure." That's when he realized her gaze bungeed between
the bed and the floor.

"I'll sleep on the floor. Don't worry." Why hadn't he thought about
what she'd gone through, being held by Bruzon, raped by the monster?
What an idiot.

Pink tinged her cheeks. "I—I..." She shrugged.

Canyon moved to her side. "Roark, it's for our safety that we share
a room. It'd attract too much attention to have separate rooms. And...I
didn't have enough for two rooms."

She tucked her head.

"I'm not going to let him find you."

That pulled the warm caramel eyes to his. He could see the pleading
as those beautiful orbs watered in the hopes that what he said would be

true. Lips pursed, she bobbed her head, seemingly unconvinced.

"We need supplies. I won't be gone long."

Panic shoved into her face. "You're going to leave me?"

"Roark," he said as he threw the tunic back on. "I wouldn't leave if I didn't think it was best. One outsider is noticeable. Two is glaring."

"Yeah. . ." Swallowing, she nodded. "You're right."

"Lock the door behind me—all of them. Move the dresser in front if you need to." He crouched to see into her eyes. "Okay?"

Again, she nodded.

Canyon opened the door and automatically flipped the lock on the handle. He stepped into the hall, waiting as the door clicked shut behind him.

Thunk!

Dead bolt.

Shink!

Chain.

When his foot hit the first step, he heard the scraping of the dresser as Roark moved it into place. He hustled downstairs and out onto the boardwalk. He crossed the street, resisting the urge to look up at the window to see if she was watching. It wouldn't surprise him if she stood at the window the entire time he was there. He hoped not—she should shower and grab some rack time. Every bit helped.

Within a few minutes, he stood under a lazily circling ceiling fan in a store. Not a sporting goods store, but it had bottled water, a canvas bag they could use as a backpack, and granola bars. He eyed a pair of radios. Too expensive. If they didn't have to fly under the radar, he could use the credit card, but he was sure any credit purchases would send Bruzon's army straight into the heart of the town.

Tugging his waterlogged wallet from his pocket, he spotted a leather necklace with a yellow coral sun dangling from a white crystal. *No, just get what you need and get back.* But somehow, it ended up in his pile. He paid for the items, stuffing the water and bars into the pack. Pocketing the necklace, he started back up the street toward the hotel.

Glancing at his watch, he decided to go ahead and grab a couple of meals. They could eat in the room, get to sleep early, and be out before sunup. At the bar he placed the order and waited. The massive flatscreen TV on the far wall seemed oddly out of place in this dump, but who was he to begrudge them a Saturday afternoon game of *fútbol*?

Yet it was the man sitting on the other side that made him pause. Though the patron hadn't looked at him, Canyon felt sure he'd seen the guy somewhere else. Head down, shoulders slumped, the man stared into a glass of amber liquid.

Recognition slammed into him. No. . .it couldn't be. Thankfully, the man hadn't spotted Canyon. That was good. He needed to keep it that way.

Just then, the man looked up—straight at him. He frowned.

Move!

A woman in a multicolored dress walked toward Canyon with his food. He thanked her and started out of the restaurant, aiming for the stairs.

"Midas, that you?"

Canyon turned, steeling himself and feigning surprise. "Brick?" He extended a hand but closed his heart. This smelled rotten. "What're you doing here?"

"I could ask you the same thing, man." Brick sported a several-day beard and the stench of alcohol. "My *abuelo* died. Left me his farm. Just up the hill."

"Farm?" The surprise was real this time. "Since when do you farm?" The guy had been one of the best Green Berets he'd trained.

"Don't." The man grunted. "That's why I'm drowning myself in whiskey. The farm's failing. Losing it all." The man slapped Canyon's arm. "Never mind about me. What're you doing here? Way out of your territory, aren't you?"

"Yeah, I guess I am."

Brick frowned. "You in trouble?"

"Not really, just trekking. Trying to get to Caracas to meet up with some friends."

"Hey, I could drive you down, unless you want the alone time. I know how you used to be about that."

Mind racing, Canyon considered the man's words. He'd known Brick for years in the Army. Then the guy got out. Never heard from him again. "You sure about that? Isn't it far?"

"Only three or four hours' drive. On foot, another day at least." Brick thumped Canyon's shoulder. "I'll be here at seven in the morning. That too early?"

"No, no, that'd be great." Was he making a mistake? "Where'd you say your farm was?"

"End of the street, take the first dirt road. Hang a right. Up the hill."

Canyon would check out the farm story, and if Navas was telling the truth, they'd wait and catch a ride into town. If not, they'd be long gone before dawn.

CHAPTER 19

"D o you trust him, this Brick guy?" Sitting at the lopsided table, Dani tugged the end of the oversized tunic beneath the comforter, knowing she was covered but still feeling undressed.

After showering, she'd washed her clothes and hung them over the door to dry. She should let her fears rest. Canyon hadn't even blinked at her attire—or lack thereof—when he returned with the supplies and found her like this. Still, she eyed her jeans and shirt hanging over the door drying.

"I did, five years ago."

Chewing another bite, she considered not having to hike for another day. It was almost too much to hope for. "What about now?"

Meal finished, he tossed his empty bowl in the trash and crossed to the other side of the room. There he yanked off his vest and removed his tactical shirt. Bare-chested, he shrugged. "Not sure."

Mercy! Her mouth went dry. And not out of fear of being alone with a man. But dry mouthed from the strange things he did to her mind and body. For a second, she couldn't help but marvel that here, with Canyon, she wasn't thrust into the past, terrified of being raped. Being with him didn't feel suffocating. How weird—wonderful! She'd been on the verge of hysterics with Range. Why wasn't she terrified with Canyon?

Although she dragged her gaze away from his well-muscled body, it rebelled. Soaked in the— Whoa. Wait. What really snagged her attention—more than his incredible physique—were the tattoos, especially the one emblazoned over his heart. Three small crosses and the words: *Always Remember*. What did that mean?

Conversation. Steer it back. "Then, what do we do?"

He stepped into the bathroom, oblivious to her scrutiny, and that's when a few spots that looked like melted skin on his back glared at her. Bullet scars. "I'll ask around. If the people know him, we'll take the ride." He shut the door, severing her independent study of his body.

The tub handles squeaked in the bathroom. Soon, the sound of water tumbling over porcelain reached her ears.

Hair still wet, Dani finished the meal of beans, rice, chicken, and bananas, all smothered in a sauce with shredded meat. She glanced at her jeans and T-shirt hanging over the closet door, praying they'd be dry come morning. Though the yellow tunic was dry, it was also several sizes too big and hung loose on her. It might be comfortable to sleep in, but it was hot, which meant she couldn't wear it for hiking. She prayed this guy Canyon met worked out.

But wasn't it straining credulity that a man Canyon knew from his Special Forces days just happened to live in the village where they'd taken refuge?

A peal of thunder shook the walls and floor beneath her feet.

Dani groaned. Again?

Through the open window, rain pelted the dingy curtain. After she set her half of the torn foam box in the trash, Dani closed the window and pulled the shade. As she passed the mirror, she caught her dulled reflection. Ugh. Did she really look that bad? Fingering her hair dry, she yawned, but her mind hadn't let go of his friend.

Within minutes Canyon opened the door. In his half-dried tactical pants and still-bare chest, he draped his shirt over the bathroom door just as she had done with hers. She tried not to stare at his toned abs, the scars on his shoulder and back. Right now her attention should be on something else. That guy downstairs. "I'm not sure we should trust this friend of yours."

"Good. You're thinking instead of reacting." He plodded out. "But a little recon will tell me if he can be useful." He hesitated, his right pec flexing as he tossed something on the bed. "Do I need to put a shirt on?"

Dani blinked and looked away but not before seeing the smile on his face. "Why are you grinning?" Was he teasing her for staring?

He held out his palm. A brown leather cord held a beautiful shell pendant in the shape of a sun.

She drew in a breath. "It's so pretty."

"Good. I got it for you."

Seriously? "Why?"

Pinching the clasps, he held it out, as if wanting to put it on her.

"Because we've had too much rain and too little sun, so. . ."

Dani lifted her hair and turned her back to him, craning her neck as he slipped it on. "My own piece of sunshine."

"Exactly." His fingers tickled the nape of her neck, then slid down her shoulders.

Fingering the pendant next to her mom's rose, she stared at him in the mirror. Strange feelings roiled through her, the biggest of which was uncertainty. The man she'd held up as a hero bore wounds with no tangible scars. He was broken, hiding things. And out there on the street, he'd avoided her kisses. But would he buy her a necklace if he didn't return her feelings?

Canyon's smile faded.

"Thank you," she said, though it took every ounce of concentration. She shifted toward him, locked in his magnetic gaze.

Electricity filled the air as his fingers trailed along her jaw. But he shook his head and curled his hand into a fist. "Sorry."

His apology sliced through her, yanking out every last vestige of hope. Heart thumping, she unleashed her venom. "I'm sorry I can't please you. I'm sorry I'm not good enough that you'd want to fight for me."

"Roark, listen—"

"No. I'm sick of this. I can't figure out how you feel about me. One second you seem ready to kiss me senseless, then the next you're Tarzan herding Jane through the jungle." She shrugged, fighting off the tears. "Did you not hear what I said out there? And you have no response to that? Or is your silence the only response I can expect?"

"Roark, we've been through a lot since landing here. It's understandable that you think you like me—"

"*Think* I like you?" Her voice shrieked through the room. "I said I *love* you. And this isn't some stupid transference or Stockholm syndrome or whatever. I've loved you since the day you showed up at the hearing. I felt it, Canyon. It's real, not made up." She felt the ache at the back of her throat again. "Why won't you believe me? Or is it just easy for you to step aside and hand me to Range?"

Canyon jerked. "Easy?" He shuffled closer. "This isn't *easy*. It's pure hell."

Defiance sparked in her chest as she spun away from him, feeling petulant. "Good, then you know a little of what I've felt."

He stalked toward her. "You think I like turning off what I feel for you—?"

"So, you *do* feel?"

He scowled down at her. "Of course I feel. Just because. . ." Canyon shifted around. Paced as he ran both hands through his short crop. He looked back at her. "I—" Elbows back, hands fisted, he seemed ready to punch something or someone. His breathing grew labored. "It *kills* me each time I have to step out of the way so he can have a chance—"

"Have to?" Her eyes stung. "Why do you *have* to step out of the way?"

The ridge over his eyes knotted. "In high school," he said, his voice quiet and hoarse as he slumped against the dresser and folded his arms. "I was a class-A jerk."

"Not much has changed."

He shot her a glare, and she couldn't help but toss him an impish smile.

"I had everything—voted most popular, homecoming king, football captain—you name it. Always had to be bigger, better, stronger than everyone else. It drove me, controlled me." Hands on the dresser he let out a long breath. "I stole Range's girlfriend right before prom."

She let her shoulders drop. "That's mean, but I don't understand what that has do—"

"She was the only girl Range ever liked or asked out. To him, she *did* hang the sun, the moon, the stars—the whole freakin' galaxy." Canyon shrugged. "I was mad and jealous because Mom and everyone made such a big deal over it. My getting scouted for baseball—something I'd wanted more than anything out of life—nobody cared about because Range finally had a girlfriend. So I stole her to spite him."

"That's why. . . ?"

"He planned to marry her." He seemed to deflate. "I was a stupid twenty-year-old grunt. Reckless and self-centered." He swallowed— hard. "My idiocy ruined my relationship with my family. I vowed to never make that mistake again. So when you showed up, I got waved off. I haven't been able to live that down, and I don't think Range ever forgave me for stealing his girlfriend."

Her chin trembled. "Why am I not worth stealing?"

Did she really say that? Or really look as childish as she felt? It had to be the exhaustion and stress dragging out all her horrible character traits. The dresser rattled as he pushed off it. When he started toward her, she held out a hand. "No. Don't." She sucked in a long breath, shook her head, then let it out. "Forget I said that."

Canyon paused, hands fisted.

"I'm tired and not thinking straight." Wrecked. It was the only word she could find to describe the look on his face. And it was because of what she said. Glancing around the room she searched for something to redirect their attention. "It's dark. Weren't you going to check on that farm?"

He said nothing.

"Maybe you should go now."

Relief and yet heartache strangled her when he quietly turned, grabbed his shirt and vest, then climbed out the window.

Near Bruzon's Facility
5 May

Stacked along the perimeter fence, Max knelt and stared down the sights of his M4 as Squirt and Aladdin connected the device, effectively bypassing the electricity humming through the steel-cabled gate.

A crackle in his earpiece sped up his heart. A signal from Cowboy. He motioned to Squirt and Aladdin, who ceased working and pulled back. The warning hadn't given them the time they'd need to take cover. Max anticipated the guard's attention.

Within seconds, the overweight man slumped to the ground.

Aladdin leapt back to work. A few more strokes on his digital readout and the current ran around the device, affording them an opening in the circuitry and fence. Squirt cut through the cable.

Max slid through and scrambled to the guard. He lifted the man's earpiece and handed it off to Squirt, who tucked it into his ear. Even in the darkness, Max saw the man's eyes dart back and forth. Squirt adjusted it, then gave a nod. With Aladdin's help, they dragged the guard out of the secured area into the tree line. While Max and Aladdin kept watch, Squirt changed into the guy's uniform.

No need for anyone to find the guard and realize someone had entered. Hopefully by the time the man's body or absence was discovered, they'd be on a helo, or at least, on their way out. They sprinted back to the opening, crawled through, then Aladdin secured the fence so the opening wasn't noticeable at first glance or through binoculars. Max keyed his mic, and a confirmation crackled through the coms.

Half-bent, they darted to the first building, slid along its rear side, then stacked up again by the parking garage. Using hand signals, he ordered Aladdin to the vehicle parked two yards from the back entrance. Max scanned the open area as the former assassin hustled across the paved lot.

Sweat spiraling down his back and neck, Max drew in a breath—

192

one full of thick, humid air. A tap on his shoulder sent him sprinting across the cement. Back to back with Aladdin, Max could count on Squirt to pull up the rear. A former SEAL like him, Squirt would get the job done and not complain. A brother in arms in more ways than one. They both had the same training, the same focus. Even if the guy did talk a bit funny.

They leapfrogged from one vehicle to another, steadily closing in on the building. Max rushed the last few yards to the secret entrance, eye on the door. *God, give Your angels charge over me. . .and mine. Protect us. Guide us.*

A blast of light shattered the night.

He threw himself into a roll. Came up next to a small transformer. Heart pounding, he waited. Around his boots, the light groped the cement, the rocks. . .the small patch of grass. Crouched, he pressed his back against the grate of the steel box and ducked.

The beam danced back and forth. Maintaining eye contact with Squirt and Aladdin gave him confidence the spotlight was randomly searching, not targeting them because Squirt wasn't taking aim at someone. Max blew out a few short breaths to gain a normal rhythm.

Darkness blanketed the night again. *Move!* He lunged toward the building and plastered his back against the steel wall. Once the others slid up next to him, Max keyed his mic to indicate they were in position to penetrate. The response from Cowboy seconds later allowed him to breathe a little easier—the snipers had them in view. At least for the next minute or two. Once they breached the facility, they'd be dark—on their own. At that point, the snipers and the Kid would hoof it out of here because once inside, the others would have no way to extract Max's team if they were caught.

So, don't get caught.

Small Venezuelan Village

It'd only taken minutes to find the dirt road and another fifteen to trek up to the farm. Satisfied, Canyon headed back. Agony had a new name tonight—Roark. She'd all but ripped his heart from his chest asking why she wasn't worth stealing.

God forgive him, he'd steal her in a heartbeat. The fallout would be ugly. Real ugly. He toyed with her offer to talk to Range. That wouldn't work—Range would think Canyon had put her up to it. Besides, he didn't want her caught in the middle any more than she already was. This was his fault. He had to pony up and own it.

But if he thought he had even one chance of happiness with her, he'd do it. Life hadn't looked upon him favorably in a long time. Look at his career, his family, Tres Kruces—fragile pieces that trembled beneath his touch.

Regardless, he wouldn't want a woman like Roark to set her heart on him when she had no inkling of the damage he could inflict. She might have an idea after seeing him kill that VFA soldier—but that damage was intentional. The other was unintentional and a thousand times worse. Trouble just seemed to follow him like a lost puppy.

"For I know the plans I have for you. . .plans to prosper you and not to harm you, plans to give you hope and a future."

The words stilled Canyon. Though he wasn't a Scripture-quoting Christian the way Cowboy was—and now even Max—Canyon knew the words were from God.

But could God really stem the havoc?

Stupid question, especially if he believed God was all-powerful. And he did. But how did that fit into the established norm Canyon had lived?

Sorting those thoughts and slinking through the shadows, he kept to the alley and dark patches of the village as he made his way back to the hotel. Back to Roark. Plans. God had plans for him? Seriously?

Bet I can screw them up like I do everything else.

What would Roark say? How would she handle it if he told her about the past? He'd told her about Mariah and she hadn't blinked. Or maybe she was just really good at hiding her feelings. After all, she was a politician's daughter.

She'd never talk to him again, not if he told her. . .*everything*. It was best to keep her at arm's length. Let her think he was this hero that he wasn't.

That! That right there was the reason he wanted her to know everything. So she'd stop looking at him, believing he was this good, ideal man. Canyon fisted both hands and squeezed. Why couldn't he be that man? Be her hero, sweep her off her feet?

A car chugged by, pushing him into the shadows, and only then did he realize he'd been standing in the rain across the street from the hotel, staring up at the window. Light glowed amber through the drawn shade. Was she still awake? Probably. Which meant more talking. . .

Coward.

He crossed the street, climbed up on the bed of a truck parked off-center of the small balcony, then leapt up. The world spun and he dropped hard against the truck. Canyon shook his head, the wooziness away, then tried again. This time he gripped the ledge and hauled himself up over the lip. Crouched in the corner, he nudged the window open and slipped inside.

Roark stood near the door, hand on the knob as if ready to run, questions bouncing in her expectant gaze.

He removed the tunic, then peeled out of the vest. "Farm's there, truck in the drive, just like he said."

Her rigid posture softened. "So, we go with him—get a ride. No more stupid jungle or rain." She sighed and hurried into the bathroom, then returned and handed him a towel. "Can you believe it? We're this close"—she held her thumb and forefinger so they were almost touching—"to being home."

Sloughing the water from his face and neck, Canyon avoided looking at her long, toned legs. She'd hidden them during dinner and after his shower. But apparently in her panic to run if he was an intruder, she'd abandoned propriety.

"I can't wait to get home." She laughed as she folded her legs under her on the bed and drew the cover over them. "I never thought I'd be glad to see my dad again."

"I'm still not."

Defiance flashed through her face. She snatched something from the bed and threw it at him.

He snagged it from the air. Granola bar. He wagged it at her. "This is our nourishment till we get to safe haven, highness. Might want to be more careful in case something goes wrong."

"Why can't you just believe things will go *right*?"

"I'm being realistic, considering options."

"You're being pessimistic." She flung another one at him. "We have a ticket out of here."

He caught that one, too. "Anything can go wrong. *In all things prepared*," he said, repeating the Nightshade motto, but when another bar sailed through the air, he rushed her.

She screamed and dove away but not before pitching another at him.

It beaned his face as he tackled her. He dragged her back, attempting to pin her. Digging his fingers into her sides, he tickled her.

Roark threw her head back and laughed. "Stop, stop!" And she shoved another bar at his face.

"You're an obnoxious brat."

Indignation marched across her face. "I am not!" Pawing for more bars, she sputtered when her hair spilled into her face. She tried to blow it away but met with little success.

"One-hundred percent pure brat." Wrestling to keep her from whacking him with more granola, he finally pinned her. "Crazy, fiery, strong." He swept aside the hair that had fallen into her face. Her beautiful face. High cheekbones. Silky-soft complexion. Pink smiling lips. . .

Canyon's gaze flicked to hers.

Expectation hung there with her captive breath. He shouldn't—

Roark froze, rigid. As if she understood what streaked through his mind. Then slowly, she relaxed. Tilted her head toward his. His lips dusted hers, testing, firm but gentle. A sigh escaped her. Canyon eased back, his mind warring with his actions.

Don't do this. Honor her. Treat her right.

Her hand cupped the back of his head, and that was all he needed.

Canyon captured her mouth with his and pulled her into his embrace. Exhilarated with her response, he deepened the kiss and relaxed against her. How long had he wanted this, wanted Roark yet stepped aside? She smelled so good, melting into his kiss. Tasted so sweet. Canyon kissed her again, deeper, more passionately. He traced her leg and drew the hem of the tunic upward.

DAY SIX

Secure Facility, Virginia
10:10:58

*I*s it true, Bayani?"

His blue eyes that always sparkled like our river, clouded. "It is." He frowned. "The orders came through last night. It's been verified." On his jaw, the muscle popped. "My men and I pull out in eight days."

Awa came out of his seat. "We knew this day would come." Hands behind his back, he paced. In all the years I have known Awa, I have not seen his expression so. . .grieved. Though not given to feelings, he had grown to love Bayani as the son I had not been able to give him.

Bayani hung his head. "Yes, sir."

"What of Chesa?"

"It is complicated, sir. My world is very different. I fear she would not be happy off this island." Bayani rubbed his fisted hand. "I don't know if it's right to ask her to leave you and her people."

Chesa lunged forward. "You are my people, Bayani. Have I not done well with your warriors, learned your ways?"

Bayani smiled. "You have. But Chesa, as I tried to explain, things are very different back there." He turned his attention back to Awa. "If you feel she will do well, I will do everything in my power to return for her."

"Return?" Chesa's question shrieked through the air.

Bayani did not look at her. "First, I must return and request permission for her to come back with me. For now"—his gaze moved to Chesa—"you must stay here."

"She belongs with you, Bayani. Not here anymore." Awa studied the outsider seated at his feet. "Then you will return for her?"

"As soon as I can, sir. She's my woman."

Bayani had learned our ways well. I would even say he loved our ways, our people, our island. Our Chesa.

197

CHAPTER 20

Small Village Hotel
7 May

Canyon jerked upright. Darkness swam mean circles around his buzzed brain. Where. . .where was he? Unfamiliar and damp, the room sat veiled in the secrecy of night. Something had snatched him from his sleep. What was it? He shifted—and froze. Groaned.

Roark lay curled in the sheets beside him.

He shoved himself from the bed and dressed as faint images leapt and tumbled through his mind. Raging passion. Abandon. . .

Horror gripped Canyon as he held his T-shirt. "No." Disbelief choked him. "No, no, no, no. . ." he whispered, afraid he'd wake her. And why did his head feel like an M1 Abrams tank had trampled it?

His gaze darted back to the curvy form. No. He'd promised to protect her. He wanted to treat her right, with respect. Canyon spun away, sickened.

Oh God, please don't let it be true. Why did it feel more like a bad dream than reality? If he'd slept with her, wouldn't he remember it better, stronger?

But there was no other explanation to finding himself naked in bed with her. Shame and nausea roiled through him. *What have I done?*

To the side, he heard a soft noise. Roark. Her bare shoulder bounced under the tease of moonlight coming from the open curtains.

Everything in him coiled in on itself and died. He'd tried again. Failed. Again.

Make it right. He swallowed. "Roark?" He couldn't even say it. "I. . ." Couldn't. . .talk. But he had to. He'd messed up. *Bad.* "I'm sorry."

She pulled herself upright, carefully holding the sheet in place. Head down, she slumped on the bed. Her shoulders bounced more.

Canyon reached for her but then drew back his hand and roughed it over his face. He turned toward the window, as if somehow he could make this disaster go away. "What I did. . .it was so wrong. I'm sorry."

"Why?"

He faced her, surprised to find her dressed and standing on the other side of the bed. Defiant—but that bore out of hurt and rejection. "Because—"

"Because you didn't want it—me?"

Confusion pounded Canyon. "Are you insane?"

"Yes, apparently I am. I just gave everything to a man I thought loved me." Her chin wobbled. "Did you know that except for the kiss at your mom's house, I'd never kissed anyone?"

He stood there, stunned. Hating himself. Wishing he could wind back time. There were words for guys like him. Words he couldn't repeat. But they fit. To a *T*. "I suppose you think I'm no better than Bruzon."

A shuddering breath. "He took what he wanted and then had no use for me. Is that what you did?"

Assaulted by the accusation and acid in her words, Canyon jerked his gaze to hers. "Roark, no—" A noise by the balcony drew him up. He snatched his SOG from the nearby chair.

"What's wrong?"

Besides me sleeping with you? Besides me breaking my promise? "Heard something."

As he reached the window—

Creak!

Instincts blazed and he jerked back.

A rifle butt flew into his face.

⚜

"Give me good news, Navas."

"We have the girl. And a bonus."

Humberto laughed so loud his side hurt. "You are worth every peso, my friend."

"And then some."

"Don't get greedy." He glanced out the window of the hotel. "You know where to hold them. I'll return soon. But remember, the girl is mine!"

"I can see why. But the location—not a good idea. The Americans know of the facility."

"They think they know."

"No. . .they *know*."

Humberto hesitated for the first time in many months. "How are you so sure?" he said with a snarl, fed up that the man had already taken so much control.

"They're here."

"They're—you're sure?" He leaned forward, already envisioning his brainchild sluicing off into the ocean. Millions of dollars. . .gone. "How can you be sure?"

"I'm looking at them."

Bruzon's Facility
7 May

A guard came around the corner. Eyes wide, the man reached for his weapon.

Max drove a hard right into his face. As the guard crumpled, Aladdin fired a tranq into his leg. Max gave him a nod, honoring not only his quick wit in figuring out the way into this facility through the underground system, but for this work drugging the guard.

Squirt hurried to a door marked *Mantenimiento* and, using the key card from the uniform he'd snagged, opened it. Aladdin fired a tranquilizer into the man's neck. They rushed into the depths of the facility.

Bound and cover. Bound and cover.

Lather. Rinse. Repeat.

In the semidarkened hall, Max's unease grew as they leapfrogged down one level after another. *Too easy.* His team must've felt it, too—they'd slowed in sync with him. Even with Squirt in the uniform of one of Bruzon's guards, Max had played it safe and they'd done their best to avoid contact. Only as a last resort would they attempt to pass Squirt off as a local and he and Aladdin as hostages. With the security badge from the guard's uniform, they'd cleared six levels so far. Squirt's microcam recorded the path.

Only a matter of time before it registered with some whiz in the control room that this guard should be a hundred feet topside and walking a perimeter. Not heading down into the prison—assuming it was really there as the girl had said—and the hidden weapons facility.

Oh man. All too aware of what assuming did, Max pulled up against the wall. They had two options: one, go ahead with the plan and do what they do best—fight their way down and back. Two, alter course and pray they could tackle the more difficult route without fatalities.

Squirt and Aladdin drew up alongside, backs to his, as they kept a sharp lookout for tangos.

"Eyes open. Too easy," he whispered. "Plan B."

A nod, then Squirt moved forward. The less talk the better. The less interaction the better. But this was obscene. Told Max they were about to walk into a trap. As they descended the stairs in the same bound-and-cover fashion they'd used for the last ten minutes, he worked through scenarios. His head could get the best of him, playing out deadly games with the enemy. What should be down in the facility was lab rats—both four-legged and two-legged kind—and a few sleepy guards. He hoped.

Roark had said Bruzon held prisoners in niches that padded the facility's reactor, which should be a multistoried structure. . .if it existed. Not that he doubted her. Okay, he did. It was the spec ops in him. Plan for contingencies. Be prepared and all that.

Ahead, Squirt snapped a fist in the air.

Max held his position and waited, tilting his head a little more toward his weapon, ready to align the sights center mass on a target. Adrenaline spiraled through his veins, pumping hard.

Squirt spun toward him, ferocity in his expression as he motioned for the weapons.

Handing over the weapons, Max and Aladdin assumed the role of captives.

The door burst open.

Max slammed his fist into Squirt's face. The man stumbled, dropped the weapons, and dove into Max. Within seconds, two guards pounced on Max and pinned him to the cement floor. Cold steel pressed against his temple.

"¡No, él los quiere vivo!" Squirt shouted.

Straining his measly Spanish knowledge from high school, Max tried to make out the meaning. *Vivo.* That meant life—alive!

The gun withdrew. Yes. Alive. He wants us alive. *I'd like to stay that way.*

A boot stomped against his face but left enough room that Max could see the three men crowding the door. One, the clear leader and grinning, patted Squirt's shoulder. This better work. Putting Squirt in the lead meant Max and Aladdin were now prisoners about to get locked in a cement coffin.

The thought angered him. He struggled against his captors, giving his best performance against the men dressed head to toe in tactical gear. Not military uniforms. Guerillas or. . .? Regardless, Max could only hope Squirt's dark features and Spanish could bypass this snafu. Eventually get them out of here—and with what they needed.

Squirt straightened and met the others head-on. *"Lo siento, han sido muy difícil de controlar."*

Though Max didn't know what that phrase meant, the wicked grin Squirt flashed at Aladdin, who was still slumped unconscious against the wall, seemed telling enough.

A man—what was familiar about that guy?—stepped forward, eyeing Max and Aladdin. *"¿A dónde los lleva?"*

"A la cárcel abajo."

Donde—where. *Cárcel*—duh, prison. Max at least caught that much of the conversation. Which meant this is where they'd learn if the information Roark gave about prison being below and on the same level with the WMD facility was true or not.

"Solamente dos? Pensé que había más soldados."

Dos meant two. *Mas soldados.* . .more soldiers. The guard must've expected more soldiers. When the man's gaze again scraped over Max and Aladdin, uncertainty marked his expression and his hand moved to the holstered weapon. Max's gut cinched a notch. He prayed they wouldn't get patted down. That the goons would assume Squirt had done his job and retrieved weapons and knives.

Squirt shrugged, then nodded to the men who still held Max against the concrete. *"¡Consígalos abajo!"* he shouted, pointing to the stairs.

Shoulders aching as the men hauled him upright, Max eyed Aladdin getting dragged down a level and into a hall marked only with steel doors. The prison. As they peered through the small barred window, he grinned. Just like the girl said. An expansive room with equipment that no business would need. A revolutionary general bent on nuclear power? Yeah. He swatted Aladdin's shoulder. "Get stills."

Aladdin started snapping away while Max took environmentals. He didn't know what the symbols meant, but it lit up like a flashlight. He pressed the RECORD button.

Aladdin stepped back and stowed the spy camera they'd been given—ultrasmall, ultrasharp, and ultraconcealable.

"That door." Aladdin nodded to a steel door with a larger security panel. "That's the way to the bays and the full lab, at least according to the schematics."

"Then that's our exit. We can get the last of what we need as we leave." Max looked down the hall to the left and right.

Now. How did they get out of here?

"Wait-wait-wait."

Leaves and branches crunched as Colton tapped Legend, who slowed and looked back at the Kid. Expectancy of danger hung in the air, thicker than the rain ready to unleash again.

The Kid held up a finger. "Noise…" Eyes surrounded by camo grease darted back and forth as he turned a very slow circle. "I thought—"

Snap!

The Kid spun. So did Cowboy, his MEU .45 at the ready. Legend slid in next to him, his M4 stabbing Cowboy's periphery. Legend gave the signal to spread out. Sidestepping, Cowboy probed the surrounding darkness.

Moonlight flickered through an opening in the overhead canopy of foliage—and with a gentle breeze filtered the shapes of a half-dozen men. Heading straight toward them. Heavily armed.

CHAPTER 21

Bruzon's Facility
7 May

Panic swirled and clamped around her heart. Dani wrestled, yelped, as the guards wrangled her down the stairs and into the hold. The same hold she'd spent 180 days in last year.

"Get your dirty hands off me," she bit out as two guards lifted her off her feet and hauled her the last couple of yards to the cell. With grunts, they thrust her into the dank coffin.

No! She would not let this happen again. She spun and dove toward them.

A meaty hand collided with her cheek. The impact knocked her backward. Adrenaline shoved her forward. Dani leaned back and nailed the guard with a roundhouse. Though he stumbled, his overweight form barely jiggled from the kick. He glowered then squatted, prepared to launch at her.

"No la tóque. ¡Ella es Bruzon!"

If, as he said, she was Bruzon's, then even she knew the general would deal cruelly with anyone who touched her. That had been his way when she'd been his captive before. As sickening as the thought was, it gave her hope because apparently Bruzon wasn't in the area, or he would've been here to claim her. That meant she had time.

Time to find Canyon.

Forget him. He called her insane and *apologized* for sleeping with her. Even now the words seared in her memory. She'd loved him, gave him *everything*. He didn't even want her to tell Range that she loved Canyon. What did that mean?

Hands tied, Dani dragged her gaze to the man in the doorway. She remembered him from last time: Bruzon's right-hand guy. A violent, uncaring brute. Extremely loyal to the general and no one else.

With a quick breath, she blew the strands of hair from her view. She held her ground, glaring at the reeking, overweight guard, wishing—daring—him to try something. Feet apart, she stood ready to fight again. Just as she would at every opportunity.

"*¡Deje solo!*" As the cell emptied at his order to leave her alone, he locked his gaze on her.

"Navas."

He cocked his head and offered a hint of a smile. "Miss Roark. Nice to have you back."

"I'll escape. You know I will. Let's not waste our time with formalities."

This time, he grinned. "I can see why he lost focus and fell for you. He always liked the tough ones." He chuckled. "Thanks for the help."

Bruzon. Bile rose in her throat at the thought of that perverted old man. She'd spent enough days as his prisoner. She wasn't about to do it again. This man before her should know that mentioning Bruzon would only make her more willing to fight for her freedom. If he had the brains he seemed to have, he'd know Bruzon didn't matter to her. . . which was exactly the point.

He wasn't talking about the general. *"Thanks for the help."*

Canyon.

Dani's heart lurched. "Where is he?" She took a step forward, remembering the way they'd dragged Canyon's limp body from the room, blood leaving a trail from his broken nose. She'd never forget the resounding crack that echoed as he thudded onto the floor, unconscious. "Did you kill him?"

Navas smiled. Laughed. Then backed out.

Clank! The door slammed shut. A steel frame slid into place, sealing her in the room, cutting her off. She banged against the hard plastic window that blurred her view. Even though it wouldn't do any good, she wanted to scream at the man—he'd never care.

Scream for Canyon—he'd never hear her.

Scream at God for the injustice.

Turned around, she slumped against the door and buried her face in her hands. Cold cement pulsed aches through her bare feet and up into her ankles, beneath the still-damp jeans and burgundy shirt she'd slipped on just seconds before the guerillas burst into the room.

Weighted by the memory, Dani pushed herself to the corner—refusing the cot with its pillow and blanket, no doubt lice infected. She slid along the wall to the floor and hugged her knees, remembering what had been the most wonderful night of her life. Giving herself to Canyon. . .being in his arms, feeling his passion fueled her own until all her reservations, all her fears evaporated. He'd been so tender, so loving. . . not like. . .not like Bruzon.

"I suppose you think I'm no better than Bruzon."

He'd apologized. Said he messed up. Why did Canyon feel being with her was a mistake?

Okay, yes—unequivocally, it'd been wrong for them to make love, unmarried. She knew his beliefs, knew her own though she hadn't attended church since her mother's death. Did it bother him more that he felt he violated God's law, or that he'd violated the family-invoked law about not cutting in on Range?

Or had he regretted being with *her*? She hated herself for wanting to be with him, should've known that only left her feeling used up. Empty. Give a man your heart, become a pawn. Like her mother. Like her sister. Dani *knew* better.

She clenched her eyes shut as the memories collided, tumbling over one another. Bruzon. Canyon. "No," she ground out. The difference had been night and day. One brutal and violating. The other passionate and loving.

"He always liked the tough ones." Navas's words skidded into her turmoil, plying new fears from her. That man knew Canyon. It hit her then. He was the contact, the one Canyon met in the bar—Brick?

Which meant it was a setup. But. . .how? Nobody knew they were in the area except, well, the whole governing body who'd tasked her with proving her own innocence. Yet only General Lambert knew their precise location and the date they'd left. And then she and Canyon had slid off the side of a mountain, been tossed down a river, then crawled back in the jungle. How on earth could anyone ever figure out their location?

Olin wouldn't betray her. He'd been like an uncle to her, a close friend to her mother. Dani had seen more compassion and concern in his eyes than she ever saw in her own father's. Not that her dad ever mistreated her. Unless you considered being inattentive and a workaholic mistreatment; in which case, he'd be a model example.

And now? Now she was right back where all this started. The four stained gray walls were a long way from home. She'd vowed to never come back, knowing—*knowing*—she'd end up in Bruzon's clutches again. No. What she feared was ending up in his *bed* again. She'd kill herself before that happened this time.

Then why are you sitting here moping?

A strange noise howled through the prison, drawing her gaze up to where the sound drifted through the tiny vent. What was that? As if she had to ask. It was entirely too familiar. Torture. A shudder rippled through her. What if. . .what if that was Canyon?

Fresh determination washed through her. She'd get out of the cell, find Canyon—they could sort out what happened at the hotel later—and escape. She'd done it once before. She could—and would—do it again.

Dani glanced around the cell, eyes fastening on the cot. *Morons.*

Bruzon's Facility
7 May

Warmth slid across his brow. Over the bridge of his nose, a dark droplet raced into his eye. Canyon blinked, gritting against the pain that radiated through every cell of his body. Arms outstretched and tied down, he clenched his fists. Thigh muscles tightened, he tensed against the fire that shot through his leg.

"How many men on your team?" Navas stood in the corner, arms folded.

Fury that he knew the man torturing him fed his resistance. *Calm down. Relax, you'll last longer.* He allowed the tension to defuse. Focused on Roark—no. No, he couldn't do that. It'd only strain his focus, wondering where she was being held, was she hurt, was she being ferried to Bruzon?

"Midas." The man moved closer and planted a hand beside Canyon's head. "Just tell me what I need and you can go."

Eyes on the blaring light overhead, Canyon refused to be baited or lied to. He knew how this worked.

"With the girl."

His gaze diverted to his captor.

"That's what you want, right? To leave with the girl?" Navas nodded. "Thought so."

Canyon cursed himself for giving away his feelings for Roark, for giving anything to this traitor. "I trained you," he said through gritted teeth. "We were a team."

"And now we aren't." Navas indicated to someone out of range. "You killed his son. Think he's just going to let you walk out of here alive?"

A hum filled the air. Movement to the side as Navas stepped back. Electricity spiked through Canyon's arms. The acrid odor of burning flesh snaked into his nostrils. Canyon jerked his attention away. Locked his jaw as every muscle vibrated from the bolts of electricity. His teeth rattled. He worked to make sure he didn't bite his tongue off.

Navas's jaw tightened. "How many men?"

Limp, Canyon shook his head and let himself whimper. Finally, he wet his lips, closed his eyes, and with a grunt he said, "Six."

Navas stilled, surprise rippling through his dark complexion.

"Oh, wait." Canyon spit blood from his mouth. "I forgot about Grumpy." He met the man's gaze. "Make it seven."

Navas pushed away and stalked from the room.

"Finish him," someone said.

A hood whooshed over Canyon's head. Darkness devoured him. Splashing sounded nearby. Waterboarding!

"You're a traitor, Juan Navas! May God have mercy on—"

The hood plastered against his face. Oxygen sucked out. Water rushed in. He couldn't breathe. Couldn't get away. The cold deluge continued. Canyon writhed, trying to get away. But couldn't. It went in through his nose. He turned his head. But there was no getting away. He choked. Gagged—mistake! It let more water in. His lungs were filling.

Can't breathe. . .

He regurgitated. The vomit had nowhere to go inside the hood. *Drowning—in my own vomit!* The smell nauseated him. He retched again. Water still soaked every available space. He choked on that acidic bile and water. Somewhere. . .from something or someone, a demonic howl seared the air.

No, it wasn't someone else. It was him—his soul screaming.

Lambert Residence, Maryland
8 May

"My team's in."

"Thank you." Olin replaced the phone on its cradle. Surrounded by mounds of papers, files, and top-secret information, he stared at nothing in particular—unless you counted the past. Would that he could turn back the hands of time, undo mistakes, undo long-cemented fractures in his character. He'd learned from them, but not soon enough to prevent the damage, the carnage eating him like a disease.

Rubbing his knuckles over his lip, he allowed himself to mentally trace the steps the teams should take to extract Nightshade and Danielle. Go into the facility with so much stealth and force, the Venezuelans would never know what hit them or why—at least, not until it was too late. Nightshade would be recovered, and no one would be the wiser about who the men were or why they were there. Danielle would safely return to Virginia, and he'd make sure the pundits couldn't touch her again.

He leaned forward and withdrew his wallet from his back pocket. Opening it, he ignored the whisper of his conscience that urged him to avoid slipping into the past. All the same, his finger dug into the innermost fold and plucked out a tattered photo. Even twenty-plus years later, those brown eyes glistened at him.

Someone. . .someone had set up the team. Someone knew where they were going and had people in place to make sure the mission failed. To make sure Danielle didn't come back. That's what this was about, wasn't it? He'd always been able to smell a trap, a job meant to cover someone's fat behind after they'd stepped in a big pile of—

"You're up late tonight." Draped in a silk nightgown, Charlotte oozed gracefulness as she leaned against the doorjamb.

He'd always vowed Grace Kelly had nothing on his wife, but tonight, the concern etching deep lines in her brows smothered him with guilt. In his line of work, she knew better than to ask specifics. But they'd constructed their own codes around the truth to help her know what he was dealing with.

"Yes, forgive me?" Olin tucked the photo beneath a stack of papers and glanced at the clock, his fogged-in brain struggling to comprehend the time. Three? Was it really that late?

"Every time." Charlotte hesitated near the door, her easy smile turning upside down. "Is everything okay?"

Tonight, it was no use hiding behind codes and half truths. She knew, thanks to the media, what was happening down in Venezuela. "It's Danielle."

Stiffening, she drew straight. And the knife in his heart dug a little deeper. "Is. . .is she okay?" She stepped from the halo of light outside his office and drifted inside, wrapping her arms around her waist. She knew. . .oh, she knew his failings. All of them.

Olin sighed. "Honestly, I don't know. She and one of the men got separated from the team. They haven't located them yet."

She came to his side and rested her long fingers on his shoulders. "God will take care of her, Olin. Leave her in His care." She pressed her lips to the top of his head. "And those men are the best, you said so."

He patted her hand, but the comfort that should have come from those words fell short of the mark. Though he wanted to remind his wife that he'd made a promise a decade ago, he couldn't. It'd only open old wounds. . .wounds he'd tried desperately to let heal.

Her finger raked his desk, then she sailed out of the room. As she did, he realized she had not merely touched his desk. No, it was more than that. She'd touched something on his desk. A tattered edge. Of the past. Of his guilt.

DAY SEVEN

Secure Facility, Virginia
16:32:08

Sir!" *One of the outsiders jogged through the village, trailed by several more and the dark ones. "Sir, we've got a problem."*

Bayani turned from the final instructions to Maut and Tem-Tem. *"Easy there, Mav. What's up?"*

"There are tanks, Jeeps, and hundreds of warriors and others headed this way."

I turned to Awa, whose face went as pale as Bayani's. *"What can this mean?"*

"Seems the new team has upset someone." Bayani hefted his big gun. *"Let's—"*

"No, sir." Mav gulped a breath. *"We don't have enough. We go up against them and with those armaments—we're dead."*

"An air strike."

Bayani turned to the big Spaniard he had punched and put in his place two weeks ago. *"That's not how we work."* He pointed to his outsiders. *"Get our gear piled up and ready."*

"On it," the man said and took two men with him.

"What is an air strike, Bayani?" Awa knew the answer; I could see the fear of it on his face.

"Bombs, from an airplane." Bayani glowered at the dark one. *"And it's not happening. They're already too close and if we do this—it could injure this village."*

"If we don't call in a strike, we won't be doing any kind of work." The Spaniard looked around. *"And neither will any of these people. What do you say, Bayani? Going to kill your woman?"*

Words of war. Taunting. Cruel. Meant to get the thing this man desired. I was not sure if Bayani knew this man's purpose, or if Bayani felt there were

211

no other options. Regardless, he knew that this strike was not a very good choice.

I knew this big man's heart. There had been others like him before. Like the warrior who had nearly killed my Chesa. This man wanted that strike.

The old woman shuddered; her breathing came in gulps.

Matt leaned forward to pause the recording. "Are you well, Mrs. Mercado?"

She patted his hand, and a shaky smile trembled beneath wrinkles. "Not for years, Major Rubart."

"Do you feel up to continuing?" He shifted, agonizing over the idea of her wanting to stop. The doctors feared she would die. Without this testimony. . . "We can take a break, if you need it."

"Major," Carrie Hartwicke whispered. "We can't afford—"

He snapped up a hand and silenced her as he lifted the older woman's hand. "We don't want to rush you. Transporting you took a greater toll than we all expected. But I know you understand how important the information you have is to us."

Weariness seeped past Corazine's resolve. She sighed and seemed to drift to sleep.

Matt's heart chugged. "Mrs. Mercado?"

A withering breath. "No. No, I must continue. For Chesa." Her smile wavered again. "I wonder, who will I see first—Bayani or Chesa?"

Matt wasn't sure what to say. The question seemed incongruent with the whole deposition. "Bring her some water." He watched as the doctor pressed a dampened cloth to the woman's face. Really, there was nothing to do but keep her alive and comfortable for as long as they could. She would die, the doctor had said, regardless of their efforts.

"No," she said, her voice gaining strength. "I must finish before I go. See?" She sighed. "I'm a fighter. Awa always say that."

"Okay." Matt eased back into his chair at the small table and clicked the small device next to his computer. "We're ready when you are." He nodded. "It's recording."

CHAPTER 22

Bruzon's Facility, Venezuela
8 May

Whirring vibrated through the walls. . .the ceiling. . .the ground. Max capitalized on the sound and closed his eyes, allowing it to lull him into a light sleep. Yet not sleeping—he focused on the sounds, the patterns happening outside the cell. They should be good for another twenty minutes before another guard came by to check.

Twenty-six hours. They'd been locked up in here for more than a day. His mind drifted to Squirt, imagining what the man must be facing if he hadn't freed them already.

"Movement."

At Aladdin's voice, Max hiked to his feet and positioned himself on the other side of the door. Through the light seeping through the small square window, Aladdin's face glowed. "Two guards with—" His lips flattened and nostrils flared. "He's blown."

Not good.

Creaking and groaning stabbed the air.

"Stand back!" A guard shouted, aiming his weapon at Max.

Back-stepping, Max made his way to the middle of the cell, hands up, noting Aladdin did the same.

Seconds later, two more guards wedged through the door, an unconscious Squirt dragged across the cement between them. With the heavy ammo trained on them, Max didn't move. But he knew that with his tactics and Aladdin's, they could take this crew. However, with a man down, they needed to assess the situation. And find a route out of this place.

The door cranked shut.

Max dropped to a knee and placed two fingers along Squirt's neck as Aladdin traced hands along Squirt's body checking for injuries.

"Alive, pulse thready."

"No noticeable breaks or swe—" Aladdin leaned over Squirt and tugged the prone body up and to the side. "He bit one." He turned Squirt onto his back and planted a hand against the gunshot wound in the abdomen. Worried eyes rose to Max. "He won't last the night."

"Then we better get out of here before then." He scowled. "I'm not losing a guy."

Blackness snapped through the facility.

Max hesitated, glancing up but seeing nothing in the darkened cell. "Think that's the rest of the team?"

"Better be." Things weren't right. Getting ambushed during insertion—Midas had been right. Then he and the girl took the mudslide out of reach. Then getting captured. Now Squirt. Max was ready to turn the tide in their favor. "I've had enough surprises."

"Well. . ." Aladdin's voice sounded strained. And near the door again.

Max tensed. When had Aladdin moved?

"Better get ready. Generator has dull lights. I see nearly a dozen men drifting through the hall. Straight toward us. And they're armed."

A dozen? Nightshade didn't have a dozen even with the girl.

"Get back." Scooting into the corner and dragging Squirt's heavy bulk with him made Max feel like a scared rabbit. But the face of his beautiful wife and chubby-cheeked son compelled him to fight. If need be—to the death.

"They banked off."

Fear whooshed out of him. He set Squirt to the side and slumped against the wall. "That was—"

A scream knifed the air.

Spine stiff, Max slid along the cement wall to the door until his fingers grazed the steel hinges. "What's happening?"

Tat-tat-tat!

He paused at the rate of fire and pitch. An M4. American? A series of thuds and bangs carried through the prison. Shouts. More gunfire.

"Someone's unhappy," Aladdin mumbled.

"We have to get out of here."

"With the door locked?"

There was that. "Can you flag someone?"

"Too dark."

Hand fisted, Max rammed it against the door. That's it! He shifted and kicked the door. The jolt thumped through his leg. He did it again.

If they made enough noise...

"Wait-wait. Stop. They're coming."

Max stilled then returned to the wall, noting everything had once more fallen silent.

This had the smell and feel of a tactical strike. But. . .who was striking? Not Nightshade. They only had three men left on the outside. Though he couldn't hear Aladdin move, he saw the flicker of light against the man's skin for a second.

Boom!

A gust of hot wind. *Thud-clank-thud!* Air bled light, red and dull, revealing the door lying inside the room near the far wall. Several shapes slid into the room bringing more light.

Max spotted a leg-holstered gun. If he could reach it—

The uniformed man spun toward him.

Fight or die. Fight or die. Max lunged.

A fist plowed into his shoulder.

Max slammed a right hook into the man's gut.

"Friendly! Friendly!"

Wrestling in the arms of a soldier, Max finally connected the voice—Legend's. The soldier he'd locked around the waist snarled in his ear, "Step off."

Hands out, Max pushed back and straightened.

"Triton, he's ours. It's good."

"Legend?"

"Let's go, Boss. We found Midas; we've got him."

"He was here?"

"Yeah," Legend said. "Pretty messed up though."

"I'm fine," came the familiar growl from between clenched teeth and fat eyes. "We have to find Roark. She's here."

"She's not," said a smaller—but not by much—version of Legend. Triton, Max guessed.

Hand to his head, Midas looked like he'd collapse if the wall moved. "They brought us here at the same time. I'm not leaving without her."

"Already been through this." Triton nodded to one of his men.

Another soldier brandished a needle. When the guy moved toward Midas, an arm snaked around his throat and held him in a choke hold.

"Put it down," Aladdin ordered as he peered over the man's shoulder.

Surprise lit through Max at the stealth of that man. But Aladdin was right. "You're not drugging my man."

Triton scowled. "Exactly ten minutes to rendezvous with our only ride out of here."

"I'm not leaving without her," Midas reiterated, the growl stronger now.

"She's part of my team." Max added his assent to Midas's claim. "If she's here, we find her."

With a nod, Midas thanked him. They were a team, they—

Pain flickered through Midas's eyes and he hauled in a breath. Slowly, his shoulder rolled around the corner. He pitched forward, limp.

Max lunged and caught him, confused as he supported the man's dead weight. "Midas!" Only then did he see the dart in Canyon's neck. He snapped his gaze to the leader of the faction.

Triton shrugged. "Sorry. We've got orders, too."

Spine pressed against the wall near the door, Dani waited in the darkness as the guards shouted outside her cell. *Come and find out where I went.* Poised to the side of the door, she held the broken cot leg she'd used to shatter the lightbulb. Light leapt into the cell through the small Plexiglas window. The ground sparkled. She prayed the guards didn't notice the glass from the shattered bulb, which should give her a few more options.

Shink!

The outside lock disengaged.

Creak!

The door groaned open.

Steadying herself, she waited. . .waited. . .finally a guard stepped in. She brought the leg down across the base of his neck. A sickening crack echoed through the cement block.

The guard crumpled as she spun away, assuming a defensive posture for the other two who rushed into the room, M16s at the ready, weapon-mounted lights fracturing the darkness.

She dove forward.

Muzzle flash ignited the room, sparking.

With a gasp, she stilled.

Navas sauntered in, toed the unconscious man with his boot, then looked at Dani. "If you try that again, I'll have them kill you."

Nice try. "If you touch me Bruzon will kill you."

A sneer slithered into his face. "Are you that anxious to return to his bed?"

Fury rose up within Dani. Baiting her was one thing. Taunting another. She raised the cot leg and shoved every ounce of strength behind it.

Quick as lightning, he lunged. The flat part of his hand sliced the air and smacked her throat. Dani fell back. Unable to breathe, she flipped onto her side, holding her throat. Groping for air.

Navas knelt beside her. "If you ever try that again, I *will* kill you."

Trachea constricted, she gasped. Sucked hard for air that didn't exist. Her temples throbbed under the deprivation.

He set a netbook in front of her and pressed PLAY.

Unbelievably, she watched as red lights bathed the images of the facility as a dozen men snaked through.

"Your hero—do you see him?"

Throat aching, she rubbed it and ignored the burn ignited in her heart. Yes, she recognized Canyon's face.

"He left you."

As precious oxygen bled into her throat and lungs, Dani turned wide eyes to him. "No."

"Yes, look at the images. A spec-ops team extracted him last night."

Dani shook her head, tears stinging her eyes.

"Why did they leave you, Danielle?" He grunted. "Why did *he* leave you?"

For a second she forgot to breathe.

"Let's go. Bring her."

The pain of not breathing paled to the pain of a breaking heart.

Lambert Residence, Maryland
8 May

"What aren't you telling me, Bob?"

The connection simmered with muttering and clattering. "Never could hide anything from you."

"Then let's not ruin our friendship now." Olin stood from his recliner and started toward his office, mentally noting Charlotte set down her newspaper. No doubt her wife alarms blazed.

"She's not here."

His slippered feet shuffled to a stop on the hardwood floor. Something akin to an arctic blast rushed through his veins, freezing his muscles, his heart. "What do you mean she's not there?" He had to mentally push himself across the threshold and close the door quietly and slowly so he didn't worry Charlotte.

217

As he moved to his desk he grew concerned when his friend did not answer. "Bob?"

"That's some team you've got there."

Bob's comment wasn't the compliment it appeared to be. "What happened?" Palm on the desk, Olin eased into the chair, heart and mind racing.

"The dark-haired guy running that op?"

Had to be Max. "They call him Frogman."

"That's the one. He turned my hangar into a fight club about an hour ago."

Definitely Max. Strange and rancid, dread swirled through his gut. Max, angry? What happened? "He has a temper—"

"And a solid right hook."

But there was one thing about Max that worried Olin—he held his warrior brothers in the highest regard. For Max to attack someone sent to extract him meant one thing: He felt a code had been violated.

"You'll understand that I can't much elaborate, but. . . Who am I kidding? The man whose facility we penetrated? His reach stretches around the globe, as you know. So it should be no surprise to hear he'd gotten to one of my men."

"One—"

"Now, don't worry. He's in a cell, and your man gave him a few new lumps to consider." Bob huffed and groaned. "Can't say a lot, things are. . . well, I've got brass breathing down my neck." The phone muffled and Bob shouted something. "Listen, Olin, things are a mess. I gotta go."

"Bob." He worked to control his voice, his temper. "Where is Danielle?"

"That's what I've been trying to say—my guy left her there. Said she belonged to the general."

Fire roared down Olin's spine. He pushed to his feet, vision bleeding red. "Get my team back down there."

"No can do. We've been put on a no-fly hold for the next twenty-four hours because of this fiasco."

"Danielle doesn't have twenty-four hours."

"Sorry, Olin. It's out of my hands."

Naval Base, Cuba
14 May

Boulders sat on his eyes. At least, that's how it felt. Canyon groaned and pulled himself to the side, attempting to sit up. Pain spiked through his head and shoulder. He dropped back. A strange rustling made him still. Squinting, he glanced around the room. . .

I can open my eyes. Why weren't they swollen shut?

"Easy there," Max's soothing but entirely too loud voice snapped through the void. "You're hooked up to a few boxes."

Beeping and hissing of machines broke into Canyon's awareness. He shifted, pried open his eyes—even though he opened them, the brightness in the room pressed against the back of his corneas.

He lifted his arm and looked at the head of the needle whose length disappeared beneath his skin. Then traced the tube up to a bag. Squinting didn't help him focus, but he guessed the bag served as hydration. The beeping came from the blood-pressure monitor attached to his finger.

The room could've been a cage for all he knew. Gray bled against gray in a dull menagerie of materials—gray concrete, gray metal, gray mattress, gray lamp—lights! He winced and jerked, making his head swim. He had to align everything, get his mind back in the game. The last thing he knew—

"Roark." He grunted as he pulled himself up off the mattress. "Where is—?"

"Your head looks like someone used it for soccer."

Canyon snorted at Max's comment as he wobbled on the edge of the bed. Palm against his head, he tried to think past the thundering in his skull. "Torture and waterboarding do that." He winced at the fire in his temple. "Where. . .where am I? How's Roark?"

They were safe now. It'd been too close, getting captured then extracted by the spec-ops team. He'd never forgive himself if something happened to her again. There were a lot of things to make right. The first thing was setting things right with her. Marry her, if she'd have him. Not out of guilt—yes, he'd been wrong to make love to her out of wedlock. He felt like a heel. Like scum. If his past had been any indication, he'd pay for the mistake somehow. The thought rankled him. She deserved so much better than someone like him, but he didn't want her to have anyone else. He wanted the rest of their lives to spend together.

You don't deserve her or a happy ending.

A door squeaked open. "Ah, good." A man in a white lab coat strode in. "I thought you should be rousing."

Head down, Canyon peered up through his brows, feeling very hungover. "What'd you give me?" He also noted Max had not answered his questions. And that worried him. He locked gazes with the team leader.

"That's saline." The doctor removed an electrode taped to Canyon's shoulder and one from his chest, then removed the finger cuff. The shrill beeping stopped.

"Saline?" Canyon rubbed the spot where the tape had pulled against his flesh. "And I feel like roadkill?" It didn't add up.

The door opened again. In streamed Legend, Cowboy, the Kid, and Aladdin. They joined Max against the wall. "Hey, guys. . ." Nobody smiled. Nobody talked. What was with the lineup? "Where's Squirt?"

"Recovering."

A thought struck him: His question about Roark hadn't been answered. Which meant. . .Roark. . . If that electrode was still stuck over his heart, the team would hear his ramping heart rate. The only thing keeping him on the gurney were the spinning circles called the floor. "Anyone going to tell me what's going on? Where's Roark? How is she?"

In the silence that pervaded the moment, Canyon knew something wasn't right. Though he studied his teammates, he couldn't pin down what was wrong. "What's going on?"

"Hydrocodone detox." Max stepped from the grouping, arms folded over his chest.

"Hydrocodone?" Hot and cold swirled in Canyon's gut, mixed with dread and guilt, as his brain dumped all coherent thought. How did they know?

Straddling a metal stool, the doc clasped his hands. "You're a medic—remember, it's a semisynthetic opioid derived from either of two naturally occurring opiates, codeine and thebaine."

Canyon glared. "I know *what* it is. Why are you—?" He pushed his attention to the team leader. "Detox. What do you mean?"

A black storm cloud rushed over Max's face as he squared his shoulders and lowered his chin. Fight mode. "Why don't you explain to me"—he bobbed his head to the other men—"to the team, why you had high levels of hydrocodone in your system?"

They couldn't know. "This is insane. They drugged me. I'm a medic."

"Which gives you access to the drug, am I correct?"

Canyon swallowed—hard. Max had it figured out. How, he didn't know because he'd kept it concealed from everyone, even his family. Worked around it. Benefitted from it. Okay, so he forgot a few things. Didn't get bothered by other things. Who cared?

His mind swam—he'd taken a few just before that rifle butt. But he didn't care about that. He could handle the drugs. He'd taken them long enough. What he couldn't deal with was the pain in his back. Or the pain knowing they were ignoring what happened during the extraction. "Roark. Where is she?"

"No!" Max shouted, his voice echoing through the room. "This is about you. And us. How long have you been on them?"

"This is a waste of time."

"Own up to it, Midas." Legend stood tall and straight, his barrel chest seeming much bigger than usual.

Canyon came off the gurney. Ignored the wobbling in his knees. "Where's Roark—is she okay? It's not a hard question."

"Neither is mine." Max let out a slow, heavy breath. "How long have you been on them?"

Rubbing his face only reminded Canyon of his broken nose. He gently shook his head and studied the cracks in the cement. It was no use. Going up against Max was as useful as trying to milk a tank. "Since I landed in the hospital with a broken back after. . .a mission gone wrong." He gulped; he'd never told anyone. The explosion in that village had broken more than his back though.

"And?"

The men in this room. . .they deserved to know. But he couldn't. That order from the panel forbade his revealing the secret.

"And what!?" Never hope Max would back down.

"They help me forget."

"Forget what?" Max shouted.

"Everything! The pain, the past, the mistakes—"

Max lunged, grabbed him by the shirt, and yanked him up. "Your responsibility? Your duties to this team? How to do your mission right?" Amid Max's shouts, metal clattered against the floor.

The IV tower toppled. The needle tugged against his arm. Pinned to the wall, he felt like a limp doll.

"Tell me!" Max growled and thudded his arms against Canyon's chest for emphasis. "How'd they capture you?"

"It just happened."

"No." Pits of fury boiled in place of Max's eyes. "You're always the one who smells a trap, always feels when the wind changes. And I'm supposed to believe you didn't hear them come up on you? Where was your head? Was it the drugs?"

Canyon diverted his gaze, guilt chugging through his veins. Why. . .

why hadn't he thought of that? Was it the drugs? Or was it the high of passion that lingered after that night?

Vaguely he remembered Roark mentioning the pills he'd taken. How many *had* he taken?

"You put her life on the line! You jeopardized the mission." Forearm pressed against Canyon's chest again, Max tightened his lips. "You failed, Metcalfe. You *failed*."

Thud! The back of Canyon's head banged the cement as quick as Max released him.

Canyon braced himself, gripping his knees as he bent over. But that made his face feel like it would fall off. Guilt. *Screwup*. Yeah, no surprise there. "I just—" He hadn't felt this bad in. . .years. Oh man, he needed a pill. The thought crackled through his conscience. "I feel hammered."

Wheels clanked against the floor as the doctor shifted. "You're experiencing the aftereffects of a detox using the accelerated neuro-regulation, or ANR. You should be thankful, really. This provides the rate of highest success for opiate dependency." Understanding lurked in the blue eyes of the physician. "You aren't the first soldier addicted to painkillers. We have done in a matter of days what would've taken months—and a much lower success rate—in a traditional rehab detox program."

"Detox?" If he was detoxed, why did he feel like he'd been used for a punching bag?

"It may have actually worked in your favor that you were drugged during your torture. Your body was more relaxed due to the analgesic effect of the hydrocodone."

"Don't get the wrong idea; it wasn't a good thing. You've been strapped to that table, unconscious, while the doc here worked the drugs from your system," Legend explained. "It's been six long days."

Canyon froze. "Six days?"

"Yes." No backing down when it came to Max.

The doc rolled the stool toward the wall, then stood. "The first two you weren't in a physical condition to endure the treatment, especially not with the drug they hit you with to drag you back here. Then four days for the detox therapy."

Another scowl from Max. "But if I had it my way, you'd have gone through it the hard way, sweat it out for weeks. You deserve that."

"It was our concern for the girl that made us choose this route."

Like the mud that slid down the mountain and tossed him into a pit of chaos, Canyon saw the world collapse once again. The doc's face went pale. Cowboy came off the wall. Aladdin mumbled something. The Kid shifted nervously.

Max shot a dagger at the doc, who made a quick exit.

"What. . .?" Canyon took a step toward them. "What did he mean?" His head pounded with the rapid increase of his blood pressure. Anger gripped his chest. "I'll ask one more time before this gets ugly," he said low and slow, eyeing every man in the room. "Where is Roark?"

"Clear out." Max motioned to the others. "Midas—"

"Is. She. Here?"

Undaunted, unfazed, Max stood there as the Kid, Squirt, and Aladdin filed out. The door shut. "No."

"Where...she...you left her behind?" Everything in Canyon drained out like a massive hole in the hull of a tanker. Then refueled midair crumble. They left her. Unbelievable. He'd been drugged, dragged out unwillingly. They walked out.

Pivoting, he saw the concern etched into Cowboy's face, the anticipation leeching through Max's body language. Legend standing tall but the remorse was there, too.

They were braced for a fight. And by God, he'd give them one.

Canyon grabbed the pole on the floor and swung around. Max ducked. The metal clanged against the wall. Vibrations tremored up his arm. He spun and threw the pole. The line snapped tight and yanked the IV from his arm.

Blood squirted from where the needle came free. The spike of pain enlivened him.

"You left her! I promised her, *promised*."

"We had no choice."

Canyon launched himself at Max.

CHAPTER 23

*C*rack!

Max stumbled back. Recovered. Instinct drove a hard right at Midas. *Stand down.* Man, he did not want to do this, fight his own guy. "Hey." He shoved a hand out to hold off Canyon's next punch. *"Hey!"*

Fury glowed through Canyon's eyes as he hauled back for another punch. From behind, Legend grabbed his fist, twisted his arm down, under and around. He shoved Canyon against the wall, pressing his face against the concrete. "Stand down or so help me. . ."

Ghosts had nothing on the tormented expression in Canyon's pale face as he grunted against Legend's firm grasp. *There's more here than he's telling us.* Then again, wasn't that always the case with the former Green Beret? Yet if that were true, they had to give the guy some space.

"Leave him."

At Max's order, Legend eased back, a hand still clamped on Canyon's wrist and one on his shoulder. Finally, the big guy released him.

Canyon flipped around, shoulders supporting him as he wobbled and let out a half groan/cry. "Roark was terrified. *Terrified* this would happen." His face reddened. "She trusted us. Trusted *me.*"

Something streaked down his face. The storm, the fury that one of Max's own had been doping, subsided when he realized those were tears trekking down his cheeks.

Canyon batted the tears—looked at his hand, then. . .slumped. Slowly his brow smoothed out, his eyebrows rose, and his eyes widened as if he'd remembered something. "Oh God. . .please, no." He slid down the wall and cradled his head in his heads. And sobbed.

That noise grabbed Max's chest in a fist hold. Unable to watch

224

Midas fall apart, Max strode from the room with the others. Something happened at the end of that confrontation. Something that made Canyon lose hope. Outside, he stopped short. The door closed behind him.

"What happened, at the end?" he asked over his shoulder to Cowboy and Legend.

"No idea, man." Legend huffed.

"But it was *bad*." Leaning against the wall, Cowboy shook his head. "I've *never* seen Midas rattled like that."

"We have to go back," the Kid came toward them. "Find the girl."

Max snapped his attention to the Kid. "Not till we hear from the Old Man."

The Kid balked. "That's some kind of messed up. You saw him—"

With a sudden move toward the Kid, Max commanded the guy's silence. "I know what I saw!" This was the old Max. The one that hit first, regretted later.

"This is bunk." The Kid spun and stomped off. Halfway down the hall, he turned and walked backward. "No man left behind. We broke the code, ya know?" He pivoted and continued, the darkness swallowing him.

"He's right." Cowboy's tone was somber, defeated. "I can't live with this."

"None of us can," Legend added. "But we have no supplies, Squirt's laid up in recovery, and we don't have a way to get back down there."

"Lambert is out of contact." Max's jaw muscle popped. "Even if we managed to get hold of the Old Man, it's a no-fly zone right now. We'd get shot down."

"Excuse me." Straightening, Aladdin uncrossed his arms. He considered each of them for what felt like an eternity. "Not too long ago, you men hammered me with words about being a team, being there for each other."

Legend seemed to grow several inches in height and around his chest.

"So, would someone like to explain to me why you're all whining and complaining when a woman—granted, she's not technically part of the team, but we were all responsible for her and one of our own is in love with her—is being left behind?" Aladdin met each man's gaze. "Tell me, where's this team spirit all of you crammed down my throat?"

Legend smoothed a hand over his bald head. "He's right, and it pains me to admit that, know what I'm saying?"

Max sighed. "I'll try the Old Man again."

Naval Base, Cuba
15 May

Metal creaking pried open his eyes. The room, tilted on its side, glowed under the light of a single bulb. Canyon groaned as he pushed himself off the floor. Pain of the excruciating kind wormed through his limbs and gut. Head throbbing, he glanced around. Alone.

It should be his penance for the rest of his life because despite vehement promises, he'd left Roark. Where was she now? Had Bruzon returned to—?

Growling, Canyon flung his hand out and hit the leg of the bed. They'd held him here for days. To detox him! Wasted precious time— that could have, *should* have, been spent finding Roark—to address something that could wait a week. A month. Years. The rest of his life. Medicating helped him get through things.

Okay, so it wasn't right. But he'd faced reality enough to know he didn't want to again.

Tough. He had to face the fact that Roark would hate him forever.

She'd trusted him. Implicitly.

He'd failed her. Completely.

He would make it right, no matter what.

And he'd start right now. Escape this place, find a way back to the facility, get her out of there, and spend from here to eternity apologizing and making it up to her.

On his feet, he propped himself against the wall. Being vertical increased the throb in his skull. Good. Squinting past the pain, he looked at the door. *Get out. Get Roark. Get home.* Peeling himself off the wall, he gritted his teeth. Ten paces to the threshold. Canyon turned the knob. Maybe the other way would work. He tried. No-go.

He stood back and traced the frame. Locked? Why would they lock him in?

They knew I'd escape.

Well, he wasn't giving up. Not till he was dead. Roark needed him. And he wouldn't let a locked door stop him. He turned around and spotted the window on the opposite wall. He grinned and stumbled over to it, his mind vowing the thing was probably welded shut.

Squeak!

The window pushed out.

Too easy. After another glance at the door, he hauled himself up through the window. On the ledge, he hesitated. At least a ten-foot drop. He'd seen enough ACL and MCL injuries to know this could hurt. A lot. But if he stayed here, Roark stayed there.

With a grunt, he leapt from the window.

Canyon landed, feet together, knees bent, rolled out of it, and came up jogging. Though his body screamed for the bed he'd just left, his heart and mind screamed for Roark. How he'd get anywhere, he wasn't sure. Unless he suddenly acquired chopper- or airplane-flying skills, he would have to take a pilot hostage. Not cool.

Still, he aimed for the row of hangars at the far end of the base. Halfway across, sweat poured down his back. His legs slurred—wait, could they do that? Oh man. His mind was whacked. So maybe his body hadn't quite recovered from the torture and detox.

Light spilled out from only one of the buildings.

As he sneaked up to the bay doors, he hesitated. No weapon. No means. Ruled out bargaining with the pilot. Or what if it was a mechanic in there banging around?

He took a step—

A man emerged and gave a shout.

Canyon clapped a hand over his mouth and leaned down to whisper in the guy's ear. "Quiet."

Hands lifted. A muffled "Hey, it's me" slipped past his hold.

The man's face registered. "Kid." He blinked and released him. "What're you doing here?" Canyon braced himself against a barrel by the door.

Shorter than him by a head, the Kid made up for it in gumption. A cocky grin split the big mouth. " 'Bout time you got here. I started wondering if I'd have to drag you out of there."

"What?"

"You're going after your girl, right?"

"She's not my girl."

"Riiight." The Kid laughed, then grew serious. "Who do you think left your door unlocked?"

"The door was locked."

"Oh. Sorry. I—they told me it was locked, so I thought I unlocked it." The Kid scowled up at Canyon. "Then how'd you get out?"

Canyon shoved past him and admired the Black Hawk sitting outside the hangar. Fast enough but also loud. If he could jump out— not entirely the best maneuver, but it would work. Without a pilot, it didn't matter.

"This baby'll get you there. Can't promise about getting back though."

"Is the pilot around?"

Indignation crawled over the Kid's face. "Who do you think you're looking at?"

"Seriously?" Canyon patted the Kid's shoulder. "Can you get me to the facility?"

"Facility?" The Kid stretched his jaw as the warm May air tussled his dark hair. "Nah, man. You want the dude's estate. He's having a big meeting there with a bunch of dignitaries."

Staring at the stark black hull, he envisioned it. Roark would be Bruzon's trophy. Would he flaunt her before his guests? No. . .no, he couldn't afford to do that. Canyon dragged a hand over the Black Hawk's nose.

"How're you gonna get out?"

"We'll get out." He wasn't sure how, but the biggest hurdle was finding her.

The Kid must've seen the shock that rolled through Canyon because he rolled his eyes and donned a helmet. "Climb in."

In the cockpit, Canyon watched as the Kid powered up the craft. "How long have you been a pilot?"

"Long enough."

"I didn't know."

He flipped a switch, then another. "There's a lot you guys don't know about me. All you do is throw me in water, smack my head, and laugh at me."

"If you get me there, I'll never laugh again."

"Promises, promises." The Kid shrugged as the rotors began to whine, then screech right into a full roar. "Besides, I might get booted from the team after this."

With the copilot's headset on, Canyon glanced at the Kid. "Then why are you doing this?"

"Why are you?"

Roark. "I keep my promises."

"Yeah, well, me, too. I mean, it's about honor. Leaving her there? Major uncool." The bird vibrated beneath them. "I can't live with myself knowing we did that, especially to her."

Canyon clamped a hand on the Kid's shoulder. "Thank you, Marshall."

Green lights glared off the Kid's eyes—eyes that shone with appreciation of the recognition Canyon had just shown. "Don't thank me yet." A few more switches. "We have to get off this base and not get shot down. Imagine Hamer's going to hit the roof when he sees one of his birds taking off."

"Then fly fast and low."

"You got it."

Phone pressed to his ear, Max waited as it rang. Legend, Aladdin, and Cowboy clustered around him with Squirt, who sat in a chair looking piqued. Expectation hung thick and heady. A dozen rings and still no answer. The fourth time. He shook his head to the guys and started to pull it away from his face.

"Hello?"

Tensed, Max clapped the phone to his ear again. "Hello?"

"Yes?"

At the feminine voice, he shifted away from the guys and looked down at the desk. "Who is this?"

"You call a secure line and ask that?" Age and grace coated the voice—but also. . .stress.

"Authenticate," Max demanded.

"I. . .I can't. I'm. . .I'm the better half."

He hung up. Looked at the guys. "Something's wrong."

"What just happened?" Legend asked.

"It wasn't the Old Man. A woman answered. She called herself the better half."

"His wife?" Cowboy angled forward. "The Old Man's wife answered?"

"What does that mean?" Legend scowled. "What's she doing answering *that* phone?"

"If that is his wife," Aladdin said, "then she would know that phone is off-limits."

Legend's brows rose into his forehead. "Which means she—"

"Wanted to talk to me." Max dialed again.

The line rang.

"Oh, thank God." She sniffled into the phone. "When you hung up—"

"I need the Old Man."

"Who are you?"

They were playing a deadly game, but if something happened to Lambert. . . "Nightshade Alpha. I need to speak to the Old Man."

"Nightshade," she said, her voice trembling. "You know where the last mission was, correct?"

Max hesitated. They were *on* the last mission—Venezuela. "Yes, ma'am. Could you please put the Old Man on the line?"

"Where the last mission was—that's where you'll find him. That's all I know."

Confusion riddled Max's brain. "Ma'am?"

A shrieking siren pierced his eardrums. Max looked around and pointed to the window as lights swirled through the night. Aladdin checked the window, then darted out of the room just as vibrations trembled through the room, drowning out what the woman said.

"Ma'am," he shouted into the phone. "Repeat—where is the Old Man?"

"Bring him home, Nightshade." Another sob. "Please." The connection severed.

"What'd she say?"

"That the Old Man was where the last mission was?"

"What mission? *Ours?*" Legend's deep voice growled.

Max cursed. God forgive him, but he did. Hands on the desk, he clenched his eyes.

"Frogman, what's up?" Cowboy asked.

Sirens wailed through the night—something was wrong on the base. The air raid howling told Max this mission, which had gone horribly wrong since they'd crossed into Venezuelan airspace, had tanked. And now, they didn't even have their resources.

"The Old Man's gone rogue."

Aladdin burst back into the room, eyes wide. "You'd better come."

Max paused. Could anything else really go wrong?

"The Kid and Midas are under arrest."

Bruzon's Estate, Venezuela
15 May

"Get away from me, you piece of dirt!"

Taunting laughter spiraled through the humid air as Bruzon strolled across the courtyard.

Dani tugged on the wrist restraints, trying to free herself from the post. A hitching post. An old-fashioned hitching post and they'd tied her to it.

"Danielle, my pet." Bruzon's medals clanked as he laughed and sauntered toward her. "Why are you so violent, so filled with fire?" More laughter.

Behind him trailed a lithe woman who closed the ten-foot wood fence that separated them from the rest of his compound. He'd brought Dani to his home. And that terrified her. The facility was sterile, reeked of antiseptic. Here, the separation between the two seemed. . .well, she wasn't sure what, but it just felt more. . .personal here.

"I'm no pet of yours," she said in a low voice, jerking against the post. The shackle cut into her wrist but she pulled harder. Steel bit into her flesh. That paled to the way this monster bit into her soul.

"Get away from me." She whirled around, using the anchor of the post that chained her as a counterbalance and thrust a roundhouse kick at his chest.

He drew back, surprised, but then guffawed.

A guard rushed her and slammed his rifle into her face.

Her head whipped back. Momentum carried her into the dirt.

"You are a prize!" Bruzon grabbed the lithe woman behind him and pulled her in front of himself. "You see Catalina? She was once almost as wild as you, Danielle." He clutched the woman's face tight, puckering her lips and cheeks. "Now look at her. Beautiful, elegant"—his hand traced down her side and hips—"tame. Obedient." Bruzon tossed her aside, grabbed Dani by the hair.

Fire prickled at every root on her scalp as he hauled her to her feet. Swallowing the scream, she clamped a chained hand over his to stem the pain.

"You are mine, Danielle." His breath reeked of spices and liquor. "And I will break you, too. If it takes me *years*."

Holding on to his hand, she stared right into his muddy eyes—and drove her knee into his groin.

He doubled over and moaned.

She whipped back, away. The chains jerked her arms taut, forbidding escape. Again she thrashed against her bonds, frantic, desperate to get free.

To her surprise. . .he laughed. The sickening sound growing as he slowly rose to his full height. "Why are you not this wild in bed, Danielle?"

The fight drained out of her. No. That's what he wanted—to capture her mind, smother her soul. "Forget it. You can't take anything from me again." A bald-faced lie but it felt good saying it. She shook her head, backed up till her arms were outstretched.

"Navas tells me you have taken a lover."

Canyon. He knew about Canyon? How was that possible?

He snickered. "But I removed him from the equation."

A swarm of heat swirled through her torso. What did he mean, removed Canyon from the equation?

Another snicker. He raised his arms. "Now, you belong only to me."

Frantic, she snapped her chained hands backward. One broke free. Stunning her. And Bruzon. Guards poured out of the shadows. Thrust her to the ground. Dani let herself laugh. If they were already failing, if they could not keep her bound. . .she might have hope after all.

Pinned beneath several of them, she felt the shackle reattach, then another clamped onto her arm. When the men moved aside, Dani pulled herself onto her knees and slumped against the post. "Why? Why are you doing this to me?"

"You stole something from me."

The blueprints.

"And they never believed you." He chuckled. "But you still violated my trust."

"Trust?" she scoffed.

"And that must be repaid. The world must know that nobody can steal from me and get away with it." The playfulness leeched out of him. He snapped his fingers. "Please, Senator, come and explain things"—a man stepped from beneath a shade tree—"to your daughter."

Dani froze as her father stepped into the light. "Dad!"

Malice painted a wicked mural over his face.

"Dad?" Her pulse puttered to a stop as he stood there, unmoving. "Help me! Make him let me go. Tell him the U.S. will make sure he's dead."

Bruzon leaned toward her father and offered him a cigar. "What do you think, Mike? Should we help her?"

To her shock, her father accepted the cigar, lit it, then jeered. "She's just like her mother." Her father turned and stalked out of sight.

Shock pinned her to the hard earth. Just like her mother? What did that mean? "Dad!" She rushed forward, only to have her arms ripped backward. "Don't leave me!" The rain and thunder drowned her screams. "Help me, Daddy!" She stilled, the chains clinking as she lowered her hands. And in that moment she knew. . .

I'm alone.

DAY SEVEN

Secure Facility, Virginia
19:15:21

*N*ow. . .*where. . . ? Oh yes. The strike. The very word terrified our warriors. We had seen such things close by. Villages burned. Bodies burned. Ground burned.*

"No, no air strike," Bayani said again to the big Spaniard.

"Listen." He grabbed Bayani's shirt. "We can take the people up into the mountain. Get them to safety, but the strike—"

Bayani shoved the man back. "We both know they wouldn't be clear of the site in time."

"It's our only choice."

"I said no."

Bayani and the others made choice to fight. The big dark man told our warriors to run and get more weapons. Bayani, who still looked confused or upset, told the women and children to get supplies. So we hurry, hurry. We all run here and there to get ready. The children and women and I prepared to climb into the hills. While we packed up, I heard noise. Like fights. And more noise like big thunder.

Through the reeds, I saw Bayani and his outsiders searching the skies. A feeling came to my stomach that made me feel sick. As I stepped outside, I saw Bayani's face go very angry. Red angry. He shouted at his outsiders. They started running. I knew something very bad wrong. I ran to find Chesa. She and I saw Bayani coming very fast toward us. He was screaming, shouting. But we must get. . .

I cannot go on. I cannot.

"Please, Mrs. Mercado." Matt leaned over the bed and mopped the silky skin with a cool cloth. "I know it's tiring, but please finish."

She tried to swallow but gasped. Tears streaked down her face as

233

she shook her head. "No, it hurt too much." A wail ripped through her, awakening the child.

Carrie eased into the woman's personal space, speaking softly, holding her face and comforting her.

"Remember, Mrs. Mercado," Matt began, hating himself for reminding her, for pushing her. But the truth hovered on the aged lips. "For Chesa."

Carrie eased a glass of water and straw toward her.

Mrs. Mercado took a sip and slumped back. Her arthritic hand curled around the little girl's body at her side. "For Bay. . .ni. Tal. . .say."

"Yes."

"The bombs they come." She shuddered. "Everyone die. But not me. Not Chesa." Her watery brown eyes drifted to the ceiling. "Bayani try to save us, but the bomb blew him backward. Fire like a wall held me and Chesa back. The outsiders picked up Bayani and carried him to helicopter and they leave." Her chin trembled. "Chesa and I go hide from the Higanti and Muslim, scared they kill us. We wait for a long time for Bayani to come back." Sniffles overtook her as they morphed into outright sobs. "We not see him again."

"Mrs. Mercado?" Matt began slowly, hoping he wasn't pushing too far. He'd tried to allow the elderly woman to take this at her own pace, but her focus in telling the story was for her daughter, for her people.

Matt needed more specific information. His purpose was clearing Canyon Metcalfe. Finding the *truth*. "Who is Bayani, Mrs. Mercado? Can you tell us?"

"I tell you." She smoothed the dark hair of the three-year-old cuddled against her side.

Matt waited, then realized she meant she'd *already* told him. "I. . .I don't understand."

The woman blinked. "He soldier who come, who fight and teach our sons to fight."

"Yes, but—" How did he ask this without confusing her? "Do you know his Christian name?"

She shook her head. "He no tell his name. Awa give him name when they first come."

"Did this Bayani order the strike on Tres Kruces, Mrs. Mercado?" Major Hartwicke asked softly but firmly.

It might seem insensitive. But time—and apparently Mrs. Mercado's life—was short.

Silence hung in the gap, deafening and rank.

More tears. Her eyes squeezed closed. Then all the tightness in her face vanished. She went limp. Her pulse flatlined.

CHAPTER 24

Bruzon Estate, Venezuela
16 May

T his way, sir."

Olin Lambert fell into step behind the Latina who escorted him across the marble foyer. With a practiced gaze, he did a split-second recon on what lay before him. Four possibilities: to the right, a dimly lit hall that seemed to dead end into another hall. The same on the left. Directly ahead and down two steps provided the last set of options: a sweeping staircase that stretched to an upper level, guarded by marble sentries lining a hall that disappeared into darkness. Somewhere up there, light spilled from a lone source.

But it was the last path that the woman took. Down three steps onto a tiled inner terrace complete with a fountain, plants, and brightly colored tiled benches. A teasing mist coiled around him as they maneuvered around the fountain and flanked left, under the stairs. Carpet now quieted his steps.

Somewhere in the maze of lavish excess Danielle languished.

His heart thumped at the thought.

"Here you are, sir." She placed a delicate hand on the gold swirl handle and pressed down. With a click the door swung inward.

A cacophony of voices swarmed them.

"*Gracias*," Olin said as he entered the room and took in those gathered. Politicians, dignitaries, prime ministers, secretaries, but no senator seeking veep.

"General Lambert?" A man in a slick suit moved toward him. "What a surprise!"

"Minister Ochoa, forgive me. My trip was unplanned but. . ." He glanced around the room. Had he missed Senator Roark? "As I'm sure you know, our government is anxious to see these talks go well. Colombia has long argued over your borders and claimed you're encroaching. These talks will prove what we already know—you're innocent, of course."

"Indeed." Ochoa turned back to the others. "Would you—?"

"Forgive me." Lambert pressed a hand against his lower side and whispered, "I haven't had a minute's break since getting off that jet. Do you know where I can. . . ?"

Ochoa laughed. "Of course. Down the hall, directly past the fountain. You can't miss it." He started away then stopped. "Oh, and be sure not to deviate. Bruzon has a pretty rough welcome committee."

"Understood." All too well, in fact. Bruzon had things to hide, and if the society here realized that, he'd never get his agenda past them.

But Olin didn't care. He was here for one purpose—to find Danielle.

Swiftly he made his way back to the foyer. Bruzon wasn't stupid enough to stow Danielle here in the house. So the most likely place. . .not out front. The driver had come up from the south to the house. Olin had seen nothing but open fields till the high wall barricaded the house from the rest of the world.

As he drifted into the open foyer, a form moved from a shadowy alcove.

Olin pushed himself in the direction of the bathroom, hustling when a shout erupted behind him. In the bathroom, he locked the door and slumped against the wall. Panting, he prayed he didn't die of a heart attack. There was a reason the team called him Old Man—he was too old for field tactics. One reason he should've left this little venture to Nightshade.

But he couldn't risk Danielle's safety. She'd been missing a week already. He had to find her; he owed it to Jacqueline. He'd never forgive himself if he failed.

A few seconds later, he flushed the toilet. Washing his hands, he formulated his plan. With the guard out there, he'd have to play it cool. Figure a way to search the house without arousing attention or suspicion. Opening the door, he feigned surprise as a guard appeared before him. "Oh!"

"You should be in the meeting!"

"Manuel, be kind to our guests," a woman spoke from the side.

The guard flinched, then gave a curt bow and tucked himself into the shadows.

Olin met a pair of incredibly beautiful eyes, the soft yellow glow of the hall lights caressing her face. "Thank you. I didn't realize it was against the rules to relieve myself."

Her face remained stony. "*Perdón.*" She stared at him. Hard. "They are used to my husband's barked orders. We do not entertain here often enough. Come, we should return you to the meeting before you are missed."

As they walked back to the foyer, he noticed she'd slowed. Not a lot, but enough to seem to delay their course. "And how do you like my home, General?"

"It rivals the palaces of the most notable."

Her chin rose a notch, but the expression in her gaze seemed to speak disgust instead of pride. "Have you seen the pool?"

The guard, who'd remained with them, jerked forward. "*Se van a permanecer en la biblioteca.*"

"*¡Silencio!*" The woman could kill with that expression. But then her face softened. "Come, it's my favorite part of the house."

So Bruzon wanted everyone to stay in the library. Since it would be foolish for the man to have anything illegal at this home while the delegates were here, the only conclusion filling Olin's mind was that he had Danielle on the grounds. And. . .it would make sense, wouldn't it? If this woman, the lady of the house, wanted Danielle found.

Olin's pulse sped. What if this woman knew why he was here?

"There." She nodded as they navigated around a cluster of brown leather sofas and a fire pit. As they moved, reflections from the lit pool danced on the ceiling of the room and over the walls. "Is it not beautiful?"

Indeed. Olympic size. Surrounded by a lush garden of flowers and shrubs, meticulously manicured. A gazebo anchored the right corner.

"The waterfall is my favorite aspect."

Olin's attention shifted to the far left.

"Would you believe there's a hidden path behind there?"

His breath caught in his throat. Though he felt her gaze on him, he did not meet it for fear of giving himself away. Thrilling at the idea that behind there. . .a hidden path. To what? Was that where Bruzon had hidden Danielle?

Two forms emerged from the cascading waters.

A quick, quiet intake of breath. "We should return," the woman said.

Though he felt her tug at his arm, Olin could not tear his gaze away. Molars clamped, he worked to temper the fury bubbling up his spine. Bruzon strode toward the covered patio, laughing, talking. . .with none other than Senator Roark.

"Hurry!"

Olin threw a glance over his shoulder, surprised to find the woman a dozen feet away and motioning to him frantically. With one more look at the three men heading his way, he pulled away from the doors. Six large strides carried him to the woman's side.

"Catalina!"

The booming voice froze her. She gasped.

"What are you doing—?"

"Lambert!" Michael Roark stormed across the living room. "What are *you* doing here?"

Had it been Bruzon who yelled at him, the reaction might've been different. But it was Roark. His old nemesis. And the man demanded respect that was not earned.

Olin slowly turned. "Michael." He smoothed his jacket, which bore the medals of years of service and combat. "Nice to see you again." A nod to the host. "General Bruzon, thank you for the warm welcome. This young lady—"

"She is my *wife*."

Which meant her little excursion with Olin might cost the woman her life. Unless. . . "You should be proud of her, General. She found me admiring your artwork in here and insisted I return to the meeting."

The hesitation seemed to buy points with the burly leader. "If you'll excuse me."

Had the man held her hostage the way he'd done with Danielle? Were the children a product of that captivity?

Michael spun. "What are you doing here? You have no business here. This is politician's work, not war. This is my job."

"Then why aren't you doing it?" Olin would brook no argument. "I spoke with the president directly. You've filed no report since your arrival here a week ago."

"I am not his puppet. When my report is ready—"

"Your disregard for executive orders puts your loyalty in question." Olin let his gaze drift to the pool. "Among other things."

"What does that mean?"

"We are in the home of the very man suspected of kidnapping and raping Danielle." Olin rolled around to face the man and inched closer. "And you're cavorting and laughing with him, taking a tour of the grounds. Hmm. . ." He stroked his chin. "Wonder what you found behind that wall and hidden passage."

Michael grabbed Olin's jacket and yanked him forward. "I'm not afraid of you anymore, Olin. I don't answer to you, and I don't care what you think." With a slight shove, he released him, his lip curled.

"Understand, Michael," Olin said as he started away. "If I find you knew what Bruzon did to Danielle—or if I find out"—*Careful. Don't tip your hand*—"I will personally—"

"You don't have what it takes, you washed-up four-star."

Oh. If only the man knew. Olin's glare morphed into a sneer. And he walked away.

Naval Base, Cuba

Early morning air embraced Max as he hustled across the air base that had come alive with the sirens and searchlights. He jogged toward Colonel Hamer. "What's going on?"

The sirens droned.

"Your men, that's what happened." Hamer shot daggers from his eyes as he stomped toward a building. "You hear that C-130 powering up? That's your personal escort back to the States."

"Whoa, hang on a minute—"

"No, son. I'm afraid not." Hamer pushed through a door and stomped down steel-grate steps. Through another door, Max hustling to keep up. "Your men are loose cannons, and I can't risk an international incident. Now, my men here will walk you to that plane." He sneered. "Or carry you." Arms folded over a toned chest, the colonel dared them to challenge him. "Your call."

"Look," Max said. "We need to get this back under control." Man, did they ever. This was like trying to drink from a fire hydrant. Any more bad news and they'd drown.

"Oh, we're getting it under control all right." The older man's eyes twinkled as he motioned behind Max.

He spun and found Midas and the Kid sitting on low-slung cots, their hands cuffed. Clenching his fists, Max wished he could reach through the bars and strangle the two. But first, he had to stop the colonel from shipping off the whole team. "Colonel, listen, I've…I have a legitimate concern that the general has gone rogue."

Though the news hit Hamer hard, the iron colonel shook his head. "I sure hope not. But that doesn't change things." He wagged a finger at the Kid and Midas. "They were stealing government property. Do you realize what kind of hell would've broken loose if they'd made it into

Venezuelan airspace during a lockdown?"

Max pinched his lips together, livid. "Look, send them back."

"No!" Midas's shout blasted into Max.

Max glared at the man. "But let me and the others stay. As soon as you get the green light, drop us in there." He inched closer. "Lambert won't survive. He needs us."

Hamer hesitated, then looked at the cell. "No, no can do. Blame whomever you'd like. Your men in that cell. Your fists. The good general. But it's not happening. You're all on that C-130 out of here in twenty."

Max drew back. "My fists?"

"You put one of my guys in the hospital."

"He was compromised, put the lives of my team—"

"Your fists tell me you're a loose cannon. Their actions tell me you all are. This is a military installation, and we'll have the devil to pay if you cause any more trouble." He pivoted, negotiated a path around the rest of the team, and left. "Get 'em off my base, Major."

A man stepped through the door with two armed guards. He unlocked the cell and eased back the door. "This way, gentlemen. Orders are STK, so please don't make us."

Shoot to kill.

Yeah, Max would kill all right. And he'd start with Midas and the Kid.

CHAPTER 25

34,000 Feet Above the Atlantic Ocean
17 May

Numbing vibrations wormed through his legs as he stared down at the red lines cut around his wrists. The cuffs had been tight, but nothing like the feeling in his chest knowing that each minute flung them hundreds of miles farther from Roark. That she was alone there, most likely in the claws of Bruzon. What that sicko did to her the first time roared through Canyon's mind, furious that onboard this plane, bound for the States, he could do nothing to stop the man.

Like a fast-forwarding mental projector, complete with *whirrp* noises and flickering stills, his brain showed him horrible scenarios of what could be happening to Roark right now. Beaten. Raped. Beaten. Humiliated. Raped. Canyon clenched his fist tighter and tighter.

Something hit his booted foot.

Canyon ignored it, knowing the two facing rows of web seating rigged in the forward section of the cargo hold in the C-130 Hercules made it impossible not to trip and bump the others. Besides, he wouldn't look any of them in the eye for a while. Not without a fight.

Leaning forward dumped all the blood to the edema around his eyes and nose. But he didn't care. A dull pain compared to what Roark probably faced. He pinched his lips and crinkled his nose—eliciting more pain. Fist balled again, he honed in on the image of her, of kissing her.

Bruzon cut into the mental image. He laughed. Hit Roark. Shoved her to the ground...

Both fists balled, Canyon pressed them against his forehead and tried to squeeze the puke out of his mind. He'd kill Bruzon. Kill Max and the others for leaving her there.

Thud! His toe tingled from the hard hit.

Without lifting his head, he snapped his gaze to the other boot, but there were two within striking distance. He glanced up. Cowboy and Aladdin. Red halos wreathed the faces of both men, whose heads were propped on the webbing, eyes closed.

He dropped his gaze and pushed back against the seat. Unlike them, he couldn't sleep. Not with Roark missing.

Somehow. . .some way. . .he had to get back down there. Find her and get her to safety. There had to be a way.

As fat clouds and minutes slipped by, he searched for a plan. Why had God allowed this to happen to Roark? She was an angel, the most intelligent and beautiful woman he'd ever met. Everyone in his family saw that, which is why they told Canyon to steer clear. Someone like her belonged with his little brother who never screwed up, who did everything right and won everyone's heart.

Except Roark's.

"I love you, Canyon." Why hadn't he returned the words?

Because he hadn't been sure. Or maybe she was right—it was fear. Fear of failing her. Which he had.

Where was she now? What was happening?

He gripped his head. Thinking about that would drive him mad. Head in his hands, he clenched his eyes, pain pinching his nose. He worked through options, trying to find a way back. Hopping a flight wouldn't work. The military probably wouldn't let them board another aircraft for a very long time.

"Listen up," an airman shouted from the front. "Touchdown in twenty. You'll be escorted off the base. If you attempt to return, you will be arrested and charges filed."

Black fury pressed into Canyon's already foul mood. Criminals. They were treating them like common criminals. He glanced to the side and got nailed with one of the ugliest glares he'd ever seen come from Max.

Let the guy be ticked. He'd know a little of what Canyon felt, considering they'd dragged him across several bodies of water and hundreds of miles from Roark.

Augh! Fingers threaded, he squeezed hard. Several knuckles cracked.

His ears popped as they descended toward the base. Tires screeched on the landing strip at Langley AFB, and he could just imagine the blackened skid marks—so similar to those left on his heart for abandoning Roark.

Hang on, Roark. Somehow. . .somehow I'll find you.

Passport was still good. He could catch a flight down to Venezuela, rent a vehicle. Somehow get some weapons. Would any of his former GB buddies help? Too bad Navas was an enemy combatant. Canyon would have looked the guy up in a heartbeat. But if he could get down there, he'd make sure to look the guy up. . .and settle the score.

"Revenge is mine."

Canyon tensed, sensing God's warning. Yet wouldn't God use someone to carry out that judgment? *My name's first on the volunteer list.*

They disembarked and military police herded them into the back of a truck like cattle. Climbing aboard behind Cowboy, Canyon kept his head down and mouth shut. Less chance of a fight, of widening the gap that had stretched between him and the men he'd begun to think of as brothers.

He snorted.

Yeah, just like brothers. He and Range hadn't exactly been the best of friends. Competitive, argumentative, combative.

Axles groaned and creaked as the truck lumbered across the base toward the barbed-wire perimeter. Darkness huddled in ambush on the other side. Waiting for the team. Waiting for the Air Force to abandon them.

"How're we getting back to the Shack?" the Kid hollered over the engine and wind noise.

Nobody answered. Not out of rudeness but because discussing options in front of anyone outside the team wasn't the smartest plan. Most likely one of the team would call in a favor and they'd get a ride to the warehouse. Canyon? He intended to hoof it back there. Work off some of this steam through strenuous exercise.

Brakes squeaked and ground as the diesel truck chugged to a stop at the gate.

MPs hopped out, released the tailgate, then waved the team off. Once disembarked, the police trailed the team through the security checkpoint and stood there, watching.

"Start walking and don't talk." Max pointed west.

No one talked. Canyon sure wasn't going to look at anyone. They probably hated him. He hated them for leaving Roark, for not fighting back when the spec-ops team drugged him.

Halos of light marked a gas station perched on a corner leading to the base.

"I'll make a call." Legend headed toward the dingy building straddling the far corner of the parking lot.

Canyon started walking. He'd find a way home. Find a way back to Roark. Even if it killed him.

"Metcalfe." Max's voice stabbed the night, stabbed Canyon's tenuous control of his anger.

Keep walking. If he stopped, one of two things would happen: They'd talk him into listening and doing things their way. Or. . .there'd be a fight.

"Just leave him alone," the Kid's voice joined in.

"Back off, Kid," Max growled.

"No, this is—"

"Back off. I mean it. You're in hot water as it is."

"Leave him alone," Canyon said as he came around, staring at the man he now held responsible for this disaster.

"What?" Max said. "You ready to talk?"

Oh but no. He wouldn't step into that trap. He shook his head, turned, and crossed the street. Rocks and dirt crunched beneath his boots.

"What?" Max called, all too close. "You going to abandon the team again?"

Canyon hesitated. Forced himself to keep walking. He'd had covert operatives try to beat the Tres Kruces information out of him. A little taunting from a guy like Max wouldn't win.

"I saw you stewing on the plane. You're blaming us for the mission failure, for not getting Roark back safely."

Yeah, you got that right.

"But the blame rests on one man—you!"

Canyon rounded. Fury colored his vision red to find Max less than five feet behind. "What?!"

"If you hadn't been doping and hadn't gone off half-cocked—"

"Augh!" Canyon pounced. As he did, his brain registered the others sprinting across the road toward the ensuing fight. He dove into Max's gut.

Oof.

Pinning the guy, Canyon threw a hard right into his face.

Hands hauled him off the team leader. Squirt and Cowboy held his arms tight. "Stand down, Midas." Brows tight, lips flat, Cowboy stared between Max and Canyon.

Behind them, Legend jogged across the street.

Canyon wrestled free of the others, straightened his shirt with a shrug. "You don't know the first thing about loyalty, Max." He stretched his neck. "Tell me, what would *you* have done if we'd left Sydney on that island two years ago?"

The fury in Max's expression waned.

"Yeah. Exactly." Canyon pivoted and met a wall of bodies. "Abandon the team? Yeah, I'll do that in a heartbeat if the men I trust can't put their own butts on the line for a defenseless objective."

He shoved between Squirt and Aladdin into the clearing. Then he paused and looked back. "Never thought the guy with the most guts on this team would be the Kid." To Marshall he said, "Thanks, Kid. I'll never forget it."

Halfway across the open field, he heard: "You're off the team!"

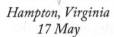

Hampton, Virginia
17 May

Max's pulse hollowed out his hearing. Had Midas heard him? He stretched his jaw as he watched the most stoic member of the team disappear into the night.

"Hey." Cowboy faced him, hand on Max's shoulder. "Let's. . .give him time."

"Time to what? Come up with another harebrained idea and get us locked up again?"

"No, time to cool down."

"I've never seen Midas like that, know what I'm saying?" Legend smoothed a hand over his bald head. "The guy is always on level ground. Even ticked off, he keeps his cool. That? That's something I never thought I'd see."

"So what? We overlook his negligence on the mission, his attempt to steal a chopper from the Air Force"—Max stuck a finger in the Kid's face—"we'll deal with that later"—then continued—"and act like it's no big deal?"

"We're all tired. A lot went wrong down there, starting with the mudslide," Cowboy said. "Let's get some rack time, then figure out where to go from here."

Were they serious? It was like nobody cared that Midas had broken nearly every protocol and rule.

"What would you have done if we'd left Sydney?"

Midas hit a nerve. Max remembered all too well the fire roaring through his body at the thought of Sydney coming under attack by Muslim radicals, watching the fireball eating up trees and huts and knowing she was down there. When Cowboy and Legend had told him he couldn't go after her, he'd wanted to kill them.

The outrage over Midas's reaction and actions dumped. Was Danielle Roark *that* important to Midas? When did that happen? *That's it.* That's what he wasn't telling them.

Headlights struck the team as a vehicle rounded a bend in the road. Legend slapped Max's shoulder. "There's our ride."

A white van pulled to the curb. A half hour later, the team strode into the Shack.

"I think we need to do something," the Kid said. "She's down there. With that piece of work Bruzon. Anyone with a brain knows that's not good."

Max snatched a towel from his locker. "Tell me, Kid, how do we get down there?"

"Lambert—"

"Missing."

"Get a flight—"

"Flights take money and passports. Hamer had ours put on hold."

The Kid shifted. Looked around at the others, who said nothing but bore the weight of the dire situation. "We can't just do nothing—again."

"I don't plan to."

Startled blue-gray eyes came to Max's. The Kid wet his lips and checked the rest of the team again. "Then we're going to do something?"

Secure Facility, Virginia
18 May

"Holy cow! Can you believe this?"

Fist against his lips, Major Matt Rubart paced outside the hospital room, his brain buzzed. When he'd gotten the anonymous tip about Corazine Mercado, he'd been pumped about finding more clues. Excited to add a new layer to this case that oozed conspiracy and thousand-watt trouble. What he hadn't expected was the nuclear blast of information she provided. In the last two days, she'd filled gaps lurking within the case file with affectionate anecdotes and mirth over the antics of Bayani and Chesa.

"Foreign nationals...training..." He dragged a hand over his mouth. "It doesn't make sense, Carrie. Why were Green Berets training Latino nationals in the Philippines? We have forces down there working *with* Filipino special forces, but not on our own like this, out in a village. It's...it doesn't make sense."

Major Carrie Hartwicke met him with a rueful smile. "I'd say someone was passing notes—and I'm talking G-notes—under the congressional table."

Matt frowned. "You realize what you're saying."

"Do you realize what I'm *not* saying?"

Eyeing her warily, Matt stowed the ideas tumbling through his head. If this was true, if the Special Forces unit stationed there had been ordered to train an enemy's enemy...the ramifications blew his mind. But then again, it also explained so much. Like why someone wanted the whole Tres Kruces fiasco swept under the Capitol Hill carpet. No senator or congressman or woman would want something like that hanging over their heads at reelection time.

But the anticipation that nearly made him giddy was that this would also prove Canyon Metcalfe wasn't guilty.

Which would score major points with Willow.

That is, if Matt could prove it. But the sweet woman had nearly died giving her story. And if it hadn't been for their location—inside a hospital—she'd have died.

"What now? She's on life support. The docs think she won't regain consciousness."

Matt rubbed his knuckles over his lips, staring at the dark gray flecks in the linoleum. "We have more than we did two weeks ago."

"True, but we don't have the proof to clear Metcalfe. And some of her story sounded elaborated."

"It sounds legit."

Major Hartwicke studied him. "Then you believe her?"

"She knows too much for it not to be true."

"Half of what she said isn't in the report."

"Exactly. She filled in the holes we've been guessing at for the last forty months."

"Yes, but thinking that and leaping off the bridge with her story is a huge risk." She reached back and freed her hair from the bun. "Listen, Matt. If we go to the Brass with this story, first of all, the press is going to be all over it."

"Nobody knows."

"You can be really naive sometimes." She glowered. "You and I both know they'll be all over it."

"Not naive. I just don't see demons behind every wall." He raked his hand through his hair and pushed to his feet. "How can *you*, in good conscience, *not* want to pursue this? An innocent man has been wrongly accused, convicted, and borne the punishment of a crime he didn't commit."

"We don't know he's innocent."

Matt considered his friend and CID partner. She'd always been challenging, negotiating troubling thoughts and theories, and it'd worked well for them, but this time. . .something felt different. "Carrie, what's with the misgivings? You're the one who was all over this like white on rice. You said we should throw ourselves in the Atlantic if we didn't try to get her back here."

After a long sigh, she slumped into a chair. "I've been thinking about it—a lot. Whoever did this to Metcalfe, whoever buried the truth—they won't want that coming out."

His mood darkened. That was it? She was cowering? "So. . .what? We sit on it? Let Canyon bear the burden of everyone thinking he massacred an entire village?"

"Matt," Carrie said with a hiss. "Nobody knows, remember? The Brass buried it. They made it go away. It made the papers once then died out. Besides, we aren't even sure who this Bayani is yet—"

"Give me a break, Hartwicke! Bayani has to be Canyon."

"I know. I just wanted to hear it from the old lady's lips."

Matt eased back. "Interesting that Canyon never reported marrying the chief's daughter."

"Well, it's frowned upon but there aren't any laws against it."

Matt nodded.

"So. . .the little girl. . ."

Roughing a hand over his face, he groaned. "Mrs. Mercado never said which of her daughters gave birth to Tala. And even in her testimony, she said Chesa never conceived."

He dropped his gaze, thinking of what Canyon had gone through. Remembering the man who'd stood before him nearly thirty months ago during his one-year review—haunted, ticked off, and adamantly silent. They'd really gotten to him. Spooked the Green Beret. "Pretty convenient, isn't it?"

Carrie's brown eyes rose to his. She cocked her head to the side. "I know that look."

"Why would they bury it? Yeah, sure, it looks bad, but if what Corazine said is true, our men were training foreign nationals. What if that wasn't on the up-and-up?"

She seemed startled and straightened. "Like?"

"Like, the enemy of my enemy is my friend."

CHAPTER 26

Bruzon's Estate, Venezuela
20 May

I am still surprised you came all the way down here, General Lambert." Humberto rested an arm around the old man's shoulder. "We are making good progress with the talks."

"Progress?" Lambert's bushy eyebrows arched. "General Bruzon, it's chaos in those meetings. Every one of them wants their piece of the pie."

Humberto guffawed. "Then they will be very disappointed when they learn we are serving cake. I will walk you out." He removed his arm and let his gaze hit the man trailing him. The man who'd warned him about Lambert's presence. The man who had returned from hunting for the incompetent team who'd returned Danielle to him.

Humberto smiled. Imbeciles. They thought they could protect her. Keep her safe—in *his* country! He'd shown them. Just as he would show this arrogant joint chief.

His fingers itched to curl around the wrinkled neck and squeeze the life right out of the general. Instead, the calm, confident expression of his right hand, Navas, kept him at peace. Humberto had played this game much longer than anyone else. And so close to victory this night, he could not afford to be impetuous.

No, he would not allow an imbecilic American to thwart his attention.

He clapped a hand over the man's shoulder as he guided him to the main courtyard, where cars sat idling. "You will return in the morning, General, for another day of talks, despite the boredom?"

Olin Lambert turned and nodded. "Of course, General Bruzon." Blue eyes twinkled under the glare of the well-lit area. "I wouldn't miss it."

Humberto held up the 1965 bottle of wine he'd plucked from the cellar stores for the general, who'd manipulated the conversation earlier with the Madame Secretary so she would ask for a tour of his home. A simple but *in*effective attempt on the part of the general to try to locate Danielle.

Did the man really think Humberto would keep her under the same roof? No wonder the Americans were losing the war.

"Thank you." Lambert accepted the wine. "I look forward to sharing this with my wife." He tucked himself into the car.

"Excellent. I hope she enjoys it." Alone. Because the old man would be dead before he ever returned to American soil.

Humberto waited as the car slid through the gates. "He wasn't on the original list?"

"I memorized every name," Navas said from behind. "He shouldn't have been here."

"Indeed," Humberto said, his eyes on the gate but his mind on the past. On a formidable foe who had been responsible for shutting down the secret training of Bruzon's militia in the Philippines. He'd inflicted a blow to the man, but he'd recovered and sailed to the top of his career ladder. But. . .that wasn't the same man, tormented with worry over a young woman. "He's lost his touch. A shame."

Humberto drew up his shoulders and let out a sigh as he turned to his man. "Know why I like you, Juan Navas? You aren't afraid to dirty your hands."

The man smirked. "A little soap and water. . ."

This time, the laugh was belly jouncing. "Lambert is resourceful. Perhaps too resourceful. He is a worthy adversary. He has the *cojones* to come out here and try to do things his way."

"Unlike some people."

He shot a side glance to Navas. He referred to the man who had been a long-time conduit to access whatever Humberto needed— Senator Michael Roark. "And his resources seem to know what they're doing. Your face is a mess."

Navas's gaze narrowed. "Do not mistake a black eye as a sign that you are in danger. I will not let them get close to you."

"Oh, that I do not doubt. No, I am not worried here. I have more security, more guns than the president himself." He smoothed his hair back. "Besides, if they get in, I will kill you myself."

"You can try."

Surprise pinned him to the ground. Humberto once again considered his man. Then laughed hard. "This—*this* is why I chose you,

Navas; you are cold-blooded. Now. . ." Humberto clapped his hands, then sloughed them together. "I think I'd like to see Danielle now. A little fun, eh?"

Smirking, Navas shook and lowered his head.

"General." The minister rushed toward them. "Come, we must confer about these border talks."

Humberto groaned. He wanted to visit the feisty American girl. He sighed. "Very well." He had time—after all, her father had delivered her himself.

"Oh, Navas?"

The man met his gaze.

"You know what to do, yes?"

"Lambert will be dead by morning."

Canyon's Condo, Virginia
21 May

Rushing, Canyon stepped into the early morning sunshine as the beeping of his security alarm echoed through the day. He locked the doors and turned.

Something shoved toward his face.

Instinct drove his fist out—but he pulled it back just seconds before it hit a woman.

"Captain Metcalfe," she said as she held a microphone. "What do you know about Tres Kruces?"

His pulse stuttered at her question, then launched through his veins as he recognized the female reporter who had made his life a living hell in the aftermath of TK.

"Back off." He ducked and hurried toward his Camaro, cursing whoever had unleashed the hounds of hell on his life again. He'd played by the rules—ones someone had apparently broken since they'd promised him it'd "all go away."

Right. Tell that to the nightmares.

"Why won't you talk to us? What are you hiding, Captain?"

Canyon slid behind the wheel, started the engine.

Tap! Tap! The reporter knocked on his window. "Is it true someone has come forward to clear your name? Or has that information proven your guilt?"

Teeth ground, he pressed a foot on the brake and revved the gas.

The reporter's eyes widened and she scurried out of the way.

Gut churning, he backed into the street and then slammed the gear into DRIVE. What on earth had set them off again? Why bother him? It was dead and buried. Like Chesa. Watching the reporter shrink in his rearview mirror gave him incredible pleasure. Still, he'd have to find out who did this. Who opened Pandora's box?

Canyon shook it off. First things first. He had to focus on the plan that had come to him in a dream. A glorious chance. But one that would really force him to put "it" on the line. As he drove, he plotted. Planned. Prepared.

A half hour later, he stood on Croatan Beach, warm sand beneath his bare feet. He leaned against his red Camaro and squinted at the sparkling waters. Just sitting here, watching the waves, the tension seemed to lessen. But there was now an edge to this view because it held a new meaning for him with Roark.

"This is a surfboard."

"Gee, really? I wouldn't have guessed."

Grief siphoned strength from his muscles. It'd been four days since the team had returned. One since he'd gone to the airport and tried to buy a flight down to Venezuela. But at the ticket counter, the agent told him his passport had been placed under a no-fly status. Ticked, he stormed out. Everything he'd tried to date had failed. And with repercussions.

Maybe that's part of the problem. When was the last time he prayed—with a yielded heart?

God. . .I need help. You know better than anyone. Help me get her back safely.

"What do you want?"

The urge to stand straight burst through Canyon, but he remained in position. Looking relaxed as his little brother stepped in front of him. "Thanks for coming."

"Well, like you said on the phone, you've never asked me for a favor in your life." Range drew closer, hands in the pockets of his jeans. "What's this about?"

Canyon tilted his head. "In the Coast Guard, there are things you see and do that you're not allowed to talk about, right?"

"Of all the—" Range scratched the side of his face. "If you needed a blinding flash of the obvious, Google it."

"Am I right?"

He threw a hand up. "Of course. We encounter things all the time that go no further than our reports."

Canyon nodded. "Then you'll appreciate it when I say that what I'm telling you could not only end my career, but could put me in jail or get me killed."

Snorting, Range shifted around, as if looking for a reason to leave. "I don't believe this. Do you still have some hero complex? You're not a Green Beret anymore."

"You're right, I'm not." Canyon looked to the waters, squinting again. "Two years ago, I was recruited into an organization. My missions range in variety, but they're all deadly and insanely sensitive."

The condescension lessened as Range eyed him and the bruises still evident on his face. "Why are you telling me this?"

Here goes nothing. Or everything.

Canyon pushed off the car and stood in front of Range. "I was on the team that took Roark back to Venezuela."

Color leeched from Range's face. "Wh–what happened?"

"Someone betrayed her. We got ambushed and captured. A team extracted me but left her behind—intentionally."

Range's expression hardened.

"You were there, at the hearing." Canyon inched closer to his brother. "You heard from her own mouth what that brute did to her."

Swallowing, Range tore his eyes from Canyon and started walking. "How do you know she was left intentionally?"

"The people who captured us knew exactly where we were, at every turn."

"A tracking device?"

Canyon's mind spun. He hadn't thought through it. But that made sense. "Look, we don't have time for questions. She's down there, in Bruzon's hands again." He tugged on Range's shoulder and brought him around. "Think about what you found when you pulled her from that yacht. Remember. . ."

His brother shoved him back, face contorted. "I don't need *you* to tell me what I saw!"

Hands up, Canyon paused. Good. Good. His little brother's anger meant he cared, meant his heart was engaged. Passion would take them far. Then Canyon's skill in the jungle would get them the rest of the way.

Range whipped back toward the lapping waters and huffed. "Why are you telling me this?"

"I need to get back down there, to find her and bring her home."

"Have your team take you."

"I can't. We've been grounded."

"Like that would stop a black-ops group."

Canyon glanced down.

"What aren't you telling me?"

"I was kicked off the team. Even if we weren't grounded, I'm on my own."

Range blinked. "Kicked you—why?"

Teeth grinding, Canyon tried to work down his frustration. "We're wasting time."

"Then tell me why they kicked you off."

With a grunt, Canyon said, "I tried to steal a chopper to go after Roark when I found out what happened. The base commander sent us packing. They blame me for the mission failure."

His brother's disapproving gaze raked over him for several long minutes. Gulls squawked and laughter drifted on the air thickened by the scent of the ocean and carried with it the laughter of families from the crowded hot spot. "What do I have to do with this?"

Finally. Progress. "You're assigned to the U.S. Virgin Islands territory, right?"

"Sector San Juan," Range corrected then frowned. "Actually, no. After Danielle left, I got promoted and offered my choice of stations. I wanted to stay closer, so I work Baltimore now."

Stay closer. . .to Roark.

Biting back a curse, Canyon spun away. *God, where are You? I screwed up and I'm trying to make it right.* "She's down there, Range. With Bruzon. He'll rape her till she's dead."

His brother's gaze darkened.

"Put aside this stuff between us. Please. Help me get her back here."

Range's lips flattened as he stared at Canyon for several long minutes. Finally, "I know the lieutenant in command over that sector. He's a friend."

Relief dumped the angst from his body.

"I'll do this—on one condition, Canyon."

Did anything matter besides getting her back? "Go on."

"If I go down there, if I put my career on the line—because that's what it's going to take to get you on that cutter—I'm going with you. When we return, you back off. Let her recover."

The old combative nature rose up. "You mean back off so you can have a go at her?"

Range held fast.

There had to be another way.

No. There wasn't. To bring back the girl he loved, he'd have to surrender everything he felt for her. "Her life is in danger and you're going to blackmail me?"

Suddenly, his brother seemed like he was twelve years old again, his expression vulnerable and innocent. "I've never felt this way about anyone."

Neither have I. And God help him if Range found out about him and Roark.

"What, do you have a ring picked out already?" Canyon tried to laugh it off, but he saw the answer in his brother's deadpan expression. Canyon grunted. "You're unbelievable."

But nothing mattered except getting her back. "Are you really going to stand there and say you won't help her if I don't agree? Is that how much you care about her?"

"You know I won't do that."

Innards coiled and poised to erupt, Canyon tamped down his frustration. It was futile to argue with Range—they'd gone in circles all their lives. "We have to put this aside and focus on getting her back. Her safety is all that matters."

"Agreed." Range stood resolute. "Just give me your word you'll stop trying to sabotage my relationship with her."

"Sabotage?!" Relationship? Was the dude kidding? *Who* did Roark kiss? *Who* did she say made her feel safe? *Who* did she make love to? He blinked.

Now who seemed like he was twelve? "This is asinine. It isn't for us to decide—it's up to her." He wanted to curse. "We might as well treat her like a dog and throw bones to see who can get her to kiss him first."

"I think you already won that contest. I saw you kiss her on the back porch."

Heart rammed into his throat, Canyon looked at his brother.

The hurt was clear and loud. "Now, agree to back off."

Canyon shoved his hands against the sides of his head. "Is that—?" Minutes were ticking off Roark's life. "Fine." Everything in him collapsed as he agreed. "Let's just get her back."

Jacobs Residence, Richmond, Virginia
22 May

"You were right."

Cell phone to his ear, Max rolled away from the warmth of his sleeping wife. Sitting on the edge of the mattress gave him a second to weave through his mental banks of information. "What'd you find?"

"He contacted his brother," Squirt said. "They agreed to go after the girl."

Max groaned and pushed to his feet. "Scramble the team. Let's stop him before he gets in trouble again."

"I think it might be too late."

Hand on a pair of jeans, Max froze. "Why?"

"They just boarded a Cessna bound for the Virgin Islands."

CHAPTER 27

USCGC Fallon, Somewhere in the Caribbean
22 May

A river of mud raced down the angry mountain straight for him. Canyon braced himself, holding Roark tightly. She turned to him, eyes wide as a tree joined the rampage. "I can't do this."

"You can," he shouted over the raging elements.

"I'm tired of fighting. It's no use. I told you what I'd do if I got caught again."

"But you're not caught. You're here, with me. You're safe."

"I'm not—look."

Canyon glanced over his shoulder. Hundreds of VFA poured out of the trees, weapons pointed at them. "We're going to get away." Something shifted in his hands. He jerked back to Roark—the line that tethered them hung limp, slapping against the churning earth.

Roark had cut it. She cut the tether! Feet perched on the edge of the river, she jumped.

"No!" Canyon jolted upright.

Thunk!

"Augh!" Holding his head, he slumped back on the thin mattress and let his breathing even out. "Just a dream," he whispered to the gray ceiling lurking less than twelve inches above. The same ceiling he'd bonked his head against.

The dream—nightmare was more like it—tormented him. She'd jumped to her death in the dream. And she'd vowed in real life to kill herself if Bruzon took her again.

"God, please. . .don't let her." Ragged, he covered his eyes with his hand. "Keep her safe. Give me a chance to redeem myself."

Tight and confined, the enclosed bunk suffocated him, right along with the thought of what Bruzon would do to Roark. Canyon slid from the bunk and dropped to the steel floor.

The cutter pitched to one side. And so did his stomach. He balanced himself as he maneuvered away from the fold-down guest berth. From the galley he grabbed some coffee and slipped up to a table in the mess. Cradling the foam cup, he stared into the steaming black pool.

Would he get her out? What if they didn't get there in time?

Please, Roark. . .hold on.

The cutter pitched again, sloshing hot coffee over his hand. Canyon shook it out and gave up. He tossed the cup in the trash and climbed the almost vertical steel steps to the upper level. Stuffing his arms through the black jacket, he skirted the pilothouse and moved to the side of the ship where he could watch the waves tumble over one another, as if fighting to be the first to devour the cutter.

Sort of like him and Range fighting over Roark. His brother had worked miracles, convincing a buddy who owed him a favor to run them down to San Juan in his small plane, where Range's longtime friend Lieutenant Browne allowed them to board the cutter, which was patrolling the coastline—coincidentally the same route that would take them toward Venezuelan waters. Which just so happened to be where Canyon would rendezvous with a Special Forces buddy who'd moved there with his wife. The guy would get Canyon and Range to Piñago, the city outside Bruzon's estate and roughly twenty klicks from Caracas. A lot of steps that meant a lot could go wrong.

What's new?

Churning waters rose and fell, crashing into the hull of the *Fallon*. Canyon gripped the rail. Salty spray misted his face. And with it, the choking sensation of hopelessness doused him. Everything had already gone wrong. What did he expect to find when he got there? Was Roark even alive still? It hit him then that Roark had been in these waters, clinging to a makeshift raft.

He shook his head, amazed once again at her incredible bravery. *No wonder I love her.*

His heart chugged.

Love? He didn't know the first thing about love. Didn't want to. Yeah, she'd declared her love for him, denied her love for his brother, and he'd taken her innocence, but love? Love. . .what was love?

"I am love."

Canyon swallowed.

"Greater love has no one than this: to lay down one's life for one's friends."

He'd give anything for her. His own life, if needed. Was that love?

260

No. He'd screwed it up. The one chance to do right and he'd failed. Roark deserved Range. *He* was a hero.

Yet. . .everything in Canyon surged and railed at the idea.

A swish startled him and jerked his attention to his right. Range stood in a USCG jacket, hands in the pockets. Feet apart, his brother seemed at home on the tumultuous waters.

"I'm impressed," Range said.

Canyon eyed him but not for long. Too many accusations. Too many fights.

"Most people would puke up their guts on a day like this." His gaze rose to the sky. "It's going to get nasty."

Small talk. Canyon wasn't in the mood. His brother had forced him to relinquish all claim to Roark to save her life. The thought infuriated him.

"Browne pulled me into the pilothouse."

Uh-oh.

"Before I got promoted, we were constantly picking illegals out of the water. They were fleeing the border wars between Colombia and Venezuela. There's been an unusual show of force, skilled force, among the VFA." Range sighed. "Anyway, with the area being in a lockdown due to border talks and an apparent attempt by some rogue group to insert into the area"—Range didn't divert his attention from the waters but Canyon felt the implication—"Browne's a bit nervous. It'd be a bad idea if one of those rogue warriors was on his boat."

Canyon smirked at the doublespeak. "No kidding. Really bad idea."

"That's what Browne said."

The smile in his brother's voice brought Canyon's gaze to him. Then to the pilothouse that had a 360-degree tinted window well that allowed the crew uninhibited views of the surrounding area.

"He also said you seem haunted. I tried to tell him it was just the telltale green hue of the broken nose someone gave you, but he didn't agree."

Canyon pushed his gaze back to the water.

"What aren't you telling me?"

Besides the fact I was doped out of my mind and made love to Roark? "I told you everything I know: Roark was taken captive and is with Bruzon again." All at the hands of a man he'd trained. What was Navas doing in the service of a dictator-seeking general like Bruzon? How had an American-trained SF guy ended up. . .

Canyon stilled. *Skilled* soldiers. As in American-trained soldiers?

Was this Tres Kruces all over again? American SF training the enemies of an enemy to change the political tide in U.S. favor? Slowly he straightened. He motioned toward his brother. The lockdown. . .the arms talks. Was there a list of who was attending that?

"Hey," Canyon said, turning the idea over in his mind. "Is there a computer I can use?"

Range hesitated but nodded. "In the mess hall."

Canyon smacked his brother's shoulder as he hustled past him, through the hatch and back down the steep stairs into the main deck. At the terminal, he searched the Web for news on the border talks. As he scanned a CougarNews article, his breath hitched into this throat as one name stood out: Senator Michael Roark, D. MD.

Canyon whipped his phone from the holster, and his fingers froze over the keypad. It'd been years since he'd entered this number. The man could have him strung up. Or he could help. Canyon hit SEND and pressed the phone to his ear.

"Authenticate."

Leaning his shoulders toward the wall, he burrowed into the alcove, seeking anonymity aboard the cutter. "Mike Indigo Delta Alpha Sierra Golf Bravo One Sierra Foxtrot."

"You no longer exist," the voice intoned.

His jaw tightened. "It makes disappearing easier."

"I like talking to ghosts." A chuckle seeped through the line. "Pleasure or business?"

"Remember Tango Kilo?"

"Of course."

"I think we have a repeat."

"A lot of innocent people could die if that's true. But how is that my problem?"

Canyon glanced around, relieved to see the empty mess hall. "There is a common name between the two: Senator Michael Roark."

"Mm, tasty. Quite a favorite among the GOP at the moment." The operative was hedging, indirectly saying this would be very touchy and cause an uproar.

"The VFA have suddenly swung the tide in their favor. Just like Tango Kilo. Someone gave me bad intel four years ago, nearly a hundred people died, and I took the blame while two men walked away guilt free. I won't stand idly by while they nuke some poor country."

"Sorry, Midas. No-go. It's too touchy. I need to protect myself and my assets."

"No. Listen—"

Click.

Furious, Canyon banged the phone back into its cradle. "Am I cursed?" he shouted.

CHAPTER 28

34,000 Feet over Miranda, Venezuela
22 May

Icy, sharp fingers of the cold atmosphere ripped at his body as the ground rushed up at him. Overhead, the cargo plane that Canyon had jumped from continued on its journey to the capital city with nobody the wiser to its secret deployment. He pulled the cords and the chute deployed. Within minutes, he landed hard and rolled.

He launched to his feet, wincing at the oh-so-familiar streak of pain in his spine. Chopping the cords and nylon chute he balled it up, his feet dragging against the strong winds. White flapped against the expanse of green. *Might as well be a freakin' strobe light!*

Panic hammered through his pulse, spiking his adrenaline. "Range, help me with the chute!" He battled the chute, which seemed to have a mind of its own. A few more pulls and he should have it collapsed.

A low moan nearby snatched his attention. Canyon glanced over his shoulder as he wrapped up the lifesaving nylon. Range lay facing away. Another moan.

Chute secured, he jogged over to his brother. "Hey, we need to get into—"

Face contorted, Range rolled to the side, hands extended toward his leg—the leg that sat an unnatural angle.

Crap! Canyon dropped the chute and slumped to a knee. "Lie still." Carefully he probed the injury.

Range howled. "I can't. . .move my foot." He cursed and sputtered. "It's killing me."

Smooth move, Ex-Lax. Go rogue. Steal into enemy territory with a brother *not* trained in spec ops. Jump out of a cargo plane. And land, blowing Range's leg.

Canyon bit against the condemnation as he tried to stabilize the leg, his brother hurling curses like he'd never heard. "I promise I won't tell Mom I heard that."

Behind them came trouble—a vehicle. Joints squeaked and popped, the engine roaring as it apparently went airborne. When he checked his six, he spotted a Jeep bounding over the hills and disappearing in the small valleys as it raced closer.

"We have to move." Canyon stuffed the chute into Range's arms. "Hold that."

Range stiffened. "Is this going to hurt?"

"Like hell." Canyon hooked him into a fireman's carry and rushed to the trees. After a few diversionary turns and switchbacks, he settled his brother against a tree.

"You need. . .to get. . .away," Range ground out, his face a puddle of tears and sweat. He jerked to the side and retched, waving Canyon off. "Go. I shouldn't have come. It was my jealousy, me wanting to control—"

"Shut up." Canyon bent and dug into his pack, his hearing on the twang of a dirt bike, his medical training on the twisted leg. He withdrew an inflatable splint and slipped it over the leg.

Arching from the tree, Range grunted. Then slumped back with a long hiss.

Canyon gave him two tablets. "Ibuprofen." He stowed his gear.

"I'm telling you, man—" His complexion paled.

A scent sailed on the wind.

Canyon clamped a hand over Range's mouth. Shoulders hunched and head cocked to the side gave him the perfect angle to hear the goings-on behind them.

Grease. Oil. Gasoline.

Amazing how those smells reeked in the luxury of a freshly washed jungle.

Silent terror screeched through Range's face, tugging at Canyon's heart. Hitting the tree, he cursed himself. Everything he'd done in the last few weeks had screwed up. By trekking out on his own, he'd really screwed things up. Almost got his brother killed jumping. What else could go wrong?

Snap!

Canyon whirled, coming straight up, drawing his weapon around in front of him.

A fist flew at him. Canyon ducked—but not soon enough. Knuckles grazed his cheek. His head whipped back, the foliage blurring. Though he staggered, Canyon seized his attacker.

"Navas!" The man who'd betrayed him. Tortured him. Using those memories fueled his fight, drove his fist at the guy.

"You never learned when to give up," Navas growled and dove at Canyon's gut.

Air seemed to levitate him, nudging him back several feet. Pain darted through his neck and back. A weight pressed in against his throat as Navas pinned him against a tree.

Canyon swung a left.

The hit connected. Drove Navas back.

Another right. Left.

Range. The thought pulled Canyon's attention to his brother. Propped against the trunk, head lobbed to one side, he looked unconscious. Dead.

No.

Thud! Something hit him in the head. Sent him spinning. He flipped over. Navas dropped on top of him.

Forearm constricting Canyon's windpipe, Navas stuffed a gun in under his chin. "Who's teaching who now? Really, Midas—dropping in on a white chute? Why not bring a spotlight?"

Whom. Canyon wished he could say it, rattle the guy. But the bulging pressure from the O_2 deprivation left him weak. Hands cupped against the guy's arm, he pushed.

"Know how long I've wanted to do this?" Dark wild eyes glowed down on him.

Suffocating beneath the man's grip, Canyon thrashed, trying to kick him in the back. Trying to get his legs wrapped around him.

His temples pounded. A strange wheeze escaped his lungs.

Navas jammed the muzzle harder against the soft spot. "Thought you were smarter. You had your chance to escape but you come back. Brought your general. That sweet thing worth your life?"

Canyon rammed his fist into the guy's kidneys.

A strained groan accompanied a shift in Navas's weight. Enough for Canyon to haul in a breath.

Red-faced and neck bulging, Navas returned. Angrier. He rammed his forearm against Canyon's throat, once again cutting off his oxygen. "You piece—you know what I'm going to do to you and that white-haired fool?" Small talk left behind, he rammed a fist into Canyon's head.

Agony and confusion wrapped Canyon in a tight vise. General?

White haired? Slowly, he pushed onto all fours, waiting, expecting the guy to pummel him again. As he stood, Canyon knew he was being baited.

"My team will get to Isla de Margarita and silence that warmonger once and for all." He drove a fist into Canyon's face.

Blood spurted. Slid back down Canyon's nasal passage. . .air cut off by the blood gushing out. No air.

Navas sneered. "See? You taught me well, Midas. There won't be any more mistakes this time. My men will take care of the old man while Bruzon takes his pleasure with Danielle." The way he dragged out her name, a sick, haunting whisper. . .

Canyon clawed at Navas's face. Slapped. Hit. Punched. Wanted to curse him. But even his ears hurt now. The edges of his vision ghosted as Canyon struggled to breathe.

He chuckled. "Finders, keepers, pal."

I'll kill you. Gray seeped across his eyes, closing out the world. Closing out life. *God. . .help me!*

In the void devouring him—a shout.

Navas glanced back.

With all that Canyon had left in him, he threw a hard right into the guy's face. Navas flipped backward. . .off Canyon. Crumpled in a pile on the floor of the jungle.

Hauling in deep, painful breaths, Canyon rolled onto his stomach. Fingers dug into the warm earth as he sucked in more and more air, his lungs screaming against the deprivation.

Crawling onto all fours, he coughed and looked at Navas. On his belly, the traitor lay unmoving, blood spilling into the earth from his nose.

Nose for a nose, pal. Canyon dragged himself to the man's prone figure. Wrapped his fingers around the weapon, lifted it, and slammed it into Navas's temple.

Struggling to his feet, he wavered. Stilled. Then forced a foot forward as he tucked the weapon at the small of his back. He stumbled to his brother. "Range." Raw fire lit down his throat as his hand dropped heavily on his brother's shoulder. "Range."

No response.

Hoisting Range up again proved harder, but Canyon did it. He trudged back in the direction from which Navas had come, searching for the Jeep he'd seen the guy driving. It only took a few minutes to get Range into the passenger seat. Revving the engine, Canyon's mind thumbed through the information Navas had revealed. He drove away from the trees.

Frogman. Nightshade. The team. Roark. He'd failed them. Though he tried to make it right, he failed again. Failed better.

Bruzon had Roark. Sickening and infuriating but no surprise.

The big surprise was the general Navas mentioned. White haired. Old man. The only white-haired general interested in Roark would be Lambert. But that didn't make any sense. Coming down here would blow the team's cover. It would put Lambert in trouble.

Correction. It put Lambert in the direct line of fire of the VFA.

If Canyon went after Roark, the rebels would kill Lambert. But if he went after Lambert, Roark could disappear forever.

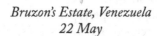

Bruzon's Estate, Venezuela
22 May

"Out!"

Handcuffed, drenched from the rain, and frantic, Dani writhed against the guard as he shouted at the servant by the fireplace. He wrangled Dani into the room. Metal pinched her wrists as she struggled to free herself, growling.

"I said get out," he shouted.

"Sí, *señor.*" The servant girl gathered rags and a bucket from around the fireplace, placed a huge arrangement of lilies and other flowers in front of the sparkling glass doors, then hurried out.

Dani kicked and jerked as he hauled her across the marble floor. "No, let go!" She stuffed her foot against the bedpost, wedging herself between him and the bed.

The man's curse skidded along her neck as he gripped her around the waist and hoisted her off the floor.

She arched her back and whipped her head against his.

Another curse.

Then he released her. She tripped and pitched forward, colliding with the nightstand. *Think!* Pain darted through her temple. Spots danced across her vision. Her arm jerked to the side.

Shink.

When she looked up, horror gripped her by the throat as he yanked her other hand. He'd anchored her to the post at the head of the bed. On her feet, she jerked against her binding. "No, don't do this."

He pivoted and left her alone.

No, no, no. She couldn't do this again. Bent almost in half, stretched over the nightstand and her hands chained to the headboard, Dani refused to touch that bed.

Where was God? Where was Canyon?

It's a miracle Bruzon hasn't touched me yet.

Perhaps, but he would. Soon. He was on his way up here right now.

She thrashed, trying to break the post that held the chains. No good. Her gaze skimmed the room, searching for a way out, a way to get free.

Her gaze hit something shiny. . .a letter opener sat on the small desk. Iron resolution carved a painful path down her soul.

And there was only one way to get that opener. Digging her nails into the knots of the laces on her boots, Dani stole a peek over her shoulder, checking to verify the door hadn't opened. She freed the knot, loosened the laces, pried off the boot, then tugged off the sweat-and-rain-soaked sock.

Black dirt dug in and around her toenails. She swung her torso around. Holding the tall post, she stretched her leg toward the secretary desk. Canyon might've left—*abandoned* her—but her promise to him still stood.

Her toes scraped the edge of the desk. Straining, she stretched closer. Cold metal brushed her toe. Yes! A little closer. If she let go of the post, using her fingertips for balance against the headboard, she'd reach it. She propped herself and once again arched toward the desk with her toes. Her sister had always taunted Dani about her big feet, about the second toe that was bigger than the others, but it had its usefulness.

Her toes curled around the letter opener. She wiggled until it sat wedged between those two odd-sized digits and squeezed them together. Slowly she brought her leg back around and gripped the opener. Alexandra could laugh all she wanted. This letter opener was her way to freedom. In her hand, it took on new meaning.

Thumb caressing the tiny teeth of the blade, she knew for this to end, she'd have to end it. *I told you I'd kill myself first.* Anything rather than be taken by the brute again.

Forehead resting on her arm, Dani fought the onslaught of tears. Why? Why had Canyon not rescued her in the facility? She'd told him she loved him, accepted him, believed him. . .

Fifteen thousand tears could not erase the raw ache pulsing through her body. Defeat threatened her standard kick-butt refusal to become a victim. Shackled for thirty hours to a post while the sun blazed, the rain pelted, and the night fell left her courage wilted like the flowers in front of the fireplace.

She turned the blade so it faced her. But then. . .the problem presented itself. She'd have to get on the bed since her hands wouldn't stretch this far to reach her torso. Even if she moved the nightstand, there's still be too much of a gap.

On the bed.

With a furtive glance to the door, she placed a foot on the bed. Checked the door again, her heart thundering like the storm outside. It had rained nearly the whole stupid little adventure. Just like her life—all rain and no sunshine.

My own personal sun.

A sob racked her, remembering the gift Canyon had given her. Hand closed around the choker, she felt the cold necklace her father had given her there as well. Two pieces of her heart. . .shattered.

Dani climbed onto the bed. Feet situated firmly gave her the resistance necessary. Was suicide a sin? While she may not wish to inhabit this world any longer, she didn't want to burn in hell for eternity.

"It is the most atrocious of acts, mija."

"Why, Mama?"

"Because it breaks God's heart to see His child throw away the most precious gift He has given—life!"

Cheeks wet, Dani wavered, her knees feeling worse than putty as she swayed, both internally and physically. She pressed her temple to the headboard and sniffled. Tears dripped off her cheeks and fell onto the white pillow, each drop a piece of her identity. With a soft moan she wished for a miracle but knew she was on her own.

Just like before. Like always.

"You are not alone."

The whisper caressed her wounded soul.

"Oh, God. . ." she whispered, her throat burning. She wanted to believe that. Oh, did she ever! With every desperate, frantic beat of her of heart. Maybe God was watching out for her. Dare she hope?

But if she didn't do this, she'd be his prisoner. How could God expect her to stay where nobody loved her? Where she wasn't wanted? Where a man abused her so violently? Surely He didn't expect her to again be captive and subject to the whims of a sadist.

Voices from the hall sneaked under the threshold.

Now or never.

Resolve surfaced. Dani sucked in a shuddering breath and regained her position. "Forgive me, Father." She wiped the tears and drew in a shuddering breath.

With a resounding click, the latch released.

CHAPTER 29

Isla de Margarita Hotel
22 May

Y ou're a dead man."

Muzzle pressed against the back of his head, Olin Lambert strained to see in the mirror over the hotel desk where he sat. He'd expected an attempt on his life; Bruzon had been too friendly earlier. And that Navas...

Still, the feel of the steel barrel and the animosity pouring off the man's words tensed Olin's muscles as his mind darted to his wife. Charlotte. Poor Charlotte. She had believed in him when he wasn't worth believing in.

Could he negotiate this man down? "Whatever you were promised..." Not that he'd pay or bargain his way out of this, but he had to try something. The team. Danielle. Again he tried to peer into the mirror, but the darkness and all-black attire concealed the intruder's identity.

"I ought to kill you for what you did."

The man had a point to make. Wanted to spill his guts about it. Olin hesitated, his gaze skidding over the pocked and marred wood desk. "Tell me what I did."

"You blew our cover, Old Man."

Two phrases—*our cover* and *Old Man*—brought Olin's eyes up. Like an old movie, blue eyes glistened in the darkness. "Midas?"

Midas grabbed the back of his collar and jerked Olin up. "You compromised the team."

"No!" He shook his head. "No such thing has happened."

"They're coming for you. Navas told me." Midas nudged the weapon. "If they take you, they'll torture your old butt till they drag out our identities."

272

"Never—*never* will I betray the team."

Weight rammed into the back of his neck. "Too late! Navas knew about you, knew where you were staying."

"Because I told them. They think I'm on a diplomatic mission." The man was stoked on fury. Olin had to bring him down, distract him.

Midas flipped him around, pressed his arm against Olin's chest, and aimed the gun at his temple. "Stop trying to turn this on me. You're screwing everything up. They know you're after Roark and they know about the team."

"No." Olin breathed in deeply as Midas drew the weapon back. "That's where you're wrong. They know nothing of the team. Danielle— that can't be helped."

"Why's that?"

"Because. . .because her father is here. He's behind this snafu."

Midas lowered his weapon. "Go on."

"Michael Roark is obsessed with one thing: furthering his career. Bruzon, I believe has been helping him. Before I flew down, Sokoleski broke—he gave proof that he's been working with Bruzon to supply missiles and fissile material. And his right-hand man—"

"Navas."

Olin paused, frowned. "How do you know about Navas?"

"I trained him. Guess he's gone rogue."

"You can say that again. Bruzon doesn't eat, sleep, or drink without consulting Navas."

"It still doesn't add up."

"Sure it does. Bruzon—"

"Why are you here, Old Man?" Midas's breath skidded along Olin's cheek.

"I told you. I came down here because of Danielle, because of a promise I made to her mother." Olin pressed his palms against the armoire, not wanting to frustrate Wolfsbane more. "When I found out the team had been locked down, I played my diplomatic card to find her."

Midas flung him around. Torment wreaked havoc in those blue eyes. But amid that torment lurked a raging beast. Gun in hand, Midas shifted and shook his head. "No. That doesn't add up. You wouldn't even put your tail on the line for us." Seemingly bolstered by his own realization, Midas straightened and pointed the weapon at Olin again. "Bruzon knew we were coming." His stormy eyes bounced to Olin's. "Tell me it wasn't you. Did you turn on us?"

"Of course not!"

"Bull!" Canyon lunged forward. "Nightshade is black ops. We don't exist in your paper-clean world. You could walk away, wipe your hands, and nobody would be the wiser." Like a schoolyard bully, Midas was on him, clenching his shirt in a fist. "Somebody betrayed Roark and ratted us out. Betrayed the team, exposed our locations. I'm going to make sure they eat a bullet. If it wasn't you— Why. Are You. Here?" He shoved him.

Olin stumbled backward. "I told you. I promised her mother"—he gulped air as the back of the couch clipped his knees, dropping him onto the thin cushions—"I'd protect her."

For a moment the man seemed ready to yield, but then with a slow shake of his head, he lifted his Glock and aimed it at Olin. "Nice try, Old Man," he snarled. "We're out of time."

In the trigger well, Canyon's finger eased back.

"She's. . .she's my daughter."

No way. Canyon stood mute as he eyed the man he'd long admired and respected. White hair glistened under the warm glow of a side wall sconce light as the general composed himself. The light caught his wedding band.

The Old Man scooted to the edge of the couch, elbows on his knees, hands fisted. "Bet you didn't see that one coming." Despite the humor in his voice, there was none in his eyes. Regret. Sorrow. Ache.

"You realize what you're saying?"

Defiance gleamed in the blue eyes set in a weathered face lined with the imprints of time and experience. "I know perfectly what I'm saying— and what one stupid mistake cost me over the course of my life."

He could relate to that. Weapon down, Canyon slumped against the desk, numb. "I don't understand. Roark. . ." The Old Man's daughter? He tried to push his mind past that, to consider the consequences, but every thought rebounded. "How?"

"It doesn't matter."

"Yeah," Canyon muttered, his brain reengaging. "Yeah, it does matter."

"Why?"

"Because if you were unfaithful to your wife," Canyon said, "that calls into question your character and your loyalty to the team, to me— even Roark."

Whoa. Saying her name made a lot of things make sense. The

biggest of which was why the general had come down here. To save Roark—his daughter.

The Old Man's head lowered, and he let out a long sigh. "My character *was* in question—twenty-seven years ago. I met a young diplomatic aide married to a freshman senator."

He ran a hand over his face and groaned as he stood and paced. "I violated my oath of marriage and my oath as an officer. My infidelity affected me deeply. I tried at first to compensate for that sin, but God made it clear I had to leave it on the altar of forgiveness, move on." He looked at Canyon pointedly, and Canyon couldn't help but wonder if his sin with Roark was written on his face.

"I have never broken those vows since. Though God and my wife forgave me, it took years for that rift to repair in our relationship. It nearly ruined my marriage—imagine, putting a decades-old marriage back together."

Canyon could relate. He'd slept with Roark, and now he felt as if the world had upended. Every effort to find her and get her back had tanked. Majorly.

"Jacqueline was pregnant—with my child."

Canyon lowered himself into the chair the Old Man had occupied earlier. "Does Roark know?"

"No. Jacqueline made me promise I would never tell Danielle or insert myself into her life." He attempted a smile that did not even flick past his lips. "To Danielle, I am merely her mother's old friend and her godfather."

Whoa. Roark. Her mother. The senator— "Her father."

The general hesitated.

"Does he know that he's not her father?"

"Yes. And he vowed to hate me with his dying breath." General Lambert drew in a deep breath. "And I believe it is Michael Roark who betrayed the team—and Danielle." The embers of hatred were kindled with that phrase.

"What proof do you have?" Canyon had already put together some keys to this puzzle, but he wanted to hear the Old Man's thoughts. Wanted to know if they had enough to take the slimeball down.

"I've been in this business far too long to imagine things and leap without looking." Lambert's face seemed enlivened. "I saw him with Bruzon walking from a hidden garden, where I believe they have Danielle locked up."

Something wild churned in Canyon's gut. He'd already voiced

unfathomable ideas in the last few minutes. Why not a few more? "You think. . .you think he knows about Roark being there?"

"I know he knows."

No way. What father would do that to his own child? Canyon scrounged for a plausible explanation. "Maybe he's trying to get information, so he can get her back." Did he sound as idiotic as that question felt?

Lambert sniffed. "Michael Roark no more wants Danielle back than he wants you or me to return to the States alive."

Fire lit through his already foul mood. "Why do you think *he* ratted out the team?"

"Besides me and Nightshade, nobody else knew when she was leaving." The Old Man stood and walked to the bedroom door. "Who— is that your brother?"

"Yeah. He helped me get back here, busted up his leg dropping in."

"I'm sure he wants to get Danielle back as much as I do."

Hot and roiling, a cauldron of jealousy ignited in Canyon's gut. But he didn't want to talk about it. Canyon straightened. "I have a theory about the senator."

Though a smile seemed to tiptoe off the general's lips, he nodded. "I'm all ears."

"You know about Tres Kruces."

Something strange flickered in the general's eyes but he said nothing.

Canyon unloaded his heavy burden, the one that involved Tres Kruces and the village massacre. The training of the foreigner soldiers— illegally. And the name connected to them all. "I think Senator Roark has been in bed with Bruzon for a very long time."

"I believe your theory is correct. The only problem is that Michael can wave off his relationship with the socialist general by saying he's building alliances on behalf of the U.S. Unless we have proof of his wrongdoing—"

"I saw him at Tres Kruces. I think. He was younger, came in with the last group. Checked things, then left."

"That's not proof. And according to them, you gave the coordinates. You're responsible—"

"I gave coordinates for a location a klick away!" He stuffed his hand through his hair. At least, he thought he had. One minute he heard the screaming bomb. Then he heard screaming people—shrieking in pain.

"Not one of your men could provide evidence of your innocence.

Opening that mess up without the necessary proof will annihilate your chances of ever clearing your name."

Canyon jabbed his hand over his head. "*This* is why I hate politics." Forget it. This wasn't about Canyon anyway. He had one goal. "We need to get Roark."

"Midas," the Old Man said. "We need the team."

"Then we're out of luck. Max removed me from the team after I punched him."

Lambert chuckled. "You really are keyed up. Very unlike you." His light expression grew somber. "Midas, what's your interest here? There's a lot more passion behind this mission than just wanting to complete it."

Yielding information could be trouble, especially if Range overheard. Canyon wouldn't make that mistake. "I promised Roark I would not go back without her." He gritted his teeth. "I'm going to keep that promise."

"Didn't they have you in custody—for drug addiction?"

It surprised him that the Old Man knew, but he shouldn't have been—nothing was sacred in the military. "I'm fine. And if you aren't willing to do what's necessary to get your own daughter back—"

"Don't try that, young man." The general strode toward him, purpose defining each step. "I may be old and I may be slower than I used to be, but I am still a four-star general who is aware of human avoidance techniques." His nostrils flared. "You attempted to steal government property, involved a young man who is naive enough to follow you, then you illegally penetrated this country, brought your brother—all without considering the ramifications. Danielle is no safer because of your abandonment of the team—"

Canyon reared back and slammed a fist toward the general. It sailed past him and barreled through the wall. "*Don't* lecture me," he growled. "They *drugged* me and eliminated any chance I had to get her back. And that boy you called naive? He's more a man than anyone else on the team. The Kid's the only one who saw what happened and called it wrong. He's the only one who stepped up to the plate to try to help get her back. And if you knew my brother, you'd know there was no stopping him from coming on this mission. Besides, nobody else would help."

"Did you give them the chance?"

"They had their chance when they walked out of that facility on their own two feet without Roark." The growl worked its way through his lungs. "I would not have left there without her."

"Maybe staying there jeopardized too many lives."

"She was terrified and trusted me."

"You? Or the team?"

Canyon faltered.

"She trusted you or the team?"

"Me—the team. I will die to make sure she comes home safely."

"Why? Why is there so much passion behind your determination to bring her home?"

"Because it's my character, my reputation on the line."

The general laughed and shook his head. "Nice try. But this time, *I'm* not buying it." Lambert got in his face again. "Are you in love with my daughter, Midas? Is that what this is about?"

Creak.

Navas's men! Canyon snapped his gaze to the door and yanked his weapon to the ready.

Crack! The door flew inward.

Behind the chair Lambert had occupied seconds earlier, Canyon hunkered and aimed. His pulse jammed as a half dozen men poured into the room. He fired at the first guy.

Point man's shoulder whipped back. He stumbled backward into two more black-as-night men who rushed in with AK-47s. Wood splintered off the doorframe leading to the bedroom. Plaster peppered Canyon's face. No way would he survive this without a few extra holes.

Lord God, have mercy on me!

Considering his options, he flinched as a familiar sound registered.

Thump. Thump. Clink. . .clink. . . The canister rolled through the door and out into the living area.

Flash-bang!

Canyon curled in on himself, nose in the corner, and shielded his face and ears.

Boom!

An invisible force shoved into his back. Slammed his head into the wall. Everything went white. His hearing hollowed out.

CHAPTER 30

Miranda, Venezuela
22 May

He whipped out his hand and clamped onto the arm clutching his. Blinking, Canyon groaned against the light stabbing the back of his eyes.

"Easy." A familiar voice warbled strangely against his burst eardrums. "On your feet."

Seconds felt like hours as his brain formed a coherent thought. Again, he strained to see past the cloud and blurry images. "Frogman?" Two more shapes loomed behind the former Navy SEAL. "What the...?"

"Easy there, golden boy." Aladdin's voice, hollow and warbled, held humor as a touch rested on his shoulder.

"Aladdin? What're you guys doing here?" In fact, shouldn't he be stateside?

"Saving your sorry butt."

"I can see that—well, no, I can't." Shame covered him as thick as the mist that made everything more like a creepy M. Night Shyamalan movie. "The flash-bang."

"It'll pass, just give it a minute."

"Trouble en route," Frogman's voice cut through the blanket of confusion. "Move out!"

"Here." Aladdin hooked Canyon's arm over his shoulder and led him away...from what, Canyon wasn't sure. His mind had drowned and become disoriented in the concussive effect of the flash-bang.

Cool air swirled and rushed over his face and body, soothing and yet taunting. Out of safety. Out in the open. "We taking a trip on your flying carpet?"

"You really need some new jokes."

Still half-blind, Canyon chuckled as he placed his trust in the hands of his friend.

"Place your trust in Me."

How. . .how exactly does one do that, God? He'd been trained as a highly skilled, lethal soldier. Trained to take control before things took control of him. But maybe that's why things had screwed up so bad.

The iron fire escape rattled beneath his feet as he made his way down. "Wait." His brain caught up with him. "My brother."

"Don't worry about it."

His vision cleared with each step, his mind chugging along. In a truck, they rode for a while, jostled and tossed about like ice in a blender. As they dumped onto a slick patch of grass, Canyon let his gaze shift to the sky. Hazy stars swirled against a black canvas. They spun, whirling.

"Just relax. We're about ten klicks south of the city," Max said, his voice calm and firm as he guided Canyon to the ground. "Sorry about the flash-bang."

"A bit of a surprise."

"It was necessary. Cowboy had his sights on too many tangos."

Fingers pressed to his forehead—there was too much pain to pinch the bridge of his broken nose—Canyon hauled his brain, body, and emotions into focus. A strange chirruping bled into his awareness as he stared up at a starless night. Almost sounded like cicadas.

"Wait." His heart rapid-fired as he looked at the men standing around. "My brother."

"Your what?" A dark mass next to Max coalesced into the form of Legend.

Man, he couldn't wait for his vision to clear completely. "My brother." Canyon glanced around, blinking, straining through the darkness. "He was in the bed."

"Oh." Legend's face fell. "Man, we didn't know. We grabbed you and got out of there. No time to deliberate over the extra bodies."

Canyon shoved to his feet. The world whipped around and tilted. He swung out a hand for balance.

"Easy," Cowboy said with a chuckle as he braced him. "Ignore Legend. Your brother's asleep over there."

Amid Legend's laugh, Canyon saw the bedrolled form on the ground. Slowly Canyon's pulse evened out as his gaze connected with the general. *"Are you in love with my daughter?"*

Canyon glared at Legend, who laughed behind a fisted hand. "You're a riot."

"Sorry." Legend laughed again and nudged a laugh-tear from his eyes. "That was too rich to pass up."

Cradling his head did little to alleviate the squall pummeling him. "What're you guys doing here anyway?"

"We heard about this guy chasing some woman down to South America, trying to get himself killed," Squirt said. "All half-cocked with no backup."

"Not sure what he thinks he's doing, going all Lone Ranger on us." The Kid seemed to have grown up a few years as he sat next to Legend. "But it's what we do. Of course, I'm missing a hot date chasing this rogue."

"I had jury duty." Squirt smirked.

"My nephew begged me to take him sailing."

The taunting, meant to ease the tension, only increased Canyon's. "I'm doing what's right. I never asked you to come down here."

Max frowned at him. "We work as a team, plan as a team, move as a team. Always."

Elbows propped on his knees, Canyon peered from beneath his brows at the team leader. "A bit hard to do when you're removed from said team."

Hard, unmoving eyes held his. "You looking to get kicked off again?"

"That mean I'm back on the team?"

"Give the boy a cookie!" Legend clapped.

Silence held the moment captive. They seemed ready to move beyond what happened the last time they were in this godforsaken jungle. But Canyon wasn't sure he was ready to let it go. He felt betrayed. Abandoned. Discarded.

Just like my dad.

Grinding his molars, he steepled his fingers and looked down at his boots. Knots rolled through his shoulders and neck as he chose his words carefully. Threatening was pointless. Slowly he lifted his head and met the gaze of each team member. "You need to know where I stand. I'd never leave one of you behind, and I won't leave her. I'm here till this is done, till Roark's home."

With a long sigh, Legend leaned forward and rested his forearms on his thighs. "Look, it needs to be said: None of us likes what happened. The mission got screwed up. Were we wrong to let them drag you out of there and leave her?" Legend shrugged. "God knows. Did we have a choice?" Another shrug. "To me, no. I didn't want to be pumped full of a drug and kill my ability to function. What they did to you was wrong. And they paid—thanks to Frogman's fists."

Surprise tugged Canyon back as he looked to Frogman, whose steady gaze met him. Max had fought someone? On his behalf?

"But right now, priority one is getting your girl back." Legend's deep voice rattled through the hot night air. "A divided team cannot succeed. Let's put this behind us."

It was the right thing to do no matter how the dice rolled.

A rustling to the side drew his attention. Sitting up, Range watched him—intently. So much so that Canyon heard an unspoken question of disbelief. His mind scissored back to Legend's words. In fact, two words. *Your girl.*

And it hit him that his brother's expression wasn't intense curiosity, but rather fierce determination. A reminder that Canyon had promised to back off once they got home.

The guys would never understand the bargain he'd made out of desperation to find Roark. The thought of getting her back and letting her go flipped through his gut and struck a nerve that radiated from his brain to his heart. Maybe Roark would hold out for him.

Frogman's eyes held a mischievous gleam. "You ready to do this?"

With a quiet resolution carving itself through Canyon's soul, he nodded. He straightened and nodded again, this time stronger. "Let's hit it."

The first hint of a smile crossed Max's face. "First—Old Man, we've got a rendezvous set up to get you out of here. No way we can do this with you down here."

"I'm here. Let me be of use."

"Sorry," Max said. "You've blown our covers and any further exposure puts us another inch in the grave."

Canyon watched the Old Man and saw an intense grief and vulnerability skate into the weathered features. Lambert held a secret almost as bad as Canyon's. And the team didn't know. Though he didn't like the decision Frogman handed down, it was clear Lambert wouldn't argue.

"Take Midas's brother," Max said.

"No!" Range's voice shot through the discussion.

Max glared.

Legend pointed at Range and shook his head. "Sorry, little man, you don't have a say. You're a liability."

Range hobbled over to Canyon, grunting as he held his splinted leg. "You can't let them do this. I got you down here."

Canyon clenched his jaw tight.

"Tell them." Range leaned in closer. "You promised—"

"No." White-hot fire spread down Canyon's spine. "What I promised is that I'd back off once she was back home. What I didn't promise was that you'd be on every aspect of the mission." He jerked his brother aside as he looked at the others. "They're right, Range. You'd slow us down, and you'd be a flaming beacon to the VFA."

Range opened his mouth.

"Trust me."

Conflicted eyes held his, but what Canyon saw almost leveled him.

"Why'd he call her 'your girl'?"

Canyon swallowed, glancing to Legend, now engrossed in talks with Frogman and Squirt.

Range gripped Canyon's vest. "So help me if you steal her—"

He slapped his brother's hand free. "Back off, Range. I swore I'd give you room, and I'll do it, even if it kills me." Breathing was a chore. He glared at his little brother. "Not for you. For Roark. So she has a chance to say who she wants."

His brother's mouth gaped. "You. . .you really want her, don't you?"

"What I want is Roark safe on American soil. Safe out of Bruzon's hands."

"You *are* in love with her." Range shook his head. "Did you turn her away from me, Canyon?"

"What matters right now is that if you want her alive to make a decision, then you have to get out of the way." His chest rose and fell hard as the words left his lips.

Torment colored Range's face, even in the darkness. Finally through gritted teeth he said, "I don't like this."

Foul and rank, his displeasure pushed Canyon away from his brother. "Don't have to." He sure didn't like the idea of rescuing Roark to bring her home to his brother. "This is the way it works."

"It's not your brother who I love, okay?"

Canyon fisted a hand. Would she still feel that way once he got her back? Or would she hate him eternally for deserting her? For—as she wrongly suggested—using her and leaving her?

And maybe it'd seal the coffin on their relationship.

"Gather up," Max said. "Here's the plan. . ."

Bruzon's Estate, Venezuela
22 May

The door opened. Dani's heart catapulted into her throat, choking. Hours ago, she'd thought Bruzon had finally come but it'd been a guard, retrieving something from an adjoining room. He sneered at her and left. She'd worked the letter opener on the cuffs, but to no avail.

Now that voices approached once more, she gripped the opener tighter—it slipped. She frowned and panicked as the handle grew slick in her sweaty palm. Couldn't get a solid grasp. The door opened. She glanced back. At the hulk of a man towering over the threshold.

A scowl spread over Bruzon's ruddy face. "What are you doing?" In that split second his gaze bounced from her face to her hands. His eyes bulged. "No!"

Dani whipped back to her task. She clasped both hands around the letter opener—

It slipped again. Plopped onto the pillow. . .slid out of view.

"No," she gasped and dropped to her knees on the mattress to catch it.

A weight slammed into her back. Her cheek hit the headboard. *Thud!* Pain darted across her face and neck.

"You little witch!" Bruzon's hand dug into her hair and yanked her head backward.

She wailed as he flopped her onto the bed, her hands twisted and anchored overhead. Her joints stretched and pulled.

"What? You think killing yourself will help?" Foul and reeking of liquor, his breath blew into her face. "It just makes you all the more fun."

Dani recoiled. She kicked up her legs. Connected with the back of his head.

He cursed. But the action only seemed to invigorate him. A sick grin seeped into his jowls. Without mercy, he ripped her shirt off. Like tearing toilet paper, the arms detached from the rest of the material due to her restraints.

Feeling the chilled air-conditioned air against her bare abdomen speared her with panic. Dani screamed and thrashed. The shackles sliced into her soft flesh, searing, but the pain didn't come within a mile of what radiated through her soul. If she didn't stop him. . . "No!" Hair tangled over her wet face. Heat rushed through her face, embarrassment bleeding into fury. "Get off me!"

He clapped a hand over her mouth.

Dani chomped into his palm.

He cursed again. Smacked her hard. The sting stirred her conviction to escape. Gone was the girl who believed compliance would make the bad things stop. Gone was the girl who clung to vain hope that someone would save her. In many ways, she found the girl she'd lost a year ago. Nobody saved her. Not back then. Not today—especially not Canyon.

Besides, she would not be Bruzon's pleasure toy. She wouldn't endure him. Ever. Again. "You stinking, fat pig." She arched her back and rocked her body to dislodge his weight.

Bruzon pawed at her, determined to have his way. He dropped on her, a breathy, sickening laugh seeping though his chest.

Dani railed at the feeling of his hands running over her body. Over her will. Then, like from an old dragon, came a fiery, smothering sensation. She remembered it—fear drowning her in panic. If she didn't somehow regain control of herself, of her fear, she'd pass out. Just as she had dozens of times before as his captive. If she yielded to this, he could do whatever he wanted. Dani again thrust her legs into his head.

Muttering more curses, Bruzon wrestled, grunting as he battled to secure her beneath his bulk. He hauled back and punched her.

Stars and spots leapt into her vision. But in the second that his hands went to the button on her jeans she jolted out of it. Yet her strength was failing, the energy pouring out of her limbs. "No! Please, no. . ." She was losing. . . A whimper.

Bruzon leered at her.

Distant shouts stilled the beast atop her.

"General! General!" a man's yell carried through the house, probably from the stairs—feet pounded against the wood. . .closer. . closer still.

Bruzon launched off the bed and rushed across the room. He flung open the door. "¿Qué pasó?"

"Sir." Navas appeared and looked into the room at her.

Cold shame turned Dani away, cowering in her bra and jeans. Her gaze hit something near the fireplace. What? A bottle. It wasn't just a bottle, but a *vinegar* bottle. Maybe the servant had been cleaning the smoke stains from the fireplace.

Hope surged within her tactical brain, and she knew in that second she might have a way out of here. Her gaze jumped to the metal keyhole on the marble mantel. Gas powered. *Yes!*

Now to find peroxide. Dani curled into the headboard. Ignoring the blood streaking down her arm, she pushed wet, matted hair from her face to see into the bathroom.

"What is it?" Bruzon demanded.

"It's Catalina. She's. . .gone. Escaped."

His wife? Bruzon's wife *escaped*? What did that mean? Why would someone's wife escape? Okay, stupid question. Anyone with a brain would want to flee that man. Regardless, Dani needed peroxide. Combined with the vinegar, the peroxide provided the hope of creating an ignition source—of course, she'd need fire, which she hoped to get from the gas fireplace and a spark. . .

"Find her!" Bruzon stuffed his hands into his shirt as he stepped out of the room and pulled the door closed.

This was her chance. Heart racing, Dani shoved from the bed and wedged herself between the nightstand and wall. Staring at the sleeves that hung at her elbows, she wanted to crumble. Blend into the corner and fall apart. Instead, she saw the cord to the lamp. A spark. Could she get a spark from that somehow?

A scraping jerked her around.

In the wall near the secretary desk, a panel slid back. Catalina emerged, face radiant. "It's time." She rushed to the bed and produced a key.

Confusion entombed Dani as the woman joined her. "Time for what?"

"To get out of here. You must come with me. I can help you."

"If he catches us—"

"He will not." Catalina raised her chin and her brown eyes shone. "I've made sure." She nodded to Dani's cuffed hands and slipped the key into the catch.

The shackles fell away and with it the suffocation of captivity.

Catalina looked at Dani's bare torso. *"Un momento."* She rushed to another room.

Seizing the chance, Dani darted into the bathroom and searched the cabinets. If Catalina could get them out of here, then she could fry Bruzon, make sure he never hurt another girl or person again. Frustration coaxed out a foul mood as she considered the contents of the cabinet. He had everything in there—bandages, rubbing alcohol. . .

Aha! She snatched the bottle and hurried into the bedroom. She flung back the glass doors and reached into the firebox. With a yank on the coiled cable running from the wall, she angled the cord toward the front. She dumped the flowers on the floor then carefully poured the vinegar and hydrogen peroxide in.

A gasp from behind. "What are you doing?"

"What I do best—blowing this place up." Once the flame started, it'd ignite the peracetic acid she'd made by combining the two chemicals. That would then rupture the gas line. It'd go global within minutes if not seconds.

"Why would you do this?"

Dani jerked and looked at Catalina. "To make sure he never hurts anyone again."

A rush of air preceded the girl dropping to her side. "You cannot!"

"How can you say that? Look what's he done to you, to me."

She clapped a hand on Dani's forearm. "Please." Wide eyes begged her. "I have family here. Friends. They are *good* people. And killing him does not make the pain in here"—she tapped Dani's chest—"go away."

Maybe. But a sense of vindication and justice would be gained. Still. . .she didn't want to be a killer, and as much as she didn't want to admit it, Catalina was right—the pain wouldn't go away. Might dim it a bit, but she'd have to live with the murder of every servant in this house for the rest of her life.

Defeated, Dani gave a slow nod.

"Hurry! Before he returns." Catalina stood and held out a blue button-down. "Here. Put it on as we go." With a prod, she nudged Dani into the passage.

Chilled and damp, darkness enveloped her.

CHAPTER 31

Bruzon's Estate
22 May

Crack!

Lightning snaked through the sky and turned night to day for three long seconds. At least, for Max and the others who stood exposed and illuminated for those three seconds. Holding his position by a small shed, he leaned against it and squinted against the bright flash. Ahead five meters, Midas scrambled for cover behind a transformer box.

Within seconds, darkness snapped across the compound.

M4 cradled in his arms, Max hustled through the trees. Shadows skittered to his three o'clock and gave him peace of mind knowing the others were on target.

Screaming sirens pierced the night.

The alarms shoved him against a tree. At his six, Aladdin gave a firm nod. *All good.* Peering around the bark, Max scanned the estate, assessing potential hazards and routes. The lights on the pool could reveal one of his men. Gazebo and patio furniture could provide concealment.

Floodlights flicked on. Shouts erupted. Concealed in the shadows on the courtyard's perimeter he looked across the chlorinated water and checked both sides of the house as thunder growled through the heavy clouds. VFA soldiers poured out of every door and crevice. They darted north—the front of the house.

They know we're here. Max's heart raced. Hold up. No. All the firepower was headed away from Nightshade, not toward them. *What's going on?*

Use it. They had the perfect distraction.

He keyed his mic. "Cowboy, you got thermals?" With Cowboy and Legend hidden in the hills, they had their sixes covered.

"Roger."

"What do you see?"

The void of night held them hostage as they waited for Cowboy's assessment. "I'm blind. Walls must be dense concrete or thick metal."

Via hand signals, Max sent Canyon, Squirt, and the Kid ahead, praying the HUMINT provided by Lambert was solid, that beyond the back wall of the house sat another structure, one that most likely held the girl. They moved quickly, the swish of their tactical pants barely noticeable with the chaos tumbling out of the mansion.

Using the bound-and-cover tactic of clearing, the guys moved swiftly as Max held his position outside, monitoring the direction from which they'd come. As a trio of "clear" came through the coms, Max knew he'd been right. Somehow, Lambert had gotten bad information.

Minutes delivered the Kid, Squirt, and Canyon back to the point of entry. Their plan had contained the contingency that the girl wouldn't be here. Next step: the main house. That meant the most danger, too.

With a split-second assessment, he picked his next source of cover—a dozen feet northeast of his present location. He darted into a cluster of trees.

Thwap! Thwap!

Bark leapt at him, biting his cheek. He ducked and dived at the tree. "Taking fire!"

"What is happening?"

"The demons of hell have been unleashed." Humberto stormed through his home and rubbed at his temple where a headache roared to life. What was that god-awful smell?

Behind him, the telltale scritch of Michael Roark's expensive shoes sounded. "I thought we were safe here. You said—"

"It seems someone is trying to interrupt my schedule."

"What schedule is that?"

Bruzon snickered at the edge of the foyer, his hand on the brass knob leading to the pool patio. "Come, Michael. You are a naive fool but you're not that stupid. The nukes."

The man's face paled. "What nukes?" He shuffled forward. "You said it was a ruse."

"And you said you'd get me the money I needed."

"I did get you that mon—" He clamped his mouth shut. "No! What're you planning to do?" He shook his hands in front of himself, eyes wild. "Never mind. I don't want to know."

"Why?" Bruzon let his laugh echo off the marble floors. "Are you afraid of what you've helped bring about? Tsk-tsk." He laughed again at the way the puffed-up American had fed right into his hands. "Michael, I will be sure to thank you before I launch. And for the pleasure of your daughter."

The man's face reddened. "You can't do this to me!"

"But I already did." Bruzon looked to Navas, who'd paced them and waited quietly, as he had for so many years. He gave a somber nod and turned as the man withdrew a Smith & Wesson revolver.

"No!" The senator lunged toward Humberto.

Even as Navas caught him, wrangled him into a stranglehold, Humberto could not help but admire the stealth and skill of his man.

With a nod toward the french doors, Navas said, "Toss him to the American dogs. They can finish him."

An idea. A good one. Except. . . "No, they are more likely to drag his sorry carcass back to America and put him on trial." He sneered at the man. "And this one will squeal like a stuck pig." He lifted his chin. "Finish him."

As Humberto stepped into the frenzy of the attack, the loud bang of the revolver followed him. He smiled. It'd been too easy. The Americans were just too easy.

As Canyon rushed for cover, two lithe women crouch-ran along a hedgerow. Hidden from the gunmen—and if he judged the angle right, the rest of the team—the women made swift progress. Shadows, the cacophony of battle, and the lightning stabbing the tortured sky made it difficult to see the women. But. . . He squinted. They both had long, dark hair. A grunt ricocheted across his hope of finding Roark. Dark hair. Brown eyes. Like 98 percent of women in this country.

But then it hit him where the women were headed. Toward the hidden complex the Old Man told them about. Which was also the same direction away from the estate and away from the city. Why would they head that way?

One of the women tripped and went down. The other skidded to a stop and rushed back—her face clear. And beautiful.

"Roark!" Her name leapt from his lips before he could stop it. He jerked back into the shadows, eyeing the building, the shooters, hoping he hadn't drawn their attention and fire.

To his nine, dark shadows coalesced into men. Bruzon and Navas— that no-good *traitor!*—running straight for the women.

He darted a look to Roark, who tried to help the other woman from the ground. Had she seen the men? Couldn't have. She wasn't moving fast enough. What if Bruzon caught her again? Or Navas? Canyon's breath lodged in his throat.

Shouts. He snapped his attention back to the house, to the men. Bruzon hollered, but the din engulfing the grounds swallowed his words. Navas lifted a weapon and aimed it at her. Adrenaline raced through Canyon's limbs as he watched the scene unfold. If Roark didn't wake up, she'd get shot. Killed.

Panic flung his heart out into the open—and apparently, his body went with it.

But it was too late. Bruzon raced up on Roark. Slipped an arm around her throat and hauled her backward, away from the second woman. Screams pierced the night.

Canyon snapped his weapon to the ready. "Bruzon!" Aligning his sights on Navas, he waited for the guy to swing toward him.

Bruzon came around, Roark caught in a choke hold as a gun swung toward Canyon. "Let me leave or I'll kill her."

"Let her go!" Canyon locked his gaze on the man. If Canyon fired, though, he could hit Roark.

"No. She is why you're here. She is why the general came, yes?" Bruzon's face beaded with sweat. "We both leave and she lives."

"Not happening!" Frogman's voice came from two meters to Canyon's left. "Let her go. We will take you down."

"You won't because you want her to live."

"You're dead, Bruzon." Frogman inched forward, his M4 trained on the psychotic man.

Canyon's hands grew slick watching Roark, her frantic—but controlled—fear as the man negotiated the space between the team and the house.

When Bruzon shifted and started back toward the patio, Canyon fired a warning shot over the man's head. "Stop!"

A spark flew—and flared blue. *What caused that?*

"We have a sniper ready to put a bullet in your skull, Bruzon."

"You won't kill me. Your dirty secrets will be exploited."

Where's Navas? Where'd he go? Canyon tried to use his peripheral vision to locate the traitor, but the guy had bled into the darkness.

"Frogman," Cowboy's quiet, formal voice cut into the chaos. "Line of sight is obstructed."

Read: Shooting Bruzon could nail Roark.

Frogman edged closer.

291

Bruzon swung toward him. "Stop or I'll kill her." He glanced over his shoulder. "Navas!"

"It ends tonight," Canyon shouted.

"Navas!"

The general had lost his back.

Canyon rolled onward another two feet.

"Come closer and I will kill her." A wicked gleam lit through the man's face.

Canyon fired.

A bright flash winked at him—east side of the house. Navas! He'd fired.

White light blasted through Canyon's senses.

Boom!

A fiery inferno devoured his vision. Blinded him. Air sucked out like a hypervacuum. Then rolled back. Plowed him backward. Lifted him into the air. Flung him around and slammed him into the earth.

"Augh!" As he pulled himself off the ground, Canyon rapidly assessed his aches. Nothing broken. A few bruises come morning, but he was okay. Staggering to his feet, he realized day had turned into morning.

No, not morning.

He peered toward the house—and jerked away at the intensity.

Fire roared into the sky. Wood sizzled and crackled.

A ball of fire vaulted into the air, licking the branches. It danced through the black of night. Smoke snaked out in angry tendrils, reaching for him. Choking him. An explosion. The spot where Roark had stood sizzled and popped beneath the fury of the fire.

"No!"

No, she couldn't be gone. She couldn't. . .

"Roark!" He rushed forward. His leg buckled but he stumbled toward the flames. Numb. Angry. "*Rooooaarrrk!*"

CHAPTER 32

Debris littered the yard as fire streaked through the heavens. Heat so intense his weapon warmed in his hand, the flames roared and danced.

Hands on his head, Canyon dropped to his knees. Nothing but rubble, smoke, and ash remained where Roark had stood two seconds earlier. "No!" The half groan-half scream radiated through his chest. The release proved painful. There was no relief here.

"God, no. . ." Holding his head, he felt the wetness sliding down his face. Didn't care. She was gone. Dead. No way she could survive that blast. *This is my fault.* She wouldn't even have been here if he'd put this whole mission in God's hands. Not in his own. Not trusted in himself when his trust should've been in God.

If he'd been alert. If he'd. . .prayed.

Canyon stumbled past the guilt. "Roark!" He trembled, pushed forward, reaching for the fire. On his feet, he tripped but straightened. "Roark, where are you?"

Hands gripped him and yanked him back.

"Let me go! She's there," he growled. "She's got to be."

"It's no good," Squirt said, shoulder pressed against Canyon's stomach as he held him back. "It's no good. You can't do anything. She's gone."

Agony matched the explosion. *"Noooo!"* Canyon rammed a fist into the man's neck. Squirt went sideways and fell away, enabling Canyon to step over him. "Find her. She's got to be here." *Had* to be. "God, help me! Help her!"

"I am a refuge and help, an ever-present help in times of trouble."

At the words, heat radiated through Canyon, reassuring. "Show me—Roark!"

"Midas!"

The shout to his three yanked him around. More than two yards off, Aladdin knelt beside a chunk of roof and timber that lay on the ground.

His man called, "I...I don't think she's breathing."

Beneath the pile, Roark's head and shoulders peeked out.

Canyon sprinted over the yard, wiggling out of his pack as he did. He threw himself to his knees, skidding over the grass to her side.

Squirt and Aladdin hoisted the large piece of the roof aside.

A support beam lay across Roark's chest. Canyon's gut twisted and churned at her neck cocked at an angle. Unconscious and dust—lots of dust—covering her face, she lay silent and still. As he shifted closer, he tensed at the dirt and drywall that coated her beautiful face. Coated her nose and open mouth. As if she'd been gasping for air and inhaling the gritty stuff.

Unable to discern a breath, he wondered if she was breathing. Panic rolled through his chest, lodging itself against his own agony. He wiped off her mouth and...stilled. Blue. Canyon jammed two fingers against her carotid artery. Head tucked, he focused on locating her pulse. Ignoring the men trying to move the beam off her. From the fire and screams.

C'mon, c'mon...where are you?

His breath backed into his throat at the almost imperceptible thump. Thready. She was dying. He'd have to straighten her neck to open her air passage. But if she had a neck injury, he could permanently paralyze her.

Better than dead.

Canyon placed his hands on the sides of her face, reached beneath her head—where the slickness of blood dribbled against his fingers— and gently straightened her neck and head.

A moan wheezed through her chest. Her eyes fluttered.

"Roark." Breathing in the ash-laden air made it difficult, but watching her collapse on him like this made it impossible. "Roark, can you hear me?"

Her head shifted—and he held it firm. "Don't move. Are you hurting?"

Words slurred and faint, Roark mumbled something.

"I can't hear you. What hurts, Roark?" He looked up as Frogman and the Kid raced toward him. "Medevac!"

"En route." Frogman dropped to his knees. "What can I do?"

"SAM Splint." Holding her neck still, Canyon nodded to the pack.

Frogman dug through the supplies and found the gray-and-black splint material. He shifted to Roark's head. "Roark, don't move." As Canyon held her head in place, Frogman carefully wrapped the aluminum-padded material around her neck.

Squirt bent toward them, hands on the end of the beam. "Will it hurt her more?"

"Move it," Frogman said.

Once her neck was set, Canyon used a portable suction to clear the blood and saliva from her mouth and throat. He swept a penlight over her pupils, listened to her lungs, then gently palpated her abdomen. "Roark," he said as he lifted her hand. "Squeeze my hand."

Relief swirled at the squeeze—faint but present. He repeated the same on the other side. After taking her respiration counts, he checked her blood pressure. Noticed her drifting.

He checked her pulse. He pressed his finger under her jaw, letting the din around them drown out. He pressed firmer. Where...where was it? His gaze slid into her chest. Agonal breathing.

"We need to bag her."

It wasn't supposed to happen this way. He was the one who screwed up. He should be lying on his back, struggling to breathe. Not Roark.

"Roark. Stay with me, baby."

Unintelligible, slurred words seeped from her mouth. She coughed. Her face knotted in pain. "...neck...can't..." She breathed, long and painful. Then, nothing.

"IV." Canyon nodded to Frogman who plucked the large-bore needle and tubing from the pack as Canyon slid a j-hook into her mouth to keep her teeth apart.

"Not supposed to happen this way," he muttered as he intubated her. "C'mon, Roark. Don't do this to me." He worked quickly under the light of the blaze consuming the house as he slid another large-bore IV into her arm and let it run wide open. Noting the blisters over her flesh, he cringed and prayed those weren't what he thought—second-possibly third-degree burns.

Another cough.

"Tell me what's hurting. You're still wearing the necklace I gave you?" He needed something—anything—to keep her this side of eternity. But it felt like he was fighting a losing battle. When he checked her pulse this time, his own heart stuttered.

"We're losing her." Everything in him slid off the cliff of despair. "Roark!"

The *thwump-twump-thwump* of a chopper droned past the quieting flames.

"Roark, breathe!" He manually pumped air into her lungs. To Frogman,

"Compressions!" Frogman leapt in and together they keep her alive.

Wind whipped his clothes and face, torrential, stirring up the smoke and fanning the fire.

"C'mon, Roark. Breathe, baby! Don't do this to me."

Hands pawed at him.

He resisted, concentrating on saving her life.

"Midas, move!" Frogman shouted over the scream of the chopper.

A man in digitized camo squatted next to Roark with an immobilization board. He bobbed his head for Midas to clear out. "We've got her."

Beside him, a gloved hand slid over his, taking over.

Reluctant to stand aside, Canyon eased out of the way. Within seconds, the two medics had Roark on the board, strapped down. The lead medic keyed his mic. "Base, we're coming in with a female, mid-twenties, possible spinal injury, no pulse."

Undisclosed Location in Virginia
22 May

"Did you talk to Lambert?"

Matt Rubart stood at the door, watching through the small square window as the little girl played with one of the agency's psychologists. "Hasn't returned my calls."

Hartwicke frowned. "It's been almost a week."

Matt nodded, admiring the resilient child with a beautiful smile. "Look at her. She's oblivious to what's happening."

"Yeah, what's that?"

Unfazed by Hartwicke's antagonism, Matt answered. "Her world has been torn apart and turned upside down, her grandmother is dying two doors down, she's about to become a ward of the state, has no family or siblings. . ." Matt let out a deep sigh. "If we can't get this done—"

"No." She shoved a finger in his face. "You're the one always telling me not to go there. We focus. Get the truth. Flip the case."

"Truth?" He pried himself off the doorjamb. "Carrie, the woman is dying! She's so sick she can't give us any more. Our chances of clearing—"

"Shut up."

"No, I'm not going to—"

She whacked his gut. "Shut. Up." The bit-out words surprised him, then she nodded over his shoulder. "Hi, Willow."

Dichotomous feelings erupted in Matt as he turned: Dread that his case could be exposed. Thrill that the most beautiful and intelligent woman he'd ever met stood just outside the elevator doors. He harnessed his wayward thoughts. "What're you doing here?"

Willow Metcalfe sauntered down the hall, suspicion dancing over her stunning features. "Hello to you, too." She shot an appraising look to Hartwicke. "Carrie."

Hartwicke pinned Matt with a glare. "Ten minutes."

He shifted nervously, praying Willow hadn't heard him and that the psychologist wouldn't come out anytime soon. The last thing they needed was for Willow to see the little girl. It was a long shot, but he had to find out if she'd overheard them. "I thought we were meeting for dinner."

Willow's pink lips wavered into a smile. "Uh-huh."

"What?"

Her gaze darted around as the smile fell.

Bent, he looked into her eyes. "Willow, what's wrong?"

She huffed. "Our date was last week." Hurt played a mean serenade in her blue eyes. "I haven't heard from you in ten days," she whispered.

"That's not true." His pulsed skidded around her pained words. "I called you—"

Lips tight, she stuffed something between them. A baggie.

Only then did he see the toothbrush wrapped within. "You brought it." Relief rushed through him. "Great. Thanks."

She hid the windows to her soul as he tried to take the toothbrush. But she wouldn't release the baggie. Slowly, her eyes came to his. "What have you found?"

Defeat hung a choke collar around his progress. "You know I can't discuss my cases."

More hurt. No, worse—disappointment. "It's about my brother and you can't tell me?"

"I can't even tell your brother."

Something flickered through her irises. "Then, no toothbrush."

"Willow, please—don't. I can get it with a subpoena." Fail. What'd he'd meant as a joke flatlined as soon as it left the tip of his tongue.

Her eyes widened. She stuffed the brush at him, spun around, and stalked off.

Way to wreck it, Rubart! "Willow, I was teasing."

The clicking of her heels quickened over the slick floors. Matt had to jog to catch up with her. "Willow." Gently, he caught her arm and pulled her around.

Tears streaked down her face.

Surprise forced him to retreat a step. Then regret had him taking her into his arms. "I'm sorry. It was a joke—a bad one." Hand cupping her face, he thumbed away the tears. "I didn't mean to hurt you."

"Well, you've done a brilliant job."

Schink. Click. Thud.

They both glanced to the side as Dr. Calla and Tala emerged. He must've tensed or something because Willow noticed. Her gaze bounced to his. She went rigid. Her eyes wide. He heard the quick intake of breath as her mouth dropped open. Her gaze went to the toothbrush.

In the seconds it took for her to blink and look back to the girl, a woman and a man with a shoulder-mounted camera stepped out of the fire escape well. Reporters. Unbelievable! How did they know?

"Hey!" He pointed to them. "Out!"

Light burst from the camera as the guy honed in on Matt and subsequently Willow. The woman, dressed in a silk blouse, fitted blazer, and shorts, spoke. "Major Rubart, there are reports— Connor, there!" She pointed to Dr. Calla.

Matt leapt between the camera and the hall where Calla and Tala vanished into a room. "Leave now or I'll have you arrested." He motioned Willow toward him. She came willingly, her blank expression evident that she was still in shock over the thoughts taking shape in her quick mind.

Undaunted, the reporter pointed the fat mic toward Willow. "What is your name?"

"Wil—"

"No! Enough. Out of here or I'll have you arrested."

"Is that a threat?"

"It's a promise."

And in that split second, Willow gasped and met his gaze. "Paternity test."

CHAPTER 33

Naval Base Hospital, Cuba
23 May

He'd seen that look before, but Canyon was not in the mood to placate Max Jacobs. Not this time. Not with Roark's life hanging in the balance. So he paced. Up the hall that reeked of antiseptic cleaners, bandages, and—God, forgive him—death. Past the thrumming vending machines. Past the rest of the team, crashed on the floor of the family waiting area.

It's my fault.

If he'd had his head in the game, if he'd not been weak and stupid, she never would've ended up back in Bruzon's hands. Nearly three weeks in his hands!

Down the hall. Past the snores sailing from the team. Past the vending machines. Back to the two plastic chairs sitting beside the doors. The chairs that the nurses, smiling and flirting with him and Max, had delivered.

"It's killing me."

"Good."

Canyon turned, not realizing he'd spoken his thoughts out loud. "Good?"

Max pushed upright, then slumped against the orange chair. "Ready to talk?"

Pivoting, Canyon trekked back up the hall. Vending machines. Family waiting area.

Down the hall.

Thwap!

He stopped and looked up—his heart speedballing into his throat. Dressed head to toe in green scrubs, the man removed a face mask. Was that one of the doctors?

"Are you gentlemen waiting on word about the young woman?"

Canyon rushed forward, thumbing the weapon holstered at his leg. "How is she?"

"Are you the medic who came in with her?"

Though he nodded, Canyon cringed at the look in the doc's eyes. "Yes, sir."

"Dr. Calvert." Wizened eyes considered him as he offered a hand, which Canyon shook. "Good work out there in the field. You probably saved her life."

Dare he hope? Canyon leaned forward. "Then. . .then she's okay?"

"Have a seat," he said as he propped himself against the wall across from the chairs. " 'Okay' is relative." Dr. Calvert slid the paper cap off his head and stifled a yawn. "She's stabilized, breathing on her own. We'll get her back to the States. There, they'll run some tests."

Canyon scooted to the edge of his seat. "What kind of tests?"

"There are some abnormalities we can't account for, like her blood pressure keeps dropping. Then there's the injury to her neck." Dr. Calvert pressed the back of his hand over his mouth as he yawned. "Sorry. Anyway, there's too much swelling right now to know what sort of damage she received. We've sedated her for the flight back, but there, they'll do an X-ray and an MRI to determine if she has a spinal injury, cracked vertebrae, or whatever."

As a nurse emerged from the operating room, Dr. Calvert pushed off the wall. He accepted a chart from her, read something, then scribbled on the paper.

"They're prepping her for transport now," the nurse said.

"Thank you." Calvert looked to Canyon. "I'll need your combat-casualty card before you leave."

The report on what he'd done to save Roark's life. "Of course." He nodded toward the room. "She's going now?"

"An order faxed in seconds ago for her to be shipped stateside *stat*." Calvert glanced at the paper. "Signed off by a General Lambert."

Canyon nodded toward the doors. "Can I see her?"

"Give us about ten minutes."

Canyon hung his head. Raked both hands over his short crop. Relief and exhaustion pulled at him. She would make it. She'd fought her way through the surgery and come out alive.

From the family waiting room, Legend rounded the corner, rubbing his face as he lumbered toward them. "We're outta here in fifteen." He held up a phone.

Orders from Lambert, no doubt.

"That leaves you five minutes." Max slapped a hand on his shoulder. "Make 'em count."

When they allowed him into the room eight minutes later, Canyon had the jitters. He'd seen a lot of trauma in combat. But he'd never seen the woman he loved lying on a table.

Loved? His heart rapid-fired as he moved around the table. Covered in thermal blankets, chocolate brown hair spilled around her round face in a halo, Roark looked peaceful. As if she were sleeping. A cannula taped to her face provided oxygen as she remained unconscious. Beeping and blips pervaded the sterility, plucking his nerves.

Alongside the gurney, he stared down at the most amazing woman he'd ever known. "Hey. . ." Canyon swept a hand along her face. "Glad you decided not to chicken out."

A tightness began in his chest and constricted as he stood there.

"Excuse me." The feminine voice drew him around. He found three medical personnel behind him. "We need to move her, but Dr. Calvert said you were the medic."

Canyon nodded.

She handed him the chart. "We're running behind. Would you mind filling in the information from the combat-casualty card?"

"Sure." Canyon took the file as the two men unlocked the wheels of the gurney and wheeled Roark from the room.

Canyon pulled the paper he'd filled out during the two-hour wait in the hall and recorded the information on the sheet. Penning his name and SSN would tag him to the mission. That was a no-go. He'd have to skip it.

As he stood there, his gaze tracked over the charts. The hastily scribbled drugs. The reports from the hospital labs. Everything normal. But somehow, reading the information and results gave him a strange peace. Helped him cope. Helped him see the tangible results of his efforts in the field.

He flipped another page.

Air trapped in his lungs. Cold washed over him as his gaze stumbled over the words.

What the. . .?

He read it again.

So he *had* been too late.

Canyon swallowed hard. Slapped the file closed. Threw it on the table. And stalked out of the room.

CHAPTER 34

Undisclosed Location in Virginia
1 June

Breaking news to a soldier or family member was never easy. But today, considering his connection to the Metcalfe family, Matt Rubart stood poised to deliver a revelation that could so affect Canyon's life that the trickle-down would impact Matt's as well. That wasn't his gauge, but it certainly played into his planning and perfecting the scenario in which he now stood. If only he could tell Canyon that they'd cleared his name regarding Tres Kruces, give him a free pass out of this inferno that had engulfed his life. But he couldn't. And that ate at him.

Carrie came toward him, holding Tala in her arms. "We had a good night's sleep." She smoothed the little girl's long black hair.

He heard the hidden message: Tala's young mind was adjusting quickly to the loss of her grandmother.

Hollow and loud, a thunk at the other end of the long hallway caught Matt's attention. General Lambert strode down the hall with a woman in a conservative blue dress and heels. Matt waited in the welcome area of the now-empty family center. Carrie set the girl down, and from a bag on her shoulder she pulled several toys, a drink cup, and a snack.

He hoped the tide turned in Canyon's life. But would today's interview and news end it? Or make it worse?

In uniform, Matt snapped a salute.

The general responded. "Good afternoon, Major Rubart. This is a colleague of mine, Dr. Avery, the psychiatrist I told you about."

Matt shook the woman's hand. "Dr. Avery. Thank you for coming."

"So." General Lambert pointed to Tala. "This is the little girl?"

"Yes, sir. She has been staying with Major Hartwicke and her family."

Dr. Avery joined Carrie and the girl, talking quietly.

Angling his shoulder so the ladies couldn't hear, Matt leaned into the general. "I know you're disappointed that I can't clear Canyon—"

"Easy there, son." Lambert patted his shoulder. "All things in their time. I trust you'll find what we need."

"I do believe we have enough to, at the least, lessen the charges—"

"No." Lambert's normally tender eyes flamed. "If you cannot clear him, leave it alone."

"But the news—"

"It'll go away." Hand still on Matt's shoulder, his gaze on the little girl. "It's not just about him anymore. If we complicate things, if the surface is disturbed and we can't absolutely eradicate this, then he could lose everything." He nodded toward the girl. "Am I clear, Major?"

"But, sir, he's not guilty."

"I know that. You know that. And so does someone else."

"You want me to—"

"Digging a grave doesn't require a mouth."

In other words, keep digging but keep your mouth shut. Their attention drifted to Tala as they waited in the stark-quiet of the building. Finally Matt shifted and glanced toward the entrance. "Will he come?"

Lambert nodded, watching the ladies.

"I'm worried about his reaction."

A laugh. "Rest assured, this won't be pretty. As far as Canyon knows, everyone died."

The hard-core facts hit Matt. He had to keep that in focus. Remember what Canyon would be thinking. What the guy must've felt, thinking everyone died.

Dark and in shadow, a form lumbered along the hall. Canyon stepped into the light. Dressed in slacks and a shirt, he strode toward them, purposefully. His gaze hit Matt's. Then the general's.

Face hard, Canyon stopped in the middle of the open corridor, shook his head. "No." He turned. "This isn't happening."

"I assure you, Mr. Metcalfe," the general said, "you will want to hear what the major has to say."

Wariness crowded his taut expression. Stiff and clearly furious, Canyon slowly joined them. "I have nothing to say, Major Rubart."

"That's okay." Matt extended his hand. "Thank you for coming. Have a seat."

Canyon glared, ignored the hand, and remained on his feet. He glanced at the girl, frowned, then pushed his attention back to the table where a laptop sat.

Matt sat on the sofa in the seating group and perched himself on the edge of the leather cushion. "As you are aware—"

"Is it your fault?" Hatred cut through the cool air like a scythe. "Are you the reason the media's climbing down my throat again?"

"Canyon—"

"No." His jaw muscle popped. "I did what I was told to do. I kept my mouth shut. Now, it's all over the news again. Whose fault is that?"

Talking, *trying* to talk him down would do no good, and Matt understood why Canyon was keyed up. He would be, too. Without a word, Matt turned the laptop toward Canyon, reached over the raised screen, and hit the touch pad.

Lip curled, Canyon said, "What is this?"

Matt folded his hands and glanced at Lambert.

The video started, silencing the room.

Canyon blinked and froze. His lips parted and his shoulders pulled forward as Corazine Mercado's voice broke the tension. Angling to the side, he dropped into a chair, riveted to the screen. "When was this?"

"Last week."

"Impossible. She's dead!" Red streaked Canyon's eyes. "Cora." He grabbed the laptop and dragged it closer. "She's. . .she's dead. She died. . .four years ago." His voice a whisper, Canyon steepled his fingers and touched them to his lips.

But he fell quiet again as the aged voice recounted the story of interaction between a Special Forces team and her village. Matt assessed and monitored Canyon's reactions very closely, partially to gauge his emotional state, but also to see if anything she said was contrary to what he remembered.

When silent tears streaked down Canyon's stubbled face, Matt had his answer. It was true. Everything Corazine Mercado testified to was true. Minutes ticked by as Canyon, enrapt, watched the woman. Twice, he reached out and touched the screen. Sorrow gouged painful lines in the former Green Beret's face.

Willow had said that Canyon came back from that mission changed—quieter, withdrawn. And knowing the story, knowing he'd invested his heart and life and found companionship in the arms of a young woman. . .*no wonder*.

As the story pitched in intensity, Canyon slapped the screen shut. "Stop." He shook his head. "I can't. I can't. . ." His voice cracked. "No more."

Was that because he feared what might've been told? Or was it just too painful?

"Canyon." Only as General Lambert took the lead in the conversation did Matt even notice the psychiatrist now sat next to Canyon. "Mrs. Mercado repeatedly mentioned someone named Bayani. That name is not in any report or record. Do you know who he was?"

Tormented eyes staggered to the general. "Me." He pawed at the tears, face red. "It was the name Awa gave me. It means 'hero.'" A sob ripped through him. A soft snort mixed with more tears. "I'm no hero."

"Canyon, I know this is painful—"

"You have *no* idea." Canyon glared at the general through red-rimmed eyes and tight, quivering lips.

"You're right. But your report never mentioned a union between you and the chief's daughter."

The strength that held the man's neck up collapsed. He cradled his head in his hands. "Chesa." With a groan, he eased back against the chair. "The sweetest, most naive...innocent..." He dragged in a ragged breath and pushed to his feet.

Matt and the general shared a glance, and in it, Matt knew to let the man have some space. This was a lot to digest. And it was only the beginning. He didn't want the guy blowing a fuse, so they had to take this slow.

Along the bank of windows, blinds closed, Canyon stood. "What do you want? Why are you doing this?" Reverie lost, he turned, a storm in his expression. "Leave it. Leave it alone. Leave them—buried." He shoved a finger at Matt. "You people told me to keep my trap shut, so I did. Now leave me alone!"

Matt held out a piece of paper. There was no other way to do this.

Belligerently wary, Canyon snatched it from his hand. "What is this?" He glanced down. Frowned. "I don't... What...?"

"It's a paternity test."

"For whom?" His tone was shrill and implied the absurdity he no doubt felt. But his gaze gradually drifted to the girl, who had stopped playing and now watched him with frightened blue eyes.

"Your daughter."

A scoffing laugh sparked against the tension. "Nice try. I don't know what game you're playing—"

"She is your ch—"

"No!" Canyon stabbed a finger toward Matt again. "See, this is where I know you're wrong. The one sore spot in my marriage to Chesa:

She never got pregnant. It was painful and humiliating, a point of honor among our—the people."

"When Mrs. Mercado came to us," Hartwicke's quiet calm voice sliced into the tension, "she repeatedly said she was doing it for Chesa and the child." Hartwicke stood. "She fought to get to the States, to find us, so she could tell her story—and bring Tala to her father."

"I am *not* her father."

"How do you think she got blue eyes—blue eyes, like yours?"

Canyon waved a hand back and forth. "No." He held his head as if feeling faint. "No, this isn't true. Chesa *died* in that fire, and I *know* she never had my child—I was there! She died! What part of dead don't you people get?"

Hartwicke lifted Tala, who clung to her. "I know that's what you were told, but Chesa didn't die that day. She couldn't have because this child *is* yours."

"We conducted a paternity test using your toothbrush and a swab of Tala's inner cheek." Matt found no pleasure in blowing the man's mind. "The results have a 98.5 percent certainty. Tala is your daughter."

Merciful God, help! It couldn't be true. Chesa had cried nearly every night in his arms, agonizing that she'd never carried his child. He tried to convince her that it didn't matter, that he would still honor her, but it did no good.

Yet even as he looked at the little girl playing on the carpet, he saw. . . "Chesa." Face wreathed in innocence. Beautiful round cheeks. Jet-black hair. Where. . .hold up. To birth this child she had to be— He jerked his gaze to the CID agents. "Where is she? Where is Chesa?"

"I'm sorry." Rubart paled. "She died, Canyon. Corazine told us she lived only long enough to bring Tala into the world."

His head spun. His world crumbled. Again. Was there no mercy? Chesa had the baby she wanted, and she would never see her grow up. A pressure built around his chest, his heart.

Something touched his arm. He jerked, disoriented. Yanked from the past and painful memories into the present laden with painful truths. Pain. . .why was there always pain?

"Canyon, are you okay?"

The shrink chick who'd visited the Shack—what was her name?—stood beside him.

"Yeah. . .sure. . .no." He stuffed his hands on his belt. "This can't be.

I mean, wouldn't I feel something for her? A connection or something?"
The way I feel with Roark.

Roark. Oh man. What would she think? What must everyone in this room think? That he'd killed all those people. The people who had embraced him as a *warrior*. A hero. And he'd failed them. Every one of them. Including Awa, Corazine, and Chesa. . .who was pregnant?

He swayed and grabbed the chair. "Why are you doing this?" Numb, he dropped into the leather cushions. "Corazine—where is she? Why bring this girl to me?" What a stupid thing to say. Canyon buried his face in his hands. *This can't be happening.* "Don't you people see this is stupid? I mess things up. Everything I touch, it doesn't turn to gold. It turns to rot. Look at Tres Kruces, look at my whole freakin' life! Why on earth would you put a child with a man like me?"

"We have more testimony from Corazine," Rubart said. "She insists you were not responsible for what happened to the village."

He pulled his head out of the quagmire of the past. "She. . .but how?" That made no sense. How would Corazine know?

Matt sighed. "She wasn't detailed, but I think we might have a shot at clearing your name."

"No!" General Lambert lunged to his feet. "I told you to bury that until we have more details and proof—cold, hard proof."

Rubart's expression darkened. "He has the right to know what we have."

Surprise lit through Canyon at the way the two argued. But his mind hooked on one thing. "Of course she wasn't detailed. Cora wasn't a soldier. She was a sweet woman who didn't know military procedure. She didn't know I gave the coordinates—"

"Explain that to me."

Canyon held Rubart's gaze. "I disagreed with the strike, but when we were being overrun by radicals, I gave coordinates. I thought. . .I thought they were for a location more than a mile away. But. . ." He shrugged. "I don't know. The bombs hit the village. Perfect strike. Don't you get it? Cora loved me; she wouldn't want to believe I made *that* mistake."

Matt opened the laptop, accessed the video, and forwarded it to the segment he'd marked. He played it. Then motioned to the screen. "Right there, she says you were not responsible."

"That's it?" Canyon struggled to his feet, biting through the pain that leeched into his chest again. "This is. . .this is bull!"

"Aren't you interested in—?"

"*Don't* go there." Canyon shook a finger at Rubart. "Think about what you're doing—shoving this girl into my life and opening this Pandora's box from hell. Are you out of your mind? They'll put me away, then where does that leave her?"

"That is exactly what I told Major Rubart." General Lambert's chest was heaving. "No, we will not do anything with the little we have, Canyon. I promise you that. If we cannot find more, then things stay as they are."

Rubart planted his hands on his hips, that crisp uniform tidy and sparkling. The man should try getting his hands dirty. "So, what? You don't want your own daughter?"

Canyon smirked. "I never figured you for a politician, Rubart."

"I am trying to find the truth, Canyon."

"Just. . .leave it alone." Exhaustion weighted his limbs. He sat in the chair, staring at the little girl. Kneading the tension in his forehead, he watched the girl. "How old is she?" Three. . .wouldn't she be about three? That'd fit the time line. Right?

Major Hartwicke crouched next to the girl, wrapping her arm around the yellow-and-white daisy dress. "Three." She touched the tip of the girl's chin. "And she speaks English." Hartwicke looked at him. "Mrs. Mercado told us *Bayani* taught them all English."

A sour taste squirted over his tongue, remembering how determined the chief and his wife were for their people to know the language. His heart constricted at the way the little girl laughed with the major, a chin-tucked coy smile-laugh.

Just like Chesa.

He snapped his eyes shut. *Chesa. . .*

She was alive. She was alive and I left her. She was alive, I left her, and she was pregnant. Oh, Lord God, forgive me!

"Leave us." Canyon stroked his head with his fingers, a new volatile ache whipping through him.

Once the others had cleared out, the little girl hesitated and looked around. Her gaze finally rested on him. Though something in him wanted to shove her away, deny the whole mess, he realized this was his chance. His chance to make it up to Chesa. To honor her memory by taking care of their daughter.

"Hi."

Eerily, she looked at him with eyes he saw in the mirror every day. *The Metcalfe blues.* He pushed out of the chair and eased himself onto the carpet next to her. "You have my eyes," he mumbled.

That chin-tuck smile melted his heart. "Lola said I have my daddy's eyes."

Emotion thickened his throat and he strained to swallow. Two things plucked the image of the wonderful woman who'd treated him like a son: *Lola*—the Filipino name for grandmother. And "daddy's eyes."

My eyes.

He smirked. "Yeah." He brushed the hair from her face and off her shoulder. When he did, a chain necklace caught his attention. As he touched the tiny ball beads, his heart skipped a beat. Then two.

He tugged it free. When a dog tag dangled in his hand, he sucked in a breath as he closed a fist around the tag.

"It's all I have, Chesa."

Brown eyes captivated his mind. "It is all the more special."

She'd worn his dog tags proudly since he had no ring to give her for their wedding ceremony. And she'd had them on the day she died.

The day I left her.

New agony wormed through his mind. Abandoning his wife when she was pregnant. Never seeing her belly grow large. Or seeing her give birth, seeing their daughter come into the world. Was she a quiet tormentor the way his mom had said he was? Or did she come in kicking and screaming?

He dreaded facing Roark now. Might as well squeeze lemon into that sucking chest wound. He'd complied with the agreement he'd made with Range. And it'd killed him not to visit the hospital. Not to call and see how she was doing. But he had to give her room.

Or was it the lab results that kept him away?

The girl patted his shoulder. "Are you my daddy? Lola said we were going to find my daddy."

Pulse spiraling adrenaline-laced panic, Canyon stilled. Daddy. Yeah. Exactly how did that work? *What if that test is wrong?* A vehemence rooted itself in Canyon's heart. This little girl was Awa and Cora's granddaughter, which meant, even if he wasn't her father, he was the only family she had now.

"Yeah, I am." He blew out a breath. Owning up to it was half the battle.

At that, she chin-tucked again and eased into his arms. As if she'd done it all her life, she snuggled into him. In her hair, he could smell Chesa, that unique body scent he could've tracked like a bloodhound. Finally, something in his life had not ended in total ruin. Holding Tala flooded him with so many fond memories. . .and peace. He closed his eyes and inhaled. With a smile, he pressed a kiss to her crown.

Twisted. Weird. But so good.

I don't deserve her, God.

"Love is not earned. It's given."

CHAPTER 35

Walter Reed Army Medical Center,
Washington, D.C.
20 June

Hꜰow many fingers do you see?"

Dani sighed. "Four."

The doctor moved his hand but kept the same fingers up. "And now?"

"Four."

He penned something in her file, tossed it aside, then scooted his stool toward where she sat on the edge, wearing pajama pants and an ARMY sweatshirt. She'd adamantly refused to wear a hospital gown and have her backside bared.

Two weeks ago, she wondered if she'd ever walk again. Although her neck and back ached, she felt stronger and more capable. She'd awakened the first time surrounded by General Lambert, her sister, and Range Metcalfe. Though a nice welcome, it wasn't the one she wanted.

Canyon had been strangely absent. And nobody talked about him—or anything that had happened down in Venezuela, for that fact. She heard their hushed conversations about her father—found dead, execution-style. Apparently everyone expected her to bemoan her father's death. But they weren't there when he turned his back on her. Mourning him? No. What she mourned was spending weeks without seeing Canyon. *"Roark. Stay with me, baby."* His words, as life tried to sneak out of her lungs, were burned into her memory.

He'd not stepped foot in this hospital. But Range had visited every day, brought flowers, stuffed animals, and cards.

Dr. Henderson smiled up at her as they sat alone in her room. "How about the dizzy spells, Danielle? Are you still experiencing those?"

"Occasionally." She glanced down at the doc, who didn't look old enough to wear that white medical coat. "Is that from the neck sprain?" When the brace had come off, she'd started walking around more, until the room swirled and tilted. And that brought nausea.

Hesitation held the room captive, then he let out a quick puff of air. "No."

"Then what?"

Hands clasped in front of him, Dr. Henderson pinched his lips together. "Are you having any other. . .unusual symptoms?"

Dani shook her head and shrugged. "Should I be?" What if being thrown across Bruzon's lawn had damaged her brain or. . . ? "Is something wrong with me?"

"No, not particularly. The MRI came back clear once the swelling went down." He stood and shoved the stool back. It thudded against the wall, the metal clanking. "Just a moment, please."

What's going on? He opened the door, stepped into the hall—still holding the door open—then returned. With General Lambert. And Frogman. And an attractive brunette, whose belly was rounded with the expectancy of a child.

Um, okay. What's with the entourage?

"Hello, Danielle." The general greeted her with a gentle kiss on the forehead. "I'd like you to meet Sydney Jacobs, Max's wife."

Standing, Dani blinked and stilled against the light-headedness that threatened. Once it passed, she recovered and extended her hand. "Nice to meet you."

"I've heard a lot about you." The strength in her hand belied Sydney's sweet voice.

General Lambert threaded his fingers. "Danielle, we'd like to ask you some questions."

Uh-oh. She thought this smelled like a setup. "Okay." She eased back onto the bed and lifted the glass of orange juice from her tray and sipped.

"Not to be indelicate," General Lambert said, "but we need to know. When you were held by Bruzon during this last mission, were you raped?"

Hauling in a breath and swallowing OJ at the same time—bad idea! She coughed. Sputtered. Choked. Her eyes stung and watered. She felt like she could hack up a lung. Awkward silence bled into the chilled room. Thumping her chest, she shook her head and cleared her throat. "Sorry." She cleared her throat again. "No, no, he didn't rape me this time."

WOLFSBANE

"You're certain?"

Startled at the question, Dani looked at Max.

So did Sydney, who scowled at her husband.

"Sorry." He covered his mouth with a fist. "I mean, did anyone else... were you...?"

"Was I raped by someone else?" Dani almost wanted to laugh at the way the guy stammered. "No."

Lambert frowned and looked to Max, then to her. He angled toward the doctor, away from Dani, then whispered something. Max joined them, muttering to the general. Henderson's head wagged as he mumbled something to the other two.

Sydney shifted awkwardly and offered an apologetic smile.

Dani couldn't take it anymore. "Is there something wrong?"

The three men conferred—albeit quietly—then Lambert emerged from the pack. "Danielle, as you know, it's SOP to run a lab kit when a patient is brought into a hospital."

She shrugged. "I'm sure my kit was pretty thick. I was almost dead."

"Yes..." Lambert came closer, his expression knotted. "Danielle..." He slid his hands into his pockets. "One of the tests they run on every female—"

"Even if you're a Catholic nun, we run a pregnancy test." Henderson's chuckle earned him glares from Max and the general.

Something thumped against her chest. Hard. Startling. Her mind flicked to Canyon. To that night at the hotel. To their fight afterward. No... Heat washed through her face and neck. Her mind scrambled for proof that it couldn't be true.

When...when was her last monthly? She racked her brain to come up with a date. It all blurred into one massive nightmare she'd worked hard to forget.

Lambert said, "Your test was positive."

"Tha–that can't be." She swallowed, gulped the adrenaline rushing through her veins. "It's a mistake."

Dr. Henderson offered a sad smile. "I'm sorry. We did run a second one, just in case. But there are no false positives with the tests. Negative, yes. But not positive. Those tests use the hormone..."

As his clinical explanation droned on, Dani buried her face in her hands. His words were lost as she fully comprehended what they were saying, why Lambert had brought Max's wife—to comfort her after they broke the news.

I'm pregnant.

313

"Dani," Max's gruff voice cut through her shock. "I need to ask: This baby—does it belong to someone on my team?"

Wild panic streaked through her. No. No, she wouldn't out him like this.

Wait.

Was *this* why Canyon hadn't come to see her? Was it because he knew and didn't want her—or the baby? The thought felt like a kick in the gut. Tears streamed down her cheeks. She pressed her face into her pillow propped against the elevated mattress.

"Danielle—"

"Leave me alone," she cried through her hands, hating the way the general's voice sounded. Filled with sympathy. Concern. "Go away." She drew up her legs onto the bed and cried.

She'd been a wreck since regaining consciousness, morose that he hadn't come to see her. Now she knew why.

Richmond, Virginia
22 June

"I'm sorry but the number you've reached is no longer in service."

Canyon flung the phone against the passenger door of his Camaro. Why did it feel like his last hope of seeing Roark had been severed? Though he'd promised Range he wouldn't see or talk to her, he couldn't live with that bargain. He was going crazy out of his mind not knowing how she was doing. Max told him her recovery, though slow, was good. From Lambert he'd learned she was still in the hospital. But beyond that. . .nada.

Now, her cell wasn't working.

"Daddy, are you mad?"

Still unused to being a father, he chided himself for acting out in front of Tala. "It's oka—" He clamped down on the words as he spotted the cluster of vans and cars encamped at the entrance to the driveway. "Bloodsuckers," he mumbled.

Two sawhorses blocked the drive, an armed security guard directly behind them. Canyon flashed his lights, signaling the guard, then gunned the engine. The guard launched into action and whipped the blockade aside just as Canyon nailed the driveway before anyone could get in the way or stop him. Or frighten Tala by mobbing the car. The tires spun and spit pebbles toward the camera crews and reporters.

Guilty pleasure rumbled within him at the shouts of protest and cries. "Stay out of my life."

In the garage, he let down the door before he climbed out.

"Hey, there's the man of the hour!"

Sandwiched between the car door and frame of the Camaro, Canyon caught Stone's hand-slap-back-slap hug. "Thanks, man. It's good to be home." He glanced toward the back entry to the kitchen. "Is everyone here?"

"Just as you asked. Even Brooke, which is amazing these days."

Stomach twisted and knotted, Canyon hesitated. What would they think? Honestly, he just wanted to talk to Roark, tell her about Tala, get the past behind them and try to start a future.

"You okay, Canyon?"

"Yeah. Sure."

"Then let's get inside. Mom's got a million foodstuffs and we're all starving."

"Right." He shifted and bent down, reaching for the seat lever. He flipped the front seat forward and bent into the car.

"Need help with anything?"

Man, this sucked. Canyon angled himself in and unbuckled the five-point harness then slipped the straps off Tala's shoulders. . .and hesitated.

With the way his mother loved kids, he didn't doubt for a second she'd take to Tala. The question, the fear that sucked at his courage, was what she would think of *him*. Especially since he couldn't tell them anything or explain where Tala had come from.

They'd just write him off as a loose cannon again. *Loose Canyon.* Silent tormentor.

He brushed Tala's hair from her face and smiled. "How can they not love you?" he whispered and pulled her into his arms. Backing out, he steeled himself against Stone's reaction. Slowly he came around, eyes pinned to his older brother.

Stone blinked, eyes widening, mouth parting.

Canyon felt sick.

"Not exactly what I expected you to bring out of your car."

"You and me both." Canyon moved for the stairs. Swirling nausea coated the back of his throat with an acidic taste. Up three steps and through the door, he entered the kitchen. Willow and Brooke turned with wide smiles that somehow widened as his younger sister squealed.

"Oh my goodness, she's adorable!" Willow rushed forward and

scooped Tala from him.

"No, Willow, lea—" He tried to maintain his hold, but it broke when she spun away with the three-year-old.

"Who is this beautiful angel?"

Tala arched over Willow's shoulder and screamed, "Daddy!"

The room froze as Tala's crying invaded the home.

Willow's wide eyes found his. *"Daddy?"*

"What on earth is going on in—?" His mother's words dropped like a brick. Hand to her throat, confusion scraped through her sweet face and rubbed Canyon's heart raw. Confusion bled into what he thought was understanding, then into disappointment.

Retrieving his now-crying daughter, Canyon motioned toward the living room. "Please. Let's sit down and talk."

"Here," Brooke's soft voice said from beside him.

Canyon glanced down and found a cookie being offered to a sniffling Tala. "Thanks." He took the cookie and tucked it in her hands. "It's okay, baby."

Stone gathered Leif and Range from the back forty, and soon, the entire family had gathered around the fireplace. Canyon eased himself into one of the recliners, perched on the edge with Tala on his knee.

She took one look around the room, at the expectant and anxious expressions, then slumped against his chest. How did he do this, tell his family that this was his daughter? How had Rubart done it—oh yes, with the paternity test. It'd shocked Canyon stupid so he couldn't object anymore. But that wouldn't work with his family, especially not his mother. She'd slap him into next week. Then Stone would throw him into the next one for upsetting their mother. But he could feel their gazes, feel their questions. . .and their condemnation.

Tala fidgeted on his lap, repositioning herself so she laid against his chest in a way that she could look at the others. Then she flipped her head the other direction and burrowed into his hold. Awkwardly, he held her.

"What is her name?" His mom eased closer, sitting on the edge of the coffee table, smoothing a hand along Tala's brown leg and sandaled foot.

"Tala." He hadn't really thought about her full name. "Tala Metcalfe."

His mom paused.

"Tala's my daughter." Man, that sounded hollow. Void of emotion. But there was no other way to say it. "It's important to me that you believe her birth was legitimate."

"Why is she just now here with you?"

"She. . ." Canyon realized to answer that, he'd violate the gag order. "I can't answer that. But she has no one left to take care of her but me." He'd gone over and over this, sorting what he could say and what he couldn't. To his regret, too little could be said of this revelation. "I didn't even know she existed until yesterday. There's not much else I can say."

Unspoken questions peppered the air but no one probed or pushed. They'd been through this before with TK. Instead of drilling him with questions they knew he couldn't answer, his family did what they did best: rallied. Within a half hour, his mom and sisters had negotiated with Tala to go into the kitchen to get some dinner and dessert, but the round blue eyes never left his for long.

Leif and Range said nothing and did nothing. They'd been too blown away, he guessed. But Stone sat on the edge of the table where their mom sat earlier, watching Canyon.

"The last thing I ever expected or wanted was to be a father." He felt evil for even saying that, but it was true. And he wrestled with the confession.

"She's a cute kid, looks Filipino." Leave it to Stone to play lawyer and dig out the truth without making Canyon break his vow.

Leif grabbed a soda from an end table. "*Half* Filipino." He shrugged when Canyon peered up at him. "She has the Metcalfe blues."

When Leif and Range finally left, Canyon scooted closer to his older brother. "Stone, I think you get it, get what happened. I don't want the family thinking I had loose morals away from home."

Right. Like when you slept with Roark on the mission?

Canyon hung his head. "I deserve a lot of things—a lot of *bad* things for my screwups—but Tala deserves a better father than someone like me."

"Would her mother agree with that?"

Chesa. . . He looked away, pained at the thought, and pinched the bridge of his nose.

"Canyon," Stone said, taking on that authoritative tone Canyon usually hated. "We all make mistakes. It's what we do after them that determines our character." He glanced at Tala. "You seem to be doing your best to take care of the little angel."

"I don't know the first thing about being a dad!"

"Who ever does? I didn't when Jack was born."

Fists balled, Canyon inched forward some more. "But I'm a soldier, a fighter." A Class-A screwup. "Not a domestic type. A fighter, Stone."

Blue eyes resonated with understanding but also with something more. "If she survived what I think she did, she's a fighter, too. And so was her mother."

Let's just hope I don't kill her like I did her mother.

CHAPTER 36

Walter Reed Army Medical Center,
Washington, D.C.
25 June

Y ou're not going to drag me here every day, are you?" Though Sydney glared at him, Max shrugged. "Don't like hospitals."

"You were in one for Dillon's birth. And what about this guy?" She rubbed her belly as they stepped into the elevator. "You'll be there for his birth, too, right?"

The questions weren't fair. He'd spent plenty of time in sterile chop shops getting patched up. Besides, being there for the birth of his sons was one thing. Being here for someone else's problems. . .well, shouldn't someone else do that?

"Canyon should be doing this."

Sydney darted him a look. "Don't you dare say that in front of her. She's torn up as it is that he hasn't visited her since they returned—a month!" She punched the button for the fifth floor.

"I ought to drag his sorry butt here."

"Don't. It needs to be his doing, not yours." She scratched her belly. "And remember, she hasn't said directly that the baby is his."

"And she hasn't *in*directly said it isn't."

Sydney rolled her eyes as the doors whooshed back. "Play nice, Max."

"Me? Nice?"

In the room, Sydney and Danielle fell into an easy conversation, like the fast friends they'd become. General Lambert rose from his seat and eased himself out of the conversation and toward Max. "Her sister just left a few minutes ago," he whispered. "I didn't want to leave her alone. Grab some coffee with me?"

"Sure." Anything to avoid sitting here like a marble statue while the two women did their girl thing.

As they headed to the family waiting area where four vending machines anchored a wall, Lambert gave Max a backhanded pat. "Heard from the panel regarding Danielle—they're dropping the charges. Our government is sending teams en masse to check out that facility."

"The same one they said didn't exist?"

Lambert chuckled. "Seems our evidence was enough—that and information from an intel source, though nobody will tell me who or what they said."

"Isn't that the way the government works?"

"No kidding." Lambert fed the machine his money, then selected his drink. "Still no word from Midas. I'll throttle that young man."

"Get in line." Max's growl echoed through the hall but then he paused, considering the Old Man. How'd he know about Danielle and Midas?

"It's unusual for him. I mean, I know he's quiet, but this—complete silence and disregard for her well-being—it's not the same young man who held a gun to my head thinking I sabotaged the mission and Danielle's life."

Max couldn't help but arch his brow. "Held a gun to your head?"

Once the cup dropped into the tray and started filling with the hot brew, Lambert sighed. "When Canyon found me down there, he behaved like a rabid dog. I'd never seen him out of control like that—so angry, volatile. I'd expect that from you, but him?" The Old Man shook his head. "He kept saying he had to get her back, that he'd promised. There was something in his voice, his eyes that told me his determination wasn't just about the. . ." He dragged a hand over his face. "He was tormented. I knew something had happened between them, even asked him if he was in love with my—with Danielle."

Max nodded, quietly refusing the coffee Lambert offered to buy.

Steam rose in a lazy spiral over the insulated paper cup. "What about you? How'd you know about them?" He lifted it as they strolled down the hall.

"Same thing, out of control. When we got him back and he found out she wasn't with us." Max shrugged. "He actually punched me." He made a *tss* noise and wagged his head. "Stole the chopper." He folded his arms and slumped against the wall as they waited for Sydney to come out. "Gun to your head. . .then the guy vanishes into the night? Doesn't make sense."

"Agreed," Lambert said. "Thanks again for bringing your wife.

Danielle has really enjoyed her company and friendship. The doctors are talking of releasing her."

"Good. Yeah, Sydney likes this stuff, wants to start a group since we've got a regular *Leave It to Beaver* team. Ya know, a wives' thing." Max shuddered. Why women wanted to get together and yak, he didn't know.

Lambert snickered. "That is happening, isn't it, the men finding their matches. Interesting." A laugh-snort plied a smile from the Old Man's face.

Cowboy got his girl on a mission. Now it seemed Canyon had found his girl—but would it work out? The dude crossed some serious lines and shirked duties. A heavy talk was on the horizon.

But when did they have time for sex? That mudslide...the prison. "A lot went wrong on the mission."

"Indeed." Worn and tired-looking, the Old Man yawned. "There's a lot to clean up as well."

"One thing can't be cleaned up."

Lambert shifted. "Danielle's pregnancy." He shuffled back down the hall toward her room. "Think he'll make good on this?"

"If he wants to stay on the team."

Lambert nodded. "You're going to—"

"Make him own up? Absolutely. If he doesn't, I removed him once..."

"The poor guy."

"Poor guy?!" Indignation chomped through Max. "He—"

"There's a lot you don't know, Frogman." He clicked his tongue. "Hate to say it that coldly, but it's true. Have you watched the news? Seen what's upended his life again?"

Max bit back the urge to curse, to say he didn't care what was happening. But the reeking truth had emblazoned itself over the Old Man's face. "I *live* the news."

Lambert smirked. "Tres Kruces."

Max nodded, remembering the media blitz over that nightmare. He'd never been so thankful for the integrity of his own team as he—and nearly every man on a spec-ops team—watched the team stripped naked, metaphorically, in front of God and country of their green berets.

His breath caught in his throat. Green Beret. "That was Midas?"

"Yes." He sighed. "And no. Was he blamed? Yes. Was he guilty?" Lambert ran his hand through his snow-white hair. "I don't believe so. A witness fought her way here, a survivor from the village. We were exhilarated to have someone counter the sworn testimony against Captain Metcalfe. She told us just about everything. . ." He let out a long exhale. "But died before providing critical evidence."

"So, the media got wind of this new witness?"

"We don't know what tipped them off. But they're crawling all over it like maggots on a carcass. If you ask me, the timing was a little too convenient. I think Michael Roark may have started the maelstrom. And once again, Canyon is eating cameras and nosy reporters for lunch," Lambert said.

"I'm surprised the Venezuela stuff hasn't hit the fan—you sure made that go away fast."

"I swore I would."

The door to the room swung open and yanked both men straight.

Sydney's normally olive complexion bore a pale sheen. "Get the doctor. She's bleeding."

Without a word, Lambert rushed down the hall toward the nurse's station.

"You okay?" Max joined his wife, scowling at her pallor.

With a nervous smile, Sydney nodded. "You know I'm not good with blood."

He wasn't convinced that was all that bothered her.

"I better go back in." She kissed him and slipped back into the room.

The dark door bore a number and a narrow slip of glass. Through it, he saw Sydney standing next to the bed holding Danielle's hand. Cold air swirled around Max, taunting as he stood alone in the corridor. Stuff like this. . .this is why he hated hospitals. They made him feel powerless.

Thuds reverberated through the hall, pulling Max's gaze over his shoulder. Dr. Henderson and the Old Man hurried toward him.

"Have you called Midas?"

"Think he needs to know?" Max unholstered his phone and started dialing.

"I think she needs him." Lambert stared after the doctor, who disappeared into the room.

Max sent the AHOD text to Canyon, refusing to even talk to the guy. Send an AHOD and he'd show. Tell Canyon he was needed at the hospital, no telling.

Over the next fifteen minutes, several more staffers entered and exited. Some with equipment. Some with scowls and dirty—bloodied—linens. And every time that door opened, cries and sniffles seeped into his awareness.

If there was too much trauma, the doc would send Syd out, right? He'd be considerate, watch out for the other pregnant woman?

Running a hand over his head and down the back of his neck, Max turned in a circle, feeling like he could literally climb the walls. "Come on, Syd. . .what's going on in there?"

"I'm sure she's fine," Lambert mumbled.

"She's as thickheaded as me. She'd stay there even if she was dead on her feet." And until she was convinced Danielle could be left alone. Or had fallen asleep. Or. . .something.

Shoes clicked against the highly waxed floor, drawing his attention to the other end of the hall. Dressed in head-to-toe navy, Range Metcalfe strode toward them with a bouquet of flowers and an elegantly wrapped gift box.

With a low growl, Max rolled his shoulder around and focused on the room. His gut cinched when he realized the curtain about the bed had been drawn. That was a bad sign, right?

"Evening, gentlemen."

Max's mood worsened at the all-too-chipper voice of Midas's brother.

The Old Man shook Metcalfe's hand. "You might want to come back tomorrow. She's not feeling well."

Range's brow furrowed. "Is something wrong?"

"Just a bit out of sorts," Lambert said. "Nothing a little rest won't cure. I'll be sure to tell her you came by." He pointed to the flowers and candy. "Would you like me to deliver them to her?"

"Uh, sure." Uncertainty marked Range's reaction.

Down the hall, fast steps echoed through the ward. Max tensed as Canyon jogged around the corner, his face screwed tight.

Range turned. The guy's shoulders rose several inches. "What're you doing here?"

Ignoring his brother and breathing hard, Canyon looked at Max. "What's wrong? Why'd you page me here?"

Lambert put an arm around Range and deliberately led him away from them.

Max seized the distance. "Accountability."

Shaking his head and trying to take an even breath, Canyon frowned. "Come again?"

"What happened down there, Midas?"

Arms to the side, he shrugged. "What. . .I thought something was wrong. Am I missing something?"

"You got her pregnant, Midas."

✦

"What?" Canyon stumbled back. "No. She was raped. Bruzon."

"She wasn't. Not this time." Fiery eyes darkened. "You knew she was pregnant!"

"I. . .down there, at the base, yeah I saw the lab results. I thought. . . I thought she was raped and he got her pregnant."

Max glowered. "You sick puke! That's why you haven't been here?"

"No, I haven't come because. . .well, it doesn't matter." She wasn't raped?

"You're right. You failed. And now she's in there right now bleeding—probably miscarrying your baby."

Knees buckling, Canyon almost didn't feel himself falling. He flung a hand out and caught himself. "You. . .no. . ." Mouth dry, he pushed his gaze to the door. "Is she okay?"

Max snarled. "Doc's in there now. We don't know."

How. . .why didn't she tell him it was his? Call him? *Because you haven't talked to her since returning.* A month. It'd been pure hell. Every waking thought filled with her. Every dream serenading her into his life. And then smothered because of his vow to Range.

"I want to see her."

"Midas."

The wizened voice stilled him as Lambert came toward him. "Let's wait, shall we, to see what the doctor has to say?"

Hand on the door, Canyon hesitated. What if she didn't want to see him? *Would* she even see him? What if she hated him now more than ever? He'd made good on his promise to Range, and it might've cost him the only woman he'd ever loved.

Propped against the wall, his hand curled into a fist. "I *need* to see her."

"Canyon, son." The Old Man stepped closer. "Let's make sure she's in a condition to receive visitors, hmm?"

Tears stung. Burned. Slipped free thinking of her in there bleeding, possibly hemorrhaging as she lost the baby—*their* baby.

His eyes snapped closed. *What have I done?* Agony writhed through his chest. He'd spent the last four weeks holding back, keeping his distance. And she'd never had the chance to tell him. Unacceptable.

He'd abandoned her long enough.

Canyon jerked open the door.

"Midas!"

A woman—Max's wife—stood against the wall, her stomach round. Her eyes widened as he strode into the room, using long powerful strides. Knowing if he slowed he'd chicken out, he ignored her panicked expression.

She rushed toward him. "Please, she's already distraught—"

Canyon glared but kept moving.

He came around the edge of the curtain.

Writing on a clipboard, the doctor stood at the foot of the bed.

On her side, Roark lay clutching a ratty tissue. Blotchy red spots covered her face, apparently from heavy crying. Self-loathing took on a new name: Canyon. He'd done this to her. Put her in this position.

Maybe he should leave. Before she saw him. Before he upset her more.

He took a step away.

"Who are you?" The doctor's voice snapped through the room.

Canyon looked at the doc. Glanced at the bed.

Roark's gaze collided with his.

CHAPTER 37

Relief warred with fear. Dani rolled off her shoulder, twisting her body at an odd angle that enabled her to see Canyon. Her heart rate bleeped through the room, thanks to the machine attached to her finger. The man who'd captured her heart—unflappable, gentle, quiet—stood at the foot of the bed, staring at her. Hard. By his taut expression and stance, she guessed he'd been told about the baby. What was he thinking? What she saw in his face, what was that? Was he upset? No she'd seen him angry. This wasn't anger. Sickened?

Dr. Henderson glanced between them, obviously noting the chilling silence. Finally he spoke. "You shouldn't be in here."

Nostrils flared, Canyon's eyes rolled to the doc with a warning look that dared him to interfere.

The doctor shrank away.

Canyon returned his blues to her face. "Roark."

As he stormed around the doctor, Dani felt her pulse leap. "I'm sorry," she blurted through sniffling. All the anger, all the hurt, vanished at the sight of him. Though it frustrated her, she was too tired of the drama. Too tired of fighting. She wanted peace.

The angst in his expression smoothed out, then knotted.

"Now, look," Dr. Henderson said. When he caught his shoulder, Canyon rounded on him. Wrested free.

"It's my fault," she blurted out again as he came to her side. His handsome face blurred beneath hot tears. "I didn't know."

Canyon dropped onto the edge of the mattress and scooped her into his arms.

Fingers coiled around his shirt, Dani clung to him. Tears ruptured. She buried her face in his shoulder and sobbed. "I'm sorry. I'm so sorry..."

Why was she blubbering—had to be the hormones, right?

Large, powerful hands held her firmly against his chest. "Shh." He kissed the side of her head. "It's my fault. *I'm* sorry, Roark." His biceps squeezed her in closer as he nestled his face against her neck. "I've been a fool."

"You didn't come see me. I didn't know if you were done with me, if you hated me."

He eased back and cupped her face in his hands. Ferocity filled his normally quiet demeanor. "You are the most important thing in my life."

"I am?" Her voice croaked. Did he mean that? A stuttering breath wormed through her chest as she took in his face, ignoring the stabs of pain in her neck and ribs from the explosion injuries. Was that vehemence what she'd earlier mistaken for anger?

"I've been so stupid." He smoothed her hair, his blue eyes darting over her face. "I tried to do everything in my own power, my way. And we see how good that turned out." He smirked. "I'm sorry I didn't honor you, didn't treat you better. You deserve the best. It's just that you make me crazy."

Sniffling, she gave a soft laugh and slumped against him. "I'm good at that." There, safe again in his arms, she let out another stuttering breath. "I thought you'd hate me."

"Not possible."

"Give me a few days."

He arched his back out and looked into her eyes. "I *love* you, Roark. There's no one else I want."

She threw her arms around his neck again, relieved that he was here. That she wasn't alone facing this horrible nightmare. "They think I lost the baby. I didn't even know about it, but I already feel like this is the biggest loss of my life."

Canyon held her close, his hands pressing her farther into his hold. "Shh. Together. We'll face it together. You should lie back and relax," Canyon said, his voice quiet.

Reluctantly she released him and eased against the propped mattress but held on to his arms, unwilling to let him go. "Why didn't you come see me?"

He scooted next to her. "When I found out you were left behind—"

"Found out? You walked out of there."

"I was drugged and dragged out."

Dani blinked. Swallowed. "They showed me the video."

"Roark, I don't know what they showed you, but I didn't walk out of that prison on my own willpower." His lips were flat, thin.

"You're mad?"

He smirked. Swept a hand along her face. "Not at you. At them. I'd told them I wouldn't leave you, and they put a dart in my neck and hauled me out." He craned his neck forward. "Understand—that's the *only* way they could get me out of there without you."

Disbelief wove through her but she knew he wouldn't lie. "That doesn't explain why you didn't come see me here. A month, Canyon, with bruised ribs and swelling on the brain."

"In this, I'm guilty." When she started to object, he kissed her. "Please—give me a chance." A sheepish expression stole over his face. "After they left you, the only way to get back down there and find you was to recruit help from Range."

Range? Range had helped?

"He said if I wanted his help, I had to agree to stay out of the way for the first month you were back." He offered a lame grin. "He wanted a chance with you."

"But I told you that night—"

"I know. But I was desperate to find you, knowing you're a woman of your word. You said you'd kill yourself and I knew time was short. Also, since you'd told me you loved me, not him, I figured that month he was asking for wouldn't change those feelings."

"Wow."

"But understand—the last thirty days have been the most brutal I've endured in a very long time." Another classic-Canyon smirk. "And I'm pretty sure Range hates my guts right now."

"He knows?"

A nod. "Not about the baby. But that I'm here. And I think his shattered leg didn't help; he blew it on the jump back into Venezuela."

Admiration warm and reassuring swirled through her. "So. . .you set off on a harebrained rescue attempt?"

"It wasn't harebrained." This time, a full-out grin bled into his face. "Okay, yeah. It was harebrained. But I didn't care. I had to get you back."

"You did that. . .for me?"

He leaned closer. "Yeah. Told you, you make me crazy."

Dani smiled and whispered, "Ditto."

His lips swept hers, testing at first, then firmer and loving.

Behind them, a voice cleared. Heat trickled into Dani's face as she glanced over his shoulder and saw Dr. Henderson.

"I think it's time for another sonogram." Dr. Henderson motioned to a nurse, who waited to the side with a machine. To Canyon, "If you'll give us a few minutes..."

As Canyon eased off the bed, Dani snatched his hand. "No!" Her heart thumped erratically. "I want him to stay." She looked at Canyon and threaded her fingers through his. "Please."

"Like I said, we'll face it together."

The nurse wheeled the cart closer and plugged it into an outlet. Then she constructed a small tentlike partition from Dani's waist down, protecting her modesty.

Canyon angled himself so he couldn't see what they were doing, his gaze locked on hers and her hand gripped tightly in his.

Dr. Henderson manipulated her belly, then used the probe. Belly—weird. To think, a baby had been there. She'd never known. All the things she went through... Thank God the general hadn't raped her again. It just seemed infinitely worse knowing she'd been carrying Canyon's baby.

"My mom is going to rake me over the coals for this." He shifted on his feet as the doctor worked. "Then she'll crank the heat and baste me for the next few weeks."

And a new worry folded into her bed of anxiety. What would his family think of her getting pregnant? "What will she do to me?"

"Look, what happened was wrong. I dishonored you—and I'm very sorry." He roughed a hand over his mouth. "I wanted to do things right with you, to show you I could be the good guy, the hero. My mom is not going to hold a grudge against us for this. She won't be happy, and she'll remind us of what God's Word says. But she'll say that God forgives and loves us and so does she."

With a halfhearted smile, she tried to move on. "I like your mom."

"She likes you. Of course, she thinks you're marrying one of her sons, but she's thinking of the wrong son."

Marrying?

"Okay."

They both stilled, Canyon's confidence and playfulness gone at the sound of Dr. Henderson's voice, who came to the side of the bed where the raised rail provided the perfect prop for his hands. He looked at Canyon. "Are you the one responsible for putting this young lady in this position?"

Though she expected Canyon to rail or argue, he merely straightened—his face a shade darker with the crimson flush—and nodded, their hands still joined. "Yes, sir."

But Dani wouldn't tolerate him getting berated. "What's the verdict,

Doc? Am I okay? Will you release me to go home?" She'd been waiting for that news the last several days.

"One thing at a time." He let out a sigh. "Your uterine wall is still agitated." He glanced between them. "Using the probe, I was able to see a heartbeat. But there's still some bleeding."

"Heartbeat?" Canyon's face now paled.

A twinkle came to the doctor's eye. "I am cautiously optimistic the pregnancy is viable."

"Viable?" Dani whispered, her heart tripping and tumbling. "You mean. . ."

"You're still pregnant."

"I need to tell you about someone."

Wariness crowded out Roark's near-euphoric expression as she stepped from the bathroom where she'd changed into jeans and a sweatshirt. Canyon watched her glide across the room, his heart full. . . of trepidation.

"That sounds ominous." She brushed her hair from her face and sat on the bed, then began putting on her socks and shoes.

Here goes. . .everything. From a chair, Canyon recounted the events of Tres Kruces, told her about his tribal ceremony with Chesa, and about Tala, the daughter he'd just met a week ago.

"So, you're becoming a father for the second time." Jealousy and anger leeched into her words.

"It's messed up, I know." Elbows on his knees, he rubbed his knuckles. "I had no idea about Chesa. I thought she died there." He shook his head. "It's like my whole life is dumping all my screwups on my head at once. I deserve it, but I feel like I'm stumbling through it all right now."

"But you were married to her?"

He nodded, hating that he had to tell her now, in the middle of their own personal drama. Too, he had this perfect moment of bliss— confirming his love for Roark, her echoing the sentiments, then the doctor announcing she was still pregnant.

Shoes tied, she crossed her arms. "Did you love her?" More jealousy.

Canyon's eye twitched. He pushed against the back of the chair and sat straight. "I was a cocky, midtwenties Green Beret captain. I married her out of obligation and duty, but there was a definite attraction. It became more. Did I love her?" He shrugged, looking sheepish. "Yeah.

I did. But. . .Roark, it's got nothing on what I feel for you. If anything happened to you, I don't think I could go on."

Her eyes became pools of melting caramel.

Canyon pivoted his position and lowered himself next to her, liking her jealousy but hating that she questioned her place in his life. "You don't look good in green." He kissed her again. "It's you and me. No one else."

"Tala."

Okay, there was her.

"And our baby."

Our baby. Whoa. What a mouthful. He smoothed a hand over her head and hair.

She sniffled. "It's a tad crowded already."

His pulse misfired. "What're you saying?"

Her eyes bounced to his as a tear slipped over her lid. "Besides the fact that I'm a hormonal wreck?" A smile wavered on her lips. "We'll need a big house."

Air whooshed from his lungs. He smirked. "It's definitely not my first option for newlyweds."

"Newlyweds?"

That knock-her-breath-out cockeyed grin gleamed back at her. "Yeah."

Her spunky nature reared its head over the cloud of doom trying to strangle their lives. "If you want me to marry you, I expect a decent proposal. And a ring." A gleam stole into her eye. "A big one."

Lambert Resident, Maryland
26 June

"People—and when I say people, I mean politician people who could make our lives really ugly—are not happy."

Olin sipped from a mug, the steam spiraling up and warming his face. "That's never bothered you before."

"True." The man laughed. "It's been weeks since the incident, and they're still digging for a connection."

"Let them dig. There's nothing to connect, thanks to you."

"There is a curious piece of evidence—Bruzon did not die from the explosion. He was shot through the head. The bullet retrieved was from a revolver."

"A revolver? Only those wanting to make a statement use those anymore."

"I guess the killer made a statement." The man sighed. "I have to say, Lambert, this team of yours. . .I'm impressed. If you want to hire them out—"

"Sorry, but they're not mercenaries."

"So you say, so you say, old friend. At least you got the images you needed to clear the girl and prove what was happening right under our noses. Good job. Oh—one thing. Keep your eyes open. There might be a small problem."

News like this from an asset made Olin shift at his desk and ease back, the leather high-backed chair creaking as he did. "Go on."

"We're missing a body."

Olin pulled forward, reaching for a pen. "Who?"

"Navas."

Olin hung up. That wasn't a small problem. That was a deadly problem. Navas knew the team, knew Canyon's name. And that meant he could come back for retribution.

CHAPTER 38

En Route to Metcalfe Residence, Virginia
1 July

W ait." Dani's heart jammed into her throat as they turned onto the street that led to his mother's home. "Pull over."

"What? We're almost—"

She stabbed a finger to the curb. "Pull over. Now."

Canyon guided the Camaro to the side of the street and shifted the gear into Park. "What's wrong? Are you in pain?"

"Yes." She blinked. "No, not that kind of pain anyway." She glanced down at her jeans, and her gaze invariably went to her tummy.

"Roark?"

What would his mother think of her? "What if she hates me?"

"Who?"

"Your mother! She's Mrs. Perfection—strong, she's raised five kids, she believes so firmly in God, and she's always so. . .happy. Peaceful."

He cupped her face. "Roark. . ." He smiled. "You're so much like my mom, it isn't funny. Your strength, your character—"

"I'm pregnant with your baby—outside of marriage. That's not character!" Maybe this was one of the reasons the Bible said not to have sex outside of marriage. "Why. . .why does the Bible say not to do that?"

Canyon's relaxed expression tightened.

"I'm serious, Canyon. Help me understand this. I was raised Catholic, but I see people all the time—"

"I don't want to be 'people' to you. I want to be set apart, for God." He held out his hands and seemed to pat the air. "Okay, the way I see it is this is about measuring a level of commitment. By having sex outside of marriage, the commitment comes into question."

"No, I never—"

"Tell me"—his voice crackled with intensity—"that you didn't

333

question my commitment to you after we slept together. Tell me you didn't wonder if I wasn't coming back."

The heat drained from her face.

"By breaking my promise to God, by not obeying His command, I opened a vulnerability in our relationship that should never have existed. I hurt you." His words sounded thick. Painful. "That is not acceptable."

She swallowed.

"It's not just hard rules by an omnipotent God who wants to spoil our fun. He knows us better than we know ourselves. He knows the future—we don't. I never could've predicted we would get captured, that we'd be separated. That you'd sit there in a prison wondering if I took what I wanted and left."

A tear slipped loose. He'd read her soul. Read her pain. She just wanted things to be better. She wasn't a fool—she knew Canyon was an amazing and would not let go of him. But now she understood his grief because she understood more of God.

Canyon brushed the tear from her cheek. "I trust God with my life, with our future. Do you?"

Blinking away more tears, she nodded. "I think so. . . . I want to. I just don't know how."

He smirked. "You and me both. It's an every-day, every-minute journey. But we're going to do this together. And that peace you see in my mom, Roark?" He leaned closer, his brow knotted. "That's the Lord, her letting Him have control even when things turn out different than she hoped." He bent forward and kissed her. "Now, let's go test that theory."

They drove to the house and climbed out of the car. Canyon helped her up the steps from the garage that led into the laundry room, then to the kitchen. Inside, the din quickly died down. Small feet padded over the wood floors.

"Daddy!"

Canyon bent and hoisted a little girl into his arms and planted a kiss on her cheek. "How's my girl?" He turned to Dani. "Meet Tala, ball of boundless energy."

Jealousy slithered through Dani's veins. "Hey, sweetie."

"Danielle?" The sweet voice of Moira Metcalfe sailed through the home. "Is that really you, my dear?" She came forward, a white sweater draped over her thin, bony shoulders, and hugged her.

"Careful, Mom. Her ribs—"

After a gentle squeeze around Dani's shoulders, Moira turned to

Canyon. She brushed crumbs that had dribbled from Tala's animal crackers onto Canyon's black shirt. "Well, come on into the den. We're all here. Again. Just as you asked." Her gaze flicked to Dani. "We've missed you. I'm so glad you're feeling better. Can I get you anything?"

A lifeline?

Why was it pleasantries often seemed not so pleasant? As they endured the welcomes by his family, Canyon noticed his palms sweating.

"Tell ya what," Stone said with a wink to Dani. "This is the last family meeting I'm attending till the Fourth."

"Thanks for enduring it." Canyon glanced at his future bride. Though his heart swelled at the thought, the feeling burst knowing they were about to let everyone down. He caught Roark's hand and led her to the overstuffed sofa, easing her onto the cushions so she didn't jar her back. She peeked up at him, a flush filling her face.

He lowered himself onto the couch next to her and drew Tala to his side as he met his family's smiling faces. Well, save Range. Face red, brow tangled, he scowled at something. Canyon followed his gaze. . .to his hand threaded with Roark's. *Great.* But he wasn't letting go—it would look like guilt and then Roark would feel abandoned.

It didn't matter anymore. They were together. Range would be ticked off.

He shot a nervous glance to Stone, who whispered something to his son, Jack, who bolted up the stairs. Leif slouched in one of the recliners, his attention on the muted football game. Stone stuffed a pillow behind Mom's back as Willow handed Roark a glass of water, then joined his brother and mother.

No Brooke. Interesting.

"Well," Canyon said as he tore his gaze away. "There's no soft way to break this, so. . . I've made a lot of mistakes."

A snort from the side drew his attention. Canyon knew it could only come from Range, but his brother wouldn't meet his gaze.

Get it over with. "As you know, almost two months ago, Roark went back down to Venezuela. This time, however, I was on the escort team." His mouth went dry. He checked his mom and felt his stomach clinch at the absolute trust and pride he saw there. That would be gone in a few seconds. "I have no excuses for my behavior. But I intend to own up to the mistakes."

"Dude, what mistakes?" Leif chuckled, and when Stone glared at the youngest clan member, Leif's smile fell.

Sloughing his hands together as if he could slough off the guilt and shame, Canyon went for the straightforward approach. "While we were down there. . ." Oh man. He so wasn't going *there*. "I betrayed. . . *everyone*." The back of his eyes burned. "Let all of you down, let"—he glanced at the beautiful woman beside him—"Roark down. I've been addicted to painkillers for the last few years, but I lied about it, lied to myself. But it got worse, and. . .it clouded my judgment—er, I'm not. . . . I made mistakes. I'm still responsible for what I did, it's just. . ."

Why couldn't he just say it, get it over with?

His mother reached across and touched his hand. "Canyon?"

He rubbed his thumb over Roark's knuckles, wishing he could rub away the mistakes. "I. . ." A metallic flavor slid over his tongue, forcing him to swallow.

"I'm pregnant," Roark said, her voice sweet and firm. "Canyon would have you think he's solely responsible, but"—her eyes locked on to his—"he's taught me a lot about owning up to mistakes."

"Then the baby. . ." Stone looked to Roark, then to Canyon, waiting for one of them to finish his sentence.

"The baby's mine."

"Oh, Canyon," his mother said at the same time Range punched to his feet with a curse.

Canyon matched him, scooting Tala next to Roark.

"Unbelievable! You piece of—" The raw emotion roiling off his little brother mirrored Canyon's. "You only did this because I wanted her."

Canyon's anger rose. "This isn't about you."

"Bull! You did this to me in high school—"

"In high school I was stupid, insane with jealousy, and I made a mistake. A horrible, tragic mistake. I know I hurt you then, and I begged your forgiveness"—Canyon's breaths came in ragged gulps— "but you've never let me live it down. In fact, you've held it over my head for the last twelve years."

"You promised me one month—"

"You *blackmailed* me to get me out of the way, so blinded by your determination to have her for yourself that you never saw what was standing right in front of you."

Range's face hardened. "Yeah, what was that?"

"A brother." His breathing went shallow. "A brother who never asked you for a thing, who did everything to placate you for the last decade, yet he stood in front of you, begging you to help save the woman we both loved."

Range swallowed.

"All you could see was your chance to push me out of the way, without thought or care for what Roark might feel or want."

"And you sure seized on that. You knew it was your way out—"

"I *knew* it was the only way to get her back—*alive!*"

When Range lunged, Roark popped between them. "Stop." She flashed a fierce glare at both of them. "Range. . .I'm sorry." She blew out a breath. "You were so kind and wonderful to me after the captivity. But you never asked me what I felt, what I wanted."

Canyon glanced down at Roark, whose cheeks were red and streaked with tears. Anger, strong and virulent, snapped through him. "I know you love Roark, but so do I."

"Your mistakes have cost me everything." Range's words bore the raw vulnerability that rested on his brother's face even now.

Shame quieted Canyon's anger. "I know. But they've done the same thing to me. . .until now." Here went nothing. "I'm not fighting the past anymore. I've tried it my way, and failed. In the last month, God's taught me a lot about placing my burdens at His feet." The words bolstered him, imbued him with strength. "I have to change. I'm tired of cowering and hiding from the mistakes, hoping they'll go away. I've got. . .I've got a family now"—*wow, that sounded wicked*—"and I need to man up."

"Don't ever talk to me again." Range stormed out the back door. The screen clapped shut, sealing the gap between his brother and him.

At the blanket of silence that fell on the room, Canyon deflated and dropped to the cushions. Beside him, Roark sniffled. He pulled her into his arms. "I'm sorry," he mumbled into her hair, feeling Tala hugging his legs.

Soon, arms came around his. His mother leaned against his shoulder. "My silent tormentor." She clucked her tongue. "Your father always said you were quiet because you were either in trouble or stirring it up."

Her words held too much punch for Canyon to smirk.

"This is a really big mess you've created," she said. "And I don't mind telling you I'm not happy about the wedge you've put between you and Range." She sighed. "But I am proud of you, son. You messed up and owned up to it."

"Yeah, that's a first." Leif chuckled.

Stone joined them. "I won't give you the lecture I feel is necessary because I see you doing the right thing, little brother." He touched Roark's shoulder. "Maybe you can hammer some sense into his thick skull. Welcome to the family, Danielle."

"I'm going to be an auntie again!" Willow embraced Roark from the other side. "So, when's the newest Metcalfe coming?"

Roark peeked up at his sister with a shaky breath. "Um…December."

"A Christmas baby." His mother smiled.

Euphoria swarmed his heartache as the family rallied. He hated the way Range had reacted but he understood. And prayed God would take care of his brother, heal his broken heart.

Canyon's phone buzzed. Though tempted to ignore it, he checked the ID. His pulse rapid-fired at the coded message. An address, followed by all-hands-on-deck.

CHAPTER 39

Lambert Residence, Maryland
2 July

Where is he?"

General Lambert stepped back from his open front door and motioned her in. Dressed in slacks and a blue button-down, he did not seem surprised to see her. "Please, come in."

Dani swept onto the marble floors and turned toward her godfather. "He said you called him last night, then he vanished. I can't reach him."

"Nor will you be able to for a few hours." He walked down the hall toward another room.

Keeping pace, Dani frowned. "Have you seen the news?"

"The question is, have you?"

Disbelief spiraled through her. "How could I not? Every channel is running pieces on him, saying he did all these horrible things."

Olin stepped onto the plush carpet, waited as she joined him, then closed the door. "And what do you believe, Danielle?"

"Canyon's the best man I've ever known."

His white, bushy eyebrow arched. "I'm glad to hear that."

"Where is he, General?"

"In custody."

The breath slammed into the back of her throat. "Custody?" And he just stood there? "How can you be so calm? Why aren't you doing something to free him?"

"Because I believe, at the moment, things are taking care of themselves." He motioned to the chair beside her. "Please, sit. I need to share some things with you."

"I want to see Canyon."

"In due time." Again, he motioned to the chair.

With a huff, Dani sat.

"What do you know of your father's role in what happened in Venezuela?"

Her stomach tightened. "He. . .he. . . I don't know." She shrugged. "He saw Bruzon had me and did nothing—he walked away from me."

"In fact, your father's guilt goes beyond walking away." He slid an envelope over the desk. "Do you remember what the panel said? That at your house they found photos containing evidence against you that painted you as complicit, not a captive?"

Dani nodded, her gaze locked on the manila envelope. "I. . .I didn't look at them. I didn't care at that point."

Olin's lips tightened. "Go ahead, take a look."

Fingers shaking, Dani reached for the evidence. She lifted it, opened the flap, and drew out the photographs. She frowned as she perused them. "It's not me. I was never there. But. . ."

"But you recognize them."

She glanced at Olin, then back to the images. "Yes. Well, a couple of them—at least, I thought I did."

He rose, strode to a cabinet in the wall-to-wall shelves, unlocked a door, and drew out a book. For a few minutes he paused, as if reconsidering, then glanced at the ceiling. He whispered something that sounded like, "Forgive me."

Dani watched him return, stand in front of her, and hold the book. "What does this have to do with Canyon?"

He smiled with a soft snort. "Besides the fact that he ordered me to tell you, threatened to kill me if I didn't? Nothing."

"I don't—why would he threaten you?"

"Because it's long overdue." Extending the book, he opened it and turned to a page.

As her gaze struck the image, she gasped. "My mother! That's right—it was a picture from her album of her on the coast of Venez. . ." Her mouth went dry. "How. . .why. . .who gave them that picture?"

"I believe Michael Roark is the one who sent that envelope, and since you are your mother's equal in shape, size, and color, he had your face added to the images."

"M–my father?" She turned a page in the album and gasped. "Why would he do this? Why would he deliberately try to sabotage me?"

"The team felt they were being tracked, and we discovered that the necklace your father gave you was in fact a tracking device."

Her hand went to her neck, where the necklace Canyon had given her now lay. "They ripped it off me."

"Evidence they didn't want anyone finding."

"My own father!" Another image. Matched perfectly to the ones given to the panel.

"No, not your father."

The photograph that lay open. . .her mother. . .her godfather—the general. Looking very cozy. When was that taken? "Is this you?" She perused the album, surprised at the number of photographs of him with her mom.

What had Olin said? She blinked and looked up at him. "I don't understand. What you do mean not my father?"

"Michael Roark did betray you; he's the one who did this." Softness trimmed his handsome, weathered face. "But, Danielle, he is not your father, not biologically."

She shook her head and drew back. "Excuse me?"

"Your mother had forbidden me from telling you, but when she was working with the embassy in her country, we had an affair."

That last word knocked the breath from her lungs. She swallowed—hard. Then stomped to her feet. "No." She flung the book back at him. "How dare you say that about my mother. She was one of the most incredible women I knew. She wouldn't have kept a secret like that from me. She loved me. She sacrificed everything to make sure I had a good life." The words died on her lips. This. . .this was why her parents had a cold, lifeless marriage. This was why her mother repeatedly told her to wait for the right man.

Dani wanted to dart out of here, curse the man in front of her, but there was an eerie similarity between his story and hers and Canyon's. Her hand went to her tummy. "Did you love her?"

"Your mother was, and always will be, very special to me." A buzzing rippled through the air. Olin glanced at his phone. "I have to answer. It's about Canyon."

Judicial Building, Virginia Beach
2 July

Though nobody could tell him what was happening in the closed-door meeting, Canyon's gut swirled with dread. Lambert's call that something was happening with the case yanked him out of the house, away from Roark and Tala. He'd stayed with Lambert last night, worrying, then bolted to the courthouse first thing. This couldn't be good.

Though he'd tried to believe Lambert's reassurances that things were turning for the better, Canyon wouldn't put his trust in that. He knew the facts of this case. They were aligned against him. Eventually he'd be behind bars. For years, if not the rest of his life.

Canyon shifted on the hardwood chair and pressed his palms to his forehead. *God, I know You're here. You've shown me that. So. . .whatever happens, not my will—which, just so You know is me living with Roark as husband and wife with our kid—but Your will. Please. Let me love her the way You designed me to love her. Not from behind bars.*

"Canyon?"

He straightened. And a beautiful sight swept toward him—Roark. On his feet, he welcomed her into his arms and held her tight. "Man, it's good to see you." He buried his face in her neck and sighed.

"Are you okay?"

"I am now." He looked at Lambert. "Tell me this is good news. I've been here for two hours. They asked me a few questions, then shut me out here."

Lambert patted his shoulder. "Let's find out."

"Canyon?" Matt Rubart stood at the door. "The judge is ready."

"What's. . .they can't put me in prison now, can they?"

Matt shrugged. "They can do a lot of things, but I don't think we have to worry about that this time."

Pulse ratcheting, Canyon was led through a back hall system and into the small courtroom. Seated at the table, he was flanked by Hartwicke and Rubart, whose rocklike expression had morphed into something. . .different.

The judge and two others entered and climbed up into their thronelike area, ready to preside over Canyon's life.

You're in control, God.

The realization spiraled through him, stronger than the painkillers that numbed him stupid. That was just the thing—he wasn't numb. He felt alive! And at peace. For the first time in his life.

"After a thorough and complete review of a last-minute testimony that has been investigated, verified, and determined to be the absolute truth, this panel has unanimously voted that *all* charges against Captain Canyon Everett Metcalfe regarding the massacre at the village known as Tres Kruces are dismissed."

Canyon's ears rang. Dismissed? He was free? *Dismissed?* Didn't she mean guilty? He was going to jail?

"Captain Metcalfe, it is with the utmost sincerity that this panel offers you a heartfelt apology and our regrets for what you have gone through. Please, have your lawyers contact the department for an appointment regarding reparations and full reinstatement."

Only as his mouth dried did Canyon realize it hung open.

A thud against his back jerked him out of the shock. He blinked and looked at Rubart who leaned over the rail. Eyes back on the judge, Canyon stammered, "Sir. Yes, sir. I'm free?"

The brooding judge smiled. "Yes, Captain, you are free."

Seriously? A smile faltered then plowed into Canyon's face. Shouts echoed through the gallery as the hearing closed. Numb, Canyon felt people tugging his shoulder. Pulling him this way. That way.

All he could do was turn to Hartwicke. "How? Who did this? Who provided the testimony? I thought everyone who survived said he couldn't verify it one way or another."

She shrugged. "A man who would not allow his face to be seen by anyone but the presiding judge gave details that nobody could've known." She smiled. "Canyon, you didn't give the wrong coordinates. Senator Roark had someone alter them and the records to place the blame on you, to divert attention away from what they were doing."

Overwhelmed, Canyon dropped into the seat, face buried in his hands. Though he heard the clatter and clicking of lenses, he didn't care. The great burden of believing he'd killed Awa and Cora—*Chesa!*—and all the others...brave, beautiful people...The guilt was gone.

Arms encircled his neck.

The delicious scent of Roark pulled him up and around as her arms encircled him. "I love you," he muttered, hearing once again the telltale click of shutters.

When he lifted his head, light caught his attention. To the side, the guard had opened the door to the waiting room, and through the opening, Canyon saw a man standing with Lambert. The dark-suited man shook Lambert's hand. Then an arm stretched into view, sleeve partially rolled up. Canyon saw a tattoo.

His breath backed into his throat. He shoved to his feet. Threw back the chair and darted around the tables. "Wait!"

The door slid shut. Mounted on the wall, a security release box glowed red. LOCKED. Canyon spun and bolted out of the room. White light slapped at the highly polished hall floor, snapping Canyon's attention to the opposite end. There, a door flapped open, leading into the bright afternoon. Silhouetted, a man's figure drifted into the sunshine.

Canyon sprinted down the hall. Slammed open the door. "Hey!" He shielded his face against the brightness as his eyes adjusted.

Halfway down the walk, a man stopped.

Unbelievable. Canyon shuffled down the steps. "It *is* you!"

Slowly the man turned round, hands in the pockets of his slacks. "I'm not here. I don't exist." He tucked himself into the shadows of the large split oak, out of plain sight.

Relief surged but then anger drowned it. "I don't get it. You tortured me. You—"

"Did unspeakable things." He looked away, the light glinting off his brown eyes. "What I do, most people can't accept or understand. People want sanitized truth. I don't belong in that world."

"Why'd you come forward now?"

"I'm dead. The man I was working for is dead. No better time than the dead, I guess you could say. Coming forward sooner would've jeopardized my mission and thousands of lives." He started away, then paused. "I am sorry. . .for everything. That I couldn't clear you sooner or stop what was happening."

Canyon wasn't sure he could accept that. Yet the man cleared him, told the truth. Only as he considered the man before him did Canyon realize all the clues he had dropped. When he'd parachuted in, the man told him the general was there. Told him the name of the hotel. He'd helped him find Roark. What else had Canyon missed? "How long were you embedded with Bruzon?"

The man shrugged. "Too long."

"I owe you my life."

"*Life* owes *you*, man." Dark eyes sparkled under the rays of the sun as he looked back to the Capitol building where Roark stood on the stoop. "You've got a pretty girl to spend it with. Do me a favor—make the best of it."

Canyon extended his hand. "Thanks, Navas."

"My pleasure, Midas."

EPILOGUE

Seven Months Later...

Dani squeezed his hand tight as she pulled forward, her legs held in place by devices that looked a lot like stirrups. Canyon cursed the thought, thinking how crude it seemed against a backdrop as beautiful as watching his child being born. Missing Tala's birth and getting to know his daughter had made him realize how much he wanted to be here, no matter what. Which is why he'd skipped the last mission with the team.

"C'mon, baby. Push hard."

Sweat blotting her face, Dani glared at him. "You want to try pushing a boulder from between your legs?"

Canyon tucked his head and tried to hide the smile.

"Just remember, this is your fault."

"Be quiet and push!" the doctor ordered.

Canyon ground his teeth against the sound of her straining and against her solid grip that bore down on him like a vise.

The doctor moved and did something, then nodded to Roark. "Ease up, take a breath, then give me one more strong one, Dani."

She tried to blow the sweat-plastered hair off her face. Canyon scraped it off. "You're a champ, Roark. I'm proud to call you my wife."

"Remind me to talk to you about that."

He chuckled. "Sorry. I'm here for good. You can't get rid of me."

"Just. . .my. . .luck." With a deep breath, she bore down.

Soon, a slimy ball of baby made his appearance. After a grunt and grimace, Owen Lambert Metcalfe slid into home base. Into life. Though he wasn't screaming and protesting, his chest moved, he had good color, and his arms swung out, alarmed at the sudden freedom birth had granted him.

Silent tormentor—just like me.

Canyon stilled. "Oh man, we're in trouble."

One Year Later...

A young, attractive platinum blond sat across from him, green eyes vibrant and piercing. She stared at him for several seconds, apparently unaware of her natural beauty but keenly aware, no doubt, of her lethal skills.

"Meeting like this is dangerous," she said as she set a disruptor between them.

Olin Lambert held her gaze. "I am not recording."

One side of her pink lips pulled upward as if he'd missed the point. "I know."

He leaned forward, resting his arms on the table.

She held her ground.

This woman trusted no one, even him, so he'd have to be more considerate. "I need you to do something for me."

"That's the way this usually works."

He slid the envelope across the table. "Top priority, eyes only. I've wired into your account the sum of five million dollars. Upon completion, you will get ten more."

"Fifteen mil." She held his gaze as she drew the manila envelope to herself. "Pricey."

"No," Olin said, a weight pinning his heart to his stomach. "Price*less*. But don't think that means you can adjust the value. If you won't take it, I know others who will."

"It's not very nice to threaten, General." She lifted the disruptor and stood. "For that much money, can I count on some danger?"

"Deadly."

A stellar smile lit her eyes. "What's the objective?"

"Secure seven men. A team—it's been disassembled."

Wolfsbane Discussion Questions

1. At the opening of *Wolfsbane*, Canyon is faced with the loss of his career and the reminder of a devastating incident that obliterated his confidence. Have you ever been at a breaking point that leaves you changed forever, desperate for God's intervention? What was it that broke you?

2. Dani's first scene shows her escape a brutal rebel general who has held her captive for several months. Sexual abuse and/or exploitation is widespread, and the numbers are higher than statistics reveal because many women, like Dani, do not seek help or feel they need help. Have you, or do you know someone who has, endured sexual abuse? What can you do to help this wound heal, or how can you be a source of comfort and security for this person?

3. A persistent theme in this story is familial relationships. It's clear from the beginning that Canyon's relationship with his brother is strained, and that Dani has a distant, at best, relationship with her father and sister. Do you have a strained or distant relationship with a family member? How has this strained relationship affected *your* relationship with God?

4. Canyon has a tattoo over his heart. What is it, and what meaning does it hold?

5. Later in the story, Dani once again finds herself abandoned. Have you ever felt abandoned or seen someone abandon another? How can Deuteronomy 31:6 and Isaiah 54:10 be of comfort during a difficult time of loneliness and despair?

6. In the story, what is the connection between Siberia and Venezuela's rogue general?

7. Chapter 15 holds quite an adventure for Dani and Canyon as they battle the elements of nature. In this chapter, Canyon uses something to tether himself to Dani, afraid to lose her, determined to be there for her. What does he use? Though this is a tangible tether, what can we use spiritually to anchor ourselves to Christ so we don't get lost in the storms of life? Is there a verse that speaks to you during difficult times? What is it?

8. The subplot of *Wolfsbane* involves the story of a village. A tragedy takes place, and the blame for it is placed on Canyon's shoulders. Have you ever been wrongly blamed for something and been dealt punishment? What does Matthew 5:39 say that could apply to a situation like this?

9. In Chapter 19, Canyon breaks a lot of his own rules and a clear biblical guideline. What is it?

10. There is an old saying: Christians are not perfect, just forgiven. As an author, I greatly wrestled with including the element in Chapter 19 because I do not condone their actions. However, I am also aware that as Christians, we fail. A lot. What Canyon and Dani did was wrong, unequivocally. Often, we even apply a measure of "weights" to sins, believing one is more sinister/evil than another. Do you believe one sin is greater than another? If so, why? If not, why not?

11. Marshall "the Kid" Vaughn has often been the brunt of jokes and made a mockery of in the series. However, in Chapter 24, he stands up to the team when he feels things have been handled unjustly. What was your reaction to this scene and why? Have you ever stood up for something you believed in when all others seemed to be against it?

12. One of the most important elements of *Wolfsbane* is accepting responsibility for our actions and resisting the urge to place the blame at someone else's feet. As the story progresses, you learn that Canyon is addicted to painkillers. This addiction often disables clear thinking and increases forgetfulness. Despite that failing on his part, Canyon does not use this as a crutch for what transpired between him and Dani. He takes responsibility and is ready to own up to his mistakes. Do you have something in your life that you're running from, that you've been unwilling to accept responsibility for? Perhaps it's driven a wedge in relationships or had unfortunate repercussions. I would encourage you to pray, to ask God to open your heart and mind. Then ask for the help of the Holy Spirit to accept forgiveness and take responsibility. What can you do in an effort toward restoration/reconciliation with God and/or with the affected parties?

ABOUT THE AUTHOR

An Army brat, Ronie Kendig married an Army veteran. They have four children and two dogs. She has a BS in Psychology, speaks to various groups, is active with the American Christian Fiction Writers (ACFW), and mentors new writers. Ronie can be found at www.roniekendig.com or www.discardedheroes.com.

DISCARDED HEROES SERIES
by Ronie Kendig

NIGHTSHADE

DIGITALIS

WOLFSBANE

COMING IN 2012
FIRETHORN

AVAILABLE WHEREVER BOOKS ARE SOLD